lock & key

gordon bonnet

part one

when you have eliminated what is impossible

. . .

Darren Ault woke in pitch darkness, which was odd, because he was fairly certain he was dead.

He brought his hands to his face, tentatively, and felt for gunshot wounds. Finding none, he sat up, blinking, and began to move his hands around. This was done with considerable trepidation. He was understandably curious about his surroundings, but at the same time, the problem with darkness is that anything could be in it with you, and you'd never know until it was too late. As far as he knew, he could be sitting in a tiger's lair, the cat's dark-adapted eyes already sizing him up and deciding which parts of him would be the tenderest. He could be in a basement, at the mercy of the gangs his mother had repeatedly warned him about during his childhood in the Capitol Hill area of Seattle. Worse still, his high school chum Lee McCaskill could still be there, somewhere, with the neat little pistol aimed at his forehead, like it had been moments ago. Only this time, Lee would be wearing night-vision goggles, so he could see him in the dark.

Or maybe all three at the same time. Just because those were unlikely scenarios didn't mean they were mutually exclusive.

But whatever horrors might await him in the dark, he couldn't sit where he was forever. For one thing, the floor felt like tile, and was hard, uncomfortable, and cold. And for another, he was, much to his own surprise, beginning to be more curious than afraid.

However impossible it seemed, he had evidently survived a shot to the noggin not only without dying, but without injury. He had felt the bullet strike his forehead—the sensation was pressure rather than pain, and over in a flash—but now there wasn't so much as a scratch on him, much less the kind of wound that a point-blank gunshot to the head would cause.

Honestly, he should have been dead, and missing a considerable portion of the top of his skull to boot.

"Wait," he said aloud. "Maybe I *am* dead. Maybe I'm a ghost."

That explanation immediately made sense to him, but it raised a host of new fears, all of which crowded about him in the darkness, vying for his attention.

"I'm dead," he repeated, trying the idea out. "I'm a ghost."

He squinted, but still could make out nothing in the dark. Were ghosts able to see? He thought they were, but who really knew about ghosts? To be propelled into the afterlife, but to find oneself unable to see, would *seriously* suck.

Maybe that was why ghosts bumped around so much. They run into things.

He got to his feet, a bit stiffly, and took one step forward. There was a whirring noise, and a loud click, and the lights came on.

He gave a feeble scream and whirled around, but there was no one there, or at least no one that he could see. More likely, it was some sort of motion-activated lighting. The light came from overhead. It had that pale, glassy look of fluorescents, but the ceilings were so impossibly high he couldn't see the fixtures.

He looked around, and recognized his surroundings instantaneously. He was between two long rows of shelves, lined with books. Only one sort of place looked like this. As unlikely as it seemed, he was in a library. This was peculiar, but preferable to tigers, gangs, or an armed Lee McCaskill, and he gave a little shudder and a sigh of relief. It still didn't remove the possibility that he was a ghost, but at least he could see, and he reasoned, philosophically, there were worse places to haunt than a library. At least he could count on its being quiet.

Even accepting the fact that he had survived a pistol shot to the cranium didn't end the mystery. However comforting it was to be in a library, it *did* bring up the inevitable question of how he'd gotten there from Lee's apartment with no apparent awareness of the passage of time. He patted his pockets. His wallet was still there, and so were his car keys, with the attached mini-flashlight and electronic air horn that his mother insisted he have.

"You never know when you might be in trouble," his mom had said, when she'd given them to him, a statement that seemed to sum up her general approach to life. "What if you get a flat tire at night? You'll need a flashlight. What if you get mugged? You could use that thing to call for help."

He had tentatively pressed the button on the little plastic square in his hand, releasing an earsplitting honk. His mother's cat leapt off the sofa, overturning a potted African violet, and ran under a chair.

"See?" his mom had said, after she'd recovered her composure. "It'll be useful. Clip the horn and the flashlight onto your car keys. I'll sleep better at night, Darren, dear."

Well, he could only hope Mom was sleeping well, because he'd just sat there in the dark for ten minutes without remembering the flashlight in his pocket.

He went up to the row of shelves on his right. They were the typical metal affairs you find in an average library, but there were several odd differences. First, they were far taller than ordinary. He looked up, squinting, and could not see the tops. They receded upwards to the vanishing point, merging with the diffuse overhead light. Second, the books were all of uniform height and coloration—bound in what looked like crimson Naugahyde—and all of the ones he could see had the same legend, printed on the spine.

RICHARD PRESTON THATCHER, born 18 March 1832, Scarborough, England.

In smaller print, beneath this, was a seemingly arbitrary series of numbers and letters.

He selected the book at the end of the shelf on his eye level, and opened it up to a random page. Each page had a date. This one was July 19, 1858. He read, "… and feeling the need to finish the job that he had left incomplete because of falling ill with influenza the previous week, he skipped the Sunday church services, and taking a ladder, went up onto his roof to continue replacing shingles that had been torn off in the storm the previous month…"

He flipped ahead a few pages. An entry for May 2, 1860 said, "… he overslept that day, and his wife was unhappy with him. He ate breakfast, finishing at a little before ten o'clock, then went out and fed the chickens. His wife had already milked the cows, and she told him that she was angry about his oversleeping…"

He went ahead a few more pages. More trivia about country life. If this was a novel, it was a singularly dull one. No dialogue, no apparent plot, just a list of the daily occurrences in the life of some country farmer in nineteenth century England.

He flipped to the last page. It only had a few lines.

"The doctor, Andrew Smithfield (TYH149087-1011) came to attend to him, but was unable to bring down his fever. He became unconscious at 3:02 in the afternoon on September 29, 1864, and died without ever regaining consciousness. His wife and all of his children, as well as Dr. Smithfield, were there."

And below that final paragraph was the cryptic phrase, END TRACKING CODE ZCV781540-4891 (ALTERNATE)

He closed the book, frowning in complete incomprehension, and put it back on the shelf. Then he looked around a little, hoping something would appear that would make sense of this place.

And that was when he noticed a third odd thing about the shelves. In between each of the sets of shelves was a handle with a black plastic grip, sticking out of a slot. Above the slot were arrows, one pointing up, one pointing down. He wasn't normally someone given to messing with things for no good reason. It never ended well. Today, however, was *not* a normal day. He reached out and yanked downward on the lever.

There was a groaning noise, as some large machine underneath the floor kicked into action, and the shelves descended into the floor, bringing new ones from above. Darren understood immediately. The shelves were on some kind of vertical conveyor belt, so the upper ones could be accessed without a ladder. You simply pulled the handle, and the shelves came to you.

He let the shelves descend for nearly a minute, curious to see if there was an end, or at least a change, to all of these rows and rows of identical books. It didn't appear that there was. But then he realized that some of the books rumbling by did have a minor difference. Running down the spine of several shelves' worth was a gold stripe.

He released the lever, and with a grating noise, the shelves stopped. He leaned forward, and studied the gold-striped volumes. The spines still had the same legend—the name Richard Preston Thatcher, with a set of numbers—but there was that little strip of gold foil pressed into the spine. He pulled the last of the gold-embossed books from the shelf, and opened it to the last page. The date was July 19, 1858. He read, "… and feeling the need to finish the job that he had left incomplete because of falling ill with influenza the previous week, he skipped the Sunday church services, and taking a ladder, went up onto his roof to continue replacing shingles that had been torn off in the storm the previous month. He had only been working for five minutes when he caught the toe of his shoe on a loose shingle, lost his balance, and fell off the roof. He broke his neck and died instantaneously."

This was followed by

END TRACKING CODE ZCV781540-8103 (ACTUAL)

There was a slight noise behind him, and he whirled around, once again giving a little shriek. The book tumbled from his fingers, and landed upside down on the floor.

Standing a few feet away from him was a young man, perhaps twenty-five years old. He had straight, white-blond hair that fell lankly across his forehead, partly obscuring his eyes, which were large, long-lashed, and pale blue. His face was narrow and clean-shaven, and he had a black stud in his right nostril and three rings in his left ear. He wore an over-large black t-shirt with a drawing of a kitten with enormous eyes, one of which had a bright blue teardrop suspended below it. The overall effect gave him the appearance of an emo elf.

"Who the fuck are you?" the elf said.

"Darren Ault. Where am I?"

The elf ignored the question. "How did you get here?"

"I don't know. Lee killed me, and then I was here. Is this heaven?"

The elf scowled. "Don't be ridiculous."

"Hell?"

"You don't seem the type that would ever do much of anything that would merit hell," the elf observed.

"Well, then, where am I?"

"You're in the Library."

"Okay, I can see that. What kind of library?"

The elf didn't answer. He turned and walked quickly down the aisle. "I'm going to kick some ass in security over this."

Darren had always hated to put anyone out, and however inadvertently, his presence seemed to be causing the elf a considerable level of distress.

"Look." He followed, jogging to catch up. "I'm sorry. I'll leave if you can tell me how."

"You can't. It's not that simple."

"Who *are* you?" Darren said, a little louder than he generally spoke.

This brought the elf to a halt. He turned and faced Darren, his bright blue eyes rolling upwards a little in disdain, and gave a harsh little sigh.

"I really don't have time for this. The idiots up in security seem to have fucked up big time, and I've got to make sure it's not worse than it seems." He looked Darren up and down. "And it seems pretty bad already. But three questions. I'll give you three questions. Then you need to shut up, stay out of the way, and let me do my job."

Darren swallowed. "What is this place?"

"It's a library."

"I know that. You told me that. What kind of library?" He put up one hand. "And that only counts as one question."

The elf sighed again. "Fine. It's the Library of Timelines. And no, I'm not going to explain what that means, because it would take too long. Next question."

"Who are you?"

"My name is Fischer. I'm the Head Librarian. Although on days like this, I wish I had listened to my father and gone into manufacturing."

"Okay, Mr. Fischer. And last... Why am I here? I'm sure I should be dead. I got shot point-blank in the forehead."

"Drop the 'Mr.' crap. It's just Fischer. And I don't know why you're here. That's one of the many things I've got to find out." He rubbed his eyes with an angry little gesture, and brushed his hair back. It immediately fell forward again. "Right after I twist off a few heads in security. And put some coffee on." He turned and walked away down the hall.

He trotted after Fischer again.

As they reached the end of the aisle, and Fischer turned right and headed toward what appeared to be an office, he muttered, "Jesus, days like this make me want to *puke*."

Fischer pushed the door open with unnecessary force, and he followed him in. The office was a mess. There was an old-fashioned mahogany desk in the middle, home to a telephone, a computer, and a number of untidy piles of paper. A filing cabinet stood in the corner, one drawer open because it was stuffed so full of folders it wouldn't close. A number of cardboard boxes sat on the floor, some with their lids askew, filled with more papers and manila folders. Fischer swiveled the desk chair around, and a large ginger tomcat vacated the chair with an aggrieved meow, then jumped up onto the desk and began to wash himself, only giving one momentary glance about the room to make sure everyone appreciated how little the disturbance had bothered his equanimity.

Fischer didn't so much sit down as drape himself over the chair, and tapped a few of the keys on the computer. There was a chiming noise as the machine roused itself from sleep. He then picked up the telephone and punched in three numbers.

After a brief pause, he said, "Maggie, can you get down here? We got a problem." There was another brief silence, and Fischer rolled his eyes. "Yeah, I know, but the filing will have to wait. We got a problem. A big problem. One I'm gonna have to talk to Fassbinder about." He frowned. "Well, of *course* it's because there's been a breach. Why else would I want to talk to Fassbinder? I don't talk to him for the stimulating conversation." He sighed. "Look, just get down here and see for yourself. And did you put the coffee on?" Only a moment's pause this time. "Good. Can you bring me a cup?"

Fischer hung the phone up, and clacked the computer keys furiously. Darren, finding himself ignored, looked around the office. There was a calendar, tacked crookedly to the wall on the other side of the room, depicting a scene from *Raiders of the Lost Ark*, but he noted with a frown that the calendar was open to the page for February 1982. A series of sticky notes were affixed to the wall next to him. These had various scrawls, most of them either too far away to read without being obvious about it, or else in a handwriting so bad as to be nearly indecipherable. He noted that one of the nearer ones read, "Fix linear time sequencing, First Battle of Bull Run, possible divergence," and almost asked Fischer what that meant, but the librarian was scowling so darkly at the computer screen that he didn't dare interrupt him.

His gaze dropped to the desk, and he noted that in the midst of the piles of paper, barely visible, was a nameplate. It read, "Archibald Fischer. Head Librarian."

He stared at the Librarian in some amazement, and spoke before he could stop himself.

"*Archibald*? Your first name is *Archibald*?"

Fischer looked up, his lips tightening and his scowl deepening even further. "I told you. My name is *Fischer*. Just plain Fischer. Now shut up and let me do my job, before I send you to the north wing, where we keep the records for medieval China, and have you spend the afternoon doing a little light reading." He looked back down, muttering, "My parents couldn't name me for my *other* grandfather. No. *Jim* wasn't *aristocratic* enough. Fuck."

Darren sat for a few moments, silent, while Fischer pounded on the computer keyboard so hard that it looks likely letters would start flying off. He reached up absently, and touched his neck. He had a nervous habit playing with a necklace he always wore, a chain with a little silver key hanging from it. The key had a filigreed, intricately carved head, and was a keepsake he valued, although it likely had little monetary value. It went to a wooden box, of uncertain but undoubtedly great age, that he'd inherited from his grandmother.

The key and chain were gone.

He frowned, dismayed, wondering where in all of his mystifying day's travels he could have lost it. But wherever it was, it was undoubtedly irretrievable at this point.

There was no use fretting about it at this point, though he knew he would anyway.

The door opened and a woman came in carrying a cup of coffee. The woman was in that indeterminate age between fifty and sixty-five. Everything about her was round—her face, her body, the severe bun into which her hair was fixed, even her glasses. Yet there was a grim cut to the lines of her face that gave her the look of a guard from a women's prison. Most people intimidated him, but this woman had a presence that radiated intimidation. It was hard to imagine *not* being intimidated by her.

The ginger tom, on the other hand, seemed to immediately recognize a kindred spirit, and jumped down off the desk and twined around her legs.

The woman gave a chilly little smile of recognition, and said in a voice with a rolling Scottish accent, "Now, don't make me spill this coffee, Ivan, there's a good puss." She set the cup down on the desk.

Fischer looked up, and gestured toward Darren.

The woman turned, noticing his presence for the first time, and scanned him from head to toe.

"See what I mean, Maggie?" Fischer said.

"Where'd you find him?"

"Nineteenth century Britain. He sort of appeared there, claiming that he was dead."

"Curious. His appearance didn't set off the security alarms?"

"Not that I know of. Of course, they could all be napping up there, as usual. I haven't checked it out yet. I blundered into him. I was heading to my office this morning, and saw the light was on, and went to investigate. He must have tripped the motion detectors. Lucky he appeared where he did. If he'd suddenly popped into existence over in the southeast corner of ancient Peru, or somewhere like that, he might have wandered for days before anyone knew he was here."

"And he simply *materialized*?"

"Actually," Darren said, "I was shot in the head, and then I materialized."

The two of them simultaneously turned their heads and glared at him, but didn't respond.

His cheeks warmed, and he muttered, "Sorry," in a small voice, and the two turned back toward each other.

Fischer shook his head. "Anyway, he says he doesn't know how he got here. Either he doesn't remember, or else he's lying."

She gave him an appraising look, one thin eyebrow raised slightly. "He hasn't the look of a spy."

"I'm *not* a spy!" He sat up straight, unable to keep himself from speaking. "Look, Maggie, I don't care what he says, I wasn't spying!"

Now both of the woman's eyebrows went up. "The Librarian calls me Maggie. *You* call me Mrs. Carmichael."

He said, "Sorry," again, and subsided into silence.

Fischer drummed his long fingers on the desk, and then took a sip of his coffee. "I think the problem here is threefold. First, how do we fix whatever monumental fuckup got him here in the first place? Second, how do we get him back where he belongs? And third, does he already know more than he should?"

"The answer to the third question is probably yes, but I

don't know what we can do about it. And honestly, Fischer, maybe you should find out more of his story. It could be relevant that he seems so insistent that he's dead."

"Maybe. If he's telling the truth. I wonder if Fassbinder still has those torture devices he swiped when he took that vacation in fifteenth century Spain? They may come in handy."

His eyes widened. "Now, wait a minute."

They turned and looked at him.

"I am telling the truth, I swear. My friend, Lee McCaskill, shot me in the forehead. I have no idea why. I was over at his apartment, having dinner, and he seemed upset about something. I asked what was wrong, and he said, 'It's nothing that this won't fix,' and pulled out a pistol and shot me in the freaking head. And I woke up here. That's really all I know."

Maggie looked at Fischer. "Have you checked the database records?"

"I was in the process of doing that when you got here." Fischer turned to him. "Full name?"

"Darren Michael Ault."

Fischer typed into the computer. Maggie went around the desk and peered over his shoulder, frowning through her thick glasses.

With a little more trepidation, he rose, and joined them. He half expected them to order him to sit down again, but they didn't, and when he looked at the screen, he saw a list of several entries for "Ault, Darren Michael," followed by a string of numbers and letters, similar to what he'd seen in the books.

"When and where were you born?"

"Seattle, Washington, September 16, 1989."

Fischer typed that in. Within seconds, the screen blinked, and the message, "NO VALID ACTUAL TRACK CODE. ACCESS ALTERNATE TRACKS?" appeared.

Both Maggie and Fischer made small noises of surprise.

"What? What does that mean?"

"Well, on its simplest level, it means that you don't exist," Fischer said. "Which makes it kind of perplexing that you're here, ruining my morning."

Maggie gestured at the screen. "Try the murderer, his alleged friend."

"What was the name of the guy who shot you?" Fischer asked, without looking up.

"Lee McCaskill."

"Middle name? Do you know birthplace or birthdate?"

"I think his middle name is Allen. Not sure if it's A-L-L-E-N or A-L-A-N. I don't know his birthdate, but he was born in Spokane, Washington."

Fischer typed in the information. There were more entries for Lee Allen McCaskill than there had been for Darren Michael Ault, but the birthplace information narrowed it down to one. Fischer clicked on the entry.

Once again, the message, "NO VALID ACTUAL TRACK CODE. ACCESS ALTERNATE TRACKS?" appeared.

"Uh-oh," Fischer said.

Maggie looked over at Darren. "Who is the current president of the United States?"

"Barack Obama."

"Of course. The gentleman with the two cute little girls. Middle name's Hussein, Fischer. I remember that horrid woman making such a big deal out of it, what's her name? Oh, yes, Ann Coulter."

Fischer typed in the information.

"NO VALID ACTUAL TRACK CODE. ACCESS ALTERNATE TRACKS?"

"Okay, this is bad." Fischer stared at Maggie, his large blue eyes wide. He looked back down, and typed in "Britney Spears," and after a few clicks, once again got the same message.

"Shit." Fischer 's voice sounded awestruck, and more than a little frightened.

"What? What's happened?" Darren said.

Fischer swiveled his chair around, and for the first time, looked him in the face. "Well, it's a bit premature to make this conclusion, only having a sample size of four, but given that it's hard to imagine an event that would include yourself, your murderer friend, President Obama, and Britney Spears that *didn't* include everyone else in the world, I'm going to hazard a guess. This McCaskill character who shot you seems to have generated some sort of temporal paradox."

"What's that?"

Fischer leaned back in his chair, closed his eyes, and didn't respond.

"It means," Maggie said in a low voice, "that somehow what your friend did made the entire population of the earth cease to exist."

Darren stared at them, and swallowed. "Um... How can that be possible?"

Fischer opened one eye, and his mouth twisted into a sardonic grimace. "Well, now, if I knew that, I wouldn't be sitting here trying to head off a migraine, would I?"

"People get killed every day, and this doesn't happen."

"True," Fischer said, still with only one eye open. He sounded like he was keeping his temper only with an effort.

"And there's nothing so special about me."

"Clearly also true."

"So why..."

"You know," Fischer interrupted, opening both eyes, "you have this annoying habit of asking questions that it's obvious no one in the room has the answers to."

"Well, perhaps," Maggie said, "that *is* the place to start. What is special about him? See how deep the paradox went. Did it begin at the instant he was shot? Or did it erase actual tracks farther back in time?"

Fischer's nod appeared grudging. "Well, that's easily enough done. I suppose it's worth checking."

He leaned forward, and typed in a box marked "Command" the phrase, "Access actual end track codes."

A screen appeared with a variety of options—"By Name?" "By Region?" "By Time?" "By Interlock With Code?"

Fischer selected "By Time?" and another screen appeared. "Time range?" it asked, followed by a place for the minute and hour in Greenwich Mean Time, day, month, and year, and a pulldown menu that said, "Plus or minus how many minutes?"

Fischer half turned toward him. "When did your alleged murder take place?"

He thought for a moment. "It was around seven-thirty PM. March 12, 2016."

"What time zone?"

"Pacific. Pacific Standard Time."

Fischer sighed harshly. "Shit. How many hours different would that be from Greenwich? I can't keep track of time zones to save my neck."

"It could be worse," Maggie said. "He could live in China. Ever since the whole country went on to the same time zone, I've not been able to remember which it is." She thought for a moment. "It would be two-thirty AM, Greenwich Mean Time."

"We really need to have IT install an autoconverter on this thing." He typed in the time and date, selected "Plus or Minus Ten Minutes" and hit enter.

There was a brief pause, and then a list of names began to appear. The first name—Wu, Li Feng, Guangzhou, China, 2:20:01 AM GMT—was quickly followed by others, all in chronological order, and the list zipped upwards almost too fast for the eye to follow.

Then it hit 2:34:05 AM GMT, and the list stopped.

Fischer sat up straight in his chair. "Whoa. Hello."

"What?" Darren said.

"Looks like at two thirty-four and five seconds, Greenwich Mean Time, on March 12, 2016, people suddenly stopped dying."

"Those are death dates?"

"Yes. At the point of death, a person's actual track becomes fixed. All the other possible outcomes or paths they might have had become locked in as alternate tracks."

"So that's what the books are…" he began.

Fischer nodded. "They're all the possible life tracks that anyone could have had. Taken as a whole, the library is a map of the potential lives of everyone in the history of the world. As people make choices, they are navigating through a field of possibilities, and selecting one path as their actual track. All of the others become alternate tracks. At death, of course, the power of choice immediately ceases. Death cancels all of the remaining alternate tracks. After that, neither they nor anyone else can do anything to change what happened."

This was the most forthcoming Fischer had been since they met, and he wanted it to continue. He chose his words carefully, and tried to use a soothing voice, such as you would use on a potentially vicious dog. "And at the moment Lee shot me, it stopped happening."

Fischer nodded again. "It looks like no actual track locking took place after the event. Put simply, no one died after that moment. From what the computer told us earlier, it seems like at that moment, all of the actual tracks evaporated—as if the entire population of the earth simply vanished. They didn't die. That would have made the computer simultaneously assign all of them actual end track codes. They simply ceased to be."

"What on earth could do that?" Maggie said.

"Good question." Fischer raised one hand in his direction without taking his eyes off the computer screen. "It looks like whatever your friend did somehow only affected people who were alive at the time of the event. It didn't go back into history, and alter the past. People who died before the event still died."

She frowned. "Are you certain about that? It seems to me a little premature to make that conclusion. If I may be so forward as to say so."

"Of course you may. You're my administrative assistant. It's your job."

"So perhaps, Fischer, you should check a few people who should have actual end track codes, who are connected to Mr. Ault here. If he's the pivot of this whole mess, perhaps it would be worth finding out if the phenomenon has had local effects, in addition to the global effect we've already noted."

Fischer looked up at her. "That's an excellent suggestion. And if we find some, perhaps it would help to figure out how this happened." He leaned back. "Do you have any near relatives who are deceased?"

Darren nodded. "Of course."

"Pick one."

"My grandmother. Katherine Jane Ault."

"Is that her married name?"

"Yes. Her maiden name was Clevenger."

"Birthdate and place?"

He bit his lip. "Um. She was born June 7, let's see…" He did some mental figuring. "1921. In Oskaloosa, Iowa."

Fischer shook his head. "Why do so many names of American cities sound like the punch line of a joke?"

He entered the information. The now-familiar message, "NO VALID ACTUAL TRACK CODE. ACCESS ALTERNATE TRACKS?" appeared.

"Well, well," Fischer said. "The plot thickens. Seems like your grandma never existed."

"That's ridiculous! My grandma only died a year ago. I used to spend Christmas vacation at her house every year. What do you mean, she never existed?"

Fischer opened his eyes wide, and speaking very slowly, said, "What I mean is: Your. Grandma. Never. Existed."

"Maybe that..." Darren started, and then stopped.

"Maybe that what?"

"Maybe that explains why my key is gone. My grandma willed me a wooden box, and the key that goes to it. I always wear the key on a chain around my neck, and I noticed it was gone. I mean, if my grandma never existed, then she can't have willed me anything, right?" He closed his eyes, and pinched the bridge of his nose between his thumb and forefinger. "Man, this stuff makes my head hurt."

"*You* should complain." Fischer's voice was a little bitter. "You only have to keep track of yourself. I have to keep track of everybody who ever existed, and also all the ones who don't. You want my job?"

"No. But still... I mean, that doesn't make sense."

"What doesn't?"

"If my grandma never existed, how can I be here? I mean, it explains why my key is gone, but I think the bigger question is why I'm still here."

"Well, first of all, you're not exactly *anywhere* at the moment." Fischer leaned back and gave him a speculative look. "We've already established that you don't exist, if you'll recall. But if somehow the event that dumped you into my lap not only erased the whole population of the earth, but also reached farther back and erased someone who *had* existed, and *had* died, this points to a more pervasive problem."

"I think that erasing the whole population of the earth is pervasive enough already," Darren observed.

"I can't argue with that," Maggie said.

"Yes, but is it a problem with only his family? Or have more people had their dead ancestors erased?"

Maggie gave a little gesture with one hand. "That is an excellent question, but I haven't the vaguest idea how we could find that out."

Fischer shrugged, and typed in "Nelson Mandela" and after adding a few clicks selecting dates and places, got a screen that said, "Actual end track code FGO883671-0708: Access Files?" Fischer clicked "No" and looked up at Maggie.

"Well, Mandela still existed."

"That's good. So, perhaps we should operate under the hypothesis that whatever it is that happened erased Darren's family, and no one else."

"Yes, but how far back? And how could we find that out? The computer records are meant to be static after an actual track is selected. It's unheard of to go back and change the past. We don't have the software to track changes to the past. They're not supposed to happen."

"Well, I think we might be able to figure part of that out. I wonder how far back Darren's grandmother's family was erased? We can do a reverse bifurcation analysis. See how long ago it was before she had an ancestor who actually existed."

"I think my brain is going to explode," Darren said. It came out sounding more pitiful than he intended.

Fischer glanced up at him. "If you start whining, I'm going to kick you right the hell out of this office. I'd think you'd be grateful that we're spending our morning trying to bring your sorry ass back into existence."

"Well, I'm *grateful*. I just don't *understand* all this."

"Once he starts the reverse bifurcation," Maggie said, "I'll have time to explain it to you. It takes a couple of hours for that software to run."

Fischer clicked an icon on the screen that said "Norton SuperBifurcator!" and there was a whirring noise as the software booted up.

A cartoon of a grinning, bespectacled man popped up. The words, "Welcome to Norton SuperBifurcator!" were in a speech bubble over his head.

"Do you want to: (1) compare alternate and actual time

tracks for points of divergence? (2) do backwards sequencing to locate points of divergence in the past? or (3) compare possible intersection points in the future? Select an option to continue."

Fischer clicked on option two.

The bespectacled cartoon man popped up, in a different position this time, with one finger pointing to another speech bubble.

"Excellent choice! That's easy, with Norton SuperBifurcator! Do you want to find past divergences by: (1) name? (2) time? or (3) event? Select an option to continue."

Fischer clicked option one. "This program is so fucking cute it makes me want to throw up my breakfast."

"Cute sells," Maggie said.

Fischer typed the name "Katherine Jane Clevenger" and hit enter.

The cartoon man reappeared, a dismayed expression on his face, both of his palms pressed to his cheeks. This time his speech bubble said, "Uh-oh! There is more than one person by that name! Do you want to select by (1) birthdate, (2) birthplace, (3) death date, (4) death place, or (5) tracking code? Select an option to continue."

"What's her birthdate again?" Fischer asked.

"June 7, 1921."

Fischer selected option one, typed in her birthdate, and hit enter.

"And last! What would you like to know? Do you want to know (1) intersection points with other individuals, (2) interactions between this individual's timeline and specific events, (3) most recent intersection point between alternate and actual tracks, or (4) advanced options? Select an option to continue."

Fischer clicked on option three.

The cartoon man appeared, seated in a chair, a broad grin on his face, his feet up on the desk. "Thanks! Sit back and relax! This should only take a minute!" A little hour glass appeared, its sand emptying downward. When it was done it flipped over, and began to empty again.

Fischer snorted. "A minute. Yeah, right. Last time I had to do this, it tied up the computer for three hours."

"Well," Maggie said, "let's not sit here and wait. I suggest we go to the staff lounge, and spend some time bringing Mr. Ault here up to speed on all of this."

Fischer started to object. "Look, Maggie, it's not as if I don't have work to do…"

Her face eased into a faint trace of a smile. "I think we've established that whatever went wrong here, it's not Mr. Ault's doing. I think we owe him as much of an explanation as we can give." She looked over at him, and one eyebrow went up a little. Whether it was in humor or in pity was impossible to tell. "And after all, we have time. At this point, we have all the time in the world. If the entire human race doesn't exist anymore, it rather puts us out of business for the moment, wouldn't you say?"

The staff lounge looked like your average staff lounge. Darren wasn't sure what to expect—perhaps something with a bit more *gravitas*, given the apparent function and scope of the Library. Some historical artifacts, maybe some tapestries on the wall or intricately carved wooden chairs. But it turned out to be a room that could have been in any of the corporate buildings in the world. Tile floor, a variety of mismatched metal-legged chairs with worn upholstery, a long folding table, a dented refrigerator, a coffee maker, a microwave that looked like it hadn't been cleaned since it was installed, and a rather moth-eaten sofa. There was a large corkboard attached to one wall with a variety of notices affixed with pushpins— there was one that said, "ATTENTION ALL STAFF

MEMBERS: All vacations to the past require WRITTEN APPLICATION WITH TWO WEEKS' NOTICE. Approval is by the Librarian's permission only. Upon return, YOU MUST CHECK IN THROUGH THE ARTIFACTS DEPARTMENT and declare and register any items you have brought back with you. NO EXCEPTIONS."

Fischer immediately went and flopped down onto the sofa, and covered both eyes with one arm, and lay there, totally motionless.

Maggie poured herself a cup of coffee, then looked up. "Coffee, Mr. Ault?"

"Um, sure, thanks."

"Cream? Sugar?"

"Two sugars, no cream."

She poured another cup, and while she was stirring in the sugar, half turned toward Darren.

"Sit. Make yourself comfortable. We'll be here for a while."

He settled in one of the metal-legged chairs, and she set his coffee in front of him, and then sat down across from him. "I'd imagine you have some questions."

He stared at her, and then took a sip of his coffee. It was stronger than he liked it, but at this point any coffee was better than no coffee. His mind was so roiling with questions that he couldn't settle on one.

"It's all pretty overwhelming," he finally said.

"I would expect so."

"So, this has never happened before?"

"What, one of you showing up here? No, no, not to my recollection. And I've worked here for... well, for a long time. Fischer is the third Librarian I've worked for. Mr. Furnival — he just retired two years ago — and before him, Doctor Rounsaville. She was a grand old lady, my, yes." The severe lines in her face softened a bit with the memory.

"And this place really keeps track of every possibility? For everyone? Everywhere?"

"Oh, yes. The Library is bigger than it appears."

"It appears pretty big to me already."

She nodded. "You've only seen the barest fraction of it."

"And you think somehow what Lee did changed the past?"

"It would appear so. But I'm not prepared to put much weight behind that theory, not yet. The reverse bifurcation should give us a bit more information."

"What is that, the reverse bifurcation, um, thingy?"

"Ah. Yes." She set down her cup. "It's simple enough in principle, but takes the computer a lot of time to do, because in practice it's extraordinarily complex. What the process does is to start with one person, living or dead, actual or alternate, and works backwards from there to find out where particular events could have occurred that led to diverging timelines. In this case, we're taking your grandmother, who didn't exist for some reason, and we're running her family tree and personal events—well, the ones she *would* have had, had she actually existed—backwards, and trying to find out how far back her family line never existed. Somewhere, an event occurred that stopped her from being born. Reverse bifurcation should pinpoint where that is." She shrugged. "Theoretically, at least. Sometimes there is more than one such event, or some confluence of particular events, that did it. Let's hope it's only one, because otherwise it can get confusing."

"More confusing than it already is."

"Oh, yes, indeed," Maggie said. "You have no idea."

"So you think that somehow, what Lee did changed something in the past?"

She nodded. "The puzzling thing is, that isn't supposed to be possible. As Fischer said, the past is supposed to be fixed.

Once a person dies, and the computer assigns him or her an end tracking code, that should be that."

"But…" Darren started, and then stopped. He frowned. "But there was a note on the wall in the office. Something about fixing a divergence in the First Battle of Bull Run. That's in the past. So things can be changed."

"Oh, yes. By *us*. Just not by *you*. We have to go back and fix things all the time. Small discrepancies, mostly, nothing that would concern anyone. We travel to the past, sometimes to work, sometimes for pleasure. But we are required to run a computer analysis before we go, to make certain that nothing we do will interfere substantively with anyone's timeline, and run a second one when we return to make sure that we did, in fact, follow the rules of non-interference. We simply keep track of people's choices. We're not supposed to *influence* them."

"So… you're not one of us… you're not…" He sputtered a little, and fell silent.

"Human? Well, yes, Mr. Ault, we are. But you are thinking rightly, to some extent. We're *different*, I'll grant. We're the Monitors." The corners of her mouth turned up slightly, which was, he was learning, as close to a smile as she ever got. "We pass amongst you, and you never know. Some of your best friends could be Monitors, and you'd be none the wiser."

He opened his eyes a little wider. "Could… could Lee McCaskill be…?" He left the question unfinished.

"A Monitor?"

There was a snorting noise from the couch, but Fischer didn't move.

"No, Mr. Ault, we would know that," Maggie said. "He's an ordinary human, like yourself."

"Could it be relevant that Lee is a physicist? He works on things like the arrow of time, and the mathematics of eight or nine dimensions, and that sort of stuff."

Fischer's arm came up, and he turned his head and scowled at Darren. "It only now occurred to you to tell us this?"

"Well, I didn't know it was relevant."

Fischer snorted again, turned his head back, and put his arm back over his eyes.

"It could be relevant," Maggie said. "Do you know if he was researching time travel?"

Darren shrugged. "I don't really know. I don't understand any of his research. He's a physicist. I run a bookstore."

"And you have no idea why he wanted to kill you?"

He shook his head. "No. None. We've been friends since elementary school. We've always gotten along fine. He's been acting a little weird for about a month, but I thought it was because of his girlfriend."

"Girlfriend?"

He nodded. "Sherry Christensen. He asked her out a few weeks ago. She seems nice. But Lee started acting really nervous after that, like something was on his mind. I thought, you know, people change when they fall for someone." He felt a little wistful. He had seen that sort of change in others, but had never had the opportunity to find out about such a phenomenon first-hand. His experience with women had been not so much unpleasant as non-existent.

"And you don't know what he was worried about?"

"No idea. I figured either he'd work it out, or eventually he'd tell me about it." He took a sip of his coffee. "Instead, he shot me in the head."

"So, it looks like whatever was bothering him must have involved you. Do you think he was concerned that you would go after his girlfriend?"

"Me? Oh, no, nothing like that. Lee knows me better than that. Besides, why would a woman go for me when she could have a tanned, athletic, handsome physicist instead?"

"Don't start with the self-pity or I'll have to throttle you," Fischer said.

"Well, it's true," Darren said, a little defiantly. "Besides, I only met Sherry twice. And it was just to say hi to, nothing more. And Lee's not the jealous type. He's devoted, but not the kind who sees every man as a threat."

"I think," Maggie said, "that the crux of the matter is to find out why Lee wanted to kill you. But that will be a little difficult to do directly, seeing that he doesn't exist anymore. And we *would* have been able to try to ascertain some of it by looking up his records and seeing what chosen actual track he was on. But now that this event has happened, we have no way of knowing which that was, out of the hundreds of millions of possible tracks he could have taken. Whatever else it did, when he shot you, it simultaneously erased all of the records of everyone alive on earth. Trying to find out what his actual track was would be like searching for one particular grain of sand on a beach."

Fischer suddenly sat up. "I have a theory."

Maggie's eyebrows raised in a silent question mark, and she and Darren both turned toward Fischer.

"Darren said that Lee is a physicist, working on issues having to do with time."

"Was," she corrected.

Fischer waved a hand at her impatiently. "I don't know what tense you'd use in this situation, and it doesn't matter. But suppose he did find out a way to travel to the past, or at least *influence* the past."

"Yes," she said.

"And, somehow, his shooting Darren will lead to a chain of circumstances in which he goes back into the past, and interferes with Darren's birth. Not only Darren's, but his distant ancestors'." Fischer's long, melancholy face grew animated. "Perhaps when he shot Darren, he escaped to the past to avoid being arrested. And his presence stops Darren's great-great-great-grandpa from knocking up his great-great-great-grandma…"

Darren recoiled a little. "Do you really have to put it that way?"

Fischer ignored him. "… and so Darren's ancestral line stops cold. He's never born. But it creates a paradox, because if he's never born, Lee never shoots him, and never escapes into the past… and so on, and so forth. Ergo, he has generated an impossible situation, and it sends all of humanity into the logical void."

Maggie looked skeptical. "In the absence of further evidence…"

"I know." Fischer still looked excited. "But it's the only thing I can think of that explains all of the evidence we've currently got. It's like Sherlock Holmes said—when you have eliminated what is impossible, whatever is left, however improbable, must be the truth."

"Well, far be it from me to argue with Sherlock Holmes," she said. "But if it's so, then how do we fix it?"

"We?" Fischer's mouth twisted in a little smile, and he looked at Darren. "Not *we*. I think we send Mr. Ault here on a little adventure."

"Me?" Darren's heart gave a thud against his ribs.

"Stands to reason," Fischer said. "Neither I nor any of my staff know what Lee McCaskill looks like. You, on the other hand, would recognize him on sight."

"But…" he said, and then closed his mouth.

Maggie's brow wrinkled with disapproval. "Honestly, Fischer, is this the wisest course of action? Sending an untrained young man… who only today found out about how all this works…"

"… and who still doesn't really understand *anything* that's going on here," Darren added.

"… and expecting him to somehow fix the biggest divergence that's happened since the Library was founded?"

"I don't know," Fischer said. "I have a feeling there's a reason he's the only member of humanity that somehow made it through this."

"Now, wait just a minute." Darren's voice was a little breathless.

Both of them turned to him.

"I am *not* some kind of adventure hero type. I'm a *book-store owner*. This isn't something that you can just... just *do*. How do you know I won't screw it up worse?"

Fischer frowned. "Things could be screwed up worse than the entire human race being wiped out of existence?"

He sagged a little. "If there's one thing I've learned, it's that things can *always* get worse."

"I don't know, Ault. Look at it this way. You're already dead, for all intents and purposes. You were shot in the head. What more can happen?"

Darren winced. "You should never ask that question. It never turns out well."

Fischer leaned back, and cupped his hands behind his head. "I don't know. It sounds like a brilliant idea to me."

"Just because *you* don't have to go." He turned to Maggie for support. "You can't think this is a good plan, Mrs. Carmichael."

She shrugged. "I've learned from working with Fischer that his intuition is seldom wrong. He may not look like a typical Librarian. Even I was a tad skeptical when I met him first. His manner of dress, and his youth. But the Board was right to hire him, of course, I shouldn't have doubted. He has brains, and more than that... he has a way about him. Uncanny. In another age, he'd be said to have the second sight."

He gazed at Fischer, who for the first time exhibited a genuine smile. He looked like a self-satisfied cat.

She gestured toward Fischer. "True, he can be overbearing, and a wee bit of an arrogant jackass at times..."

"Hey now." Fischer sat up straight, his smile dimming a little.

She turned toward him, her eyes wide and innocent. "Didn't you say I had permission to speak freely? It is my job, I believe were your precise words."

"I said that an hour ago."

"I wasn't aware of its expiration date. My apologies, sir."

"Oh, knock it off," Fischer said. "I'm right, you'll see."

"Truthfully, I've no serious doubts of that." She glanced at the clock above the corkboard. "How much longer, do you think?"

"It's only been forty minutes. I think the software will take at least another hour to run, maybe two."

"Perhaps I should take Mr. Ault here on a tour of our facility. Whilst we're waiting."

Fischer frowned. "Do you think we should? I doubt Security would approve."

"You can be assured I won't let him cause any trouble. I'll be watching him every minute."

"I won't mess with anything." He was beginning to like her, but still found her to belong to that group of people that he called "forceful personalities." Causing trouble while under her supervision would be a seriously bad idea.

"Fine," Fischer said. "I'll go up and talk to Fassbinder. I'm still wondering why Security didn't even realize we had an intruder. If I hadn't tripped over him, he might still be wandering around getting into god-knows-what."

Maggie led Darren out into the hall, and they spent the next hour ambling about the place, with her giving little explanations such as, "Here is where the records are kept for prehistoric Sub-Saharan Africa," and "If you have the leisure, once this situation is resolved, here is the wing for Medieval

Central Europe. You should read the alternate track records that describe the outcome to history if Charlemagne had died as a child. Fascinating, truly fascinating." She always referred to the current chaos as "this situation," as if it were a minor inconvenience, on par with breaking a light bulb or getting caught in traffic.

"So," he said, during a lull in the tour, while they were walking down a seemingly endless hallway, "you really think I'll be able to fix this?"

"Fischer has faith in you. I know it seems like he's angry at you, but that's his way. He would never propose such a course of action if he didn't think you were capable of doing it."

"I don't even know what I'm being expected to do."

"I suspect that he doesn't either, or not precisely. I think when the software has finished running we'll have a better idea of the specifics."

He glanced over at her. "How did you become a Monitor?"

"Become?" She sounded surprised. "You don't *become*, you simply *are*."

"But you said you and Fischer were both human."

"We are."

"So, how…" he started, and then stopped.

"In each generation, some humans are born to be Monitors. We grow up knowing it, knowing we're different. When we're old enough, we take the training, and there you are."

"When did you realize it?"

Her eyes became distant, her face relaxed a little, and for a moment he could see the girl that she had once been, before time and responsibility had lined her face. "I was five, I think. I grew up in a little village in Aberdeenshire. My parents were farmers on a smallholding, my brothers and sisters just ordinary children. I knew I was different from as early as I can remember. But when I was about five years old, I realized that

I could see into the past, and could, for myself, see into the future. I suddenly found that I could predict the outcome of my own actions ahead of time." She gave a little gesture with one hand. "Take this path through the moors, you'll stumble and bruise your shins. This one," she gestured with the other, "and you'll come home safe. I ignored those inner messages, at first, thinking they were mere fancies, till I found that they were always right. When Doctor Rounsaville became my teacher, when I was eighteen years old, and asked me to come work for the Library, it was hardly a surprise. It was as if I'd been waiting for eighteen years to find out what I'd always known."

"But why you? Why not one of your brothers or sisters, or some other little kid?"

She smiled a little. "Why *anyone* for *anything*? Why are you a bookstore owner? Why do you have brown eyes? Why is your last name Ault?"

He shook his head. "I don't have a clue."

"It's the same way here. Some of us are Monitors, others are bookstore owners or physicists or bakers or chimney sweeps. Asking why would take unraveling all of the choices for the past thousand years that led to your being born and ending up where you are. It's a question that would take another thousand years to answer. So perhaps the true answer is, it happened that way simply because it did. And maybe that's answer enough." They passed a lit window that looked into an office of some sort, and she peered in. "This is our Research and Development office. But look at the time. We should get back to Fischer's office. The software is probably finished running by now, and he'll be pacing the room like a caged lion, waiting for us."

In fact, when they got back, Fischer was once again draped in his chair in front of the computer, with Ivan the ginger tomcat curled in his lap purring wheezily. Fischer looked up as they entered, and gestured for them to join him.

"Good timing. The reverse bifurcation finished up five minutes ago. We have an answer. Or answers. Or pieces of them."

Darren followed Maggie around the back of the desk, and peered at the screen.

The cartoon man stood with his arms folded across his chest, a satisfied grin on his face. "Here are your results!" was all his speech bubble said. Below the speech bubble were about fifteen lines of text, more prosaically laid out.

CLEVENGER, KATHERINE JANE, Oskaloosa, IA, USA b. 7 June 1921

Results of Reverse Bifurcation to locate actual track interlock

Points of intersection with existing actual tracks:

1) South Uist, Hebrides, Scotland, Maíre Gillacomgain, b. 3 March 882; actual end track code = GGY837789-0098; spouse unknown; divergence occurred 16 August 903

2) Trondheim, Sør-Trøndelag, Norway, Per Olafsson, b. 19 December 1323; actual end track code = JNB615530-2822; spouse unknown; divergence occurred 12 April 1350

3) Concord, Kentucky, USA, Jane Bell, b. 30 July 1820; actual end track code PSD900654-3487; spouse unknown; divergence occurred 2 November 1844

"Curious," Maggie said.

"It is that," Fischer said, his voice animated. "Looks like there are three points where something happened that interfered with Darren's timeline. Look how far back the first one was. Early tenth century. I wonder if Lee somehow went back and killed one of Darren's ancestors in medieval Scotland, and that's what generated the paradox."

"Or stopped one from being born," she said.

Fischer nodded. "Yes."

"But why three points? You'd think one would be sufficient to render the rest of the family line nonexistent."

"Perhaps Lee fucked around with three different places in the timeline." Fischer sounded uncertain.

"That would presuppose that Lee had a great deal of knowledge about Mr. Ault's family history," Maggie said. "Given the dearth of genealogical records available before the eighteenth century, that is hard to imagine."

Fischer frowned. "I don't know."

She pointed at the screen. "And note that in each of the three divergences pinpointed, the software only could find one of the parents. The other is unknown, in each case. I've never known this software to do that."

"Me either," Fischer said. "It doesn't say, 'never married.' It says 'spouse unknown,' as if the computer knew they'd hooked up with *someone*, but ran into some sort of snag when it tried to figure out *who*. But that supports my hypothesis that something went back and interfered with the birth of Darren's ancestors. Three of them, apparently, were left spouseless, or perhaps married other people. In any case, those three divergences made it impossible for Darren's grandmother to be born, and thus Darren went *pfft*. Along with the rest of humanity." He gave a wry little smile. "God dislikes paradoxes, apparently."

"But," Darren said, "how do we know what it was that caused it? If I'm supposed to go back and fix this, how can I do that if I don't know what went wrong?"

"Well, it has to have had something to do with Lee McCaskill. We're working on the assumption that he has somehow learned how to time travel. So I'd say we should start with the earliest one, and have you go back there and snoop around and see if Lee shows up. When he does, get him to… to not do whatever it was that he was going to do."

"Well, that sounds simple." Darren shook his head, eyes wide.

"Good," Fischer said, ignoring his attempt at sarcasm.

"What if he has a gun?" He was immediately embarrassed at how weak his voice sounded.

"Well, he tried that once, and you survived," Fischer said. "So far, I think it's Darren Ault one, Lee McCaskill's gun zero."

"I don't know about this." He was rapidly running out of things to say to stall.

"Well, I do. That's why I'm the Librarian, and you're not." Fischer rubbed his hands together. "So, there we are. We'll land you a little before the date the divergence occurred," Fischer consulted the computer again, "August sixteenth, nine hundred and three. Try to find this…" Fischer looked at the computer screen again, "… Maíre Gillacomgain. She must be important. So that's that. Off you go to Scotland."

He swallowed. "Now?"

"We should wait why?"

"Um. I don't know. And besides," he said, desperation rising in him, "how can you send me to the tenth century? I mean, you can't just make me… *go* there." His eyes widened. "*Can* you?"

"Easiest thing in the world," Fischer said. "Remember, you really don't exist in any case. You have no actual track, ergo, you're nothing. Nada. Bubkis. And I can send nothing wherever I want."

Darren gave a desperate glance at Maggie, who was regarding him with some degree of sympathy. "Mrs. Carmichael, he can't… he can't…"

"Well, yes," she said. "Actually, he can."

Fischer made a little shooing gesture with his hand, and the Librarian, Maggie, Ivan the tomcat, and the Administrative Office of the Library of Timelines... all simultaneously winked out of existence.

An icy gust slapped Darren in the face, and he closed his eyes involuntarily. He opened them a moment later, however, when a wave of frigid water crested over his feet, soaking his jeans to mid-calf.

He yelped, and scrambled uphill, as another, and larger, wave foamed toward him. He avoided most of that one, and stood looking around, his eyes at first refusing to believe what he saw.

He was facing out over a rough, gray ocean, rippled with shifting, wind-driven whitecaps. A shelving slope of rough gravel and sand curved away from him in both directions. The sky was a pale, washed-out blue, with a few streaks of high cloud, and gulls kited and soared in the gusty air, calling forlornly. The sun shone, but its light seemed feeble, and provided no warmth whatsoever. Behind him was a ragged slope, with nothing but a few tufts of grass hanging on, blown nearly flat, hissing in the constant wind.

He wrapped his arms around himself. The wind sliced easily through his thin t-shirt, and salt spray spattered his glasses.

He looked up into the empty sky.

"Fischer!" he shouted. "Get me out of here!"

There was no response except from the gulls.

"Fischer!" he bellowed as loudly as he could. "I *demand* that you bring me back!"

Either Fischer couldn't hear him or else wasn't listening. The waves continued to strike the shore, the wind continued to blow, and the gulls continued to cry. Nothing else happened for several minutes.

"Oh, well, this is just *great.*" He rubbed the backs of his arms. "He sends me to medieval Scotland without a jacket. I don't even speak Gaelic, or whatever they spoke in medieval Scotland. And I'm somehow supposed to fix this stupid mess." He looked up into the sky again—the thought, *why do I think the Library is up there?* passed through his head. Probably because when he was a kid, that's where they'd told him that dead people went. He wasn't dead, but nonexistent was only one step removed.

He raised both arms to the sky and shouted, "Some Librarian you are! You send me somewhere where I don't speak the language, I don't know what I'm looking for, I don't know how to fix it even if I find it, and I *don't have a goddamn jacket!*"

Again, there was no response.

"Just *great,*" he said again, and for no very good reason, he made his way up the slope of the beach.

When he got to the top of the low hill, he saw the first sign of human habitation, a rough wooden rack, its base weighted with rocks to keep it from blowing away. It looked a little like the portable laundry rack he'd had in his apartment when he was just out of college, only rough-hewn and heavier-built. He went up to it, and was struck with a strong fishy smell.

They dried fish here. Of course. You live on a small island, fishing would be the only game in town.

He looked past the rack, and out over the barren landscape of sand, rock, and grass. There was no other sign of inhabitants.

"Dammit, Fischer!" Darren shouted again. "There's no one here! You sent me to the wrong place!"

Something pointed jabbed him in the back. He jumped a little, and turned.

Facing him was a young man of perhaps eighteen years,

who appeared to have risen up from the hillside by magic. He had long, reddish-brown hair, tied back, and narrow, aquiline features. He was clad in a plain brown garment a little like a kilt, a pair of leather sandals, and nothing else. In his hand he had a straight wooden spear tipped with a barbed metal head.

"Move," the young man said, in perfect English, "and I will spit you like a fish."

Darren made an inarticulate noise, his eyes wide.

"Are you a Viking?" the young man demanded.

"What? A Viking? Me? Lord no."

"Then why were you calling out to your Fisher God?"

Darren frowned in confusion. "What?"

"You called out to your God of Fishermen. You said, 'Fisher, you sent me to the wrong place.' The Vikings worship a God of the Deep Places, so they say."

"Him? Fischer?" He gulped. "No, no! He's not a god, he's just a guy. His *name* is Fischer. I don't *worship* him. In fact, right now, I'd like to punch him in the nose."

The man dropped his spear a little.

"Then you're not a Viking?"

"No!"

"How did you get here?"

His mind ran through various lies he could tell. None of them sounded very convincing. He settled on the truth.

"Fischer sent me here. To this island. To do something."

And that *did* sound convincing?

"Where is your boat, then?"

"Boat? I didn't come on a boat."

The spear point rose again. "This Fischer, he sent you here? With no boat to carry you? Then he is a god. No man could do such a thing."

Darren snorted. "Believe me, he's no god. He can do stuff. But that doesn't make him a god. He seems to *think* he's one, though." The words felt bitter in his mouth. He looked at the young man in some incredulity. "You speak English?"

The young man's expression was one of incomprehension. "I speak only as all here do. I do not know of *English*. Is it how they call the speech in your land?"

"Yes. But I thought... well, I didn't think they spoke that language here."

"The only other speech is that of the Vikings, which sounds to my ears like the snarling of wolves. You and I, we simply speak as our people do. Why does this surprise you?"

"I really don't feel like explaining. And I don't know if I even could, anyway. But yeah, I'm surprised, I guess."

The young man gestured with his spear. Darren flinched a little, but he was simply using the weapon as a pointer. "Do all men dress like that, where you come from?"

He looked down at his t-shirt—a souvenir of a Dave Matthews Band concert he'd attended the previous year—and his sopping wet jeans and sneakers.

"Yeah. Pretty much."

"And the..." the young man gestured toward his face. "The thing. On your face." He reached out, and tapped one of the lenses of his glasses with a fingernail, and his expression showed surprise. "The crystal covering you put over your eyes."

"They're called glasses. They help me see better."

The young man took them from the bridge of his nose. The entire scene dissolved into a diffuse blur. He saw the vague motion of the young man placing them on his own nose, and heard an exclamation of dismay.

"They blind me!" the young man said, sounding angry, or frightened, or both.

"Don't throw them away! I need them! I can't see without them!"

The glasses were shoved back onto his face, and he

reached up and straightened them. The world's clarity returned.

"Your land must be an odd place, that men there would need such a thing."

"There are no people here who don't see well?"

The young man nodded. "Certainly. Every place has its blind men. Some can see a little, others not at all. But I do not understand how those—what did you call them? glasses?—would help a blind man see."

"They just do, I don't know that I can explain it."

The young man did not seem to be interested in discussing the point—he simply appeared to accept that it was a mystery, and that was enough. He looked Darren over, his shrewd blue eyes evaluating him. Finally he appeared to make a decision. He dropped the spear point, and jabbed it into the sand next to him.

"Very well. I believe you. You are no Viking." One eyebrow rose a little. "For one thing, you are too thin around the chest and arms to be a Viking. Whatever else you may say about them, the Vikings are truly men."

He considered defending his masculinity, but decided against it. He'd made some headway, in that the spear was no longer pointed at his breastbone, and arguing over whether he or the Vikings had the most testosterone probably wouldn't help.

He shivered a little, and gave the young man a plaintive look. "Aren't you cold?"

The young man's expression became incredulous. "It is a beautiful summer afternoon. Why should I be cold?"

"Because it's freezing, and you're hardly wearing any clothes."

"You must come from a land of great warmth, if you find it cold here."

That was the first time he had ever heard Seattle described

as "a land of great warmth," but he didn't argue. "Warmer than here, anyway."

The young man nodded. "What is your name?"

"Darren Ault."

"It is a strange name. Darinauld. You have come from far away, I'd wager."

"You have no idea." He tried unsuccessfully to keep the defeated tone from his voice.

"I am called Malcolm. I live yonder. It is not far. My father will want to meet you and speak with you." He turned, and strode farther up the slope, away from the wooden rack and the view of the ocean.

"Wait a moment," he said, jogging to keep up with him. "Have you seen any other strangers in the last few days? Someone dressed like me?"

Malcolm halted, and turned, his eyes narrowing with suspicion.

"There is another from your land here?"

"There might be. He doesn't really look like me, though. He's taller, and bigger built."

Malcolm grinned. "That would describe many, I fear."

He tried to keep the exasperated look off his face. "Now, look…" he began.

Malcolm thwacked him on the back, nearly knocking him over. "Take no offense, Darinauld. I merely jest with you. I am certain that in your land, you are looked upon as a valiant warrior, and have a different woman to your bed each night."

He fought down the urge to scream. "Yeah. Whatever. I'm the pinnacle of warrior-ness, back among the fierce tribes of the land of Seattle. But listen, you have to be on the lookout for this guy. He'd be dressed kind of like me, probably. At least not in that, um,"—he gestured toward Malcolm's kilt—"skirt-thing you wear. He doesn't have glasses. And he's blond."

"A Viking?" Malcolm's voice suddenly sounded guarded again.

"No, he's not a Viking. He comes from Seattle, like I do." Darren considered for a moment. "But you might be well-advised to treat him like a Viking, if you see him. He's dangerous."

"Why would he come here?"

"I don't know. That's what I've got to find out. But he has already tried to kill me once. And if he comes here, I need to stop him. Somehow."

Malcolm's eyes had that appraising look again, and after a moment, he reached out and gave Darren another breath-chasing whack on the back with his open palm. "There is more to you than I would have expected, to look at you, Darinauld. Courage is not measured in size, in the far land of Seattle, I think. You should certainly meet my father. He may have some wisdom to share with you about this situation."

Situation. Just like Maggie always called it. What was it about Scottish people, referring to chaos and insanity as a "situation"?

Once again, Malcolm turned and strode away purposefully, Darren trotting along behind.

A ten-minute walk over the rocky, barren hillside brought them to a small cluster of low huts. It was nestled in a hollow to avoid the worst of the wind, which he was already realizing was incessant. He had warmed up a little from the exertion of keeping up with Malcolm, but was still in amazement that the young man wasn't freezing to death, given how much of his skin was exposed.

Not only was Malcolm not wearing a shirt, there was the issue of what the Scots allegedly didn't wear underneath their kilts. And about which he was definitely not going to ask.

Nothing was in evidence near the huts but a few sheep in a pen, but Malcolm shouted out a greeting, and a tall, middle-aged woman with red hair shot through with gray came out of the largest hut, carrying a wooden bowl in which she was mixing something. She gave Malcolm an austere little nod, and then looked Darren over from head to toe.

"What is that?" The woman's voice was clearly disparaging.

"His name is Darinauld, Mother," Malcolm said. "He came by strong magic from the distant land of Seattle. He is no Viking, however, and means us no harm, but is pursuing one of his countrymen who is in our land with evil intent. So he says, and I believe him."

"Do you?" Her voice was noncommittal. She gave him another appraising glance. "Do you speak, Darinauld?"

"Yes, I can speak." Even though he didn't have the slightest damned idea what he should say.

"And my son speaks truth? This one you pursue, he intends evil?"

"I think he does, yes."

"You wish to kill him, then." It didn't sound like a question.

"Well, yes. I mean, not really, I don't *want* to. I don't know. I want to stop him."

"Indeed?" the woman said. "Stop him from doing what?"

"Well... I don't know. I'm not sure." Jesus. He didn't usually sound impressive, but he was setting world records for unimpressiveness here.

The woman's right eyebrow went up a little. "If you don't know what you are trying to stop him from doing," she said, "it may be difficult to stop him from doing it."

"That's what I told Fischer!" he blurted out.

"Fischer?"

"He was praying to his god of fishermen when I first saw him," Malcolm said.

He rolled his eyes in exasperation. "No, I *told* you, Fischer is *not* a god. He did send me here, yes, and I guess it would seem like it's by magic. Hell, I suppose it *is* by magic. I don't know. But he's just a *guy*. Just a skinny guy with pierced ears and a big ego."

The woman looked at him, her eyes expressing mild curiosity but little comprehension.

Okay, they understood the language, but that didn't mean they understood anything outside of their culture. For some reason they understood each other's words, even though he thought he'd read that they spoke Gaelic or something in medieval Scotland. But if the concept didn't exist in their culture, it wouldn't make sense to them, even though they were somehow speaking the same words. So everything about the Library, the computers, the timelines, Fischer, Maggie, and Norton SuperBifurcator would sound like complete gibberish. And trying to explain it all would get him exactly nowhere.

He took a deep breath and started again. "Look, it's just that this guy, the guy I'm looking for. He's bad. He tried to kill me, and has caused, um, a lot of damage in my land. Other lands, too." Yeah, eradicating the whole human race was kind of a lot of damage. "I need to find out if he is here. His name is Lee. He's taller than me, bigger, with blond hair. And he doesn't have these things." He jiggled his glasses.

"I've seen no such stranger," the woman said. "But to follow such a man. You are braver than your appearance would tell."

"I said the same," Malcolm chimed in.

"Well," Darren said, "that's really nice of you both. But I guess, the sooner I find Lee and stop him from doing whatever it is I'm supposed to stop him from doing, the sooner I can stop complicating your day, and get back to Seattle." He paused for a moment. "I hope."

The woman set down her mixing bowl. "Malcolm, perhaps you should bring this man to your father."

"It is what I wished to do. Is he not here?"

"He is away, near the harbor. Donnacha told him that the

boats were in a day early with their catch. He and your sister brought their creels down to take back our share."

Malcolm nodded. "Will he be back soon, do you think? Would it be best to wait for him here, or meet them there?"

"They left not long ago," she said. "Perhaps if you leave now, and don't tarry, you will be able to help them carry back the creels. You can explain the stranger's story to your father on the walk back."

Malcolm nodded.

The woman looked over at him again. "And for my part, though it is perhaps not my place to say it, you have an odd manner of speech, and one that gives the impression of cowardice and ignorance."

He started to object, but the woman gave a little gesture, and he fell silent.

"I think, however, that you are neither cowardly nor ignorant, merely different. Something in your speech tells me that you are speaking the truth, or at least as much of it as you know and it is wise to speak to us, who are strangers to you. That you could tell more, I don't doubt, and for myself I do not fault you for keeping your own counsel." She looked at him, her gray eyes steady. "And you gave us your name before you knew if we were friend or enemy. We owe you the same. I am called Caitlin."

He wasn't sure what the proper medieval Scottish response to that was. *Nice to meet you, Caitlin. The pleasure is all mine. My, you've done such wonderful things with this hovel.* None of the usual sorts of platitudes seemed appropriate, and he ended up inclining his head a little in what he hoped was a respectful fashion. Caitlin acted satisfied, and without any other words, she turned and went back through the low door into the hut.

"Let us go down to the harbor and meet my father." Malcolm immediately turned and strode off down the path.

Whether it was his age, or simply his personality, Malcolm

appeared gifted with a limitless supply of physical energy. He was strong, tireless, and had the boundless enthusiasm of a golden retriever. His long, sinewy legs moving in a determined gait, his powerful arms swinging at his side, he easily outpaced Darren, who was breathless after the first minute of trying to keep up.

"What do you think your father can tell us?" Darren struggled to keep the sounds of exertion out of his voice.

"He will know if others of your land have come here. My father is wise. He speaks to others on the island, and to the fishermen who come from other islands. If your enemy has come here, he will know it." Now he half turned toward Darren, and said, his voice betraying curiosity. "What is your home like? I have never been farther than the neighboring islands. But I think that there is much to explore, out there in the world."

"That's the truth. But I haven't seen much of it. I've lived in Seattle all my life." He paused. "Seattle is a big city. Huge, really. People everywhere, and big buildings, and roads."

"Some of the men who have talked to my father have been to Scotland. Some have been as far as Wales. There are towns there, they say, that are crowded and noisy. Some have five hundred families in them." Malcolm looked back at him, a little sheepishly. "I do not ask you to believe it, and you who come from a distant land surely know better. But that is what they say."

"Five hundred families..." Darren couldn't help a smile. "That wouldn't make a thousandth part of the people in the Seattle area."

Malcolm came to a sudden stop, and turned to look at him, his face a mix of incredulity and suspicion. "Are you trying to dupe me with a falsehood, Darinauld? Just because I'm a simple islander..."

"No. It's the truth. Seattle is enormous. There are so many people that many live in huge buildings, with..." He paused.

How do you explain a multi-story apartment building to someone who lives in a one-room hut? "Like many houses, one on top of the other. Each house has many families, and there are paths to get from one set of houses to the ones above and below it."

Malcolm looked suitably astonished. "I would not like to have so many other families so close. I would feel I was suffocating. Why would you want to live in such a place?"

He didn't answer for a moment. Why *did* he want to live in Seattle? Mostly it was because it was where he always had lived. He'd never really contemplated living anywhere else.

He finally said, "I don't know. Probably because it's where I was born. I don't really know why."

Malcolm looked thoughtful. "That is a fair answer."

"I do like the fact that there are a lot of trees. It's very green. And the weather is mild, even if it rains a lot."

"Here the winters are cold. Few trees. For wood, we must cross to Scotland."

"So I see."

"But maybe you are right. Maybe you love Seattle because it is what you know. Perhaps the same is true for me. I love the island because it is beautiful and the fish are abundant in the waters, but mostly because it is home." He brightened. "Perhaps one day I will visit Seattle, and will find it beautiful also, and then I will understand why you wish to live there."

"Maybe," Darren said, and they began walking again.

After a few minutes, they crested a hill, and the path sloped down before them toward the curve of a bay. Several dark boats rested on the gravelly shore, and there were groups of people unloading the boats' contents, dragging nets onto land, and spreading them out for cleaning. There were dozens of large baskets lined up, ready to be filled with the day's catch.

Malcolm suddenly gave a shout of greeting, waved, and jogged down the hill toward the harbor. A thick-set man with an unruly mane of gray hair turned and watched Malcolm's approach.

"Father!" Malcolm shouted. "I bring a guest! He has journeyed long and hard from the distant land of Seattle, where men live in houses stacked one on another and there are trees growing everywhere, and it is always summer. He has pursued an enemy here whom he has already defeated once, and he believes that the enemy has come here to threaten our island, and he wishes to slay him so that he may return to his own land in peace." Malcolm turned, and gestured. "His name is Darinauld."

Malcolm's father turned his gaze toward him, and his blue eyes registered skepticism. "Well, that is quite a story." His voice was deep, resonant, and exuded calm and confidence. "I welcome you. My name is Dugal. Where did you put in your boat?"

Oh, shit, here we go again.

But before he could answer, Malcolm said, "He came in no boat, Father. He came here by magic."

"Magic!" Dugal said.

Malcolm nodded enthusiastically. "He has strong magic, Father, however he looks as scrawny as a plucked chicken. Look at the crystal coverings over his eyes. In his land, such things can make a blind man see!"

The skeptical look deepened. "You have impressed my son, and he speaks many words on your behalf. But perhaps you should speak for yourself, and see if you can impress me."

He swallowed, and looked at the older man's steady eyes.

Okay, now they had come to it. All of this other stuff had been practice. Screw this up, and any hope he had of getting these people to help him was done.

"Your son speaks truly." He tried to keep his voice steady and his words respectful. "He exaggerates my valor, but otherwise the story he tells is true."

"It is modestly spoken. You come from far away?"

"Very far. The other side of the world."

"It must be important, this quest of yours."

"Very important."

Dugal nodded. "And this enemy, this man you seek. He would come to our island seeking to harm us?"

"I don't know that for sure, but I suspect it. He has done a lot of harm back... back home. He tried to kill me once already. I have to stop him. Whatever happens, he can't be allowed to come here and hurt anyone. Or do *anything*, really. He needs to either leave, or..." He paused. "I guess if he won't leave, I may have to try to kill him."

Dugal nodded. "It sounds from your tale that he is worthy of death."

"I don't know. I'm not the one to make that judgment. But I do know that whatever he tries to do here, we *have* to stop him."

"And he also comes here by magic?"

"I suppose you could call it that."

"I could *call it that*? What does that mean? If it is magic, it is magic. If not, it is something else."

Darren didn't respond for a moment, desperately searching for words to explain himself. "What I mean is, it certainly *looks* magical. To anyone watching, it would have appeared like magic. But looks are deceiving."

"So it would seem, in your case."

"So, you believe him, Father?" Malcolm said.

"For now," Dugal said. "I don't hear a lie in his voice. But it is a lot to believe."

"That's the most I could ask," Darren said. "Thank you."

One corner of Dugal's mouth turned upward. "You may thank me when I have done something to aid you."

"Just being believed is nice."

"That is true. And now, perhaps you can aid us. We have creels with fish to be brought back for drying. An extra hand would not go amiss." He looked around. "Where is your sister? She is probably down the beach, making doe's eyes at Donnacha's son Cullen." He turned and bellowed, "Maíre! Come help us to carry! We are all waiting for you, lazy girl!"

Darren's head snapped around toward Dugal. "Maíre? That's your daughter's name?"

Dugal looked at him, frowning. "Yes. Why is that strange? It is a common enough name."

"Maíre Gillacomgain?"

Dugal and Malcolm stiffened, staring at him. The three men stood, stock still, in a frozen triangle, Dugal's brows drawing together like a storm cloud, Malcolm looking stunned, Darren trying to keep his face from showing the combined fear and self-reproach that seemed to rise upward from his belly.

He had been doing so well, and then he had to go and blurt out her name…

"And how," Dugal finally said, in a quiet voice, which nevertheless was heavy with suspicion, "do you know my daughter's full name?"

He swallowed, and opened his mouth to answer. He had no idea what he intended to say. But at that moment, a lithe, smiling young woman, with waist-length red hair tied at the back, came up to the three of them. "I was talking to Cullen, Father, I wasn't far away." And then she turned toward Darren, curiosity in her eyes. "Who are *you*?"

Neither Malcolm nor Dugal spoke. It seemed that the temperature between them had suddenly dropped twenty degrees.

"I asked you a question, stranger," Dugal said. "How do you know my daughter's name?"

He gave a wan smile. "Magic?"

Dugal's lips tightened. "That answer comes far too easily to your lips."

He started to protest that Malcolm was the one who had

characterized his appearance there as magic in the first place, but thought better of it. "Look. It's a long story. I'll try to explain it to you. But maybe we should take your fish-basket-things home and find a place to sit down."

Maíre laughed. "They're called creels."

Dugal looked at him, his eyes narrowing. "Well enough. But if I find that you are lying to us, you will be treated as a spy for the Vikings."

Darren swallowed. "That doesn't sound good."

"It isn't," said Malcolm.

"What is it with you people and the Vikings?" Darren lifted one of the creels, groaning a little under its weight.

"I hope you never have to find out," Malcolm said.

By the time the little huts in the valley appeared in the distance, his back ached and every muscle in his arms was burning. He was determined not to be shown up, however—even Maíre was carrying one of the creels, although she was struggling with it a little—and Dugal and Malcolm carried one each with ease.

He was getting a little sick of the scrawny jokes. Plucked chicken? Okay, he wasn't a bodybuilder, but that was a low blow. He looked over at Maíre. And especially in front of her. Damn, she was beautiful. Was there such a thing as love at first sight?

Well, lust at first sight, maybe. But he knew he'd better not even *hint* that he had the hots for this girl in front of Dugal, or he'd be missing important body parts about two seconds later.

It was a relief to reach the encampment and drop the creel to the ground, and he rubbed his numb hands while trying not to be too obvious about it. Caitlin came out of the hut and gave her husband and children the same austere nod that she had given to Darren.

Apparently they didn't do demonstrative in medieval Scotland. Worth noting.

Malcolm grinned broadly, and gestured at the full creels. "It was a good catch. We'll have our hands full, salting and drying."

Caitlin regarded her son with mild amusement. "I hear you say 'we,' and I will take that to mean that you will be helping instead of wandering the island wasting time, as you usually do."

"It's no waste, Mother. It was me who saw the Vikings ships first when they came, three years ago. And I found Darinauld, just today."

Caitlin's eyebrows rose. "Indeed! Two successes in three years of wandering. I was unjust to criticize you."

The sarcasm seemed to pass by Malcolm, and he went to the fire, and leaned over to look into the bubbling pot suspended above it. "I'm hungry."

"And there's a second miracle. You'll wait to eat with the rest of us, child."

"Before then," Dugal said grimly, "we have a matter to discuss. What has this Darinauld told you of his purpose?"

Caitlin shrugged. "Only that he was pursuing an enemy here, who came, as he did, from a distant land, and intended harm. Nothing else."

"Then perhaps you would wish to know that he revealed by accident that there is more than that in his visit here. He knew, somehow, our daughter's name before he had been told it."

Caitlin gave Dugal an inquiring look. "And have you asked him how he came by that knowledge?"

"I did. He told me that he would explain it, once we returned here. And here we are," —Dugal turned toward him —"awaiting that explanation."

Darren didn't answer for a moment. There was no sound but the crackling of the fire, and the ever-present whistling of the wind. All of their faces were turned in his direction. Malcolm expectantly, as if he really wanted there to be an explanation. Dugal filled with suspicion. Caitlin curious but reserving judgment. Maíre with a faint smile, as if merely amused at this diversion from the day's chores. If she was disturbed by the fact that it was her name that had caused all of this, and had thrust her with him into the center of attention, she didn't show it.

Finally he said, "I've told you the truth. Like Caitlin said to me earlier, as much of the truth as I could easily explain. But there is one part of it that I didn't tell you, that I have to tell you now." He stopped, swallowed, and looked at each of them in turn. "I am from Seattle, which is a distant land. I did come here by some means that I don't fully understand, and calling it magic is probably fairly accurate. I did come here trying to find a man named Lee, who has caused great harm to my land. But what I didn't tell you is that now, at this time, Seattle doesn't even exist. Seattle is a city that won't exist for a thousand years. I come from the future. In my own land, I won't even be born for another eleven centuries."

All of them simply stared at him. Had they understood a single thing he'd said?

Finally, Malcolm broke the silence. "How can a man be here who has not been born yet?"

Well, that was the question, wasn't it? How could he be here? He studied the faces of Dugal and Caitlin, and saw no real comprehension in either. "I know it sounds impossible."

"It does that," Dugal said.

"But I'm telling the truth. Look, all of you have said, at one time or another, that you thought I was telling the truth. You got to ask yourself, why would I lie? Or actually, if I *was* going to lie, wouldn't it make better sense to come up with a lie that was plausible? There's only one reason I would tell such a crazy story—if it was the truth."

Malcolm gave a smile, as if finally hitting a part of the story he understood, and looked at his parents. "Darinauld has a point, Father."

Dugal held up one hand, and his son fell silent.

"Let us say, for the moment, that you are speaking the truth. There is one thing that I do not understand."

"Only one?" Darren blurted out. "That's really good. There's about a thousand things about this that I don't understand."

Dugal also smiled a little, which he took to be a hopeful sign. "That is well said, Darinauld. I do not fully understand much of what you are saying, but I understand enough, I think, to ask a question. If your time is a thousand years hence, then to you, what you see around you would be far in the past. Our lives and deaths would be as a finished story to you. Therefore, your part in it would be, as well, as would your enemy's. It would be a memory of events long past, and as unchangeable as the past always is. How can you explain that you do not know where your enemy is, nor what he plans to do here, if it all happened in the past for you?"

He stared at Dugal. Even if the man had a tenth-century understanding of technology, and no knowledge at all of divergences or the Library of Timelines, there was no doubt that he wasn't lacking in intelligence. Darren tried to do some quick thinking, to no very great effect. No way did he want to go into the alternate timelines issue, much less Fischer's role. He barely understood all of that himself. But there seemed to be no choice but to try those waters, and hope like hell that they didn't get too deep too quickly.

"Well," he began. "I'm not sure I understand it all, myself. But I'll try to explain, at least as well as I can. There's a man I know who can somehow control where people are in time. He's the one who sent me here."

"Fischer!" Malcolm shouted out, grinning. "The one who is not a god!"

"Yes. And I only met him because something bad had already happened. Lee—the guy I am chasing—he tried to kill me, and somehow that changed things in the distant past.

Some event that's due to happen, some time in the next few days, somehow what he did changed that, and that led to everyone in my time being destroyed. We don't know why, nor what he did, nor how he got back here to do it. But Fischer's idea is that somehow Lee went back eleven hundred years into the past, and changed something, and it caused the destruction of all the people on earth. I seem to be the only one left."

"What about Fischer himself?" Caitlin asked. "He was not destroyed."

"Oh, yeah. And him. And his administrative assistant."

This last pair of words elicited a trio of blank stares.

"Administrative assistant?" Dugal said.

"It's kind of hard to explain," Darren said. "She's his, um, friend."

"His lover, you mean?" Malcolm asked, eagerly.

"Good lord, no." What would Maggie have thought if she'd overheard that? "She just helps Fischer. The two of them, and some of the people who work for them, didn't get destroyed. And don't ask me why, because I don't know. They're exempt from the rules, I guess."

"And you were sent back here to try to stop Lee from doing what he did?"

"That's the idea. But like I said to Fischer, it's going to be difficult to stop him when I don't know what he's going to do, or when. All I know is that somehow, your daughter is involved. Her name was in the records as being important. That's how I knew her name. Fischer told me."

And he was *not* telling them that supposedly, she was his ancestor. If they were freaked out before, that would put them over the top.

Dugal looked at him steadily. "It is a strange tale. But there is probably little need to say that. It would rival the fanciful tales we tell children. But you do not seem to be lying, much as I find your story hard to comprehend and even harder to believe. As you said, liars usually rely on attractive, easy deceptions. You have a strange tale which you admit you do not fully understand yourself." He turned toward his wife. "What do you think, Caitlin? Does he speak truth?"

Caitlin shrugged. "Who can know for certain? But for my part, I hear no lie in his voice, as I have said before. Perhaps a clever liar could tell such a twisted tale, thinking that we would be forced to say, 'Who could come up with such a story? It must therefore be true.' But I do not think that Darinauld is such a liar. I believe him."

Malcolm broke out into a grin. "And so do I!"

"Silence, child," Dugal said, but without anger. "You are too trusting, sometimes. I hope that you do not live to regret it. But I, too, seem to be forced to believe Darinauld, however peculiar his tale is. But we now come to the point. What is Maíre's role in this? And why does this enemy of yours wish to harm her?"

Maíre, who until now had remained silent, frowned. "What can I possibly have that he would want?" Her buoyant tones were gone. She sounded vulnerable and a little afraid.

Darren looked at her, suddenly feeling a little desperate to protect her, to keep her out of Lee's clutches.

"I don't know," he said. "I don't think Fischer did, either. It just seemed like whatever was going to happen, Maíre was in the middle of it. I don't know if he intends her harm, or if it's that something he will do will inadvertently cause her life to change paths. But it's all about her, somehow." He gazed at her open, innocent face, and felt another powerful rush of protectiveness. "We have to stop him from coming near her, I think."

"I will kill him, sooner," Malcolm said fiercely.

"I am glad to have such protectors." Maíre smiled fondly at her younger brother, and then she raised her blue eyes to Darren shyly for a moment before looking away. "Be certain that if I see any strangers dressed as you are, I will tell you at once."

"He may not be dressed as I am," Darren said. "He may have thought of that, and come dressed as one of you."

"Better, then, that you avoid all strangers," Caitlin said. "Stay away from the harbor, where there are many men you do not know, and any one of which could be the man Darinauld seeks."

"That would be wise," Dugal said.

Malcolm grinned at her. "No more flirting with Cullen."

"Cullen is nothing." Maíre gave another quick glance at Darren, almost too fast for the eye to see.

Now what could that mean?

But the moment was over, and the others had already begun to go about their chores. Once the issue was decided, it seemed, he was one of them, and that was that.

***

The rest of the afternoon was filled with labor. Darren wasn't asked to help, but he volunteered, feeling that now that he had earned these people's confidence, he owed them something in return. He'd never gutted a fish before, and his first few tries were fumbling.

Malcolm chortled, skinning the fish in his hand while barely glancing at it. "How do you eat in your land, that you don't know how to clean a fish?"

Darren grunted in annoyance as the fish he was handling slipped from his grasp and slithered its way to the ground. "In Seattle, there are people who do this sort of thing for you."

"Indeed! And why do they give you food, if you do nothing to earn it?"

How do you explain job specialization and a money-based economy to someone in the tenth century?

"Well," Darren ventured, "other people do other chores. I own a shop where there are books written by many people. People come to me to buy those books, and I use the money to buy food and other things for myself."

"Oh." Malcolm frowned. "How many books are equal to one fish?"

"Um… I suppose that depends on what kind of book, and how big the fish is."

"That makes sense."

"Does it? Good."

"Seattle must be a difficult place to live. How do you know what to do?"

"I'm really not sure. I think in a lot of ways, your way of life makes a great deal more sense."

This answer seemed to satisfy Malcolm. And within a few more tries, he had begun to get the hang of fish cleaning. He still was working at half the rate that Malcolm was, but at least fewer of them were landing on the ground.

Night came, and food was eaten around the fire. The chill deepened to the point that even Malcolm put on a shirt. Besides some of the fish he had helped to clean roasted over the fire, there was something a little like oatmeal, not remarkably delicious but hot and filling. Maíre got a woolen blanket from the hut and draped it around his shoulders. He smiled at her, but she had already turned and gone to sit at the other side of the fire, next to her mother.

"Tomorrow," Dugal said, "we should go around the island, and look for this enemy of yours, and ask others if they have seen him. I fear to have such a man walking about, doing what he will while we sleep. But there is little we could do in the dark, so I think that is our only choice. We will do what we can tomorrow to find out if he is here."

"I will come to help," Malcolm said.

"You will stay and help me salt the fish for drying," Caitlin said. "I still recall your saying 'we will salt and dry the fish' earlier, and I have no intention of letting you forget that so you can go wandering."

"Mother!" Malcolm wailed.

"Enough," Caitlin said. "Your father and Darinauld are capable of doing what must be done. They don't need a boy galloping along beside them. This is serious."

"I'm not a boy any longer, I'm a man," Malcolm said.

"Men do their share of the work, without complaint," Caitlin said. "Therefore, your place as a man is here, helping me with the rest of the catch."

"This isn't fair." The scowl was clear in Malcolm's voice, even if Darren couldn't see his face. "It was me who first found Darinauld."

"That doesn't mean he belongs to you," Caitlin said. "The matter is decided."

After dinner, the family rose and prepared for bed. Darren chose a time when Malcolm was alone, and went up to him quietly.

"Malcolm. Where is… um, your bathroom?"

"Bathroom?" Malcolm said.

"You know. Don't you have an outhouse, or something? When you need to… you know, when you have to…"

There was a moment's silence, and then a guffaw split the darkness. "You need to relieve yourself? Then go there." Malcolm gave him a little push in the direction of the ocean.

"You don't have, you know, a building or something? For privacy?"

"Your people always relieve themselves in the same place?

And indoors?" Malcolm's voice sounded incredulous. "The stink must be incredible!"

If Malcolm couldn't understand economics, what hope did Darren have to explain indoor plumbing? Looked like it was camping-style while he was here. That part hadn't occurred to him.

"No, it's not like that," was all he said, as he stumbled off into the darkness.

By the time he returned, the family had already retired indoors. No one had told him where he was to sleep, but given that the other two small buildings nearby were clearly for the animals and for storing dried food, he ducked into the low door, pushing aside a woolen hanging that had been drawn across the opening, and carefully walked inside.

He couldn't see the interior, but it was surprisingly warm and snug.

"We have made room for you." Malcolm's voice came from the darkness. "And there is an extra blanket. I told Mother that you were from a land where it was always warm, and would probably need a second covering at night."

"Thanks." He blindly moved toward Malcolm's voice. His outstretched hand touched a shoulder, and Malcolm said, "Here," and guided him toward a soft woolen mat and a pile of blankets.

He lay down and pulled up the blankets, but for a long time, sleep eluded him. There was no noise from Maíre. He would have wondered where she was if he hadn't been certain that her parents would never have let her go away, considering the threat. In ten minutes, Malcolm's breathing became deep and regular. But he couldn't relax.

Was he up to this? He had to kill Lee McCaskill if he saw him.

He couldn't wait to find out what he was going to do, because by the time he stopped to have a conversation, it would almost certainly be too late. So the only way was to kill Lee as soon as they saw him. But how could he do that? Lee was a friend.

The rational part of his mind rebelled immediately. Friend? A friend who had without hesitation shot Darren in the head. He'd clearly wanted to kill Darren, and had failed only because of some bizarre circumstance that even Fischer had yet to figure out. Lee was no friend, he was a threat, and not only a threat to Darren, a threat to everyone. He may not like it, but he had to kill him.

But could he do it? He'd come to Scotland without anything that could conceivably be used as a weapon.

Of course, Dugal and his family had weapons. Malcolm had a spear. Dugal wouldn't go out looking for Lee tomorrow without both of them being armed. He might not completely understand the threat, but he got that it *was* a threat, and he was far too smart to leave home unarmed.

So that was it? Darren had to be willing to stick a spear into his high school buddy?

And the answer came immediately. Yes. That was it.

But it sucked.

There seemed to be no arguing that point, and his inner dialogue died down. He closed his eyes, and tried again to relax, and for a few minutes, seemed to be making some headway. But then, on the other side of the hut, he heard the unmistakable noises of lovemaking.

Oh, for chrissake. Dugal and Caitlin? Right there? With Darren present? With their *kids* present?

Of course, that was the only place they could do it. They lived in a one-room hut. Darren added that to the list of things about medieval life that he had never thought about.

He tried to tune it out, but that sort of thing was remarkably hard to ignore, and they seemed to be making no particular effort to be quiet about it. And afterwards, as silence once more settled down in the little hut, he found he was so turned on that he couldn't sleep.

If it was going to be a porn soundtrack in there every night, he was going to have to sleep on the beach.

It was after midnight when he finally dropped off.

Darren woke in complete darkness. The first thing he noticed was that he had to pee. The second was that the air in the little hut didn't smell so good. In fact, it smelled fairly strongly of unwashed human. At that point, he discovered a third thing that he hadn't really considered about medieval life—the lack of showers. Of course, intellectually he knew that there were no showers in the early tenth century, but the outcome—that everyone would go around smelling horrible —had never really occurred to him. Outside, in the continuous wind, it wasn't so bad. Inside, it was pretty overwhelming.

He got up, moving quietly in order not to disturb the others, and pushed his way through the flap. The air outside was chilly and damp, and he immediately began to shiver. There was a thin pale streak on the horizon. It was perhaps an hour to sunrise. He estimated the time at five AM, but at this latitude, who could be sure?

He unzipped and thought about time. Why was he even thinking about what time it was? Here, no one cared. There were no watches or calendars. You simply did what you did, every day, all day, and the seasons came and went and you let them. No worries about opening the store at ten AM and closing it at nine PM. No worries about seeing tax day looming. No worries about Christmas shopping or preparing a huge meal for Thanksgiving. No weekends. No weeks, either. Just time, stretched out ahead and behind, like a long road with no detours.

He finished up, rezipped, and considered returning to the hut, but instead went out toward the beach, found a rock, and sat down. The salt smell was strong, but it was cleaner and more pleasant than the BO fumes in the hut. Better to be a little cold than to lie there trying not to retch.

He'd likely get used to it. He hoped so. No telling how long he'd be here.

And, now that he came to think of it, how long *was* he expected to stay? There'd been no discussion of that point. Fischer had simply waved his hand, and he had vanished in a swirl of ectoplasm. At least that was how he pictured it. Or maybe something like the sparkly transporter thing on *Star Trek*. But how much before the event in question had Fischer sent him to Scotland? The computer screen had shown that the divergence occurred on the 16th of August, 903, but who knew how many days away that was? Malcolm had referred to the time as being "a beautiful summer afternoon," but that could just as easily apply to June as August.

"I do not want to stay here for months," he said under his breath. "Stay here, looking around, waiting for something to happen, being expected to fix that something, and then getting home who-knows-how. Although I expect that if Fischer can whisk me away, he can bring me back."

He looked out over the restless whitecaps, now vaguely visible in the widening band of gold on the horizon.

"If he remembers to, that is. He acted like I was some kind of major inconvenience. I hope he doesn't forget about me or decide to leave me here."

He sat, gazing out to sea, watching the light spread, turn orange, and finally the sun peered over the edge, and a shimmering crimson pathway glittered on the surface of the ocean, reaching toward him.

Okay. It was pretty here. But damn, it was cold. Winters must be a bitch.

He heard a noise, and turned to see Malcolm coming up towards him, smiling broadly.

"It is a fine morning," he said, sitting next to Darren on the rock. "No rain or fog. A good omen for your hunt."

Darren sighed and shook his head. "I'm not looking forward to it."

"Why not? Your heart should be joyous at the thought of vanquishing your enemy."

"Well, it's not," he said flatly. He looked over at the young man. "Have you ever killed someone?"

"Me? No." Malcolm looked out to sea. "I would do it, though. I was too young when the Vikings came last, three years ago. My father fought, though. We drove them away." His face darkened. "Five islanders were killed. But they took none of our belongings, and took no slaves."

"Slaves?"

"They scour the islands for slaves. Did you not know that? Men and women. Men for laborers, and women for wives." Malcolm's brow furrowed. "They are no better than pigs."

They sat silent for a while. The long rays of the sun warmed his skin, and chased away at least a little of the night's chill.

"There are no Vikings in Seattle?" Malcolm asked.

"Well, sort of." Darren shrugged. "A lot of that area was settled by people from Norway and Sweden. So I suppose they're sort of Vikings. They don't hurt anyone, though."

"You live peaceably with them?"

"Sure. As far as I know, Norway and Sweden are now two of the most peaceful countries in the world. The Vikings have settled down, I guess."

Suddenly he looked over at Malcolm. Should he be telling the islander this? What if by telling Malcolm things about his own time he was changing the future? In all the time travel stories, they made a huge deal about not changing the past by telling people things they shouldn't know. Or changing anything, for that matter. Maybe he could cause all sorts of havoc by stepping on a bug, or something.

"When you leave," Malcolm said, interrupting his musings, "I want to go with you back to Seattle."

"Oh, lord." Darren felt a thrill of horror that his thoughts had come to life so quickly. "That's not a good idea."

"Why not?"

"You have no idea what kind of changes you'd have to deal with, if you were to go a thousand years in the future."

"I would not mind!" Malcolm protested. "I would pee in the house, like all of you do, and I would not complain about the smell!"

He waved his hand impatiently. "It's not that. It's all the other things. It's crowded and noisy. You have to spend your time indoors, working at doing things. Pointless things, most of them."

"Do you not want to go home?" Malcolm looked puzzled. "The way you are speaking of it, it sounds as if you were unhappy there."

"Well, yes. Yes and no. There are things I miss. But I don't think that our way of doing things is the only way. Or the best, even. And you..." He paused. "I don't think you would enjoy it very much."

"I do not want to spend my entire life on an island, and never see the world."

"You don't have to."

He scowled. "I don't have any choice. My grandfather raised sheep. My father raises sheep. I think my fate is to raise sheep."

"It's not the worst thing in the world."

"Nor the best," Malcolm said.

He studied Malcolm's open, honest face, and suddenly felt the same protectiveness he had felt the previous evening for his sister. He wanted to save them, to shield their world from Lee and all he represented.

And himself as well. It was his world, too. He was as much an intruder here as Lee. He was poisoning this place as surely as Lee was.

A shudder of alarm vibrated down his spine. What if the change happened because of *him*? What if it wasn't Lee at all, but because *he* came back here and changed something, and it ended up destroying the human race?

Now wait. The human race got wiped out before he got here. Well, it was actually eleven hundred years after he got here, but whatever. He ended up in the Library and found out about all this stuff beforehand, so it couldn't have been him that caused it. Right? He squinted in intense concentration. The whole thing was too much to comprehend. He didn't even know what before and after *meant* in this situation. Probably a good time to stop thinking about it.

"You look like you're in pain," Malcolm commented.

He glanced over, and saw that the young man was staring at him.

"I sort of am," he said. "I'm trying to figure all of this out."

"Do not worry." Malcolm put one hand on his shoulder. "You will find your bravery when you see your enemy. Do not doubt yourself."

"I'm doubting everything, at the moment."

By this time, blue had spread its way across the sky, interrupted only by a few high, wispy clouds. It looked to be a fine day, although still too cool for his expectations of summer. He rose, and Malcolm followed, and they went back to the hut, where they found Caitlin already up and turning the penned sheep loose into the fields. Dugal sat by the fire, which had been regenerated from the coals and was now crackling with flame. He was eating from a wooden bowl, and it was the same nondescript gruel they'd had the previous night.

Okay, here was number four on the list of things he'd never thought about. Gruel for breakfast, lunch, and dinner. It probably wasn't worth asking for a couple of eggs over easy and a cup of coffee.

Malcolm helped himself to some of the porridge from the pot hanging over the fire, and seeing that no one was offering to serve him or waiting for him to ask, he did the same, and sat down with his bowl near the fire, attempting to maneuver himself upwind of the smoke.

"Today we will circle the island, and see what news there has been," Dugal said. "There are several whom I would like to ask for news. Niall, for one. He knows everything that happens on the island, and much that is going on elsewhere."

"Niall is a busybody," Caitlin said, walking toward the fire and wiping her hands on her skirt.

"That he is, but useful nonetheless," Dugal said. "The more eyes and ears, the better. If there is a stranger on the island, Niall will have heard. He talks to everyone, and keeps in his memory even things that others would not remark upon. Rest assured, if your enemy is here, he will know."

Time to confront it. "I have no weapon."

"You came after your enemy with no weapon?" Dugal's face betrayed astonishment. "That is either an act of great courage or great foolhardiness."

"Well, neither, actually. I didn't know I was coming, I got sent. Fischer sent me away after Lee, and I didn't have time to grab a weapon." He didn't add that he probably wouldn't have in any case, but he thought it.

"I can provide you with a spear. We only have one knife that is suitable to be used as a weapon. But a spear is as good as any, from a distance, as I doubt you plan to discuss terms with him. I think in this case, a spear through the heart would serve your purpose. There is no need to talk with your enemy, and none will think you the less brave for having struck him down so, not after they hear what he did."

Darren considered his earlier thoughts about killing Lee as soon as he was spotted, and realized that he needed answers as much as he needed to stop Lee from doing whatever he was going to do. "But I do want to talk to him. I want to find out what he knows."

"But surely such a man does not deserve to be given a chance. You do not intend to spare him in any case, do you?"

"I guess not."

"Then what need for talk?"

"I want to understand."

"You are a strange one, Darinauld."

"It's important. When I go home. For me to understand what happened. You see, Lee was once a friend of mine. He and I were children together. And I do not know why he tried to kill me, or why what he did killed so many people. I know I may have to kill him. But I don't want to do it until I find out what he knows, and why he did what he did."

They readied themselves to leave at what seemed a snail's pace. Darren found it increasingly irritating that he didn't know what time it was. He hadn't realized how tied to his wristwatch he'd been. Everything in what he was now increasingly thinking of as his "old life" had been tied to time, sometimes down to the minute. Here, none of that mattered. There were only three times that mattered—the past, the future, and now. There was a vague sense of morning and afternoon, and certainly an awareness of night. Seasons changed, years passed. But the minuscule attention to the passing of time that had been part of his life for as long as he could remember simply didn't exist here.

"When are we going?" he asked Dugal as a spear was thrust into his hand.

"When we are ready," Dugal said.

Which, he reflected, was the only answer that was meaningful in this place.

It was shortly before they left that Maíre came up to Darren, while he was idling by the fire. Dugal had disappeared behind the house, and Caitlin and Malcolm were a little way off, salting fish and hanging it on racks to dry in the chilly wind. Maíre sat down next to him, and gave him a thoughtful look.

"It is probably not my place, Darinauld, but it is in my heart to speak."

"Go ahead."

"I would ask you… if you can… perhaps after this enemy of yours has been vanquished, you would wish to say here with us."

He looked at her in some surprise. "That's kind of you. But I'm not sure I'll be allowed."

"This Fischer, he will bring you back home, then?"

"I expect so. Either I'll find Lee, and probably have to kill him, or else he'll find me, and kill me. Either way, I don't think I can stay here." He gave her a shy smile. "I'd like to, though."

"I know we have not known each other long, but something in you… when I saw you, I thought that I would wish nothing more than to have you stay here on the island. Stay with us. Stay with me."

"But… I'm not one of you. I'm not an islander."

"*Pfft,*" Maíre gave a dismissive gesture with one hand. "The island boys are dull. They have no spirit. All they want…" She looked away, out toward the sea. "All they want is what every man wants. It is not wrong, that, but… that is *all* they want. When they talk to me, it is only in the hopes that I will allow them the use of my body. Nothing more. With you… you speak to me as if I were more than an empty vessel. I did not even know I wished for that, until now. To be spoken to as an equal. It is a rare gift." She cast her eyes downward.

Darren reached out and touched her face, and raised her gaze to his. "Any man should consider you his equal. Or his better. Do not let anyone condescend to you. You deserve more than that."

She took his hand. "You are kind and brave, Darinauld of Seattle. Will you not… will you ask your god, this Fischer whom you serve, if it may not be possible for you to stay here, once your task is completed? It cannot be such a big thing, to ask it."

"I don't know. Me staying here… well, it could further mess things up. Change who knows what. I'm sure he would say no."

Again she bowed her head for a moment, her expression disconsolate. "I understand. But at least I ask this much—do not forget me."

"I never will."

"Then I am content, and we will speak no more of it." She took a deep breath, and seemed to come to a decision. Her blue eyes held a fierce glitter. "Go, and vanquish this evil man who wishes you harm. You will surely prevail."

"I hope so. Although how I am going to do this is beyond me."

After a span of time that could have been one hour or three, Darren and Dugal took off on foot on the path over the hills. Each was carrying a leather sack with food and water. Niall's house was on the other side of the island, and they would not return until near sunset. Dugal walked with a steady, certain pace, using the butt-end of the spear as a walking stick, so he followed suit.

They walked in silence for some time, the only sound the

incessant hiss of the wind in the dry grass on the hilltops. Finally Dugal spoke.

"I have been considering the words you spoke yesterday." His deep voice sounded thoughtful. "And it occurs to me that there is a question that no one has asked. Have you any certainty that the one who sent you here, this Fischer, is perhaps not the one who has evil designs on our time? That perhaps Fischer and your enemy Lee could be in league against us? It seems odd, does it not, that the two of them are the only ones who can fly back and forth from the future to the past like gods, and yet are not allies?"

"I hadn't thought of that. But Fischer seemed honest to me. I felt sure that he was telling the truth."

"Thus did you feel about your friend before he attempted to kill you, did you not?"

"That's true."

"Therefore, it may be that when Lee's attempt to kill you failed, Fischer seized the chance to do away with you by sending you here." He paused. "I am only a simple man, and I do not know that what I am saying is correct. It only seems to me that there is more here than we are seeing." Dugal gave Darren a shrewd look. "I think that you are a man who trusts easily."

"I suppose so."

"It would be prudent, then, to be aware that not everything is how it seems, and when men speak, it is never certain that they are speaking the truth."

"I still don't think Fischer was lying," Darren said.

"*Not speaking the truth* is not the same thing as *lying*. Perhaps I am wrong about Fischer and Lee being in league against you. Even so, you should not necessarily trust that what Fischer has said to you is the truth. A man may tell the truth to the best of his ability, and still simply be wrong."

"He seemed to know what he was doing. And at the moment, I don't have any better explanation for what happened than the one Fischer gave me. If he was lying, or wrong about things, I'm damned if I know what direction to go. I don't see that I have much of a choice, other than to operate under the assumption that Fischer was right."

"Then let us speak no more about it. I will only say, you should not start out from the assumption that everyone is telling the truth. It is better to start out with no assumptions at all. And second, knowing one's failings is the greater part of overcoming them." Dugal gestured with the point of his spear. "But here is Niall's house. I do not doubt that he is at home. Work does not agree with him. How he manages to feed himself, I do not know, but he never seems to lack for provisions."

He followed Dugal up to a small hut, built of stone and turf, with an animal skin hanging across the opening. The remnants of a fire, long since burned down, smoldered nearby, and a wooden rack stood alongside, downwind of the smoke, with filleted fish hanging by their tails from the crossbeams.

"Niall Dubh," Dugal said in a loud voice. "If you are here, come out. Dugal Gillacomgain has need of words with you."

A moment later, a hand pushed aside the animal skin, and a very tall, very fat man ducked through the door and stood blinking in front of them. He wore a rough brown shirt and a plain kilt, tied at the waist with a rope belt, and was barefoot. His hair was black, long, and in wild disarray, and he had a scruffy mustache and beard. He looked like the product of an unholy union between a Scotsman and a grizzly bear.

"Dugal Gillacomgain." Niall yawned cavernously and scratched his crotch with a hairy, paw-like hand. "What brings you here so early?"

"Early?" Dugal said. "The sun has long been up."

"Has it? Well, I haven't." He went to what was left of his fire, picked up a stick, poked the embers without much effect, and then shrugged. "Let me get food and drink."

Niall disappeared once more into his house, and returned with bread, salted fish, and some strips of green that looked like the dried seaweed Darren had seen used to wrap sushi. He also had a large clay bottle of what turned out to be quite passable beer.

After all three men had eaten in silence, Niall belched, and wiped his hands on his kilt. "Now. What is it you want, Dugal? I do not think you have come to this side of the island for the pleasure of my company."

Dugal smiled a little. "I have a stranger here, Darinauld of Seattle. He came here by the magic of another, seeking a man who tried to kill him. I know that you get news from far and wide, and I thought that you would know if other strangers have been seen on the island."

Niall squinted at him, as if noticing him for the first time. "Seattle? Where is Seattle? I have not heard of that place. Is it an island? Or a settlement in Scotland?"

Darren shook his head. "Neither. It is very far away. On a whole different continent."

"Is it?" Niall said, sounding uninterested. "And this villain who tried to kill you, did he come from Seattle as well?"

"Yes."

"And he looks like you?"

"Not much. Well, I mean, he might be dressed like me. But he's broad-shouldered, and blond. But he's not a Viking," he added hastily.

"Not a Viking," Niall repeated. "No, I suppose not. I have never heard that the Vikings came from a place called Seattle." He looked thoughtful. "How had you angered him, that he wished to kill you?"

"I don't know. We were friends since we were children together."

"Was it over a woman? It would not be the first time a friendship ended in death because of a lover."

"No, nothing like that. Lee has a girlfriend, but I've never tried to come between them."

Niall nodded, and stroked his beard thoughtfully. "There are only a few things that men will kill for. Women, wealth, revenge, to protect themselves or their families. I think it must be one of those. Do you not agree, Dugal?"

"It is so."

"If you had no intent to steal his lover," Niall said to him, "did you intend to steal his belongings?"

"No!" Darren said.

"Had he any reason to seek revenge on you?"

"Of course not."

Niall looked at him speculatively. "And you do not look like much of a threat to anyone. It is puzzling." He frowned. "This enemy of yours, why do you think he is here? You say your home is far distant. Why would he come here, where he knows no one?"

"I do not know. The one who sent me here told me that he'd be here, and that he'd try to do something. Something bad. And that I needed to stop him. If I don't… well, apparently, it will cause all sorts of bad things back home." Darren glanced at Dugal, praying he wouldn't mention the whole coming-here-from-the-future thing. He seriously didn't feel like explaining that again.

Dugal, fortunately, didn't volunteer any further information, and Niall didn't press him with further questions.

Niall cleared his throat, hiked up his belt a little, and said, "Well, for my part, I have no knowledge of anyone on the island who shouldn't be here. Yesterday a sharp-eyed man on Donnacha's fishing boat saw Viking longboats, but they were distant and moving away. Other than that, there has been nothing out of the ordinary here."

"I thank you for your help, Niall," Dugal said. "I would warn you to keep your ears and eyes open, and if you see any who seem not to belong here, that you let us know immediately. I have discussed the matter with Darinauld, and I am convinced the threat this man represents is real. I cannot fully explain it, but I can feel it, like a weight in my mind. If this man comes here, we cannot fail to act."

"I understand," Niall said. "If he comes here, I will know."

"That is why we came to you."

More beer was brought out, and more food, and perhaps another hour passed in that way. Whatever else you could say about the Scots, they couldn't be hurried. But finally farewells were pronounced. Niall went back into his house, and Darren and Dugal walked back the way they'd come.

"It may seem to have been a long walk for nothing," Dugal said, after they'd gotten out of earshot from Niall's house. "But however Niall appears to be a fat, indolent man, he is shrewd. Nothing happens on the island that he does not find out about. He has eyes and ears everywhere." He looked over at Darren. "Of all the things Niall said, the one that concerned me the most was the Viking longboats. This is, to my knowledge, the first that they have been spotted in over a year. But I do not see what we can do about it." He walked in silence for a while, frowning in a meditative way. He finally said, "What course of action should we pursue, then?"

"I don't know." Darren scowled. "That's the frustrating part. I don't know what I'm supposed to be looking for. I don't even know when it's supposed to happen. It could be today, or it could be three months from now. There's no way to tell."

"Then we have no choice but to keep doing what must be done, let life take what course it will, and exercise patience."

"I'm not good at that."

Dugal smiled faintly. "Few men are."

By the time they approached Dugal's house, the wind had shifted, and it looked as if the weather were turning bad. Dark storm clouds lined the horizon, although the sky overhead was still blue. From the top of a hill, Darren could see the ocean, slate gray and lined with whitecaps, and he shivered a little as a gust struck them.

It was because the wind was blowing from the direction of the ocean that their first hint of something wrong was the smell of smoke. Dugal frowned, looking seaward, and his nostrils quivered.

"That is not the smell of a turf fire." Dugal's voice sounded dark with worry.

They crested the last hill. Dugal was a little ahead, and he stopped so abruptly Darren nearly walked into him. He looked down the hill, aghast.

Dugal's house was nothing but smoldering ruin. The turf shack where the sheep were housed at night was destroyed. Dugal, silent, began to walk again, and he marveled at the man's self-control. Even when he got near to what was left of his home, he didn't run.

It wasn't until they came around to what had been the front of the house that Dugal sprang forward, fell to his knees, and looked to the sky as the rain began to fall, and gave an inarticulate cry of grief.

It took a moment for Darren to realize what Dugal had seen, what was lying by the fire pit. Malcolm, his simple shirt ripped and bloody, was sprawled on his back, fallen with one leg twisted beneath him, like a dropped doll. His shoulder bore a gaping wound, and his face was white and still.

"No." Dugal touched Malcolm's face. "No, my son, no, you cannot be gone…"

Darren ran to Malcolm's side, knelt next to him, and lifted his head. To his surprise, Malcolm opened his eyes, and after a moment licked his lips and spoke weakly, in a whisper, as the rain fell around them in swirling sheets.

"They… they came ashore. There were twenty, or more. I tried to stop them. They took Mother, and Maíre. They have taken everything." He closed his eyes, and his forehead creased with a frown. "I have failed. I failed to protect them. I did not even see them coming."

Dugal bowed his head and wept, his broad chest rising and falling spasmodically.

"Which way did they take them?" Darren's heart pounded with greater anger than he'd ever felt.

"Down… down to the shore." A tear spilled from one eye, across his white cheek, merging with the rivulets of rainwater coursing down his face. "I tried to stop them. I have failed."

"No, my son." Dugal's voice was thick. "You did what you could. None can stand against those dogs."

Darren looked up at Dugal, and fury blazed in him. A tiny voice said, almost too quietly to hear over the blood pounding in his ears, *What are you doing? You're just a bookstore owner. You can't possibly be thinking…* But then he pictured Maíre's sweet, innocent face, and what would undoubtedly happen to her if she remained with the Vikings—what might already have happened.

"I have to rescue them."

Dugal looked at him incredulously. "We two? Against so many? You cannot think that we…"

"Not we. Me. You stay with Malcolm, make him comfortable. He's lost a lot of blood, but he's young and strong. He might yet survive, if you can get him somewhere warm and dry. If you leave him here by himself, in the rain…" He reached out, and clasped the older man's arm. "This is it, I know it is. I have to try to stop the Vikings from taking Maíre and Caitlin. That's what I was sent here to do."

"But this has nothing to do with the man who tried to kill you."

He shook his head. "But it *does* have to do with Maíre. When Fischer sent me, he said… he said that the key was her.

Not Lee. It was Maíre. Whatever is causing all of this, it has to do with her. Maybe... maybe Lee has joined up with the Vikings. I don't know. But whatever it is... I have to try to save her."

Dugal frowned at him. "There is more to you than I thought, Darinauld."

"Hell, there's more to me than *I* thought."

"I should go with you. Two have more chance than one alone."

"No. Two have the same chance as one. That chance is probably pretty close to zero. And if you go, you'll have to leave Malcolm, and he will certainly die. Stay here. If I'm not back by nightfall... then it will be your turn."

Darren headed off over the low hills, away from Dugal's house, toward the sound of the ocean crashing in the distance. The rain fell steadily now, blown by a gusty wind, and it was getting dark. Darren hoped this meant the Vikings who had kidnapped Caitlin and Maíre wouldn't cast off. Once they'd taken to their boats, there would be nothing he, or anyone, could do.

What exactly was he going to do in any case? He was a bookstore owner, and he looked like a plucked chicken. He had a spear, and he was going to rush in and rescue Maíre and Caitlin from a bunch of well-armed, tough, battle-hardened Vikings? Not to state the obvious, but had he lost his mind?

No, he hadn't lost his mind. The whole world had gone crazy. None of it made any sense whatsoever—from Lee trying to kill him, to the Library of Timelines, to Fischer and Maggie, to his getting thrown back to tenth century Scotland. None of it made the least bit of sense.

But that didn't mean he had to do something crazy to fit

in. What was he going to do? Walk up to a group of Vikings and say, "Hey, you need to let Maíre and Caitlin go or I'm going to be really annoyed with you. See? I have a spear."? The only thing that would delay their running him through would be they'd have to wait until they stopped guffawing in his face.

He stumbled over a tussock of grass, and cursed the fact that it was now almost pitch dark. The clouds were thick enough that the moon, even if it was up, was invisible. He could barely see his hand in front of his face. Then he remembered the little flashlight clipped onto his key ring, and pulled it out, hoping the batteries weren't dead. He switched it on, and it gave an amazingly powerful beam of light.

"Well, score one for you, Mom," he said. "I just wish you'd figured out a way to give me an umbrella that I could attach to my keys."

The rain fell in sheets, and they glittered in the beam of the flashlight like a swirling, gauzy curtain. He was soaked to the skin, and even the exertion of walking wasn't warming him. He shivered uncontrollably.

This was insane. But then Maíre's smiling face appeared in his mind, the feel of her soft skin when he'd touched her face, the way his heart had skipped a beat when she took his hand. And he kept walking.

He couldn't see the ocean, even though he was certain it had to be close. It was simply too dark. But he did see a reddish glow, a fire burning brightly despite the downpour. He reached the top of a hill, and saw, through the shimmering bands of rain, a huge bonfire, and surrounding it some dim, indistinct shapes, but clearly human.

"Well, there they are," he said. "Now what the hell do I do about it?"

He turned the flashlight beam off, and crept quietly toward the fire. The Vikings seemed not to have posted any guards, and were apparently unconcerned about the possibility of attack. He heard the noise of speech, and then a bellow of laughter, and then, clearly, "… mutton goes down well after nothing but fish for weeks."

They spoke English, too?

No, of course they didn't speak English. Whatever peculiar circumstance had allowed him to understand Maíre, Caitlin, and Dugal, despite his complete ignorance of Gaelic, must have also allowed him to understand these people despite an equally complete lack of knowledge of Old Norse.

That was handy. It gave him at least one advantage. Maybe his only advantage.

He gradually made his way up to the edge of the firelight. Several broad-chested blond men with long hair and beards both in braids stood near the fire, which sizzled and sputtered as the rain fell into it but nevertheless burned cheerfully. He frowned a moment, wondering why none of them had a helmet with horns. Didn't the Vikings all wear helmets with horns?

But other than one of them, who had what appeared to be a leather cap on, all were bare-headed. Maybe they only wore their horned helmets on special occasions or something. Then he decided it didn't matter, and tried to focus his attention on what they were saying.

"We'd be away by now if we'd attacked the other side of the island," one said. "Wind was already coming up when we landed. I told you we'd get stuck on this stinking sand bar."

"Ulf saw the sheep. If you wanted to pass up meat for dried fish, then you can give me that shank you're working on. There's plenty of fish back in the hold for you to feast on."

One of the others laughed, and the man with the leather cap gave a resounding belch. "I'd sooner be stuck here with meat than safely away with none," he said, and there was general laughter. "And what about our other prizes, eh? What about them?"

"You can have the old one, Grim," the first man said,

"long as I get the young one. She'll be worth something when we get back home, and I daresay her value won't be any less if she's used goods by the time she gets there."

The laughter bellowed forth again, and anger, a hot and entirely unfamiliar feeling, rose in Darren's heart.

"The old one has some spunk," Leather Cap said. "She kicked Olaf in the balls when he grabbed her. He'd have spilled her guts right then and there if you hadn't stopped him."

"The rule is, no killing what's valuable," the first man said. "Olaf will get over it, and it'll remind him to be more careful next time."

Where were the women? Would they have them stowed on the boat already?

He edged his way around the perimeter of the firelight, hoping to find the two women without being seen. As soon as he moved around to the side of the fire, away from the knot of Vikings discussing the day's exploits, he found that there was a low rise that screened him from view, and he slowly made his way clockwise around the fire.

The problem was, the rise also screened him from the firelight, and as a result he found Maíre and Caitlin by tripping over their feet. He fell face-first into the sand, uttered a muffled curse, and heard an exclamation in Caitlin's voice.

"Watch your step, you filthy dog," she snarled.

"Caitlin?" he whispered. "It's me. It's not a Viking, it's me, Darren."

"Darinauld?" came Maíre's voice, the excitement and hope sounding clearly.

"I've come to rescue you," he said, and he felt his way to them, found a pair of bound hands, and fumbled at untying the knots. Finally he said, "Dammit. I can't see a thing. Hang on a second." He pulled his keys out of his pocket, and switched on his flashlight.

Maíre gasped. "How… how are you making fire in your hands?"

"It's not magic," he said, working at the knots binding her hands. "But I don't have time to explain it now." He gritted his teeth. "I wish I had a knife."

"Darinauld," Caitlin observed, "you have a spear."

"Oh. Yeah." He picked up his spear, which he'd set on the ground, and used the sharp edge of the bronze point to cut the cords that bound Maíre, and then Caitlin.

"There. You're free. Dugal is with Malcolm. Malcolm's hurt but he's still alive. You should run. They won't be able to track you in the dark."

To his amazement, and intense appreciation, Maíre took his face between her hands, and kissed him squarely on the mouth. "I knew you wouldn't fail us, Darinauld. I said so to Mother."

He found himself smiling, but he didn't have time to bask in the pleasant glow the kiss left behind. "You need to hurry and get as far away as you can, so they can't track you. If you run quietly, you'll be fine. These Vikings are big, but I get the feeling they're as dumb as they are ugly."

There was a quiet sound behind him. In the glow from the flashlight, Maíre's eyes widened, and she gave a little gasp. Then he felt something pointed jab him in the back.

Oh, shit. He knew that feeling. Unfortunately.

"Perhaps I am not quite as dumb as I am ugly," a heavy, sullen voice said, and then added, "Move suddenly, and I will skewer you like a pig."

What was it with these people and their nasty analogies? He turned his head slowly, and saw, glowering down at him, the fleshy face of the Viking in the leather cap.

For a moment, no one moved. Time seemed to have stopped. Then he did something that was either smart and brave, or simply foolhardy. He threw himself to the side, and before Leather Cap could react, he aimed the beam of his flashlight into the Viking's eyes.

Blinded, Leather Cap jabbed wildly with his spear. One of the thrusts missed him by inches.

He shouted to Maíre and Caitlin, "Now! Run! I'll be okay. You need to get back to Dugal!" Both women leapt to their feet, and within seconds had vanished into the rainy darkness.

He backed away, and stood up, still keeping the flashlight in Leather Cap's eyes. The man's expression became shrewd. He'd clearly figured out that however his prey was magically making a powerful beam of light, it wasn't hurting him. Clearly, if he had been able to do more, he would. Grunting laughter, Leather Cap reared back, prepared to pitch his spear at the source of the blinding beam.

That's when Darren remembered the electronic air horn.

He felt for the button on the little plastic square, and fortunately for him, as he probably wouldn't have had a second chance, found it on the first try. He squeezed the button as hard as he could, as if the pressure of his fingers would make a difference in its volume.

An earsplitting honk filled the quiet night air. Leather Cap's spear throw went wild, and there was a whiff of wind of it as it flew past his left ear. The Viking gave an involuntary cry of fear, and his hands went to his ears.

"Evil spirit!" Leather Cap shouted, and turned and ran back toward the bonfire. "An evil spirit of the island has come!"

He watched his enemy retreat, and burst into helpless laughter.

"Yeah!" he shouted after him, and gave another celebratory honk on the air horn. "That one's from my mom! She sends her regards!"

It was only then that he remembered he was still holding

his spear in his right hand. He'd never make a real warrior. Real warriors didn't forget they were holding weapons.

He looked in the direction of the fire, and listened for the sounds of pursuit. There was heated conversation going on—it sounded like an argument—but he couldn't understand any words.

He should at least find out what they were planning. If they were going to try and capture Maíre and Caitlin, he could warn them. Maybe they could take shelter elsewhere on the island.

He shook his head. This island must be doing something to his brain. If anything like this had happened in Seattle, he'd have run in the opposite direction as fast as he could.

Well, maybe it was because Maíre didn't live in Seattle. Yeah, that could have something to do with it.

He crept toward the fire as stealthily as he could manage, and before long he could hear the conversation—or, more accurately, the fight—that was taking place.

"… brains of a dog and heart of a mouse!" one voice shouted. "Fool! Worthless cur! You let the women escape?"

"They were protected by a spirit!" said a voice that he recognized as Leather Cap. "An evil spirit with fearsome power! His single eye glowed like the sun! And he had a voice like the trumpet of Heimdall!"

"I heard the noise he made," said another man. "To my ears, it sounded like a strangled goose." There was general laughter at this, followed by an angry grunt, and the sound of shoving and fists hitting flesh.

"Stop, fools," said the first man, who was evidently the leader. "Get torches. The women cannot have gone far in the dark. We will find them and bring them back. And if we see Grim's evil spirit with one eye and a voice like a trumpet, I will stick a spear through his breastbone myself."

Sounded like his cue to exit. He briefly wondered if he could find his way back to what was left of Dugal's house in the dark, then decided that it didn't matter, that anywhere was better than here. But he had not counted on the speed with which the Vikings could move, once they'd made their minds up. He had only gone a few feet, when the leader, jogging in his direction with a torch, spotted his silhouette in the shadows.

"There is one of them!" the leader shouted. "After him!"

He stumbled forward, and tried to fumble for the flashlight, but this time the darkness and the panic defeated him. He turned to see the leader bearing down on him, eyes wild, mouth open in a broken-toothed grin of triumph, his face ruddy in the light of the torch clutched in one massive fist. His muscular right arm went back, holding a spear that looked like a tree trunk with a barbed end. Giving a great cry, the Viking threw the spear directly at his chest.

There was a moment during which he watched with strange, focused clarity as the enormous shaft sliced through the air toward him, knocking aside raindrops that glinted in the torch light. He felt like he could see air molecules moving out of the way of the razor-edged bronze tip. Then there was a sudden feeling of recoil, as if his body had been shot from a bowstring, and the entire scene—Vikings, spear, rain-drenched hillside in the dark, the wavering, sputtering torches—vanished, to be replaced by nothing at all.

part two

the keymaker

. . .

When Darren's consciousness rebooted, he found himself sitting on the floor in Fischer's office. He was soaking wet, shivering uncontrollably, and his glasses were fogged and askew. Maggie looked at him, her eyes sympathetic behind her own round eyeglasses.

"Had a nice trip?" Fischer said amiably.

Darren struggled to his feet, his teeth chattering. "Dammit, Fischer, you almost got me killed!"

"Let's focus on the word *almost*," Fischer said. "I always believe in looking on the bright side of things."

Maggie gave a little snort, which Fischer ignored.

"So, more importantly, did you find Lee?"

"No. I didn't find Lee. I did find a crapload of really ugly Vikings who did their best to kill me. I also found Maíre Gilla-comgain, but I'm not sure what I accomplished other than making sure her father was away from home, off on a wild goose chase with me, and unable to protect her and her brother and their mother when the Vikings attacked."

"Lucky thing for dear old dad, I would expect. How did the girl herself fare?"

"She and her mother got captured, but I rescued them."

He bit his lip. "Well, I think I did. You didn't let me stick around long enough to see if they got recaptured."

"You rescued them?" Fischer sounded impressed. "From Vikings? Those guys were serious badasses. Maybe I misjudged you." He paused, and then frowned at Darren, skepticism in his bright blue eyes. "Seriously? Vikings? Like, axes and horned helmets and the works?"

"I didn't see any horned helmets. And most of them seemed to have spears, not axes." He shuddered. "Great big nasty spears with sharp metal points. One of them hurled one at me, right before I came back here."

"Well, there's another stereotype shattered. Too bad. I always thought the horned helmets were a nice touch." Fischer looked at Maggie, who shrugged a little. "Anyway, it's kind of peculiar that Lee never showed up. If he didn't cause the divergence, then what did?"

"The Vikings?" His shivering was abating, and he rubbed his arms, trying to get feeling back into his limbs.

"Oh, yeah, the Vikings were great time travelers." Fischer rolled his eyes. "That's gotta be it."

Darren scowled. "Well, I don't hear you proposing any better theories."

"He has a point," Maggie said. "If Mr. McCaskill didn't show up personally to cause the divergence, it rather bashes a great hole in our idea of what caused this situation, don't you think?"

"It might be that you didn't see him. Was McCaskill traveling with the Vikings, perhaps?"

"I didn't see him there. But it was dark. He might have been there somewhere. At that point, I had other things to worry about, like how not to end up missing valuable body parts."

"Well, you seem to have managed that well enough," Fischer said. "You look mostly undamaged, although you're dripping all over the floor."

"It was raining."

"It does that in Scotland," Maggie said.

"So, how did you know to get me back right before the spear hit me?" Darren asked. "I thought I was a dead duck."

"We didn't," Fischer said. "We let the computer handle that. The computer keeps track of where you are, and pulls you back if things get a little dicey."

"And the computer always gets you out just in time?"

"Always. Lightning-fast processor. Cutting-edge technology."

"Well, there was Janowsky," Maggie said.

"Oh, yeah," Fischer said. "I'd forgotten about Janowsky."

"Janowsky? What happened to Janowsky?"

"Well..." Fischer acted a little reluctant to discuss the topic. "Janowsky was a Monitor who worked on our custodial staff. He was a bit of a thrill-seeker."

"Morbid type, if you ask me." Maggie's round face radiated disapproval.

"He wanted to take a vacation back to the eighteenth century, and experience the French Revolution first-hand." Fischer paused. "He got his wish, I guess."

"He *died*? I thought you said your computer always kept track of where you were, and could pull you back to the Library!"

"Oh, he came back to the Library," Maggie said. "Just in two separate chunks, as it were."

"Took forever to get the stain out of the carpet," Fischer said.

He looked at Fischer, horrorstruck. "That's terrible!"

"Yes, well, we've upgraded the microprocessors since then. And in any case, you survived, didn't you? Not too many people survive having a Viking chuck a spear at them. That's two attempted murders you've lived through. I would think you'd be feeling pretty confident by now."

"Well, I'm not! In fact, confident is exactly what I'm *not* feeling! You send me back to freakin' medieval Scotland, without a jacket, without any idea of what I'm doing, to try to find someone who's already tried to kill me once, and who's supposed to do something that we don't even have the first idea of what it is, and he doesn't show up but the freakin' Vikings do, and nearly kill both me and this poor sweet Scottish girl who got captured because I went off with her father to try to find someone who wasn't there, and I nearly get skewered by a spear, and you expect me to feel *confident?*" He stopped, staring at Fischer, panting a little.

"You got that whole sentence out in one breath," Fischer observed. "That was awesome."

He made a strangled, inarticulate noise of frustration.

"Look, Ault, we're trying to help you. If you're not confident, you could at least be a little *grateful.*"

"For what?"

"For trying to bring your sorry ass back into existence."

"I'm assuming, since I'm back here in the Library rather than back in my apartment, that whatever it was I accomplished in Scotland—which at the moment seems like not very much—didn't fix the problem."

"No, I'm guessing it didn't. If you had fixed everything, I suppose you would have found yourself back in Seattle, not here. But let's find out." Fischer swiveled his chair toward his computer. Let's see... what was the Scottish girl's name, again?"

"Maíre Gillacomgain."

"Right." Fischer typed the name in. "What kind of weird-ass name *is* that, anyway?"

He bristled. "She'd probably say the same thing about 'Archibald.'"

Fischer looked up at him sourly. "Shut the fuck up about Archibald, or I'm going to lock you in the top floor of the southeast wing."

"What's in the top floor of the southeast wing?"

"No one's sure," Maggie said. "All the records are written in languages no one speaks any more."

"Oh." He subsided, but gave Fischer a glare. Somehow after nearly getting spitted by a Viking, Fischer didn't seem quite so intimidating.

"Well, look at this," Fischer said, and Maggie and Darren went behind the desk.

On the screen was an entry for Maíre Gillacomgain, and after her name it said: "Actual End Track Code = GGY899410-1918, spouse unknown," followed by a list of dates and places.

"So?" he said.

"Check out the difference." With a click Fischer flipped to the screen that they'd been looking at immediately before his departure—the results that Norton SuperBifurcator had unearthed. He saw Maíre's name again, followed by "Actual End Track Code = GGY837789-0098."

"So?" he said again.

"Different end track codes." Fischer's voice had a tone that sounded as if he were talking to a very young, and rather unintelligent, child.

Darren raised his eyebrows. "So?" he said, for a third time.

"Jesus. You send this guy on an adventure, and he comes back all snarky." Fischer tapped the screen with his index finger. "Whatever you did changed the Gilla-whatever chick's end track. In other words, you altered the course of her life." Fischer typed in a command, and on the screen that appeared, he entered the two code numbers, then clicked a button that said, "Compare."

Within seconds, the computer responded.

Gillacomgain, Maíre, Actual End Track Code = GGY899410-1918, divergence with Alternate End Track Code = GGY837789-0098 occurs on 16 August 903. Cause: abduction by Olaf Gudredsson, Actual End Track Code = AJK187228-

4732. Actual End Track locked 12 December 955, South Uist, Hebrides, Scotland. Alternate End Track potential lock would have occurred on 18 August 913, Odense, Denmark. NOTE: unresolved temporal divergence associated with these track codes. Data maintenance necessary to reestablish correct tracking.

"See?" Fischer said. "There you are, then."

"There *what* is? What does all of that mean?"

Fischer snorted with annoyance. "Did one of the Vikings knock you on the head, or are you always this dense?"

"Patience, Fischer," Maggie said. "He's new to all of this, remember."

"Fine." Fischer took a deep breath. "Look at the alternate track. That's what she had before you went back in time. That was what the computer said earlier was her *actual* track. And see? She died. Ten years after she was captured, in Denmark. That's what 'end track locked' means."

"Oh, my god," he said. "That's horrible! They recaptured her?"

"No, you twit," Fischer said. "I said that *was* her actual track. As in past tense. Now it's just an alternate. Whatever you did, she got another forty-two-odd years of life because of it. And it looks like the Vikings didn't recapture her."

"Thank god. I don't think I'd have been able to forgive myself if what I'd done had made things go the other way."

"A tad smitten with her?" Fischer's mouth gave a sardonic twist. "I could tell from the moment you got back here. The way you go all misty-eyed whenever I mention her name."

"She's sweet," Darren said, a little defensively. "And gorgeous." He sagged. "Or was. I guess she died over a thousand years ago. I don't even know how to think about that."

"You shouldn't dwell on it," Fischer said. "Isn't healthy."

"She asked me to stay with her. Back there in tenth century Scotland."

"Did she? I hope you told her no."

"Well, it's not like I had much choice in the matter."

"No, I suppose not. But you know that staying there wasn't an option in any case. That's how we got into this mess in the first place, someone going back in time and fucking everything up."

Darren looked at the computer again. It was hard to imagine her entire life, boiled down to a few lines in a computer archive. Not fair.

He pointed at the last line on the screen. "What does all of that mean? 'Data maintenance necessary to reestablish correct tracking.'"

"It means the problem still hasn't been corrected," Maggie said. "The computer still has detected some sort of anomaly that it can't resolve."

"So nothing I did made any real difference."

"All of our actions, even the smallest ones, make a difference," she said. "Most of us never find out what that difference is. All choices have consequences, however insignificant they seem at the time. However, the truth of that statement is only evident here in the Library, where we can see what would have happened if we had acted otherwise. Without that information, what happens simply… happens."

"I don't know how you can stand it. If I knew all of the potential consequences of what I did, I'd never leave my apartment again."

"That, too, would be a choice, and have consequences," she said. "You can't escape it. It's the price of being human."

"Well, I don't like it."

"We'll file that in our folder labeled 'Tough Shit,'" Fischer said. "Man up. You saved this girl from being captured by the Vikings. You should be happy about that."

"I am. It's just a little overwhelming." Darren paused. "Could you see if her brother survived? He got hurt in the fight with the Vikings. He's a nice kid. I hope he didn't die from his injuries."

Fischer scowled. "I am *not* going to check on the fate of everyone you happened to meet in Scotland. Besides, the whole point of this is to set things back into their original tracks, which does *not* entail giving you all sorts of information you have no need to have."

He looked over at Maggie for support, but she gave a little shake of her head. "Fischer is right, Mr. Ault. The contents of the Library are not, in general, safe for the ordinary human. It may seem unfair, but it's a slippery slope. Finding out whether that unfortunate young man lived or died, over a thousand years ago, would help no one, least of all him. And once you felt the right to have access to that information, would you not want more? To find out the potential fates of people you care about now, people who are still alive and whose actual tracks are not yet locked? Foreknowledge of the future is a dangerous thing, Mr. Ault. If you were given that knowledge, that act alone could well alter the track you are supposed to be on. We cannot do that."

"I don't exist," he said, a little sullenly. "I don't *have* a track."

"Nevertheless, we are trying to remedy that, so we have to think ahead," Fischer said. "The answer is no."

"Fine. What do we do now?"

"I'd say the first thing to do is to find you some dry clothes," Maggie said.

"I'd be in favor of that. But I didn't exactly bring a suitcase."

"Fischer is close to your size." She looked at her boss with one eyebrow slightly raised.

"Oh, *hey* now," Fischer said. "I am *not* giving away my clothes to this guy, just because he happens to have dropped out of the sky and into our laps."

"Not give, lend. You can't send him off to Norway soaked to the skin."

"Norway?" Darren said, alarmed, but Fischer ignored him.

"Well, what if we go to the Artifacts Department and see if they have any period clothes he could wear? Or we could throw the ones he's wearing in the dryer."

"Fischer, be reasonable. He'll catch his death of cold. Remember that the second divergence happened in April of 1350, in Trondheim. Not only is that early spring, near the Arctic Circle, it's during the Little Ice Age. He'll be hypothermic twenty minutes after he gets there, even if we dry his clothes."

"I am *not* lending him my winter coat," Fischer said. "My mother got it for me at Land's End last year. It was a Christmas present."

"Wait!" Both of them stopped, and turned to look at him.

"Yes?" Fischer said.

"Norway?" Darren's voice cracked a little. "You're sending me to Norway?"

"Of course. That was where the second of the three divergences occurred."

"But look, I just got back from Scotland, and it didn't fix anything. Lee never showed. How will going to Norway be any different?"

"You changed one thing in Scotland," Fischer said. "You saved the Gilla-what's-her-name chick from being dragged off to Denmark. That could have some serious consequences. What we don't know is whether you have to fix all three divergences to reset time and bring humanity back. It certainly seems as if that's the case, given that what you did in tenth century Scotland didn't rescue the human race from the logical void. It might be that you have to clear up all three of the problems first."

"This makes no sense whatsoever." Darren tried unsuccessfully to keep a whine out of his voice.

"Now *there's* the pathetic Darren Ault we know and love," Fischer said, his mouth wry. "I'd wondered if fighting off a horde of Vikings would have improved you permanently. It's reassuring that my original impression was correct."

"Now, now, Fischer," Maggie said. "Remember what Mr. Ault has been through." She patted his damp shoulder. "You need to get into some dry clothes, or you'll catch your death *here*, much less in Norway. Fischer, I must insist. Take him to your quarters, and lend him some clothes. Warm ones, and without the usual…" she gestured at his t-shirt, adorned with a weeping cartoon kitten, "… decorations that you favor. Surely you have plain, straightforward, *warm* clothes Mr. Ault could wear, so that he won't stand out too terribly on his next journey, and won't freeze immediately upon arrival?"

Fischer scowled at her, but he seemed to know when he was defeated. "Fine." To Darren he said, "Follow me," and got up abruptly and left the room.

As he trotted after Fischer, he turned and looked over his shoulder, and said, "Thanks, Mrs. Carmichael."

And she responded, with a faint smile, "You may call me Maggie."

Fischer led Darren down a long hallway, and to an elevator. Fischer punched the "Up" button, and while they were waiting, Darren said, "I'm sorry I'm being such an inconvenience."

Fischer gave him a sidelong look. "No problem."

"No, really. I know this whole thing is pissing you off."

"That's okay, you didn't cause it," Fischer said, a little reluctantly.

There was a ding, and the doors opened. He followed the

Librarian into the elevator, and Fischer pressed the button for the ninety-sixth floor.

"This place is huge," Darren said, awed, as the elevator rocketed upwards.

"Yup."

"And you really run the whole place?"

"Yup."

"That's impressive."

"Do you always feel the need to talk incessantly?"

He started to answer, thought better of it, and shut his mouth tightly.

There was another ding, and the doors opened into a brightly-lit hallway. Fischer stepped out, and he followed. Suddenly Fischer stopped, and turned around, and looked him square in the eyes. It seemed as if the Librarian had come to some sort of decision.

"Look," he said. "I'm sorry if I'm being an asshole. Being responsible for the fates of humanity, and having the entire human race vanish on your watch, kind of ruins your day, you know? I really am not blaming it on you, and I know you're doing your best to try to repair whatever monstrous fuck-up caused all of this. You've been a good sport, and god knows I'd be complaining too, if I'd been through what just happened to you. It's more that... okay, look. I've only had this job for two years, and there was some serious concern when I was hired that I was too young to be the Head Librarian. The Board voted me in—and I understand it was by a narrow margin—but I can't afford to bollocks things up, you know? They could always fire me and find another Librarian if I blow it. And losing the entire human race... it kind of falls under the category of 'You Blew It.' The fact is, I don't know if sending you back to Scotland was the right thing to do, but it seemed like our only option. And sending you to Norway—and if that doesn't work, to the time of the third divergence, in Kentucky—

well, think of them as reconnaissance missions. Intelligence-gathering. Even if you can't fix what went wrong, you *can* find out what happened at the divergence points. That way if we can't repair the damage, at least we can go to the Board with more information than, 'Hey, guys, all of humanity seems to have been mislaid. Whoops.' So, if I'm a little testy, blame it on the fact that if I can't get this fixed, I'll probably be out on my ass." He frowned. "Of course, where I'd go, given that the entire human race is AWOL, remains to be seen."

This was the most that Fischer had said to him since his arrival in the Library, and he simply stared at the Librarian for a moment.

Then he said, "I'll help in whatever way I can."

"I guess that's all you can do," Fischer said. "It's all anyone can do."

He turned and continued down the hallway to the end, then pulled out a large set of keys, and unlocked the last door on the left.

Fischer opened the door. "My humble abode."

Darren stepped in, and looked around. Fischer's apartment looked like some hybrid between an upscale New York City penthouse and a college dorm. The carpet was plush, silvery-blue, and appeared brand new. The furniture was simple but elegant, and there was a spacious kitchen with polished maple counters and lots of shiny chrome fittings. On the other hand, the living room wall had a huge framed picture of Kurt Cobain, and there were promotional posters for Blink-182, the Stone Temple Pilots, and R.E.M. in prominent positions. A recycling bin next to the door into the kitchen was full of beer bottles, and pile of laundry sat on the floor next to the couch.

"It's kind of a mess," Fischer said. "Straightening up isn't on my radar, most days."

"No problem. My apartment isn't much better."

"I'll get you clothes. Then you can take a shower. Help yourself to a beer if you want. They're in the fridge."

He walked around the apartment, passing a bookcase that seemed to be devoted to books on quantum physics. Stephen Hawking's *A Brief History of Time* had about a dozen places bookmarked with sticky notes. A photograph of a smiling middle-aged couple stood on one of the shelves. Probably Fischer's parents, given the resemblance between Fischer and the woman, who had straight white-blonde hair and blue eyes. He wandered over to large picture windows that overlooked a rocky shoreline stretching off into the distance, with gulls wheeling in a brilliant blue sky.

At this point, Fischer walked back into the living room, carrying jeans, a long-sleeved t-shirt and sweatshirt, and a pair of boxers.

"This place is near the ocean?" he asked.

"It's not actually near anywhere," Fischer said. "I just like the ocean."

He absorbed this in silence for a moment, then decided that it wasn't any weirder than anything else he'd heard in the past few days, so he said, "Oh."

Fischer handed him the clothes, and pointed him in the direction of the bathroom. "You can use my razor if you want. You're looking a little scruffy."

He spent the next hour under a deliciously hot shower, which served the dual purpose of abolishing the last of the chill and washing off what felt like a dozen layers of grime. Afterwards, he climbed out, toweled off, and got dressed in Fischer's clothes. The pants were a little short, but otherwise the fit was close enough. His own damp, filthy clothes he carried out of the bathroom.

Fischer sat on his couch, playing *Mario Kart* on an enormous flat-screen television. He looked up as Darren entered.

"Nice place," Darren said.

"I can't complain," Fischer replied.

"How did you land this job, anyway?"

Fischer looked up at him, and set down his game controller. Mario's car went spinning off into a wall, and there was a burst of quasi-Italian imprecations from the speakers before Fischer shut it off.

"You can chuck those on the pile of laundry over there." Fischer pointed, and Darren added his dirty clothes to the pile next to the couch. "I'll have them washed and get them back to you. We should get back down to the office."

Fischer stood up, and walked out of his apartment, locking the door behind him. Darren had decided that Fischer wasn't going to answer the question, but while waiting for the elevator, the Librarian said, "I was kind of a washout in high school, you know? Never wanted to do anything but read, listen to music, and write seriously depressing stories about kids whose parents didn't understand them, and then they committed suicide and then the parents realized how much they loved their kids, but it was too late." He made a little snorting noise. "When Maggie showed up, and told me I was a Monitor, and that I should come with her, go into the training, I didn't believe her. I thought it was another one of my dad's schemes to turn me into a Productive Member of Society, by which he meant an engineer or doctor or lawyer or something."

The elevator dinged, and the doors opened. He followed Fischer in.

"I wasn't like Maggie. She knew pretty much from birth that she could see through time. I had no idea. I mean, I'd had daydreams about being able to go back and relive moments, or change the past, or whatever, but who doesn't? It wasn't until I started my training that I realized I could have done all of that, I just didn't know it at the time."

"So after you were done with the training, they made you Head Librarian?"

Fischer smiled. It was the first time Darren had seen him

do so. It softened the severe lines of his face, made him look almost childlike. "No, it didn't happen that fast. I was a rank-and-file Monitor for four years, under Mr. Furnival. Going back, doing cleanup for minor divergences, keeping track of the records, learning the computer systems. All ordinary stuff."

"It doesn't seem very ordinary."

"You'd be surprised how fast this stuff becomes... well, if not *boring*, exactly, at least mundane. Once you accept that this is the way things work, it stops seeming weird."

"I haven't gotten there, yet."

"No, I suppose not. But anyway, Mr. Furnival, I understand, had his eye on me as his successor, and Maggie thought I would be up to the job. So when he retired, I applied, and between his recommendation and Maggie's, I was offered the position."

"I'm surprised that Maggie didn't apply herself."

Fischer shrugged. "I asked her about that. She said she's much happier being an administrative assistant. Or, as she put it, 'I play a lovely second fiddle.' Everybody fits in where they're comfortable, I guess."

"Do you like your job?"

The bell sounded again, and the elevator doors opened. "I don't know. It seems a little beyond 'liking' or 'disliking,' frankly. I guess the best way to say it is that I can't imagine doing anything else."

They walked down the hallway in the direction of Fischer's office. Maggie was already there, filing manila folders in a huge and overstuffed filing cabinet. She turned and looked at them as they entered.

"Clean and dry, Mr. Ault?"

"Much better."

"I must say, those are remarkably pedestrian clothes, Fischer. I had visions of your sending Mr. Ault back to the Middle Ages wearing a Nirvana sweatshirt."

Fischer gave her a scowl. "I have ordinary clothes, Maggie."

"Evidently. I was simply unaware of them until now."

"*Anyway.* I suppose you're ready to go, then, Ault? Go check out what your buddy Lee did in fourteenth century Norway?"

"Not really. But I don't guess I have much of a choice."

"You always have choices," Maggie said.

Darren looked at her. "I suppose. I could stay nonexistent forever. Some choice." He sighed. "Okay, I guess I'm ready. Who am I looking for, again?"

"I printed out the Norton results for you, Fischer," she said. "On your desk."

"Thanks." Fischer picked up the printout. "A guy named Per Olafsson. He'd have been about twenty-seven years old or so. Lives in Trondheim. I'll land you there a couple of days before the divergence takes place, so you can have a chance to snoop around and see what's going on. Keep your eye out for Lee. I still think that the only way any of this makes sense is if Lee somehow went back and fucked around with things. I'll bet that somehow he was traveling with those Vikings, and you just didn't see him."

"Then why didn't rescuing Maíre fix the problem?" Darren asked. "There's still something screwed up back in the tenth century. The computer said so."

Fischer frowned. "I don't know. But look, maybe you have to fix all three of the divergences before everything will reset."

"Why would that be? How are they connected?"

"I don't know," Fischer said again, annoyance clear in his voice. "Let's see what happens, okay? We don't have any other working model to go on, so I think unless you want to give up now, this is pretty much our only way to go."

Darren took a deep breath. "Fine. All right, I'm ready."

Maggie looked over at Fischer. "You need to tell him before he leaves." She gave her boss a disapproving frown.

"He'll find out when he gets there." Fischer shifted from one foot to another like a child caught in a lie.

"Fischer, that's not fair," she said. "Tell him."

Fischer looked at him, and cleared his throat. "Um, maybe you should know what was happening in Norway in 1350."

"What? Was there a war or something?"

"No, no war. Just this… thing. There was this sort of… um… plague going on at the time."

Darren's eyes widened. "A plague? What kind of plague?"

"Well, it was sort of…" Fischer winced a little. "Sort of… the Black Death."

"The Black Death?" Darren's voice rose nearly an octave. "You're sending me back there during the *Black Death*?"

"Well, that's when the divergence happened. Not my choice. Just, um… watch out for rats. And fleas."

"Watch out for *fleas*? How do I watch out for *fleas*?"

"I don't know. Take lots of baths." Fischer gave him an uncomfortable smile. "Anyway, off you go. Remember, you're trying to find some guy named Per Olafsson. Ask around. There can't be many Per Olafssons."

"Now wait a minute, Fischer, you can't send me somewhere when they're in the middle of a freakin' *plague*…" But Fischer flicked his fingers at him, as if he were brushing off a fly, and the office was abruptly replaced by a chill, windy darkness and silence that seemed to his mind distinctly plague-like.

At first, Darren thought that there was something wrong with his eyes. Then he wondered if he'd materialized inside a cave, or in a dungeon. The blackness around him appeared absolute. Then he remembered his last night in Scotland, the total, cloying darkness, in the absence of any sort of artificial light source, a darkness that most modern humans never experience. But once his eyes had a minute to adjust, he realized that it wasn't completely dark. In the distance were spots of a faint, yellowish glow that could have been candles or torches. It wasn't much, but it gave his eyes something to focus on and his brain something to hope for. He walked toward them, down what seemed to be some sort of tree-lined road, although it was hard to tell in the dark.

The wind was incessant and icy. He had thought that the Hebrides in summer was cold. Here, his ears and fingertips were numb within five minutes of his arrival. His foot found a puddle, and there was a cracking sound as his sneaker broke through a rind of ice and he sank up to the ankle in frigid mud. Swearing, he pulled his shoe free, and continued to trudge toward the light, which had resolved into a collection of low buildings whose windows held oil lanterns, smoky and guttering, producing a jaundiced glow against grimy panes of glass.

"Charming place," he muttered under his breath. "All this, and the plague, too. What else can go wrong?"

And that was when he heard a sudden thudding noise, and turned just in time to be knocked flying by a running horse that struck him broadside. He was airborne for what seemed an amazing amount of time. He had time to think, *Broke my cardinal rule. Never ask "What else can go wrong?" Because the next thing you know, things go further wrong, like being trampled by a wild horse. It figures.* And then his head struck something solid, there was an explosion of fireworks inside his skull, and his consciousness winked out like a snuffed candle.

Darren opened his eyes, an uncertain amount of time afterwards, to find himself on his back on what seemed to be a straw-filled mattress, to judge by the crunching noises it made. There was no wind, but it was only marginally warmer, despite the fact that he was under some kind of covering made of singularly scratchy wool. The back of his head throbbed, and he moaned a little, tried to sit up, and almost immediately decided it wasn't a good idea.

An oil lamp, with a greasy-looking flame that illuminated almost nothing, detached itself from its perch across the room, and floated upwards through the air toward him. It finally stopped, hovering right over him, and he squinted at it. He could barely make out a gnarled hand holding it, and then, still in deep shadow, an even more gnarled face, a face neither clearly male nor clearly female, a face that looked like a shriveled apple, all creases and lumps and crags. It was framed by a few thin wisps of white hair.

A voice with the timbre of an unoiled gate said, "Don't sit up."

Darren swallowed. It hurt. "I'm not going to."

"Knocked your head a good one, you did. Shouldn't get in a horse's way, especially not Thorvald's stallion. Bloody dangerous beast, he is. Bit the tip of my great-nephew Bjorn's nose off, poor lad, all 'cause he thought to offer him a bit of a turnip. Now he wears a clamp bit on his face."

"Bjorn?"

"No, Thorvald's horse. To keep him from biting. Doesn't help poor Bjorn, but I s'pose it's better than nothing." The person with the lamp paused for a moment. "He has the devil's own time breathing on account of it."

"The horse?"

"No, Bjorn. Doctor tried to stitch his nose back together but it didn't work, and he looks like he has a lump of putty in the middle of his face. Snores something terrible. Sounds like someone strangling a goat. Keeps the whole house awake at night."

"That's a pity."

"It is that, stranger, it is that." The voice paused again. "What's your name, and where are you from? Your clothes are odd, and I'm guessing you're not from Trondheim."

"My name is Darren. Darren Ault." He left a definite pause between the two. He hadn't really minded being called "Darinauld" by Maíre and her family, but no sense encouraging the same kind of thing here.

The lamp-person gave a cackling laugh. "Darren Ault? Such a name. Darren Everything."

"What are you talking about?" He squinted at the person holding the lamp, as if bringing the face into focus would make the voice make more sense.

"Alt. Alt means 'everything.'" The voice cackled again. "So if you're 'Darren Alt,' you're 'Darren Everything.' Who gave you that name? Everyone?" This elicited a bout of laughter that only ended when it turned into a paroxysm of coughing.

"No," he said, in a weary voice. "It's just my name. I didn't know that's what it meant, and I didn't choose it."

"What was your father's name?"

"Carl."

"A fine name. So, you are Darren Carlsson. No need for more than that." The gnarled hand came down and patted his shoulder. "Well enough, Darren Carlsson. I am called Gerda Ingjaldsdottir. I'll stay with you till sunrise. Sometimes these knocks on the head can turn evil, and always when it's dark out, seems like. My granddaughter's husband's brother was kicked in the head by a mule, and he was fine at first, but that night he took badly and now all he does is cluck like a chicken. Terrible shame." Gerda *tsk*-ed under her breath. "But when it's light out, if you're still alive, I'll fix you some food and a cup of hot broth to drink. Till then, sleep if you can, and try not to die."

That seemed like good advice, and he closed his eyes, and despite the pain in his head and the clutching chill, he finally drifted off into an uneasy sleep.

———

Darren opened his eyes and turned his head painfully toward a source of cold, gray light that turned out to be a pane of glass so covered with grime that it was impossible to see through. He turned the other way, wincing a little, and saw Gerda sitting in a chair on the other side of the room, snoring softly, her lumpy chin resting on an ample, and equally lumpy, chest. She wore a loose-fitting dress of some coarse brown material, and had tucked her hands into the sleeves, so her entire body appeared wrapped in burlap. Another piece of brown cloth covered her head, with a few strands of wispy hair sticking out from beneath. She looked a bit like a cloth bag full of potatoes, with an oddly face-like, burlap-wrapped potato protruding from the top.

He sat up, which made the pounding in his head worse, and a wave of nausea swept over him. He considered throwing up, decided not to, and then swung his legs out of bed. His shoes and socks had been removed, and when his bare feet touched the icy-cold wood plank floor, he yelped a little and lifted them again.

The noise awakened Gerda, who snorted, coughed, and then opened her eyes, blinking sleepily.

"You didn't die." She yawned cavernously, exposing gums only sparsely adorned with teeth.

"Not yet."

"Always could happen." Gerda stood up. "Day's barely begun." She moved closer and leaned over him, peering at him nearsightedly. "You look like you might be all right. You haven't had any inclinations to cluck like a chicken, have you?"

"No."

"What sort of clothes are those you're wearing?"

He glanced down at Fischer's sweatshirt and jeans. "What do you mean?"

"They're brightly colored, like the fancy clothes nobles wear, but they don't seem to fit you very well."

"I borrowed them from a friend."

"Ah." This apparently satisfied her for a moment, but then she frowned and leaned forward again. "And what are those things?" She pointed. "On your face."

"They're glasses. They help me see better."

"Do they? How?"

"I don't know if I can explain it. But they work."

"My eyes are none too good. Do you think they might help me?"

He shrugged. "Could be." He handed them to her. She shoved them on her face, and then gave an exclamation of delight.

"Jesus and all the saints! It's like being young again!" She looked around the room, her face a study in wonder. "I can see every crack in the wall!" She frowned. "And every speck of dirt. I guess no blessing comes without a curse." She took the glasses off and handed them back. "Just as soon not know how filthy this place is."

He put his glasses back on.

"Are you hungry?" she asked. "Good sign you're not imminent to die, if you're hungry."

"I'm famished."

"That's good. I'll get you breakfast." Her brow furrowed. "Don't take a bad turn and die while I'm gone."

"I won't."

She was gone for only five minutes, and returned with a wooden bowl containing something steaming. She handed it to him, and he saw, with some dismay, that it was filled with porridge.

Jesus Christ. Why couldn't he get sent to a place and time where people knew how to make a decent breakfast? How hard was it to fry an egg? But he was hungry enough that he dug in, and finished the entire bowl in short order. Afterwards, his stomach seemed as if it were accepting of what he'd given it, and his headache was abating a little.

He handed the empty bowl back to her. "Thanks."

She gave her cackling laugh. "Good appetite. It's a good sign."

"Do you know someone named Per Olafsson?"

Her wrinkled face crumpled. "Per. Poor Per. Yes, I know him."

"Why do you call him 'poor Per?' He's still alive, isn't he?"

"As far as I know. I haven't checked on him this morning."

"Good. But what's wrong with him?"

"Oh, he's a poor, sad young man. He's got the second sight, you know. He's always sighing and pining for what he thinks should have happened. He's never satisfied with what he's got. Makes himself miserable, poor thing."

Darren frowned. That sounded significant. Maybe Per was a Monitor? "Wait. What do you mean, 'what should have happened?' How does he know what should have happened?"

"Now, that I don't know. He gets these fits. In church one week, he suddenly burst into tears, poor dear. He said that he felt like it was all wrong, that he should be somewhere else. But where else he would have been, of a Sunday morning, I don't know."

"Did he have any idea of what he *should* have been doing?"

"He said something about a wife, a wife he should have had." She leaned forward, and said, in a conspiratorial whisper, "He's not married, you know. Never has been. I think that's part of his problem. I probably don't need to tell you this, but if a man's secret parts don't get used, they kind of spoil, and the rot backs up into his brain and makes him crazy." She gave him a grin that exposed two yellowed teeth. "That's why I made sure to give my husband, rest his soul, plenty of opportunities."

Great. Now he was nauseated again.

"Anyway," he said, "did Per ever tell you any details? About what he thought should have happened? I mean, other than he should have been married."

"No. He seems sad all the time, poor thing, and goes on and on about how everything should be different than it is. But of course, you can ask him yourself, as soon as you feel up to it. He lives only a mile away."

"Do you think he'd mind? Would he be upset that you told me about his, um, obsession?"

"No, I'm sure he wouldn't. He talks about it to everyone who will listen. I think that the only danger will be to your spirits. He's a bit… a bit melancholy, as they call it."

After a second bowl of porridge, Darren felt as if his strength had returned sufficiently that he could venture out. He cleaned a spot on the window, and looked out into a muddy road with a field of brown grass and leafless birch trees stretching off into the distance. A few disconsolate-looking goats grazed in the field. The sky was a uniform gray, like dirty cotton. The wind was still blowing, rippling the grass, and rattling the pane. He could feel it slipping its fingers through the cracks in the wall, making him shiver. The whole place looked cold, miserable, and generally uninviting.

"Here's a jacket you can wear," Gerda said, as he was steeling himself to open the front door. "It belonged to my husband, rest his soul. He's no use for it now, being called forth into the Fields Of Lilies To Sit At The Feet Of Jesus." He could hear the capital letters.

"I'm sorry," he said.

"Oh, it's all right. In the midst of life, we are in death. But, in any case, no sense hastening your own travels into the next world. You can't go out there clad as you are, or you'll catch a chill and die." She handed him a battered coat, much worn, but lined with what appeared to be sheepskin. It looked deliciously warm, and he put it on and tied the front snugly. It was a little short in the arms, but otherwise fit well. He decided that he would wear it from now on, even indoors, unless he was still in Norway when the weather warmed up.

"Thanks," he said. "I really appreciate your taking care of me. Thanks for everything."

She patted him on the shoulder. "It's the least I could do. It was wonderful having someone to care for, and to keep me company. Ever since my dear husband died of the plague last week, I've been *that* lonely."

He goggled at her. "Your husband died last *week*? Of the *plague*?"

"Yes, and such a terrible wrench it was. He didn't suffer long, poor thing. Died in that very bed you slept in last night." She sniffed a little, and dabbed her eyes with the end of her head scarf. "So sad. He was a good man, Jon Haraldsson. A good man."

Shit. It just wasn't fair. First he survived getting shot by a homicidal physicist, and then being speared by a crazy Viking, only to catch the plague from fleas. Would the lightning-fast microprocessor get him back in time for a doctor to give him an antibiotic before he died of the Black Death?

He looked down at the coat and suddenly felt as if the sheepskin was crawling with fleas. He knew it was his imagination—well, he was *almost* certain that it was his imagination—but the feeling was maddening. He nearly took the jacket off and gave it back to Gerda, but when he looked at her ugly, kind face, he realized he couldn't do that. She wouldn't understand. And it wouldn't be nice.

Fine. Be nice, then, and die of the plague. Gerda would be upset that he died, and say about how nice a guy Darren Everything was, and wasn't it sad how he got the plague, but now he's Sitting At The Feet Of Jesus, so it's all okay. And then she'd offer the Flea-Infested Bed of Death to the next hapless traveler who came through, and it'd all happen again.

But maybe it would be okay after all. Compared to being skewered by a Viking, the Black Death was at least potentially survivable. He'd survived the Vikings, he could survive this.

Maybe Fischer was right. Maybe all of this was making him more confident.

He said his goodbyes to Gerda, who gave him a tooth-challenged smile and a sincere farewell—"Stop back any time. Don't die in the meantime."—and went out into the cold April morning to try to find the depressed, second-sighted Per Olafsson—and see if he might have a clue as to what was supposed to happen in a day or two that so decisively changed everyone's timeline.

Wrapped in the late Jon Haraldsson's warm jacket, and trying to ignore the feeling that he was being bitten by dozens of fleas, Darren walked down the road toward a cluster of low buildings in the distance that Gerda had pointed out as the home of "poor, sad Per Olafsson." The wind was incessant, the mud ubiquitous, and the sky a uniform dull gray color. He had seen photographs of Norway, and remembered their depicting crystal-blue skies over sunlit bottle-green seas, and steep hillsides lined with trees in full leaf. Those photographs, he decided, weren't taken in early April.

A twenty-minute walk brought him to the buildings. They

were dismal and brown, like everything else here, huddled together like cattle in a blizzard. Several of the buildings had no signs, and appeared to be homes. Another was clearly a tavern of some sort.

The last one in the row had a wooden plank hanging from a post in front, with words carved into it. He blinked at the sign, and had the peculiar feeling that he was looking at words in another language, a language he didn't speak.

But he realized, with some perplexity, that he could nevertheless read them. The sign said "P. Olafsson. Goldsmith, Blacksmith, Silversmith." Somehow he was reading words in Norwegian, but some hitherto-unrecognized part of his brain was simply translating them into English without any conscious thought.

It was no weirder than his ability to understand, and talk to, people who weren't speaking English. He remembered the futile struggle of trying to learn French in high school. However Fischer had accomplished this, it'd be nice if it was permanent.

The house was long and low, but had a partial second story with windows on the two sides he could see. The front was cross-timbered, made of old, cracked, unpainted wood, and there was a window in the front wall with a large oil lamp, burning steadily even though it was daytime. A greasy streak of soot trailed upwards along the glass. The whole place looked gray and downcast. But then, so did the whole country, or at least the part of it that he had thus far seen.

He pushed on the door, which was attached to the frame by a pair of intricately-wrought black iron hinges. It swung open smoothly and soundlessly. The dim interior was hung with metal objects of all sorts, from the functional—knives, axes, ladles, spoons—to the decorative—twisted silver knots and scrollwork, bracelets, necklaces, buckles—and everything in between. There was no doubt that however depressive the mysterious Per Olafsson was, he was a master of his craft.

There was a noise, and a man of about Darren's age came out from the back of the shop. As the leather curtain moved aside for a moment, there was a gust of warm air, and Darren caught a glimpse of a fire, anvils, tongs, and hammers. But the person who stood in the doorway, a curious look on his face, was about as opposite to Darren's mental image of a blacksmith as it was possible to be. This man was scarecrow-thin, and what muscles he had stood out on his arms like cords. His hair was straw-blond, raggedly cut, and looked as if it hadn't seen a brush in months. His pale blue eyes looked out at the world with a mixture of guardedness, pessimism, and resignation that made Darren's generally neurotic outlook seem positively buoyant by comparison.

"Can I help you?" The man spoke in a neutral, uninflected voice.

"Are you Per Olafsson?"

"Yes."

"I'd like to talk to you."

"Why?"

Well, that was a good question. What was he going to ask him? He certainly couldn't launch in with the I-came-from-the-future thing. Then he thought of Gerda's mention that Per was thought to have some sort of supernatural abilities, and wondered if that might provide an opening for conversation.

"I'm told you have the second sight," he said.

Per's eyes narrowed. "You're from the church, aren't you? Because if so, Father Sven already has talked to me and he says that I'm not committing a sin unless I say something that upsets everyone. And I haven't done that in months."

"No, I'm not from the church."

"Then why do you care?" Per's voice was flat.

"Because I'm interested."

Per raised an eyebrow. "No one is simply *interested*. Everyone has a reason for what they do."

He didn't answer for a moment. He got the impression

that here was someone who would know immediately if he was being lied to, evaded, or otherwise deceived. Per Olafsson seemed to view everyone with suspicion, and any confirmation of that pessimistic view of humanity by his own behavior would lead to Per's clamming up completely.

"I've been sent here by a man named Fischer, who also has the second sight." This small bending of the truth was so close to reality as to make no difference. "There is something that is going to happen, in the next few days, that has to do with you. I don't know what it is, but it may involve a man I know trying to place you in danger. I'm here to try to stop that from happening."

"Why do you care?" Per asked again.

"Because the outcome of this event will have a great effect on the future."

"You can see the future?"

He hesitated a moment before answering, "Yes."

Per's eyebrow went up again. "That was a lie."

"It was almost the truth."

"*Almost the truth* is not the same as *the truth*. Either you can see the future or you cannot."

Darren swallowed. Time to go for it.

"I can't *see* the future. I'm *from* the future."

He expected Per to react to this statement—to laugh, to become angry, to accuse him of being insane, to order him out of the shop—but Per simply nodded, and said, "I see," in a calm voice that sounded as if he'd been told nothing odder than the day's weather.

"I know it sounds strange."

Per shrugged his narrow shoulders. "It doesn't to me. I don't see time the way others do."

"I've heard that you think things should be different than they are."

"Heard? From whom?"

"From Gerda. Gerda Ingjaldsdottir."

Per scowled. "Gerda talks too much."

"It wasn't her fault. I asked her if she knew you. I only brought it up because I was staying in her house, and I thought she might know who you were. She took care of me when a horse ran over me. I asked her about you, and she said that you think that things aren't happening as they should."

"I don't think that. I know it."

"How?"

Per shrugged again. "How does anyone know anything?"

Time to try another tack. "You say you know that things should be different than they are. How *should* things be, then?"

Per gestured around him at his shop. It was the most animated Darren had yet seen him. "All of this. It's all wrong. I shouldn't be here. I should be somewhere else. Still in Trondheim, but not in this godforsaken hole of a shop. People coming to me, buying my wares. Everyone knowing my name, seeking me out."

"Your skill is obvious." He frowned. "But you could still become famous. You're young."

Per shook his head, and waved a hand at him. "No, it's not that. I'm not some apprentice who thinks he should be rich. It's more that... it's..." He sagged a little. "Never mind. I can't explain it. No one understands."

"I think I would."

The skeptical look returned. "Why would you be any different from the rest?"

"I'm from the future, remember?"

"Ah." Per's voice was thoughtful. "Yes. I'd forgotten."

"So tell me, what else should be different?"

Per looked at him for a moment, as if he were trying to determine if there could be any way Darren could be planning on using this information against him. Then he seemed to come to a decision.

"Very well. I cannot tell you how I know any of this. But I am certain of it, as certain as I am that you are standing here, that it is spring, that the sun will rise tomorrow." Per cleared his throat. "I should be married. Her name is Ingrid. She is beautiful, fresh as a flower. Her family... her family is wealthy, and have connections to nobility in Oslo. They helped me... encouraged me to bring my wares to other cities. Even as far as Copenhagen and Aarhus and Stockholm. We live in a nice house, on the hills overlooking the sea, not in this... this hovel." He said the last word bitterly, as if it tasted foul. "We have three children. Two boys, one girl."

Not "we would have had." "We have." The alternate reality was more real to Per Olafsson than the actual world.

"Do you dream about them?" Darren asked.

"Dream of them? Yes. Of course I do. But more than that. I see them. It is as if... as if..." He paused, his eyes darting back and forth. "It is as if both are happening at the same time. Right now, I stand in both worlds at once. I can see them all, see my home with Ingrid and our children, as clearly as I see you right now. The difference is, no one else sees them." His voice became sad, the first real emotion he had shown. "It is like being surrounded by the ghosts of the dead."

"That's awful."

"It is hell," Per said. "I committed no sin, and yet I live in hell, tormented by the shades of loved ones who never existed."

"It may be..." Darren stopped.

"What?"

"It may be that I am here to help fix that."

"How?" The word was flat, an accusation.

"I told you that I come from the future."

"Yes."

"The one who sent me here... he has knowledge of the alternate realities we might have lived, had we made different choices."

"This was no choice of mine." Per gestured angrily. "Why would I choose this?"

"Not you. Each of us is who he is, where he is, not only because of his own choices. The choices of others, sometimes in the distant past, have led us here. In fact, I was sent here to fix things, because another from my time went back and messed things up. In fact, he messed things up so badly that he wiped out all of humanity."

Per studied him. "Then how are you still alive?"

"I was spared. I don't know why." He shook his head. "I know it sounds ridiculous."

"No more so than what I live with every day." The silversmith paused. "And you think that perhaps one of the results of this man's actions, this man you seek, was to change my life?"

"I think so. I was told to come back here and find you." He shook his head. "But the only thing is… the event that I'm supposed to fix supposedly didn't happen yet. It's supposed to happen some time in the next day or two. But you've *always* felt like you should be living another life?"

"Always. As long as I can remember."

"I don't understand. If the divergence has already happened, how can I stop it?"

"Divergence?"

Again, there was the problem that any word that didn't exist in the vocabulary of the time wouldn't be understandable, however Fischer had somehow worked out the language issue. "The event I'm supposed to be here to change."

"Oh." Per looked thoughtful for a moment. "And you don't know what is supposed to happen?"

"No. I have no idea."

"Then it will be difficult to recognize when you see it."

He sighed. "Yeah, people have said that to me before. We think it has something to do with this man, this one I told you about who went into the past and changed things. His name is Lee. Have you seen any strangers lately? Tall, blond, muscular. Handsome fellow."

"I see strangers every day. Many of them look like the person you describe."

"Yeah, I suppose that makes sense. This is Norway, everyone's blond."

"You think he may already be here, then?"

"It's possible. On the other hand, the last time I went after him, he never showed. At least as far as I could see."

"You have chased him elsewhere?"

"Yes. Elsewhere. And elsewhen. Scotland, four-hundred-odd years ago."

Per's eyebrows went up. "You have some powerful magic."

He gave the man a wry smile. "So I've been told."

"It is a strange story you tell."

"But you believe me?"

Per gave a little shrug. "As I have said, it is no stranger than the reality I live with every day. And if I have one skill, besides the one in my hands, it is to tell when I am being lied to. I do not think you are lying. Therefore there are only two other choices—you are mad, or you are telling the truth."

"I'm not mad."

"You do not seem to be," Per said.

"I didn't expect to be believed this easily. It hasn't gone this easily with others, believe me."

"I can see that it would be hard to convince some that you are telling the truth. Many people do not want to believe that such things can happen. As for me, I wish it were not so, but I am forced to believe, it seems."

"I'm sorry that things are lousy for you," Darren said.

"As am I." Per thought for a moment, and then said, "I suppose that the best thing to do is to have you stay here with me. If, as you say, I am somehow involved in this—how did you call it, divergence?—then it makes sense for us to stay together. My house has a second bed, and I have food enough for both of us if you can help with chores such as feeding the chickens. But I do not know your name. If we are to share a roof, I am surely owed that much."

"My name is Darren." He smiled a little. "Darren Carlsson."

Per was about as striking a contrast to the vigorous, enthusiastic Malcolm Gillacomgain as it was possible to be. The entire house was wrapped in a cloud of despair, as if the depressed state of its owner was somehow affecting the space in which he lived. He worked hard, however, and with a meticulous efficiency. Darren watched him making an intricate silver pendant, and his handling of hammer, tongs, bellows, and other tools had a subtle grace and economy of motion that at least partially explained his lack of muscle. He made up for less strength by making every movement count.

Darren helped around the shop and the occupied rooms on the first floor, cleaning up, fixing food—he was relieved to find that here at least was a culture that had eggs for breakfast—and feeding the small and bedraggled flock of chickens kept in a hutch out back. But a lot of the time was spent in silence. During meals, during chores, and while working, Per showed no inclination whatsoever toward small talk.

It was near midday on his first day in Per Olafsson's household that Per finished the pendant he was working on, set it aside to cool, and went to a cabinet to select the materials for his next project. Darren dozed in a chair near the wall, preferring the smithy rather than anywhere in the rest of the house. At least the continuous fire kept the place comfortably warm. When Per opened the cabinet door, he roused, stretched, and looked at his host groggily.

Inside the cabinet were hundreds of silver keys.

His eyes opened wide. "You make keys?"

"Yes. I have studied the mechanisms of locks extensively. I often am called upon to make keys, from large iron ones for doors in manor houses, to small silver ones for ladies' jewelry boxes."

He went to look at the jingling metal keys of all shapes, sizes, and types hanging from hooks inside the cabinet. His mind went back to the little silver key that he'd worn around his neck, the one that had mysteriously vanished the day he was shot by Lee McCaskill and transported to the Library of Timelines. Although he could not be sure—none of them looked identical to the one he'd lost—the scrollwork on the handle of the keys in the cabinet looked like similar workmanship.

"I wonder…" he said, but stopped. Could this have anything to do with the divergence? The missing key… and his grandmother's wooden box. How could that have anything to do with anything?

Per looked at him curiously, but didn't say anything. He decided not to pursue the topic. He wasn't entirely sure how he would in any case. But there was something in Per's expression that made him wonder if the silversmith might understand this situation better than he did.

Gerda Ingjaldsdottir showed up at the smithy just before sunset with a plate of boiled dumplings. "I cooked more than I could eat. I decided to bring what was left for the two of you if you were still alive. Both of you could use some fattening up. The women will not look at you twice unless you have some more girth to you." She patted Darren's stomach. "Have you always looked so underfed?"

"Um… yeah, I guess."

"Did your mother not feed you well?"

"No, she fed me just fine." He glanced down at the dumplings, which looked to be as heavy and bland as her porridge. He had to eat one, though, or it'd seem rude. And after all, Gerda had rescued him when the horse ran over him. He picked one up, and bit into it, confirming his impression. It was like having a mouthful of warm Play-Doh. He thought, not for the first time, that he would have given a lot for some salt and a bottle of hot sauce—anything to give the food more flavor—but he supposed that with no supermarkets available, you had to eat what was around, whatever it tasted like.

"They're delicious," he lied.

"Gytha Larsdottir died last night," she said cheerfully. "So did Markus Christiansson. His throat was swollen up something terrible, his wife told me, poor thing. The plague isn't done with us yet, it seems."

"You know," Darren said, speaking tentatively, and a little indistinctly, through a sticky blob of dumpling dough, "you might... discourage the plague, by... by washing your bedsheets and clothing more often. Gets rid of the fleas."

Gerda looked at Per, who looked back at her and shrugged.

"Fleas?" she said, in complete incomprehension.

He swallowed. "Um... yeah. I mean, it could be... that, you know, fleas might have something to do with the plague. You know, they're filthy little creatures, maybe they're why people keep getting sick." He hoped fervently that Fischer wouldn't get wind of the fact that he'd told Per and Gerda information no medieval person would have had access to.

Gerda stared at him for a moment, and then burst out laughing. "How could little things like fleas make you sick? They're everywhere. If fleas made you sick, we'd all be Sitting At The Feet Of Jesus by now."

There she goes again. Speaking in capitalized words.

"I don't know. It's just an idea."

"A pretty foolish one," she said. "Your throat swells up

and you get feverish and cough a lot and you die. Because of *fleas*?"

"Well, it's not because of the fleas *themselves*, it's because of little creatures that live inside the fleas." He immediately regretted saying that.

Now she laughed for a full minute, and then reached up with one gnarled claw and patted his cheek.

"Poor boy. Still haven't recovered from that nasty knock on the head, have you?" She stuck the platter under his nose. "Here, have another dumpling. It'll settle your brain. The brain's for cooling the blood, you know. When you knock your brain around, your blood overheats and it makes you silly."

Never mind. Time to give up on that line of conversation.

She apparently took his lack of a response as acquiescence, and left the matter of fleas and the plague aside. "Oh, I also thought I'd mention that on the way here," she said to Per, "I saw a stranger in town. He was walking along the road, he was, carrying a big knapsack but without so much as a walking stick, and I asked him where he was from. 'No business of yours, old hag,' he said, and I said, 'What brings you here to Trondheim?' and he said, 'Naught that concerns you,' and I said, 'Why so rough in speech?' and he said, 'My reasons are my own,' and I said, 'That may well be, but a kind word is often repaid, but a harsh one repaid double,' and then he seemed to take a little thought, and said, 'Perhaps I've been too hasty,' and I said, 'Rude, I'd call it, not hasty,' and he said, 'Perhaps I could ask you for a bit of assistance,' and I said, 'What sort of assistance?' and he said, 'To give me some directions,' and I said, 'The sooner you ask, the sooner I can send you elsewhere, and the happier I'll be,' and he said something extremely rude that I'll not repeat for fear of offending you gentlemen."

Per and Darren both stared at her for a moment.

"So?" Per said.

"Oh, yes." Gerda blinked at them. "So then I said, 'What directions would you be looking for?' and he said, 'Is there a silversmith hereabouts?' and I said, 'Yes, a fine one, by the name of Per Olafsson,' and he said, 'Would he be able to make a silver key?' and I said, 'I'm sure he would,' and he said, 'Well, then, old hag, tell me where I might find this Per Olafsson,' and I said, 'Down the road yonder, and get going that way or I'll put my boot in your rear end to help you along,' and then he said another thing that I'll not repeat. But then I flung a dumpling at him, so I had the last word. He hasn't shown up here yet, has he?"

Per shook his head.

"I suspect he might. Big fellow, blond, looks like he's got a lot on his mind. Short temper."

Per's eyes met Darren's, and one of the silversmith's eyebrows rose questioningly.

"Gerda," Darren said, "can you tell me more about what this stranger looked like?"

"Brown shirt," she said.

"Other than his shirt."

"Brown trousers, too."

"I mean," he said, trying to keep the frustration out of his voice, "distinguishing marks."

"Well, now. I can't truthfully say. I didn't see any, but then, you know, most of him was covered up by the brown shirt and brown trousers. My dear husband, rest his soul, had a birthmark on his bottom that was shaped like a fish, but you'd never have known it because he rarely took his trousers off and showed anyone."

"Do you think it could be the man for whom you are seeking, Darren?" Per asked.

A shiver ran up his back. Was he finally going to confront Lee McCaskill? He'd spent his days in Scotland looking for Lee and not finding him. This time, would he simply walk in the front door? More importantly, would he have brought his gun with him?

"I don't know," he said. "It could be."

"Then perhaps your search is over," Per said, as the front door of the shop opened, and a shadowed figure stepped inside.

But it wasn't Lee McCaskill. There was some resemblance —a strong, angular face, sandy blond hair, broad shoulders. But there the similarity stopped.

Darren breathed a sigh of relief, but then had the disconcerting thought that maybe it would have been better if it *had* been Lee. Maybe then some of this would start to make some sense.

The man saw Gerda standing there, still holding her platter of dumplings, and said, "I'd have turned down the second mug of ale at the tavern if I knew you were going to arrive here first, old hag."

"And I'd have tried to get here first anyway, for the privilege of whacking you in the head with another of my dumplings," she shot back, "although it's a sorry waste of good dumplings to do so."

The man glared at her, and seemed to decide that it wasn't worth the battle. "Let us not carry our brawl into the good silversmith's shop."

"I'd be happy to carry it back into the road."

"Another time, perhaps."

"Any time you choose." She smacked the platter down on the counter and walked out of the shop, slamming the door behind her.

The man turned back to Darren and Per, who were standing watching him with some interest.

"Which of you is Per Olafsson?" the man asked.

"I am." Per reached out a hand. The man clasped Per's skinny forearm in a firm grasp, and Per reciprocated, wrapping his thin fingers part way around the man's much better-muscled wrist.

"I am called Lars Jonsson. I come from Oslo, but have traveled far abroad. I am told you do fine metalworking. Yon old hag that we just bid farewell to, she said you are the best in the region."

"I am no judge of that," Per said, "but as to my being a metalworker, that much is true."

"Modestly said. But if what I see around me is your handi-work, I think you are the man for the job."

"Perhaps. This is indeed all my work, as far as that goes. What is the job you would like done?"

Lars took off the knapsack he was wearing, untied the knot securing the top, and reached in and carefully removed a carved box, constructed of some dark wood, with finely-wrought iron hinges and a tiny iron plate in the front with a slotted hole obviously intended for a key.

Darren stared at it, sitting in Lars Jonsson's strong hands, and his heart sped up. No... it couldn't be... could it?

"Lars," Darren said. "Where did you get that box?"

Lars turned toward him, a questioning look on his face. "It belonged to my mother. The key that opened it was lost many years ago. I want to have it fitted with another key. It is part of a gift I intend for my wife-to-be. We are to be married on Midsummer Day this year."

"May I hold it?"

Lars shrugged, and said to Per, "Is this man your assistant?"

"Yes," Per said, and gave no further explanation.

Lars handed the box to Darren. He looked at it carefully, and turned it over, running his fingertips over its surface and edges. Everything about the box was familiar—the abstract carved pattern of loops and knots on the lid, the snake-like swirls that adorned the corners and edges, the incised, twisted design around the lock. However unlikely it was, he was certain. He knew every cut, every curve of the design. In his time, it was darker, the wood showing signs of age, and some of the sharp edges had worn down from centuries of use. But there was no possible doubt, no way he could be mistaken.

"Per," Darren said, "I need to speak to you privately."

Per said to Lars, "I must discuss something with my… assistant. We will talk about the job when I return."

Lars reached out and took the box from his hands—Darren let it go a little reluctantly—and then he and Per walked back into the smithy, pulling the leather curtain closed behind them after they went through.

"Per," he said, in an intense whisper, "that box belonged to my grandmother. Or *will* belong. That same box sits on a shelf in my apartment."

Once again, Per reacted without surprise. He only questioned an unfamiliar word, not the overall gist of Darren's statement, as if that were the only thing astonishing about it. "Apartment?"

"Home. In my home. An apartment is like a room in an inn, but people live there for a long time, not only for a few days."

"Ah."

"I can hardly believe it, but there's no mistaking it."

"Are you certain it is the same box? Many carved wooden boxes look similar."

"Yes, I'm sure. I remember when I was a little boy, playing with it when I went to visit my grandmother. I know every detail of it. I'm absolutely certain."

"Ah," Per said again. "That is curious. How could this box have made the journey to your time and place? Your home, it is far away, and many years hence, am I correct?"

"Yes." He still marveled at how easily Per accepted the fact of his having come from the future, but at least it was better than what he went through with Dugal and his family.

"It is strange that there is this connection between my time and yours, and between my place and yours."

"It's not just strange. It has to be important. This has to be part of why I am here."

"Perhaps." Per seemed unconvinced. "But I don't see what its significance could possibly be."

"Me either. Not yet, at least."

"How did you acquire the box? Was it a gift from your grandmother?"

"Sort of. When my grandmother died, I inherited it. It had a key that went to it, but when... when all this happened, me getting sent back in time, everyone else disappearing, everything I was telling you about yesterday, the key vanished."

Per looked at him skeptically. "How do you know you did not simply lose it, as Lars Jonsson did?"

"It was on a chain around my neck. I always wore it, even when I slept. I was very fond of my grandmother, and it reminded me of her. But when I suddenly found myself... um, when everyone else went away, everyone but myself and one or two others, like the guy who sent me here... I noticed that the key was gone."

"Could the chain have broken?"

"Maybe. But I doubt it. It simply was gone."

Per frowned. "I do not see how that could be."

"Me either. But this *has* to be significant. I mean, think about it—Lars Jonsson brings the box to you because his key vanished, and my key *also* vanished. This *can't* be a coincidence." He paused. "You know, I wonder if the key I had is the one you will make?"

"It could be." Per looked at him in a speculative fashion. "Can you think of any importance that the box could have?"

"I don't know. Not offhand. But perhaps that's part of what we need to figure out. Maybe part of the puzzle is to discover why it's important. Per, I think you need to take this job. I think this has something to do with the divergence I was sent here to fix."

"Yes, I think perhaps you are right." Per frowned thoughtfully. "What is the box used for in your time?"

"I use it for knick-knacks."

Per looked at him in complete incomprehension. "What are these… knick-knacks?"

"Just… stuff. You must have things, in your house… you know, odd items, that don't have any real purpose. Small things that aren't important but which you still don't want to lose."

"Ah. Yes. That is a funny way to call them. Knick-knacks. I have things like that, yes." Per shook his head. "But if that is all you use the box for, then how can it be significant?"

"I don't know. but it's the only connection I see between your time and mine."

"I don't understand this. It all seems very strange."

Darren shook his head. "I don't really understand, either. But what else can it be? There doesn't seem to be any other connection to go on."

"But, did you not say that this divergence, this event, had something to do with the man who you are chasing from place to place and from time to time?"

"Well, yes, I thought it did."

"I do not see how this box can have anything to do with him. Either the man you are chasing caused everything to change, or he did not. If he did, and especially if he did something far in the past, in Scotland, as you say, how can this wooden box be relevant?"

"I don't know." Darren shrugged helplessly.

"It seems to me as if you are trying to find a black cat in the dark."

The metaphor was apt, and he wilted a little. "Look, it's not like I know what I'm doing. Even the guy who sent me here, he wasn't sure what we were looking for."

"Then perhaps the man is playing you for a fool."

Per was the second one who'd suggested that. It was a chilling thought. Dugal, in fact, had thought that Fischer and Lee might be in cahoots, and that had seemed unlikely. But would it be any better, having Fischer send him all over the place, in and out of the past, because he was getting some strange jollies out of it?

Then he thought of the glimpse he'd had of a different Fischer—a guy who was trying to do his job, like everyone else, who was worried about what his bosses thought, who was afraid he'd get fired if he screwed up, who wanted to put things right, and the whole anxiety-fraught idea of Fischer as some kind of evil genius, or at the very least a cruel practical joker, collapsed.

"No," Darren said. "I'm sure of it. Fischer wants to fix what's gone wrong, both in our time and in yours. He's not trying to do anything bad, and he's not playing some sort of elaborate prank on me. And even though he's pretty powerful—he can send me where, and when, he wants—he is trying to figure all this out, just like we are. That's what he told me to do, to see if I could puzzle out what had gone wrong. He said that I should come here and scout, try to gather information, so that we can try and repair the damage. I'm sure he doesn't know the details of what caused the divergence any more than we do."

Per absorbed all of this in silence.

"However, you could be right," Darren said. "It might be that the box has nothing to do with anything, or at least anything important. But at the moment, we don't have another guess as to what might be causing all this, so we should be careful about what we do, and follow every lead we have."

"That seems prudent." For the first time, a hopeful light came into Per's eyes. "You really think... you think that perhaps, you might be able to fix my life? Give me the life I should be having?"

"I don't know. I can't promise anything."

Per considered this for a moment. "I will help you in any way I can. A faint hope is better than none, and until now, I have had no hope at all."

"Then you need to tell Lars that you'll take the job."

Per nodded. "Very well."

The two men returned to the front of the shop, where Lars Jonsson stood, fidgeting impatiently with a silver buckle hanging from a hook on the wall.

"I will do the work you ask," Per said.

"Excellent," Lars replied. "I am willing to pay you ten silver pennies for the job, provided you can be done by the day after tomorrow at this time."

"Fifteen."

"Twelve, and make it beautiful. Filigree handle."

Per reached out his hand, which was duly shook.

Lars slid the box toward Per. "I will call for it at sunset on the day after tomorrow. I am staying at the inn, yonder. I am trusting that the old hag's description of your skills was correct."

"Her name," Per said, "is Gerda Ingjaldsdottir, not 'old hag.'"

Lars smiled faintly. "As you wish, silversmith. Until I return, then." He turned and strode out of the front door.

Per turned toward Darren, his face solemn. "Well, now we shall find out if your guess is correct. I shall make a key, and then we will see what happens."

By the time Lars Jonsson left, it had fallen completely dark. Per fixed them a simple meal—a thin soup with a scanty helping of rather tough chicken, some dried fruit, and a hunk of coarse bread. It was better than porridge, although he did notice one of Gerda's dumplings sitting in his bowl, looking like a pale, lumpy frog squatting at the bottom of a pond.

"This man you have chased so far," Per said, munching thoughtfully on his bread, "what did he do, that so harmed the people of your time? How could one man have such power?"

"We believe that the whole thing started when he tried to kill me."

Per's eyebrows rose, but his voice was still as uninflected as ever. "He attempted to kill you? Why?"

"That I don't know. But I do know that the way he tried to kill me… it should have worked. It should have blown my skull apart, actually. But somehow I survived, even though the action seems to have made the rest of humanity vanish."

"There are none left in your time?"

"Only myself, and a few others. People who like you, see the weavings of time from the outside, in a way. They are called Monitors."

Per digested this in silence for a moment.

Finally he said, "These Monitors you speak of. Have they the ability to change their fates? God knows I would if I could."

"That's a good question. I suspect that they can, but I think they're forbidden from doing so."

"Forbidden? By whom?"

"I'm not sure. By the ones who govern them, I suppose. But it's a good thing they don't, or they could go back in time and change things, maybe for their own gain."

"Yes. Is this what the man… you have not told me his name. Is this what he was attempting to do?"

"His name is Lee. But unfortunately, I don't know what he was trying to accomplish, either by killing me, or by changing the past. The one who sent me here to Norway—the Monitor I told you about, a man named Fischer—he believes that after trying to kill me, Lee escaped into the past, and while there changed something that altered the fate of everyone. Fischer has a way of knowing about these things, and he told me there were three places that had been altered. One was in Scotland, four hundred years ago. One was here, and now, in Norway. The third one was in a place called Kentucky, in the far distant future. Kentucky sort of doesn't even exist yet."

He had the sudden surprised realization that he was getting to the point where he could actually explain all of this without being completely freaked out by how weird it all was. Maybe he was making progress.

Once again, Per responded to all of this without any seeming difficulty in belief. "What do I have to do with it? This is the bit of it that I do not understand. I am not from your time. And although I understand that things are not as they should be, I am not one of those people you know—how did you call them? Monitors?—who can travel back and forth through time as easily as one walks from one room into another. I am only a simple smith who is doomed to live life alone and poor. When you came here, you knew my name, and somehow here I am, caught, trapped in the midst of this as a fish is in a net." He took a sip of ale. "It is peculiar."

"I'm as much in the dark as you are about what's behind all of this. All I can do is to try to gather as much information as possible, so when I return back to my time—what's left of it, that is—I'll be able to tell Fischer what I learned, and perhaps we can fix all of this."

Per peered at him searchingly. "If you do succeed, I would only ask you this—do not forget me. I have lived my years on this earth always feeling lost, feeling that I was not where I should be, feeling that nothing that happened went the way it should. If you can help me, please. I know I am only one man, and someone who was a stranger only two days ago, and that you have the fates of many more people in your hands. My happiness may seem a small thing, by comparison." Here his voice cracked, but he regained control of himself, and he kept on. "But still, I beg of you not to forget me."

Darren met his eyes steadily. "You have my word. I will help you if it is in my power to do so."

The next day dawned with sleet and wind, and after Darren did his morning chore of feeding chickens who seemed as unhappy to be roused from sleep as he was, he went into the smithy and decided he wouldn't poke his nose outside of the house for the rest of the day unless forced.

Why couldn't the divergences have happened somewhere warmer? He shivered, even though he was in front of the blazing fire. Cozumel would have been preferable to this. Or the Riviera. Or Maui. In fact, he'd have happily gone to Maui to fix stuff.

But no, he gets sent to the Hebrides and Norway and has to freeze his ass off.

Per had already thrown more fuel onto the fire, and was working the bellows, his thin arms pumping furiously. He'd stripped to the waist, and sweat streamed down his bony frame. His ribs stood out as his chest heaved with the exertion.

Gradually, the glow from the fire intensified until it was impossible to look at the coals without squinting. They were white-hot. He picked up a blackened ceramic crucible and added a few broken chunks of silver, and then using tongs, he put the crucible into the hottest part of the fire.

A few minutes later, he retrieved the crucible—the ceramic itself was nearly white-hot—and working quickly he poured out a stream of glowing, molten silver into a ceramic mold. He repeated the process four more times.

"Making spares?" Darren asked.

"I always cast more than I need." Per set the crucible

down on a stone slab next to the fire, and leaned the tongs against the wall. He wiped the sweat from his forehead with the back of his hand. "Sometimes the blanks crack as they're cooling, or sometimes there are air bubbles. If I make several, I can be more certain that at least one will be well-formed."

While letting the key forms cool, Per retrieved the wooden box from a cabinet, and set it in front of him. He set it on its back, and selected a small tool from a leather pouch hanging by a strap from a hook on the wall. The tool was small, with a wooden handle from which projected a slender strip of metal, like a very fine knife with a bent tip.

Darren came up behind him, and Per looked up at him.

"Do you mind if I watch?"

Per shrugged, and turned back to his work. He slipped the point of the tool into the keyhole, and very gently moved the bent tip along the inside of the keyhole.

"What are you trying to do?"

Per did not look up. "The way locks work is that there is a lever inside that fits into a cut-out slot. If the key is the right shape, it lines up with the shape of the lever, and when you turn it, it fits through the slot, pushes on the lever, and releases the latch. If the key is the wrong shape, it doesn't fit through the slot. A part of the key hits projections inside the barrel of the lock, and it won't turn. I'm using this tool to feel along the inside of the barrel. There's a groove between the lever and the barrel that I can map out using the tool. This will tell me what shape the key needs to be."

"And you can feel well enough with that tool to picture what shape the key should be?"

"It usually takes me a few tries," Per said. "But I've gotten pretty good at it."

"That's extraordinary."

Per shrugged again, and picked a small piece of charcoal from the counter, and a rather ragged piece of paper, and slowly, meticulously, made sketches of keys. He worked at this for nearly a half hour, repeatedly going back to the box with his tool to check his ideas, making modifications to his sketches as he gathered information about the inside of the lock barrel.

After finishing the sketches to his satisfaction, Per pushed paper and charcoal aside, put his tool back into the leather pouch, and retrieved his cooled key blanks from the molds.

Darren watched, fascinated, as Per picked up the ceramic molds, and knocked the key blanks jingling onto the workbench, examined each one with a critical eye, tossing three of them back into the crucible with a dissatisfied snort.

Using pliers, hammer, and a punch, he shaped the best of the remaining two. First he cut away chunks of the flat blade of the key, using a bit of fine-grained sandstone to smooth the edges, and tested it repeatedly in the keyhole, moving gently and with great caution. The bits of silver he removed were carefully swept up and put back into the crucible. He wasted nothing, not even the smallest sliver.

After working for nearly an hour, he tentatively tested the key, and felt it give slightly. He said, under his breath, "Nearly right," and went back to his pliers and sandstone, bending and filing the blade with a deft hand. The next time he inserted the key, it turned smoothly, and there was a click as the latch released.

Per allowed himself a faint smile to celebrate his success. It was the first time Darren had seen him smile since his arrival. He lifted the lid of the box, and it opened silently.

The inside of the box was empty.

"Somehow," Darren said, "I expected there to be some kind of clue inside."

Per ran his hand along the inside rim of the box. "There still may be."

"Where?"

"I recognize this type of box. It was made not only for practical uses—for rich ladies to keep their jewelry in—but to transport secret messages. Spies and government officials use them. There's often a secret compartment at the back, or sometimes under the bottom plate of the box. It's got a false back or bottom, you see. That way, you can hide a message inside what appears to be an empty box. If you're searched, or if your belongings are stolen, your secret remains safe."

Per peered into the box, and tapped tentatively on the bottom.

"I haven't seen one of these in a long time. They're quite rare and expensive."

He pushed against the floor of the box, and it gave a little, and sprung back when he let go. He pushed again, harder this time, and it slid over by a fraction of an inch, and then he tipped the box over. The bottom of the box fell forward, swiveling on a tiny pair of hinges.

"I never knew that was there," Darren said. "All these years, and I never knew there was a secret compartment."

Inside was a small space, no larger than a playing card, carved into the actual bottom plate of the box.

Tucked inside was a small piece of folded paper. Per picked it up gently, and opened it while Darren watched over his shoulder. The paper was old and worn, but appeared to be blank. Per turned it over in his hand, and shrugged and set it down on the workbench.

Otherwise, the box was empty.

"How can that be?" Darren said. "There has to be *something* relevant about this."

"I don't know," Per said. "And I need to eat something before I work on finishing the key." Per set the box down, with the unfinished key still protruding from the keyhole, picked up his shirt, and walked through the leather curtain and into the living area of the shop.

They lunched off dried fish, dried fruit, a hunk of bread, and mugs of ale.

After consuming most of the meal in silence, Per asked, "What did you expect to find when the box was opened?"

"I'm not sure. Actually, I wondered if it might not be some kind of written message. Maybe a clue from the people I was with when I was in Scotland. You know, something that would link that piece of the puzzle to this one."

Per nodded thoughtfully. "It does seem to me that you are making a great many assumptions."

"I'm sure." Darren could hear the bitter tone in his own voice. "But that's partly because we've got almost no facts to go on."

"Indeed. But even considering that, I think that there is still a flaw in your reasoning."

"Really?"

Per took a sip of his ale. "Well, perhaps I have misunderstood. You have told me that this man, Lee, the one who you believe to be the cause of all of this, tried to kill you, and then escaped into the past so as to get away with his crime, and while there interfered with something that then changed history."

"Yes."

"Did you see him vanish? After he tried to kill you, did he then disappear before your eyes?"

"No. As soon as he tried to kill me, everything changed."

"Tell me in detail what happened." Per leaned back in his chair, and laced his hands across his belly.

How could this ever make sense to a man from the fourteenth century? So much had changed since then. And yet—Per seemed to understand, and accept, what had happened far more easily than he did.

Maybe that was the downside of the twenty-first century rationalist approach. When something didn't fit, the modern brain couldn't handle it. In Per's time, they didn't expect things to make sense, or at least not in the same way. It was a different way of looking at the world, far more fundamentally different than had been evident at first. It made them get it wrong sometimes—like Gerda rejecting that the plague was carried by fleas—but it did leave them more open to a lot of things that were outside of their frame of reference, things that someone from the twenty-first century would have rejected out of hand.

"Well, in my time, we have weapons called guns," Darren started, a little tentatively. "They fling a small metal ball, called a bullet, at a very high speed. It can do a great deal of damage."

"Like a sling?"

"Sort of. But far faster. Guns can kill people, if the bullets they fire hit you in the head, or in the heart. Lee fired his gun at my head, from close by, from no farther away than you are from me now."

There was that quizzical rise of the eyebrow, about the most emotion that Per ever showed. "Indeed? And you survived?"

"Without a scratch."

"And afterwards, Lee was gone."

He shook his head. "No. Afterwards, *I* was gone. I found Fischer and the other Monitors, and they told me that at the instant the gun was fired, every other human in the world ceased to exist."

"So then," Per said, "you see that your explanation cannot be correct."

"Why not?"

"Because Lee himself was destroyed, is that not so?"

"Well..." An uneasy sensation rose in the pit of his stomach, as he saw where the argument was leading. "Yes, we think that's right."

"Then if Lee, and everyone else, were destroyed the moment the weapon was fired at you, how can he have escaped into the past and changed anything? He was no longer alive to do so."

He stared at Per for a moment. "My god. How can that not have occurred to us?"

"It is a peculiar situation. When in peculiar situations, it is easy enough to miss the obvious."

"But that would mean…" He frowned, concentrating. "That would mean that it was the act of killing me that caused things to change, not something Lee *himself* did in the past."

"That seems to me to be the only possibility."

"But how can that be? I'm not important. In my home, I'm just a shop owner. People die all the time. Hell, people are *killed* all the time, and this doesn't happen. Why would his trying to kill me affect everything?"

Per drained the last of his ale. "I think that when you figure that out, you will be able to explain everything else that has happened without difficulty."

That afternoon, Darren watched Per work on the decorative shaping of the handle of the key. He didn't speak up, not until he was sure. He didn't want to feel afterwards that he had swayed Per, and perhaps induced him to make a key similar to the one that had once hung on a chain around his neck. He would never afterwards have been able to be certain that he was right, that the box and the key were identical to the ones owned by his Grandma Kathy.

But as the key took shape under Per's tools, as the twists and loops were cut into the metal, it quickly became obvious there could be no doubt. The key was identical to the one he had worn, the one willed to him by his favorite grandmother, the one mysteriously lost the night Lee had fired his gun and started him on this bizarre adventure.

As Per finished, gently sanding the rough spots on the key,

and then polishing it with a cloth to a high luster, Darren said, "That's it, Per. It's the same key."

"Is it?" Per said.

"No question."

"It is astonishing that it came to you, down through time. How far in the future is your home?"

"About six hundred and fifty years."

"To think that something I made could last so long," Per said. "I am glad. Even if none in your time know my name. It is good that something I have done will outlive me."

"I suppose that's all we can hope for."

Per nodded. "Darren, it is in my heart to ask something. Perhaps you do not know. Perhaps you know, but it would be unlawful to tell. But I must ask. You have much knowledge of the flow of time, and to my ears, it sounds as if these Monitors you know of, these ones who can control their journey in and out of time, they know a great deal more. I wish to know… my life, what is left of it… will it be long or short? Many have died since the plague struck. Nearly a third of Trondheim is gone, houses and farms empty and silent, cattle and goats and sheep running wild because there are none there to care for them, fields of grain lying rotten and unharvested for want of someone to reap it. What lies ahead for me? Do not fear to tell me if it is to be short. In many ways I would welcome death. Although, I do fear the suffering. I have seen many people die of the plague—my brother and sister, and my father. They suffered greatly, although it was over in barely a day. If this is to be my fate, I could bear it, I think. But I would like to know."

He studied Per's thin, intense face, and felt his stomach clench. He hadn't realized that Per had lost so many family members to the Black Death. Everyone did. Whole villages ceased to be when the plague swept through. And not all were as philosophical about it as Gerda. People went crazy, blamed Satan, thought it was the End Times. Some found scapegoats in the Jews and the Romani, and added to the misery by killing innocent people they thought were the cause of the disease.

"I wish I could tell you," Darren said. "So I could put your worries to rest. But I simply don't know. I'm not even sure that Fischer knows. Especially now that the entire timeline has been altered, there's no way to know for sure what happened, much less what *should* have happened." He paused. "I'm sorry."

Per looked at him in silence for a moment. "No, you need not apologize. I should not have asked you. It is perhaps best in any case. If we were to know our fate, how many of us would drive ourselves mad trying to change it? Trying to avoid the destiny God has ordained for us? I simply wish faith came more easily to me. I have spoken with Father Sven about it. Perhaps I should speak to him again." He picked up the key, and rubbed his finger across its polished surface. "In any case, I hope you may accomplish the task for which you were sent here. Whatever others may believe, I believe with all my heart that there is a path set beneath the feet of each man and woman, although we cannot see it. There is a way that we were destined to tread. And this," he gestured around him, "it is wrong. There is another path that was meant for me. And I believe that one of the reasons you have come here is to set my feet back onto the path where they should have walked."

That evening, Darren helped Per to close up shop for the night, and was shown how to tend the fire in the smithy, to cover the embers with ashes, so the glowing coals wouldn't die out at night and relighting the fire in the morning would be easier. Afterwards, he dusted the ash from his hands, leaving black smudges on the pants Fischer had loaned him.

Oh, well, if Fischer was going to send him to medieval Norway, he should expect that his clothes would come back dirty. He passed the workbench, where the box and the new silver key still sat, and glanced down at the little slip of paper Per had discovered in the secret compartment.

On its surface, which had once been blank, was now a fine tracery of writing.

He picked it up, looking at it with a frown. Could it be the same piece of paper? Had he missed the writing at first for some reason? Then he realized there must have been some sort of invisible ink on the paper, and leaving it near the dry heat of the fireplace had somehow caused it to become visible. He remembered making a simple invisible ink out of lemon juice as a child, and marveling at how writing appeared seemingly from nowhere when the paper was passed over a candle flame. He had no doubt that this was something of the same kind.

He had the same sense now as when he had looked at the sign in front of Per's shop, that he was looking at writing in a foreign language, but that the letters were rearranging themselves into English in his brain. And he read:

Siege of Novgorod failed Magnus taking sea route Stockholm to Trondheim to meet Haakon intercept there Spare none Olaf will have ship waiting Valdemar will meet you in Copenhagen with payment

He pondered this in silence for a moment, and then called out, "Um, Per? I think you'd better come take a look at this."

A moment later, Per pushed aside the curtain into the smithy, and stood there, looking at him questioningly.

He handed Per the piece of paper. "The heat of the fireplace made writing appear," Darren said. "It was evidently written using some sort of ink that is invisible until it's heated. Read what it says. I think we have a serious problem, here."

Per absorbed the contents of the note without his face betraying any emotion.

"Do you know who the note refers to?"

Per nodded, still gazing at the note. "Oh, yes. There is no doubt about that. Magnus and Haakon are the king and his son, who co-rule Norway. Magnus has been away on a crusade to Novgorod since last year, attempting to conquer territory east. There is much resentment at this, that the king was away as so many of his people were dying of the plague."

"The king couldn't have prevented that."

"No, but still, to have our country's leader away fighting in a distant place, trying to subdue a land none of us will ever see and few of us care about, while the Black Death ravages his own people, seemed blameworthy to many. His son, Haakon, has acted as go-between, but has also been away more than he has been in the country."

"And Olaf? And Valdemar?"

"Olaf is a common name, but I believe that this must refer to Olaf, the Archbishop of Trondheim. Valdemar is the king of Denmark, whom some would like to see ruling Norway and Sweden as well."

"So that means…"

"It means," Per said, "that Lars Jonsson is a traitor, and we have been assisting men who would be regicides."

"What do we do?"

Per thought for a moment, turning the paper over between his fingers. "Magnus and Haakon mean nothing to me. What does it matter to the common folk who is king? As long as they mind their high affairs of state and leave us alone, it makes no difference."

"But if this message is delivered, the king and his son may be assassinated!"

Per shrugged. "And then we will have a different king, and life will go on the same as it did before."

"But Lars Jonsson is a… a… bad guy!" he sputtered. "We can't help the bad guys!"

Per looked at him in silence for a moment. "Were they successful?"

"What do you mean?"

"The men who will try to kill King Magnus and his son. In your time, this would be in the distant past. Surely your wise men remember what happened. People always remember what happens to kings. Were Magnus and Haakon killed? Or did the plot fail?"

He shook his head. "I don't know. I studied some history in school, but I wasn't all that great at it. I failed a test one time because I couldn't remember two of the eight wives of Henry VI, and it was only after I got home that I realized that the problem was, it was actually the six wives of Henry VIII." He gave a desperate little giggle.

"I have no idea what you're talking about," Per said.

"Never mind. It hasn't happened yet." Darren swallowed. "Listen, Per, we can't afford to mess this up. Do we give Lars Jonsson back the note? Or do we destroy it? Or do we tell him that we know what he's up to?"

"The latter would be foolhardy. Neither of us seems likely to win a fight with someone of Lars Jonsson's stature, and I have no doubt he carries a weapon and would not hesitate to use it if he thought that we might interfere with his plans."

"So what do we do?"

Per picked up the piece of paper, and tucked it back in the secret compartment at the bottom of the box. "We put the note back. When Lars Jonsson comes in tomorrow to get the box and the key, we give it back to him. I get paid my twelve silver pennies. And whatever happens to the king and his son, happens."

He stared at Per in disbelief. "Look. I was sent here to try to fix something that shouldn't have happened, to repair the damage to the timeline. What if this is it? What if by ignoring this, and letting it happen, history changes and causes everything to fall apart?"

"What if by taking the note, or confronting Lars Jonsson, *that* is what changes history? You don't know."

"I do know that something was supposed to occur in the next day or so that was the important event, the divergence that we have to fix."

"But you don't know what it is." Per shook his head. "You have been sent on a fool's errand. I am sorry to say so, but it is true. You cannot change something when you do not know what it is. And even if you did know, if you somehow figured it out, then *how* do you change it? It is not as if there is only one possible outcome for any action. There are thousands of different ways that things can go.

"So even if you somehow did know that this box, and this note of Lars Jonsson's, are the thing you need to change, what then? Do you destroy the note? Do you lay in wait for Lars Jonsson, and slay him when he walks through the door? Do you tell him that you know what he is trying to do, and threaten to reveal his plan to the authorities? Do you offer to help him to kill the king and his son?

"There are more possible courses of action than anyone could count, and yet you stand there telling me that one, and only one, of these is the right one. How, then, do you decide which one is correct?" Per shook his head again, and gave Darren a sorrowful look. "I am sorry to say so, and for a time I thought it might not be true, but I see now that your friend Fischer is a fool, and he has put your life in danger for no very good reason."

He stared at Per in silence for a moment. He felt deflated, as if Per had pointed out the very thing that all of them should have seen, perhaps *did* see, but no one wanted to admit.

Finally, he said, "You yourself said that you hoped I would succeed. You said you felt that things weren't right. And now you're saying it's hopeless."

"I still do hope. If I did not, I would hang myself from yonder beam, and be done with it. But hope is itself a foolish thing, is it not? To remain hopeful when everyone around you is dying of the plague, when your own life is not what it was meant to be, and there is no way to change it? And even hope cannot blind me to the truth, that if this is the important thing, the cause of this divergence you spoke of, then I do not see how any man could decide which way to go. Perhaps your Fischer knows, and did not tell you?"

"No," he said, in a defeated voice. "I don't think he knows, either."

"Then we can only do one thing. Put the note back into the box, give it to Lars Jonsson tomorrow, and see what happens."

The next day dawned cool, but the sky was a clean, pure blue. It looked freshly-washed, and to Darren's eyes, immensely cheering after the chill gray monotony since his arrival in Norway. The sunlight lifted his mood, even though the memory of the depressing conversation of the previous evening still nagged at him. Even the chickens seemed happier, and strutted around in the slanted rays of sunshine in the little yard behind the smithy, pecking at the grains he tossed to them and making what sounded like happy chicken noises.

Per, on the other hand, was gloomier than usual, and prepared their meager breakfast in silence. Darren tried more than once to strike up a conversation, but statements such as, "The weather looks like it's improved" and "The chickens laid three eggs this morning" were answered with monosyllabic grunts, and finally he gave up.

The day crept its way slowly forward. Per worked on an intricate silver buckle that looked as if it went to a man's belt, but unlike the previous day he seemed to prefer to work without an audience, and after a while Darren decided to go for a walk.

The air was warmer than the previous day, and there was bird song in the distance, but the road was still rutted and muddy and he had to watch his step to avoid a misstep into a puddle of ice-cold water. He walked up the road to Gerda's house, and found his rescuer outside, digging in a small patch of garden in front of her ramshackle cottage.

He greeted her warmly, and she turned around and gave him a smile that was mostly gums.

"Well. Darren Carlsson. Still alive, I see?"

"The day's still young." Darren grinned at her. "There's still plenty of time to get killed later."

"That is true, my friend. That is true. But I'm glad you've come to visit. How is Per Olafsson? Still alive too, then?"

"Yes, Per's still alive. But we've got a dilemma, Gerda, and I thought I could ask your advice."

She stood up and wiped the mud off her hands onto her dress, then tried to brush the mud from her dress and succeeded in returning most of it to her hands, then shrugged.

"Can't escape mud," she said. "Kind of like death, mud is. Sticks to everything in the end. At least it's better than fleas, eh?" She poked him in the ribs and laughed at her own joke.

Darren's cheeks warmed a little. "Yeah, better than fleas. But anyway. We have a problem, and I don't know what to do about it."

"Well, why don't you come inside, and we can each have a mug of ale, and you can tell me about it, and then I'll tell you what to do."

She led him into the house, and after two mugs of ale were poured, and they were seated at the narrow table in what passed for a kitchen, Gerda said, "Now, what is the problem, Darren Carlsson?"

He told her about Per's discovery of the note, and how they'd read the writing on it, and discovered the plot to kill King Magnus and his son.

"And the Archbishop is involved?"

"It seems like it."

Gerda nodded. "Always trouble when you get religious men involved in political matters."

"My country has the same problem."

"Well, what did Per think should be done?"

"Per said we should put the note back, and give it to Lars, and let fate take its own course. He said we couldn't change matters anyway, and would likely just get ourselves killed."

"There's sense in that," she said. "If you took the note, he would know you'd found it, and probably try to kill you to save himself."

"Yes."

"He seems like a man willing to risk a great deal. To turn over the box to Per in the first place. He was counting on Per's not finding the secret compartment." She rubbed her lumpy chin thoughtfully. "He must have lost the key, and needed a replacement quickly before he met the man who is supposed to receive the message. But he also seemed to me to be an arrogant man, who assumes that he is smarter than everyone else around him. He probably thought, 'Ignorant silversmith, he will never think of looking for a secret compartment,' and then, 'Even if he finds the note, he will not know how to make the writing appear,' and then, 'Even if he figures out how to make the writing appear, he will not know how to read it,' and then 'Even if he knows how to read it, he will not understand what it means,' and then, 'Even if he understands, he will not dare to interfere.' So there you are."

She thought for a moment. "Of course, it's also possible that Lars Jonsson does not know the note is there, and is carrying it for another. Or that he is the intended recipient of the note. You have made a lot of assumptions, that because he is carrying the box, he knows what the note says."

"Per said something like that, too—that we didn't know enough to make the right decision."

"Per is probably right."

"So what should we do?"

"Well, it seems to me that the main thing here is to keep the two of you from being killed. There are two possible things to do that might avoid that fate, for the time being at least. One is to do what Per suggests, which is to put the note back into the compartment, and let Lars Jonsson go away with it, and if the king is killed, then that is what God intended, and well enough."

"And the other?"

"Replace the note with a blank slip of paper. When Lars takes the box, he will probably check to see if the note is there. He will open the secret compartment, and see a blank bit of paper, just like he expected. Because remember, if you put the original note back—the writing is now visible, right? So Lars will know you read it, or at least suspect. But if you put a blank slip of paper in the compartment, Lars will *think* it is the original note. And then he will deliver it to the man he is trying to meet. And the man will try to read the message, and there will be nothing there. When this happens, I doubt Lars will think, 'That silversmith! He must have read the note and then replaced it with a blank bit of paper!' No, he will think, 'The message is not here, it must be the one who wrote it who gave me the wrong piece of paper, or did not use his secret ink properly.' Thereby, you and Per are both saved, for now at least, and the king may be as well."

He stared at her for a moment, and then sprang up and

kissed her on the forehead. "Gerda," he said, "you're brilliant."

She blushed. "Now, you know, if my husband, rest his soul, were still alive, he'd be *that* jealous. And the two of you would have had to fight a duel to the death over me, and I'd have been grieved whichever of you had lost."

Per was less sanguine about the whole thing.

"A man like Lars Jonsson will know what has happened. And since none but us have handled the box, whoever the intended recipient of the message is—he will know who did it. These are men who are unafraid to kill a king and the men who are guarding him." But he agreed that Gerda was right. Now that the writing on the original note had been accidentally unmasked, there was no other obvious choice.

A small slip of paper, cut to the size and shape of the original, was placed in the secret compartment, the bottom panel reset, and the lid closed and locked. The original note itself went into the fireplace, where it shriveled to blackened ashes in seconds.

"There," Darren said, as the eerily familiar box and its newly-made silver key were placed on the counter in the shop to await sunset and its owner.

However resigned Per was to a bad outcome, even he seemed a little twitchy as the sun's rays slanted downward from the west. He looked through the little window into the road, but no one came. There was no sign of Lars Jonsson. The shadows lengthened, and the light glinting on the muddy surface of the road was burnished bronze, and still no one came into the shop, not Lars… nor anyone else.

"Are we remembering wrong?" Darren asked, as the last of the sun's rays vanished behind the hill west of the smith.

"Did Lars say we should bring the box to him? I remember his saying that he was staying at the inn down the road."

"No, I am certain of it. Lars said he would come here to pick up the box, and to give me my payment." Per frowned. "But I wonder if perhaps we should bring it to him, none-theless."

"The sooner we get it out of our hands, the better, as far as I can see," Darren said. "Even though the original note is gone, it's still part of a plot to overthrow the government. I think you need to get it back to Lars as soon as you can, and hopefully never see it again." He paused. "It's funny. That box always had good associations to me. It belonged to my grandmother, and she used to keep all sorts of odd stuff in it…"

"…'knick-knacks,'" Per said.

"Yeah." Darren smiled. "And my grandma was a gentle, sweet lady. I wonder what she'd have thought if she'd known it was used to carry treasonous messages about killing members of the royal family."

"I doubt if it would have made a difference to her. Every-thing, everywhere, has been touched by good people and bad, used for good purposes and evil ones. There is no object that cannot be made to serve both purposes." Per looked at him closely. "Was she a wise woman, your grandmother?"

"Very wise."

"Then she probably would have said, 'Although this box was once used to bear messages of destruction, we will now cleanse it by devoting it to good purposes.'"

"You're probably right."

"And I think you are also right, Darren Carlsson. The time has come to send the box on its way. Let us bring it down to the inn, and get it into Lars Jonsson's hands, and I will collect my twelve silver pennies. And that, we will hope, will be the end of it."

By this time, the light had mostly faded from the sky. Per

attached the new key to the box's handle with a leather cord, wrapped the box in a piece of cloth, and then lit two oil lamps, leaving one burning in the front window, and taking the other to guide their steps down the road to the inn. The walk only took five minutes, but the warmth of the day was passing fast, and the chill was seeping back in by the time they stepped through the door.

The front of the inn housed a small and rather disreputable-looking tavern. Three men, already in advanced states of inebriation, slumped over mugs, staring off into space with glum expressions. The innkeeper, a sallow, rail-thin man whose gloomy countenance made Per look ebullient by comparison, gave the two newcomers a glance and a sigh before coming over to them.

"Evening, Per Olafsson," he said. "Evening, stranger."

"His name is Darren Carlsson." Per set his lamp down on the counter. "He is staying with me for a time, and helping me in the smithy."

"Then evening, Darren Carlsson," the innkeeper said. "You don't ever come by for beer, Per, so I've no doubt you have other business here."

"Yes, Christian, I do have other business tonight, but afterwards, perhaps we could sit down and share a mug of ale with you."

"That would be pleasant. Business is much fallen off since the plague came through and killed most of my customers."

Darren gave him a wry smile. "I can see how it would have that effect."

"So tell me what business you have, and we will talk about the sorry state of affairs in these parts over mugs of beer after you have concluded it."

"I am looking for a stranger who has been staying with you for two days, a hearty, strong fellow, with a bold, sneering face, named Lars Jonsson. I have been working on a job for him, and he was to claim it and pay for it today before sunset, and he did not come. So I have come looking for him."

Christian nodded. "He is here, but I have not seen him since he ate his midday meal. I presume he is still in his room, which is yonder"—he pointed off up the stairs at the back of the room—"the door on the right. But you may want to know, his visitor may still be there."

"Visitor?"

"Another tall sneering fellow cut from much the same mold. These wealthy landholders, who can tell one from the other? He came in, much as you have, asking for Lars Jonsson, and then vanished up the stairs. I have not seen or heard either of them since."

Per's eyes met Darren's.

"This can't be good," Darren said.

Per shrugged. "Nevertheless, it is time to get this box back to its rightful owner." He set off up the stairs.

Darren followed, his heart pounding. Something was wrong, here. Something was very, very wrong.

Per knocked on the door, and a deep, commanding voice said, "Come."

Per opened the door, and walked into the dimly-lit room. He followed, a little more timidly, peering over Per's shoulder.

"I wondered if I would have to go looking for you," the man at the table said, turning and looking at them, the light from an oil lamp reflecting from his smile.

It was not Lars Jonsson. He had never seen this man before in his life.

"So, I take it that this is the secret message that was to be delivered to Erik Jorgensson in Trondheim? Excellent. This will help immensely. We can now round up and slay the rest of the traitors to our king."

"Message? What message?" Per's voice was so flat and uninflected that Darren almost believed for a moment that he wasn't lying, and had to stop himself from saying, "Remember? The one we found in the secret compartment in the bottom of the box?"

"Do not lie," the man said, his voice calm and cheerful. "See how liars are treated?" He gestured over to a corner of the room, and only then did Darren see that Lars Jonsson was, in fact, there with them. He was missing his head, which lay a little way off, still wearing a shocked expression.

"Lars Jonsson also lied to me," the man said. "He told me he knew nothing of a message. I asked him why, then, was he staying in a filthy little inn in the hills east of Trondheim, instead of enjoying the favors of his mistress and feasting on mounds of excellent food and wine in his manor in Oslo? He told me that he was here on business, and had stopped to hire a silversmith to fashion a gift for his woman."

"That is, indeed, what he told me," Per said. "I am the silversmith." He uncovered the box, and lifted the silver key, hanging from its cord.

"Ah, yes, the box," the man said. "Poor Lars. If he only hadn't lost the key, he might actually have succeeded, and as we speak already be on the way back to Oslo. But God took a hand in things, and Lars's horse stumbled in a stream and went lame, and the saddlebag came loose and fell into the water. Lars thought he'd rescued everything, but when he stopped for the night, he discovered that the key was missing. The all-important key, which opened the box containing the message for his accomplices—the message that even he could not be trusted to read."

The man looked up at Darren, and smiled. "You may know nothing of it, young silversmith, but your scrawny friend there does. I read it in his eyes. Understand this—we know all about the note, and what it said, and how it was written with magical secret ink that only appears when the paper is warmed over a flame. So fear not, the conspiracy has been thwarted. But we need the note itself, as proof that there are bigger fish in the net than yon messenger boy—" here he gestured again at Lars's headless body, "—and that those fish have the names of Olaf, Archbishop of Trondheim, and Valdemar, King of Denmark."

"I don't know what you're talking about," Per said.

"Then give me the box, and I will show you. Of course, it will be my sad duty to slay you both afterwards, but I hope you will recognize that I very much regret it."

There was a moment of complete silence, when everything seemed suspended. He stared at the man, aghast. Per was still expressionless, clutching the wooden box under his arm, and the king's guardsman, still smiling cruelly, sitting in a relaxed pose with his long legs stretched out in front of him. And then Per turned and fled, his feet clattering on the wooden stairs.

It took Darren a second more to react. He barely missed being decapitated by the man's sword, which he brought out more quickly than seemed possible. He almost met disaster a second time by stumbling in the middle of the staircase—he grabbed the handrail to save himself from falling, but it snapped off in his hand. He went airborne, narrowly avoiding smacking his head on the crossbeam at the bottom of the staircase, and landing improbably on his feet still holding the useless chunk of wood in one hand. A moment later he thundered across the front room of the inn.

"Aren't staying for a beer, then?" the innkeeper said glumly, as Darren crashed out into the road, the bellowing guardsman right behind him.

It probably would have been better if Per Olafsson had fled into the woods, or ducked into someone else's house. In the dark, it would have been difficult to find him, even for someone as experienced as the guardsman. But Per made a beeline back for the smithy. Darren saw ahead, in the pale light of the rising moon, Per's long, thin legs disappearing through the door, and heard a bolt being dropped to bar the front door behind him.

Darren gave a futile tug on the door handle. "Oh, shit. That's not good."

Fortunately, the guardsman wanted the box more than he wanted Darren. Within a few strides, he had reached him, but instead of running him through then and there, simply gave him a hard shove. He lost his balance, and fell face first into the mud. He lifted his head, wiping the grime off his face with one arm so he could see.

The guardsman stomped up to the door of the smithy, and pounded on it with one meaty fist.

"Silversmith! Give me the box, and we will talk about terms for my sparing your life."

Per's voice came from an upstairs window. "Go to hell."

"You treasonous dog. You would be an accomplice to men who would kill our king?"

"I would be an accomplice to no one," Per said calmly. "All I want is to be left alone, and to lead the life I should have led. That is all I have ever wanted. But you can't give me that. No one can. So I repeat—go to hell." And then Per laughed, for the first time that Darren had heard. "And you should know— we found the note, and destroyed it. So what you are looking for doesn't exist any more. You can kill me now, I suppose."

"Well enough," the guardsman growled, and there was the sound of breaking glass.

Behind the window was the oil lamp, still lit. The guardsman picked up the lamp, and threw it onto the wooden floor of the shop. Oil spilled out, splattering the planks with sizzling flames.

"No!" Darren shouted, struggled to his feet, and ran around to the side of the burning house. "Per! Jump from the window!"

But Per laughed again, and Darren saw his thin, pale face

looking down at him from the open upstairs window. And Per said, "No. This was your divergence, Darren Carlsson. This is what you were sent to do—to make certain that I die here. I wish you could have fixed things, but I see now that was impossible in any case. But here! Catch!"

Per flung the wooden box out of the window.

Darren caught it fumblingly, heard a metallic clink as the key, still hanging from its cord, struck the side of the box.

"Take this to your grandmother, Darren Carlsson. May it bring her better luck." Then his face disappeared from the window, as the flames climbed higher, roaring through the little house.

"Per! Come out! You can't just *die!*"

The guardsman turned, and saw him standing there holding the box. There was a glint of reflected firelight and a ringing noise as his sword was drawn.

"I will have that box, whether the note is there or not. Was the silversmith lying, churl? Did the two of you destroy the message?"

Darren backed up, his eyes huge, until he bumped into a wall behind him. There was nowhere else to go. There was a clucking noise, and he realized it was the side of the chicken shed. He was going to die, not grandly self-immolating in a fire as Per Olafsson had chosen for himself, but beheaded amongst the chicken shit. It figured.

The guardsman brought his sword up. Darren clutched the box to his chest. There was a whickering noise as the blade sliced through the air, then a blast of wind, and silence.

part three

a dog and pony show

. . .

"**G**od *damn!*" Darren screamed, and backed into a file cabinet, upsetting a precarious stack of manila folders. The entire pile slithered to the ground, dumping its contents all over the floor and startling Ivan the tomcat, who gave an annoyed hiss and trotted out of the room, every whisker radiating disapproval.

"Good afternoon to you, too," Fischer said, from his seat behind his desk, and then looked him up and down. "You're filthy."

"Oh, don't even *start* with me." Darren glared at Fischer. He was still clutching the wooden box to his chest as if it were a shield.

"Whoa, *you're* a little grumpy. Who pissed in your cornflakes?"

"I haven't *had* any cornflakes. All I've had is tasteless porridge, and dumplings that are like compressed tasteless porridge balls, and dried fish that has too much taste, if you get my drift, and I haven't even had a decent cup of coffee in *days,* and a Norwegian guy with a sword just tried to chop my head off, and if you're planning on getting me to change my clothes and sending me off to Kentucky without having a good night's sleep in a real bed, then you can go fuck yourself!"

Fischer's pale eyebrows rose. "I don't think I've heard you swear before. I didn't know you knew how."

He goggled at Fischer for a moment, and then screamed, "Fuck! Fuck fuck fuck fuck fuck!"

Maggie appeared in the door of the office, and she looked at him, mild surprise registering in her eyes. "Ah, Mr. Ault, you have the words, but you don't have the music. I suggest you pay close attention to Fischer's command of the art of the curse word. He's a master." She paused. "Would you like a cup of coffee? I think I heard you mention something about coffee before your subsequent outburst, and I just put a fresh pot on."

He stared at her for a moment, and then said, "Um, sure. Thanks."

Fischer leaned back in his chair. "So, how was the vacation in fourteenth century Norway?"

"Vacation." He plopped down in the folding chair that stood next to the wall, set the box on the floor next to him, and put his face in one hand. "It was peachy."

"What did you find out?"

"Nothing. I don't know. That an uneducated silversmith from the fourteenth century is smarter than the two of us put together."

"Really?" Fischer said. "And what did this medieval rocket scientist come up with that so impressed you?"

"Well, Fischer, what he said was that there's no way Lee can have gone back in time and screwed things up. We're chasing shadows. Whatever caused the divergences, it wasn't Lee, or at least it wasn't Lee *personally*."

"Why not?"

"Remember when you checked the computer, and tried to find Lee, and found out he'd been erased like everyone else when the first divergence happened? If he evaporated when he fired the gun at my head, along with the rest of the human race, how can it have been him who went back in times and changed things? He wasn't alive to do it."

Fischer considered this. "Hmm. Well, maybe firing the gun propelled him into the past."

He shook his head. "Won't work. Everything stopped the moment the bullet hit my forehead. He didn't have time. And in any case, why would killing me throw Lee into the past? Or accomplish anything, other than my being dead? It doesn't make any sense."

"And your silversmith friend thought of all of this?"

"Yes."

"Impressive."

"Not that it did him a lot of good. He died in a house fire."

"Sorry to hear that."

Darren stared at the Librarian for a moment, and then exploded. "Look, Fischer, you can't keep sending me places when we don't have any idea what we're doing! I've gone two different places already, and accomplished nothing what-soever. This is pointless."

"You're not going to start screaming 'fuck' at me again, are you?"

"I feel like it."

"Well, don't. It's kind of off-putting, you know? In any case, you haven't accomplished *nothing*. You gained your Scottish girlfriend an extra four decades of life, right? That's something."

"Yeah, but in Norway I seem to have cost Per Olafsson several decades, so it all comes out a wash, you know? I'm the one who suggested he go find Lars Jonsson, and the result was that this big ape of a guy burned his house down and killed him."

Maggie walked back into the room, carrying two steaming cups of coffee, and handed one to him and one to Fischer. "Two sugar, no cream, as I recall, Mr. Ault?"

"Yes," he said. "Thanks. Coffee helps."

Fischer gave him a speculative look. "Okay, why don't you tell us both what happened, besides your having a nice roll in the mud."

"That was unintentional."

"I figured."

He launched into a highly abbreviated description of his time in Norway.

"Started out your time there getting run over by a horse," Fischer said. "Not the most auspicious start I've ever heard."

"It wouldn't have happened if you hadn't landed me in the middle of a road at night."

"And no sign of Lee?"

"No. I just don't think we're approaching this the right way. Per was right, Lee was wiped out along with everyone else. There's no way he could have gone back in time and messed with things. He wasn't alive to do it."

"Hmm. This may force a revision of our theory. What do you think, Maggie?"

"I can't argue with his logic, Fischer. But I am rather curious about the artifact he brought back. May we see it, Mr. Ault?"

Darren picked up the box from where it sat on the floor and handed it to her.

"It's extraordinary work." Maggie ran her finger gently along the incised design on the lid. "As is the key. You were certainly right about one thing, Mr. Ault. Your silversmith friend was a master craftsman."

"All the more pity he died."

"Not to appear callous, but he'd have been dead by now in any case," Fischer said.

"Not in a house fire, and not senselessly," he shot back. "It didn't have to happen that way."

When Fischer responded, his voice was uncharacteristically solemn. "Nothing *has* to happen a particular way. If I've learned one thing since I started working here, it's that. Nothing *has* to happen. Everything is contingent, not only on one event or person, but on millions. Everything that had gone before led to Per Olafsson dying in that house fire. Trying to tease out one cause by itself is impossible. So you shouldn't do it. Not even so that you have something more to kick yourself with, a pastime you seem to enjoy."

Darren ignored the last comment. "But isn't that what we're trying to do? Set things back where they were, fix things back the way they should have been? That seems like a contradiction."

"Yes and no. The point is, no one should be allowed to go back and jerk things around for his own gain. The choices of an individual *have* to be made without foreknowledge of the outcome. Don't ask me why, it's just the way the system is set up. It may be that Lee McCaskill learned how to go back and fuck around with things, based on his research into time travel. If so, he *must* be stopped, and the damage he did repaired. On the other hand, it might be that your friend Per Olafsson was right, and somehow the act of killing you was what caused all of this, and Lee was as much a victim of circumstance as the rest of humanity. In that case, we need to figure out why, improbably, your death seems to have created a temporal paradox, and undo that somehow."

"Well, it's a tall order," Darren said. "And like I said, you're not sending me off to Kentucky until I've had a hot meal, a shower, and good night's sleep."

"That's only fair, Fischer," Maggie said.

"I suppose. Maggie, can you check with Fassbinder and see if there are empty quarters somewhere he can use? I guess in a pinch he could sack out on my couch, but if there's a vacant apartment, it might be better. And maybe we can find him some other clothes, so that I can have mine back." He sighed. "Although, given the shape they're in, I suspect they'll have to be burned."

As it turned out, there was an apartment on the same floor as Fischer's that was furnished but currently unoccupied.

"The former owner was a library aide who took a vacation to seventh century Arabia," Maggie explained, "and refused to return. Something about a harem, I seem to recall."

The apartment itself was spacious and well-fitted out, and like Fischer's, it had a huge picture window. This one looked out over what appeared to be high desert, the sort of scenery Darren had seen on a visit to Taos, New Mexico. He knew, from what Fischer had said, that what he was seeing wasn't real—at least not real in the way that the Seattle skyline that he saw through his own apartment window was real—and briefly wondered what would happen if he tried to open it. He decided it was inadvisable, and continued exploring.

He'd only been there for ten minutes when there was a knock on the door, and he opened it to find a dark-haired boy who looked like he couldn't have been more than fifteen holding a pair of plastic grocery sacks.

"Delivery from Mrs. Carmichael," the boy said, in a bored sort of voice.

Darren thanked him and took the bags. To his delight they contained a few simple, but important, things—soap, shampoo, bread, jam, peanut butter, a small carton of milk, and other very welcome household items.

"Mrs. Carmichael and the Librarian also said to tell you that you shouldn't leave your apartment unsupervised," the boy said.

"Oh," he answered, not quite sure how to respond. "Okay."

The boy hesitated, and Darren wondered briefly if he was waiting for a tip. The two of them stared at each other for a moment, and then the boy gave up, turning away with a scowl. Darren watched him stalk off down the hall, and then went back into the apartment, closing and locking the door behind him.

First order of business was a shower. He was filthy, and probably smelled terrible, even if the days in a place where everything and everyone smelled bad had forced his brain into dulling his olfactory senses out of enlightened self-interest.

He went into the bathroom, stripped off his clothes, and spent nearly a half hour luxuriating. He got out, dried himself off, and only then realized Fischer hadn't provided him with a change of clothes. He thought about it for a moment, looking at his muddy, sodden pile of garments, and decided that no power on earth could have persuaded him to put them back on. The air in the apartment was comfortably warm—quite a change from his days in Norway, when he had only been able to escape the chill if he was fewer than five feet from the fireplace. So he wrapped his towel around his waist, and went into the living room.

There was a huge flat-screen television on the wall, and the remote was sitting on the coffee table, along with a couple of out-of-date *Time* magazines. He picked up the remote, and turned the television on. There was an old movie on, some science fiction thing with Christopher Lloyd and Michael J. Fox, and he had gotten about five minutes into it when he fell sound asleep.

Darren was dreaming, some vague, pleasant thing that seemed not to have much more in it than a hammock, a couple of palm trees, sunshine, and a large fruity drink with an umbrella in it. The lack of plot in this dream was actually fine with him. A warm wind caressed his face, and he dangled a leg out of the hammock and pushed off gently, setting it swinging.

I could get used to this.

He took a sip of his drink. But as he did so, an unpleasant and rather insistent noise intruded. At first, he thought it was a mosquito, but if so, it was a loud and impressively deep-voiced one. The unseen insect—if insect it was—buzzed obnoxiously several times before falling silent.

He took another sip on the bendy straw, and looked around, frowning in a bemused sort of way. Then the noise came back, strident and uncomfortable, and this time succeeded in pulling him upward, and reluctantly, out of his dream, first into a cloudy semi-awake fog, and finally into the reality of the empty apartment.

The television was still going—another movie, in the middle of a strange scene in which Brad Pitt was leaping around inside a van pretending he was a monkey. He picked up the remote, fallen where it had dropped from his hand, and shut it off.

The noise came again, and this time he recognized it as the buzzer at the front door. He stood up, lost his towel, recovered it, and cinched it tightly around his waist before going to see who it was.

The person at the front door was no one he had seen ever seen before—an amiable young Asian woman, round-faced, with a ready smile. If she was disturbed by finding him standing there behind the door, wearing less than the expected amount of clothing, she was quick enough to cover it up smoothly.

"Hi," she said. "I'm Sophie. I work for the Historical Arti-facts department. Fischer sent me here for two reasons. One was to give you some clothes." She smiled, and he looked down at his bare chest and towel-covered midriff, and his cheeks heated up.

Sophie handed him a plastic shopping bag. "I understand you're going to nineteenth century Kentucky. These are period, or at least as close as we could get. They're typical of the frontier states during that time period, so chances are they won't be too far off."

"I'm not going right now, am I?" he said, a little panicked.

Sophie smiled. "No. Well, I mean, I don't make those decisions. I understand you're doing some kind of highly classified reconnaissance work, so there's no reason I'd be privy to what's going on. I only handle the artifacts end of things."

"I see."

"The other thing I was sent here for has to do with an artifact I understand you brought back from fourteenth century Norway. Fischer wants me to check it over, and to do some temporal analysis on it."

"Temporal analysis?"

"We need to make sure that anything you brought back didn't change anything critical in the future. You know— anything *could*. Technically, moving a leaf from one place to another could make a difference. In practice, of course, most things don't result in any big changes. But we need to check. I won't have to keep it long. The tests we run usually take about six hours or so. After that, and assuming it checks out, I can give it back to you."

A little reluctantly, he retrieved the box and key from the kitchen counter, where he'd left them upon entering the apartment.

"Don't worry. I'll take very good care of them."

"I'm sure," he said, and handed them to her.

"Thanks." She headed off down the hall, and he retreated into the apartment.

He set the shopping bag down on the coffee table, and pulled out the contents.

Inside was a coarsely-woven white cotton shirt, a pair of pants that felt like they were sewn from canvas, and a jacket made of fur-lined buckskin. A pair of hand-stitched leather shoes with rawhide soles sat at the bottom of the bag. A set of underclothes, neatly folded, included an undershirt and a long-legged cotton garment with a four-buttoned flap over the butt.

"Practical," he muttered, and then dropped his towel and put them on.

After he was done, he slipped the jacket on, and went and stood in front of the bathroom mirror.

"Jesus Christ," he said out loud. "I look like some kind of Davy Crockett wannabe. All I need is a coonskin cap and a musket." He turned to the side, looking at himself with a frown. At that moment, the telephone rang.

It rang five times before he found it in a niche on the wall in the kitchen. He picked it up, and said, tentatively, "Hello?"

"Settling in, Ault?" came Fischer's voice.

"Yeah. It's a nice place. But these clothes, Fischer… I dunno. They make me look sort of like some kind of frontier settler guy or something. I feel ridiculous."

"It's okay if you *feel* ridiculous, as long as you don't *look* ridiculous. When you go places, you need to try to fit in."

"I wish you'd thought of that before you sent me to Scotland and Norway."

"Hey, all of this is a work in progress, okay? We're doing our best." Fischer paused. "In any case, it's important to remember that you need to fit in where you're going, not where you currently are. I'm sure you wouldn't look ridiculous to someone from nineteenth century Kentucky."

"Whatever. In any case, is it possible I could have something more for dinner than peanut butter and jelly? I haven't had a decent meal in god-alone-knows how long."

"Actually, that's why I called you. I'm having dinner in my quarters with Maggie, so we can discuss strategy, and we thought it might be advisable to have you sit in. Also, so that you can leave a little better fed than you were before."

"Well, that sounds hopeful. When do I have to go?"

"Probably not till tomorrow morning. There's no rush,

after all. It's not like humanity is going to become any more gone."

"That's true."

"Okay, so let's say six o'clock in my apartment. I'll have food brought up. We'll eat and talk about our battle plan."

"Battle? Was there a battle going on in Kentucky in eighteen forty-four? Because I've had enough of battles."

"No. Figure of speech."

"Oh. Good."

"See you at six, then."

Darren knocked on Fischer's door at a couple of minutes before six o'clock. Fischer opened the door, looked him up and down, and then laughed for nearly a minute.

"This costume is your fault, Fischer." He couldn't keep the sullen tone from his voice.

"God, this just *slays* me." Fischer wiped his streaming eyes with the back of his hand. "The glasses definitely complete the outfit. You're like the Nerd Man of Cumberland Gap, or something."

"You are such a pain in the ass."

"I'm glad I'm not asking you to pay for dinner. You'd probably want to pay me in possum hides." And Fischer started laughing again.

"Fischer, be *nice*," came Maggie's stern voice from somewhere behind him. "It isn't as if Mr. Ault has a *choice* of what to wear."

"No, I suppose not," Fischer said, still chuckling. "Sorry, Ault. I haven't had a good laugh like that in a long time. You can't reasonably expect me not to enjoy it."

"As long as you don't keep laughing all evening," he said, and entered the apartment.

It was immediately apparent that Fischer had at least

given some attention to cleaning up. The pile of dirty laundry was gone, as were the beer bottles. The carpet looked freshly vacuumed, the kitchen counters sparkling clean. The table was set for three, and Darren's mouth watered when he saw three nicely-prepared T-bone steaks, baked potatoes, steamed broccoli, and a big bottle of red wine. A pie of some sort was cooling on a rack on the counter.

"Not some kind of vegan tofu-eater, are you?" Fischer asked.

"No," Darren said. "And honestly, even if I was, I doubt I'd stand on my principles at the moment. I haven't been this hungry in years."

The first order of business was clearly eating, and he wolfed down his steak, a baked potato lavished with butter and sour cream, and another half a potato, and a large serving of broccoli, before he even felt like looking up from his plate. Fischer and Maggie ate at more measured paces, but finally all three were at the wine-sipping stage of things.

"That was an awesome dinner, Fischer," Darren said. "Do you eat like this every night?"

"I wish," Fischer said. "Special occasions only."

"I'm a special occasion?"

Fischer glanced up at him, a little sheepishly, and then looked back down again.

Maggie set her wine glass down. "What Fischer means to say is that he's sorry for how he's treated you, and should have given more thought to your safety before he sent you all over the world, and he promises not to be such an inconsiderate jackass in the near future."

"Hey now," Fischer said. "I didn't say anything to you about the last part."

"My apologies, sir, I got carried away with myself."

Fischer snorted.

"Well, no hard feelings," Darren said.

"Good. So we are clear that if anything bad happens to you in Kentucky, it's not my fault, right?"

He looked at Fischer, his eyes narrowing with suspicion. "Why? What do you know about Kentucky that could be worse than Vikings, the Black Death, and homicidal Norwegian guys with swords?"

Fischer glanced at Maggie. "How do you handle religious mania?"

"Religious mania?" Darren couldn't keep a note of panic from entering his voice. "They weren't burning people at the stake at that point, were they?"

"Not…" Fischer hesitated. "Not that we *know* of."

"Oh, well, *that* puts my mind at rest. Why couldn't these divergences happen somewhere safe? And warm? Well, at least Kentucky is fairly warm, isn't it?"

"The divergence happened in November," Maggie said.

"Shit. This isn't fair."

"Look, Ault, rescuing the human race isn't supposed to be some kind of pleasure cruise."

"So why don't you go yourself?" he said. "Why send me? It's not like I know what I'm doing, or anything."

Fischer didn't answer, and again, there was that second-long glance up to Maggie.

"What?" Darren said. "What does that look mean? You're not dropping me there in the middle of a war or anything, are you? Because I absolutely draw the line at being shot at again. I already got shot once, and it scared the hell out of me, and no way am I going to go through that again!"

Still, neither one answered.

"Okay, what aren't you telling me?" he demanded.

"It isn't that we are unwilling to make the voyage ourselves, Mr. Ault," Maggie said. "It's more that at this point, we can't. You're right that it would be only fair for one of us to take a turn running the risks, but the Board… thinks otherwise."

"What does that mean? The Board thinks otherwise?"

"Well, Mr. Ault, the fact of the matter is, Fischer and I, and also the Head of Security and several of the other department leaders, are under investigation for malfeasance. The Board of Directors is trying to determine if the current situation was caused by our negligence, and if so, what the appropriate measures are to rectify the situation. We had thought we would have more time to investigate the situation ourselves, and potentially to launch remedial measures, but the Board became aware of what happened and has taken matters into their own hands." The corner of her mouth curled up a little. "I suppose that it was a forlorn hope that the disappearance of the entire human race would go unnoticed."

"Meaning you can't help me?"

"We can still help you, yes, but purely from an advisory standpoint. We've all had our travel privileges suspended until this matter is sorted out—to stop any of us, presumably, from escaping into the past and vanishing ourselves, in order to avoid the consequences. So we are, for all intents and purposes, under house arrest. We are still allowed access to the computer systems, so we can still assist you in your endeavors, but the sad fact is that when it comes to investigating the divergence in Kentucky, you are on your own."

He widened his eyes. "But that's terrible! None of this was your fault!"

"Nonetheless, Mr. Ault, the Board sees the oversight of the Library, and therefore the management of everyone's timelines, as our responsibility. Our sacred charge, as it were. However this situation happened, it was on our watch, and someone has to take the blame for a problem of this magnitude."

"They're looking for a fall guy," Fischer said. "Or six or seven. An opportunity to clean house."

"Although what our successors' job description would be

if this situation is not corrected remains to be seen," Maggie said.

"What will happen to you if I don't succeed?"

"Hard to tell," Fischer said. "Nothing like this has ever happened before. I just hope they don't realize that in the Artifacts Department there's a whole room full of medieval torture equipment. Although using it on Fassbinder would be ironic, in a way."

"Now, now," Maggie said.

"Hey, he's the one who's into collecting that stuff," Fischer said.

"Be that as it may," she said, "you can see that we have quite a lot depending on your success, Mr. Ault. So while we are no longer in a position to compel you to go to Kentucky, we are... encouraging you to do so. I am inclined to agree with you, that Per Olafsson's assessment of the situation—that Lee McCaskill did not *directly* go back in time and cause the divergences in question—is probably correct. But however that is, we do know something of interest happened at those three moments in time. So far, what you have learned is intriguing, but is yet to form a complete pattern of any kind. So I would like to ask you, as a personal favor for Fischer and me—would you be willing to go back to nineteenth century Kentucky and see if you can find out further information about what has destroyed the proper time sequence? If you are unwilling... I am very much afraid that we have our hands tied."

He glanced from her to Fischer, and before he could talk himself out of it, said, "Of course I'll go."

"That's pretty sporting of you, Ault," Fischer said. "I half expected you to say 'screw it' and walk out."

Darren finished his wine, and Maggie poured him another glass without being asked. "Hey, I figure that after everything I've been through, and survived, what else could happen?"

"I thought you told me it was bad luck to say that," Fischer said.

"It probably is. But so far I've survived being shot, speared, and beheaded. Based on that, I'd say that the odds are in my favor."

"Damn, Maggie, I think we've finally turned this guy into an optimist. Who'd have thought?"

"We are greatly appreciative, Mr. Ault," she said. "Your willingness to be a pawn in this strange game takes no little courage."

"Well, I want the human race back as much as you two do, and also to find out why Lee tried to kill me. I mean, I don't know if I've made this clear enough, but Lee and I were best friends. I mean, tight. He was like my big brother. And then, all of a sudden, he goes nuts. If I can figure out what happened that caused that—and if we can somehow put that right, along with everything else—it'd really make any amount of trouble worth it."

"That's great, Ault. Like Maggie said. Thanks for being willing to do this."

"There is one thing, though," Darren said.

"Yes?"

"What were you saying about 'religious mania?'"

Fischer wouldn't meet Darren's eyes. "Oh. That."

"Yeah, that. What aren't you telling me? Last time you tried to avoid telling me about the Black Death."

"Well, you didn't get it, did you? I told you there was nothing to worry about."

"Still. I *could* have. So what are you currently trying to avoid telling me?"

Fischer fidgeted with his silverware, and then looked up at him. "Maggie and I did some research while you were gone. We thought it might be helpful to check out the people involved in the third divergence. You know, just see who they were. Even though there's still some fuckup that's making us unable to tell the difference between actual and alternate tracks, we can still poke around in their records. Their files are accessible on the computer, not to mention the printed versions in the stacks."

"Okay, and what did you find out?"

"The divergence is connected to a twenty-four-year-old woman named Jane Bell, in a little rural town called Concord, Kentucky. Like the other two people the computer identified in the original search, there's something wrong with her file—some kind of disconnect with everyone else's actual track took place in November of eighteen forty-four—but her life prior to that time was easy enough to look into. It seems like Jane Bell was the daughter of an itinerant preacher named Zebulon Bell, who took his dog-and-pony show around through Kentucky, Tennessee, and the western parts of Virginia and North Carolina. She was the eldest of twelve children."

"Wow. Brother Zebulon didn't just spend his time preaching the gospel," he said.

"No, evidently not. And the sect that he belonged to… well, they didn't believe in abstaining from sex, although they did refrain from drinking, smoking, gambling, and dancing."

"Okay, so far, what's the problem? I drink occasionally, but I don't smoke or gamble, and I have two left feet so dancing is probably out even if I wanted to. What's the big deal?"

Again, there was that momentary fidgeting with his knife and fork. "Well, you know how the Quakers were nicknamed that because they quaked before the Word of the Lord, and the Shakers were called that because they got so carried away with religious fervor that they would start to tremble and collapse to the ground in a sort of holy seizure?"

"Yes."

"Well, this group was nicknamed the Whackers."

"Okay, that doesn't sound good."

"And it wasn't because they masturbated a lot."

"I figured."

"The Whackers were a small, rather exclusive group of ultra-religious evangelical Christians in the early nineteenth century," Maggie said. "They didn't call themselves that, of course. They called themselves the Church of Our Lord Jesus Christ Risen and Triumphant Through Suffering. They believed in redemption through pain—that the line from Genesis, 'Cursed is the ground because of you; through painful toil you will eat of it all the days of your life' was not a consequence of sin, but a command by God to seek out painful experiences."

"Oh, crud."

"Yes, they were a little… extreme," Maggie said. "They never numbered more than about thirty."

"For obvious reasons," Fischer said.

"During their observances, they invited other church members to hit them in various ways. Pain was considered a sacrament."

"And I suppose the computer isn't going to rescue me if I'm about to get punched in the nose."

"No, sorry."

"Crud," he said again.

"Well, that's the breaks. The frontier was a rough place."

"Yeah, but no need to make it rougher by beating each other to a pulp every Sunday to try to get closer to God."

"I suppose you've got a point," Fischer said.

"And Jane Bell was the preacher's daughter?"

"Yup."

"So no possibility of flying under the radar on that one."

"Can't see how."

"It would be easier if they just masturbated a lot," Darren said.

"That's true."

He sighed heavily. "What else did you find out? Any other

interesting ways to get me severely injured that you're not telling me about?"

"No, nothing like that. As far as the girl herself, we know that like the other two, Jane Bell should have been married but the computer can't seem to locate her spouse. If our original hypothesis is correct, it's because Jane Bell is your direct ancestor, and the divergences wiped out one line of your ancestry. Why it intersected with actual tracks in these three different spots is uncertain. It could be that the computer was looking for some way to identify the problem, and grabbed the first anomalous data it found."

"I'm descended from these crazies?" he said, a little alarmed.

"And also from Per Olafsson and Maíre What's-her-name. Again, if we're right about how this works."

"You shouldn't be upset, Mr. Ault," Maggie said. "All of us are descended from a variety of characters, both savory and unsavory. None of us have ancestry that is pure in any sense of the word, whatever the nobility and royalty would have you believe."

"And a lot of those nobles and royals were fruitcakes themselves," Fischer said. "You should read some of their timelines sometimes. They got away with some weird-ass stuff that never made it into the history books."

"I know that," Darren said. "It's just that, you know… I don't like knowing that somehow I'm associated with these people."

"No choice involved," Fischer said. "Like they say, you get to choose your friends, but you don't get to choose your relatives."

"Unfortunately. But do you have any idea what I'm supposed to do when I get there?"

"We know when the divergence occurred, and there wasn't anything in particular going on at the time, at least not in a global sense. This was pre-Civil War. It wasn't far enough west that the troubles with the Native Americans would have had any impact, at least not at that time. There weren't any battles happening there, or anything like that."

"Well, that sounds promising," he said. "At least it sounds like I won't get shot at."

"So we think that this divergence—or, more likely, all three of them—were caused by a failure of the person in question to marry. Or at least, procreate."

"This is supported by the information you got in Norway, that Per Olafsson had a sense that he should have been married and wasn't," Maggie said.

"Although how he would know that is a little troublesome," Fischer said. "People aren't supposed to have any access to their alternate timelines. They're only supposed to have awareness of the track they're actually on."

"This could explain some cases of psychic claims, perhaps," Maggie said. "If the boundaries between actual and alternate timelines are leaky, in some cases, this might provide a rational reason for such phenomena as precognition, time slips, and déjà vu."

"I still think the Long Island Medium is full of shit," Fischer said.

Maggie nodded. "And could use a different hairstylist."

"Be that as it may," Darren said, "I don't see how that helps me much."

"In the practical sense, it probably doesn't," Fischer said. "It will be a matter of going back there, and trying to see what you can find out. Since Maggie and I are under house arrest, there's not much we can do other than to tell you to be careful. There's no guarantee that when you get back, we'll still be employees of the Library. We might well be in jail, or out on the street."

"What street, Fischer?" Maggie asked.

"Metaphorically speaking, of course."

"And I still get a night's sleep in a real bed before I have to go, right?" Darren asked.

"Yes."

"Good. Although I'll probably have nightmares about going to church and getting the crap pummeled out of me, all in the Name of the Lord."

***

As it turned out, Darren's worries about a poor night's sleep were unfounded. He returned to his temporary quarters at a little before nine. He briefly considered watching television—he figured that like a comfortable bed, it might be a while before he saw one of those again—but decided the bed seemed on the whole to be more attractive. He undressed and crawled between deliciously smooth, cool, clean sheets, and despite his long nap that afternoon and his worries about the Church of Our Lord Jesus Christ Risen and Triumphant Through Suffering, was sound asleep almost instantaneously.

He awoke at a little after eight o'clock in the morning, following one of the most completely refreshing nights he could recall. He dragged himself out of bed with some reluctance, and shaved off the scruff. His bathroom had been provided with an electric razor—whether by the ever-efficient Maggie, or left behind by the previous owner, he didn't know. Afterwards, he took a shower, and with even greater reluctance donned his nineteenth century garb again.

He was digging around in the food that Maggie provided, hoping for eggs and bacon and finding instead cereal and milk, which was adequate if not quite as appealing, when the telephone rang.

"Ready to meet the congregation?" came Fischer's voice.

"No. Not till I've had breakfast. Give me a half an hour."

"I'll be down at nine to escort you to my office. There's a little more information you should have before you go."

The line went dead.

"Well," he said, "that doesn't sound good."

Fischer was nothing if not prompt. At nine o'clock sharp, there was a knock on the door, and Darren answered it, and found the Librarian standing there, clad in a scuffed pair of black denim pants and a threadbare "Collective Soul" t-shirt.

Fischer gave him a once-down, once-up look, stifled a guffaw, and then said, "Sorry. I still can't get over the outfit. Sophie really outdid herself. It's amazing. You look like the love child of Daniel Boone and Bill Nye the Science Guy."

"Go to hell, Fischer." He made an angry gesture at the Librarian's t-shirt. "At least I know what decade it actually is."

"Hey, now. Don't knock the grunge, Frontier Boy. *No* one knocks the grunge."

They headed off toward Fischer's office.

"So, what's the new information about?" he asked, as they took the long elevator ride down.

"I'll show you when we get to my office."

Maggie met them at the door with three mugs of hot coffee. "She brought it down, Fischer. I let her in."

"No problem, I figured you would."

Sitting in the middle of Fischer's untidy desk was the wooden box, its key still attached by a leather cord.

Fischer sat down in his chair and picked up the box, then rapped it tentatively with his knuckles. "Huh. So she's sure?"

"Sophie is good at what she does," Maggie said. "I don't doubt her, however peculiar it seems."

"What's this about, Fischer?" Darren asked.

Fischer held the box up in front of his face. "You see this box, Ault? Your little souvenir from your trip to Norway?"

"Yeah, I see it."

"Well, it doesn't exist."

"What the hell is that supposed to mean?"

"We're not sure. Sophie Lau, our best artifacts specialist, went over it with a fine-toothed comb. We have to do that, you know. Can't have anyone bringing things back that played some later role in history, or make some kind of big change in preexisting timelines. So we have our artifacts specialists analyze whatever is brought back to see if its removal caused a divergence. If it did, we take it back and repair the problem. If not, then all is well."

"And what about the box? Did taking it cause a divergence?"

"Nope. That's because, as far as Sophie's analysis goes, the box doesn't exist."

"But it's right there. It's in your hands."

Fischer set down the box, and it clunked solidly on the desk top. "Well, for that matter, *you* are right there, and technically you don't exist, either."

"Oh, yeah. I'd forgotten about that." Darren took a sip of coffee, hoping the caffeine would make what Fischer just said make more sense.

"So her conclusion is that removing the box did cause a divergence, but only to *itself*. Put a different way, removing the box made the box itself cease to exist, but doesn't seem to have made a difference otherwise. My contention is that it's because the timelines are already so colossally fucked up that taking the box couldn't make things any *worse*. But you do see what that means, right?"

"Not really."

"You're going to have to put it back, eventually. For one thing, if you bring the box back and keep it, then it vanishes out of the fourteenth century, and it never gets to your grandma, who therefore never wills it to you."

"Maybe that's why the key disappeared," Maggie suggested.

"That happened before I took the box."

"I'm not even sure what *before* and *after* mean in this context," Fischer said. "Probably, they're meaningless. But the fact is, once we rectify all the other divergences, one of us is going to have to go back to Norway and bring this box back home."

"To where? Lars Jonsson got his head cut off, and Per Olafsson died when they burned his house down."

"We can figure that out when the time comes. Don't forget, that's only what happened when you visited a timeline that we know got mangled by whatever Lee did. It's almost certain that when the divergences get repaired, they'll both be in a completely different track."

"Oh. Right. I keep forgetting that."

"Thinking that way takes time," Maggie said. "We are so used to seeing time as a linear progression. Seeing it as a three-dimensional network is not intuitive for most people. It is, by the way, the qualification for the job that made Fischer stand out from the other applicants—a holistic vision seemed to come to him quite naturally. Most of us face a much harder struggle to achieve that capacity."

"So, anyway, it's something to think about," Fischer said. "And you should be careful about picking up any other trinkets on your travels. You really can't be sure what result it will have."

"At the time, I wasn't even aware I still had the box in my hands," Darren said. "I was more thinking about how I was about to have my head chopped off."

"I can see how that would make other considerations lose their impact," Maggie said.

"In any case, are you ready to head off?"

Darren glared at him. "That's a poor choice of words."

"Fine. Embark. Set sail. Say *bon voyage*. Whatever. Got a good breakfast, finished your coffee, said goodbye to indoor plumbing for a while?"

He took another big swallow of coffee. "Dammit. I really don't like all this."

"Objection duly noted. Now, please fasten your seatbelt, and pay close attention to your flight attendant for the following important safety lecture."

"Fischer, stop being a pain in the ass and get this over with."

"No sense of humor, that's your problem. Okay, fine. Like the last two times, I'm going to land you there a couple of days before the divergence happens, so you can get a feel for the place. Remember, you're our scout. Learn what you can, and see if you can figure out what Jane Bell has to do with anything."

"Okay, I'll do what I can."

"Oh, and give my regards to the Whackers." Fischer wiggled his fingers at Darren, and then there came the all-too-familiar feeling of being yanked out of the Library and into nowhere.

A chilly blast of air hit Darren in the face, and he winced.

"Shit," he said, involuntarily. "Why November? Why couldn't it be July?" He looked around at the countryside he'd arrived in, and saw neither the treeless, rocky hills of the Hebrides, nor the muddy roads and low houses of a town in medieval Norway, but an open woodland that would probably have been beautiful in summer. His landing place was a grove of trees, their gray and leafless branches reaching toward a leaden sky, with a carpet of fallen leaves and clumps of tangled underbrush. A little way off, the land sloped downward, toward the gurgling of a creek.

"It'd be nice to have a map. At least last time he dropped me onto a road." He shivered, and pulled the fur-lined jacket closer around him. "Of course, that was what got me run over by a horse."

He trudged off downhill, dead leaves crunching under his feet, and soon came to the stream chattering in a rocky bed. A rim of ice clung to the edges, and streamers of dead grass trailed in the swirling water. The whole thing looked lifeless and depressing, and there was no easy way to cross the creek without getting his feet soaked, so he turned downstream. If he followed it that way it would sooner or later lead him somewhere.

"Sooner or later" turned out to be a relative term, as did "somewhere." Two hours later he was still fighting his way through thickets of hawthorn, elderberry, and honeysuckle vines, and the creek still twisted its way deeper and deeper into a valley that showed no sign of human habitation. The branches of the overhanging trees became thicker, and the tangle of underbrush denser, and he was about to give up and retrace his steps back upstream when there came a distinctly non-natural sound—a regular creaking, like a cart wheel with a rusty axle.

That sounded promising.

He followed the noise, which seemed to come from around the next bend of the stream, and soon found himself looking down at a small building that straddled the creek. It was built of moss-covered logs and roof made of moss-green wooden planks. It looked forlorn by itself in the little valley. A log dam partly blocked the stream, with a sluice down the middle through which the water poured against the blades of a large wooden mill wheel. From inside the building came the grinding of the millstones and the clunk of huge gear teeth.

"Who are you?" came a gruff and not particularly friendly voice from somewhere behind him.

He turned, and saw a very tall, lean man, with shaggy, grizzled hair, and a short beard and mustache. The man had a rifle under one arm, and a suspicious look in his eye.

"My name is Darren. Darren Ault. Is this your mill?"

"Yeah, that's my mill. Why do you want to know?"

"I'm lost."

"Even wearing them eyeglasses, you can't see where you're going?"

"No, I can see fine. I just don't know where I am."

"That's my mill," the man said again.

"I know, that's what you said. But where is this? I mean, what town?"

The man looked around him, giving an exasperated gesture. "You see a town around here?"

"No."

"Neither do I. I was only wondering if them eyeglasses might make you see things I don't."

"No, they don't."

"Good. 'Cause there ain't no town here, far as I can tell."

"What's the nearest town, then?"

"Concord. Downstream a piece."

"How far is 'a piece'?"

"I dunno. Maybe five miles. Maybe less. Right where the creek goes into the river."

"Okay."

The two men stared at each other for a while.

"I'm trying to find someone named Zebulon Bell."

"Never heard of him."

"He's a preacher. Belongs to the, um, Church of Our Lord Jesus Christ Risen and Triumphant Through Suffering."

"Oh, *that* fellow. He's crazy as a bedbug, you know."

"So I've heard."

"Why you want to find him?"

"I need to talk to him about something."

"Oh. Well, I don't know where he is. Last I heard he was camping out down near the town. Him and his traveling circus. One of 'em tried to talk me into going to one of their revival meetings, but I told him to get the hell off my land before I filled his right butt cheek with buckshot. He left pretty quick after that." He patted the stock of his gun. "Don't like it when them people try coming on my land, hoping to convert me."

"I can't blame you. From what I've heard of them, you don't want to get involved."

The man tugged on his beard. "Yeah? Then why do you want to?"

"I don't. I only want to talk to him. I don't want to join up."

"Watch out. You start talking to him, he starts making sense, is what I've heard. Thin ice."

By this time, the light was dimming. The sun, unseen behind a thick bank of clouds, was evidently sinking toward the horizon. The lower reaches of the creek were becoming indistinct in shadow.

"Look, is there a chance I could stay the night with you? Just to sleep, you understand. I wouldn't be any trouble."

The man shrugged. "Don't bother me none. You look harmless enough. And I got no one here, no family, nothing. I'd be glad of the company, to tell the truth."

"Thanks. What's your name?"

"The name's Josiah," the man said. "Josiah McCaskill."

Darren stared at him for a moment. "McCaskill?"

"Yeah." The man frowned. "You got a problem with that?"

"No. I mean… um, no. I just… I just knew someone with the name of McCaskill, once. It kind of surprised me to hear it."

"Ain't a common name," the man said. "I'm the only one hereabouts with that name, and like as not I'll be the last. Never married."

Josiah McCaskill turned out to be a good enough host. Not as suspicious as Dugal Gillacomgain had been, nor as glum as Per Olafsson. Once Darren told him that he'd shown up at the mill after getting lost in the woods, Josiah accepted his story without further question, only saying, "You got to be careful wandering around in these woods. Never know who or what you'll run into, and ain't always who or what you'd want."

What Darren had been doing in the woods, and why he wanted to talk to Zebulon Bell, didn't seem to interest him much, although his opinions of the Church of Our Lord Jesus Christ Risen and Triumphant Through Suffering were unequivocal.

"I was down in the town couple of weeks ago," Josiah told him over a meal of bread, dried venison, and dried fruit. "And I heard them Whackers at their revival meeting. You know why they call 'em *Whackers*, right?"

"I've heard," he said, munching on a slice of bread.

"They get called up to witness before the Lord, and then Brother Zebulon and the other Holy Members, as they call themselves, slap 'em across the face. And after each slap, everybody shouts 'hallelujah' like something amazing just happened. Some of the ones who really want to get close to God ask Brother Zebulon to punch 'em in the jaw or kick 'em in the shins. Brother Zebulon is perfectly happy to do it, of course."

"Does anyone ever get to punch Brother Zebulon?"

"Oh, yeah, sometimes. Got to give him that, he plays fair enough. But only the ones who have become Holy Members get to do that, and I'll bet they don't hit him too hard. You know, make a show of it for the rest. But let someone get called up the others don't like, and they beat the tar out of him."

"Sounds kind of crazy."

Josiah gave him a satisfied nod. "That's what I say. I belong to the Methodist church, and that's always been good enough for me. I don't get to town for Sunday services as often as I should, but I do enjoy me a good hymn-sing now and again. Reverend Avery, he says to me, 'Josiah McCaskill, the Lord'd love to see your face in his house more often,' and I said, 'Reverend, I figure the Lord can look at this face any time he wants to, wherever I might be, although I got to wonder why he's so fond of it, because it's kind of an ugly thing to look at, to tell the truth. I'd look at handsomer faces than this one, if I was the Lord.' Of course, what he'd said was no more than the plain fact, and I shouldn't'a made light of it. But Reverend Avery knowed I wasn't serious or meaning to blaspheme or what-have-you."

Hearing the name *McCaskill* brought his mind back to the task at hand, which once again seemed to be taking a rather unexpected turn.

"So, Josiah, you really are the only McCaskill in the area?"

"That's a fact. My grandfather came over from Scotland shortly before the War of Independence broke out. Lived all his life in North Carolina. He had four children. Three girls and a boy. My father married the daughter of an Irishman, Patrick Ryan, who worked caring for the horses of a rich-as-Croesus tobacco planter." Josiah's craggy face broke into a fond smile. "That was my mother, of course, Noreen Ryan. Sweetest woman in the world. They had only the two children, me and my sister Anna. Anna stayed in North Carolina. She married Dan Quinlan and they have seven children, and probably two dozen grandchildren by now. Me? I came out to Kentucky when I was a young man, and bought this land and built this mill. Always intended to marry and raise a family here, and when my sons were grown, leave the mill to them and move to the town and live the easy life in my last years. But it never happened."

"You never met anyone?"

Josiah shook his head. "Oh, well, there were plenty of women around, you know? But none that ever took a shine to me. I remember thinking that I wanted what my parents had. My mother, Lord rest her soul, thought my father was the king of the world in spite of money being scarce and times being hard. She never looked at another man so long as she lived. I wanted that. Not the most beautiful woman God ever made, nor the smartest, nor the richest. I just wanted someone to look at me that way. And it never happened."

"That's sad." Darren's mind went unwillingly back to the way Maíre Gillacomgain had looked at him, when she took his hand. The day he'd told her that he couldn't stay, and after his task was done, he would never see her again.

Josiah shrugged. "It's the way it went. No changing it, and no sense complaining. I work the mill, bring flour and grits and corn meal into town once a week, and make enough to buy food and keep myself clothed and fitted out here. It's not a bad life."

"So, you never have felt like you *should* have been married and had children?"

"Should have? What does that mean?"

"Like things weren't going the way they were supposed to."

"Son, there *is* no *supposed to*. Things go the way they go, and that's that. All you got to do is to take care of what you got, and be content with it, because soon it'll be gone whatever you do. I won't pine away for what I don't have, because then I won't be thankful for what I do."

"That's good sense."

"A hell of a lot better sense than them folks down at their revival meeting, beating the tar out of each other, and thinking that's what God wants 'em to do," Josiah said. "I got enough pains and aches already without letting some fellow who calls himself a holy man add to them."

The next morning, Darren had a remarkably good breakfast off of grits, rashers of bacon fried on a blackened skillet, and mugs of a dark, steaming beverage that looked and smelled like coffee. He tasted it. It was pleasantly bitter, although sweetened with some chunks of brown sugar Josiah had in a tin box in his larder.

"What is this?" Darren asked.

"Roasted chicory," Josiah said. "It's a weed that grows hereabouts. The root looks like a carrot, but if you roast it, it smells wonderful sweet, and brewed it makes a nice way to wake up on a cold morning."

He agreed, although having grown up in Seattle, he had to admit it would probably never replace real coffee with the Starbucks crowd.

As he helped wash up the breakfast dishes, the magnitude of his task suddenly came crashing down upon him once more. He wondered if he'd ever see Seattle again. What was he supposed to do, even if he could find this Jane Bell? He wasn't convinced that what he'd accomplished so far had done a damn thing to fix either of the other two divergences. Why did anyone think he was going to do any better here? It was all very well for Fischer to call it a 'reconnaissance mission,' but all the information gathering in the world wasn't going to do them much good if they couldn't use it to repair the damage Lee McCaskill had done. And what could the connection possibly be between Lee and Josiah? There had to be one, but he didn't see it. He'd just have to stick that in the mental flash drive, along with everything else, and let Fischer figure it out when he got back.

Josiah gave him some general directions. There was a path that ran parallel to the creek, but on the opposite side from where he had been walking. It would take him all the way down into Concord. But the field where Brother Zebulon and his band were camping was off to the north, along the riverbank.

"When you get to the town, you'll see a road that runs up along the river. Go north on the road for maybe a mile. You'll see 'em soon enough. They're camping there in tents, at least they was when I was there last week. I know some of the folks in the town'd like to see 'em go, Reverend Avery among 'em. Sooner or later I expect they'll get run out. I guess it's happened before, plenty of times. They go to a place, preach the gospel, beat the Spirit of the Lord into each other, and if they're lucky pick up one or two new converts. Then when the townsfolk get sick of 'em, they run 'em off, and they up stakes and move on to the next town. Leastways, that's what I've heard."

He thanked the miller for his hospitality and his advice.

"Don't mention it," Josiah said. "Like I told you, I'm glad enough for the company. Come on back by when you've had your fill of getting your face slapped."

He assured Josiah he would, and headed off uphill, and soon the mill and the chuckling creek were lost to view.

As predicted, the path was broad and obvious. It was evidently well traveled, to judge by the marks of cart wheels and horses' hooves. He briefly wondered where the path went, and who could be traveling on it often enough to keep it as beaten down as it was. Mostly, though, he was glad of a walk that didn't involve forcing his way through vine thickets, and he ambled along for some time, daydreaming a little.

So far, Kentucky had been pretty pleasant. Josiah McCaskill was a nice fellow, and he had lucked out by running into him. Maybe he did have some connection to Lee, and it was vital that he met the miller. So far, so good. Maybe he didn't have to do much more than to get some information about Zebulon Bell and his band of traveling nutjobs. Maybe he didn't really have to infiltrate their ranks, or, heaven forbid, pretend he'd converted to their religion, and then get his lights punched out. Maybe he could hang around the town, and ask a few questions. Maybe there was an inn he could stay at, in exchange for doing some chores, or something. *This seems like a nice enough place.* He wondered why he'd been so worried.

The fact that he was happily occupied with these pleasant thoughts was probably why he didn't hear the sound of running feet, and didn't even have time to react when he was tackled from the left, knocking him off the path and sending him tumbling down a bank, all the while being pummeled and grabbed by at least two pairs of hands. When he and his assailants finally came to rest, he found himself flat on his back, staring at the point of a knife, and heard a now-familiar phrase.

"Move, and I'll slice your guts open."

And he said, more exasperated than angry, "Fuck, *again*? I am *so* sick of this happening every time I go anywhere." He reached up and adjusted his glasses, and saw two grinning faces, one of them scraggly-bearded, the other clean-shaven but missing both front teeth.

"You got any money, traveler?" Gap-Tooth said.

"Do I look like I have money?"

Gap-Tooth frowned, as if this was a question that he'd once known the answer to, but couldn't quite remember.

He finally said, "Naw. I guess not."

"He could be carrying gold in his pockets," Scraggly-Beard said.

Darren snorted. "Right. I carry gold bars in every pocket when I go out for a walk. And two in each shoe."

Gap-Tooth looked at Scraggly-Beard, wonder in his eye, and Darren suddenly felt hands roughly turning his pockets out, and pulling off his shoes.

Moments later, Gap-Tooth said, "You was *lying!* You ain't got no gold bars!"

"Let's slice his guts open," Scraggly-Beard said, as if this was a new idea that had just occurred to him.

"If you do, I'll disappear. Because that's what happens

whenever anyone tries to kill me." He gestured at them with one hand. "But I invite you to try, if you really feel like it."

Gap-Tooth considered this for a moment, his mouth hanging open a little. "I bet he's lying again," he finally said, triumph in his voice.

"Could be," Scraggly-Beard said. "But maybe we should let Murrell decide. He'll know what to do with him. Maybe he's worth something to his family, and they'll pay us to give him back alive."

"Or maybe he won't be worth nothing, and we can slice his guts open then," Gap-Tooth said, sounding cheered by this prospect.

"Yeah," Scraggly-Beard said. "Let's let Murrell decide."

Gap-Tooth waved the knife in his face. "I'll stick this in you if you try to escape. So you just walk along and be nice, and I won't have to get blood all over my nice clean knife."

That'd teach him to think things were going along well. On the other hand, whatever happened, he was no longer very worried about getting killed, which seemed to be a step in the right direction. Of course, they could torture him. Fischer said the computer wouldn't save him if that happened.

Before he could ponder it too much, he was pulled roughly to his feet. The knife point prodded him in the back, and the two men pushed him off into the woods on the north side of the path.

The terrain was uneven, and much clogged by close thickets of undergrowth, so the going was slow. Once a branch snagged his jacket, and he was caught for a minute as he struggled to get unhooked from clinging thorns that were curved like cat's claws.

"Hurry on up," Gap-Tooth said, brandishing his knife.

"Well, maybe if you'd use that damn knife for something else besides threatening me, we'd hurry up a whole hell of a lot faster!" He swore loudly as one of the thorns drew blood on his hand.

"Listen at him," Scraggly-Beard said, awe in his voice. "However he looks like a schoolmaster, he swears like a soldier."

"You better watch your tongue around Murrell." Gap-Tooth still didn't move to help Darren extricate himself. "He's a preacher man, you know."

He stopped fumbling with the branches, and looked up at them, his eyes narrowing. "Does he belong to the Church of Our Lord Jesus Christ Risen and Triumphant Through Suffering?"

Gap-Tooth and Scraggly-Beard looked at each other for a moment, then burst into guffaws.

"*Them* guys?" Gap-Tooth said. "Naw, Murrell ain't one of *them* guys. He's a right certified Methodist minister, like his daddy before him."

"A very holy man." Scraggly-Beard put his hand over his heart.

"Course, his mama was an innkeeper. If you take my meaning." Gap-Tooth gave a chortle, and poked Scraggly-Beard in the ribs.

"Yeah, but you oughtn't'a mention that bit to Murrell when you meet him. Nobody says bad stuff about Murrell's mama. Poor old soul, she died while Murrell was in prison, and he was *that* upset when he found out. But Murrell's the real deal, not one of them face-slapping traveling clowns."

"Murrell knows the Bible backwards and forwards."

"Murrell can preach the gospel so good, it'll make you feel right holy when you're done listening."

"Crowds of people come to hear him preach. You can't take your eyes off him, or think about anything else when he's talking." Gap-Tooth grinned. "And that gives us time to go behind the crowds and loot all the saddlebags."

"Can you two stop singing the praises of Reverend

Murrell for a minute and help me get loose?" he snapped. "Unless you want to leave me here."

Gap-Tooth stared at him for a moment, then said, "Oh," and using his knife, cut free the last of the thorny vines that were hooked into the fur collar of his jacket.

"There." Gap-Tooth scowled, and pointed the knife in his direction. "Now hurry on up."

He gritted his teeth. He had a quick thought that on the whole, he preferred the Vikings, and then they were once more fighting their way through the underbrush.

Another twenty minutes brought them into a clearing occupied by several lean-tos, each with a piece of filthy canvas hanging over the opening tied with pieces of twine. A half-hearted campfire burned smokily in the middle of the clearing, with a blackened kettle hanging from a branch suspended over it. The noise of their arrival precipitated the opening of two of the canvas curtains, and several men ducked out of the lean-tos and came into the clearing, looking at him with interest.

"What'd you catch, Mosher?" one of them said to Gap-Tooth. "Looks like an accountant."

"I thought he looked like a schoolmaster," Mosher said. "But he ain't. You should hear him swear."

"Oh, yeah?" The man looked at Darren, his brow furrowing. "Let's hear you swear, then."

"Fuck you."

This was followed by murmurs of appreciation from the new arrivals.

"You're right, Mosher, he ain't a schoolmaster," said a man with unruly black hair, a scar up the side of his face, and a low, rather sinister voice. "Schoolmasters don't say *fuck*. The schoolmaster at my school once beat me good for saying *fuck*. Couldn't sit down for a week."

"When did you ever go to school, Crenshaw?" another man said. "You ain't never went to school."

Crenshaw gave him a nasty smile. "I made it all the way to third grade, so shut your mouth, Norris, before I shut it for you." Then he turned back to Darren. "Well, if you ain't a schoolmaster, what are you?"

"I'm a bookstore owner."

"Oh. I ain't never heard one of them swear either."

"You ain't never been in a bookstore in your life, Crenshaw," Norris said.

"That's true," Crenshaw admitted. "So, Mosher, did he have money on him?"

"Naw," Mosher said. "He said he had gold bars in his shoes, but turns out he was lying. Johnson here wanted to slice his guts open right there on the spot, but I thought it'd be better to bring him back here for the Reverend to see."

"You wanted to slice his guts open, too," Johnson said sullenly.

"Yeah, but it was me as thought of bringing him back for the Reverend to see," Mosher said.

"Was not," Johnson said. "I thought of it first. I remember saying, 'Let's let the Reverend decide.'"

"Was too," Mosher said. "You ain't got the brains God gave a pigeon, and you only remember your own name because I shout it at you all day long. So if I remember saying we should bring the schoolmaster back here to meet the Reverend, that's how it happened."

"I told you, I'm not a schoolmaster," Darren said quietly.

"Shut up," Mosher and Johnson said together.

"Any case," Crenshaw said, "probably best you brought him back for the Reverend to meet. We're too close to the town to be leaving dead bodies around for people to find."

"Where is the Reverend, anyway?" Mosher said.

"I'm right here," said a soft voice, and he and the others turned.

Standing in front of him was a man who had evidently come up to them as silently as a cat. He was about Darren's height, and although he was probably no heavier, he gave the impression of physical power. His face was lean, with a long, straight nose, dark curly hair, a short beard, and intelligent eyes that burned with a fierce, keen intensity. His face was flushed, as if with fever. The phrase *consumed to ashes by an inner fire* came to Darren's mind. He couldn't recall where he'd come across that line, but it seemed apt. A young woman with unkempt brown hair and a rather plain face set off by intense, intelligent hazel eyes, hung on his arm, and looked at him with a curious expression, like someone examining a strange species of insect.

"Reverend," Mosher said, a little breathlessly. "Look what we caught."

"I see that," Murrell said, in the same quiet voice, and then turned toward Darren. "They haven't hurt you, I hope?"

He shook his head. "I'm fine."

"Good," Murrell said. "I'm sorry if they inconvenienced you in your travels. Allow me to offer you what hospitality we can, although I'm afraid that the standards of our establishment have fallen off of late."

Crenshaw snorted laughter, but covered it up quickly.

"What are you planning on doing with me?" He hoped it didn't sound as cowardly in their ears as it did in his own.

"Do with you?" Murrell smiled a little. "We're planning on giving you food and a place to sleep. Other than that, nothing. But I would like to have a conversation with you, just as between two friends, while we eat and drink. Crenshaw, get our guest here a bowl of stew and whatever we have to drink, and some for myself as well." While speaking to Crenshaw he never took his eyes from Darren's face.

Food and drink was provided—a stew made with some unidentifiable root vegetables and equally mysterious chunks of tough meat, and a tin cup with a drink that was unmistakably corn whiskey.

"I have had to abandon the temperance of my religious

upbringing." Murrell sighed. "It is sinful, but a necessity that I trust God will overlook. Water doesn't agree with my digestion."

The two men sat on logs by the fire, and Murrell's woman sat next to him, still holding onto his arm.

Murrell took a few small, careful bites of stew. "Where were you traveling from? And what is your name? I dislike simply calling you *stranger*. It's impolite."

He briefly considered refusing to answer, and then decided it was probably unwise. Murrell had shown no signs of wanting to slice his guts open yet, and there was no sense in upsetting that status quo.

"My name is Darren Ault. And I was visiting Josiah McCaskill, and on my way down to the town, when your men tackled me." He took a sip of the corn whiskey, and coughed a little.

"Ah, yes, the good miller," Murrell said. "I have yet to make his acquaintance, although I have heard of him by reputation. I'm not from these parts, myself. My family comes from along the Harpeth River in Tennessee, and before that, from Virginia. Your family lives in Concord, then?"

"No," Darren said. "I don't have any close relatives in this area."

Nor in this century, but he didn't say that.

"So, what brings you here, then?"

"I'm trying to find a man named Zebulon Bell."

Both Murrell and the woman looked at Darren with new interest.

"Indeed?" Murrell said. "Why?"

How could he answer that? He didn't even know the answer himself. He finally said, "Because I want to join his religion."

"Do you?" Murrell said. "Have you spoken with Brother Zebulon yet?"

"No. I just heard about him."

Murrell nodded. "The Lord has guided you in this way?"

"Um… yes. Sure."

"Perhaps you have heard that I am a man of God, myself."

"Yes, one of your men told me."

"Just a humble servant of the Lord Most High. I have suffered through many travails. I have bared my back to the whip, languished in prison, and railed against God for letting me experience such agony. And He has brought me through, He and His Most Holy Word." He looked thoughtful. "There are those who call me Reverend Devil. It is not so. I am no devil, only a simple man trying to spread the gospel message."

"That's, um. That's nice."

The corners of Murrell's mouth turned upwards a little. "But about yourself. You have no family in Concord, then?"

"No."

"I see. I wondered if there was anyone we might need to inform of your stay with us."

"No one knows where I am," he said. Should he have told Murrell that? There was something hypnotic about the man that made him let down his guard.

"A pity," Murrell said, and still without taking his eyes off Darren, rubbed his hand along the inside of the woman's thigh. "A loving family is the most wonderful of God's gifts to man."

"So what are you going to do with me?" he said again.

"For now, you may relax and enjoy our hospitality. There is no need to rush to a decision, given that you have no anxious wife waiting fretfully for your safe return."

"Oh. Okay."

All of this conversation was toward no end he could see. He couldn't stay here with this creepy guy and his idiot followers. He had a divergence to get to, and it wasn't going to happen here, it was going to happen at one of Brother Zebulon's revival meetings. But how could he escape?

However friendly Murrell acted, he'd get serious quickly if he tried to run. And besides, where would he go if he started running? He couldn't retrace the path they'd taken, and all he'd likely accomplish is getting lost and starving to death in the woods.

His earlier thoughts had been accurate. He really would prefer the Vikings over these guys. Murrell gave him the heebie-jeebies.

But he said, "Okay. I'll chill here."

Murrell gave another faint smile. "An odd way of speaking, but believe I take your meaning."

As it turned out, the worst thing Darren had to contend with was boredom. The clouds burned off by mid-afternoon, and the air was cool but not uncomfortable, especially near the campfire. The men milled about, some of them sitting with their backs against tree trunks and dozing, others throwing dice and drinking whiskey. A small group came back just before sunset carrying a dead deer, a development that was greeted with shouts of acclamation.

"We'll eat well tonight, boys," Mosher shouted, when he saw them.

The deer was quickly and messily butchered, a procedure he did his best not to watch. But when some makeshift shish kabobs were fashioned using sharpened sticks, and toasted over the fire, the resulting smell made his mouth water.

Evidently, his odd conversation with Murrell had given him some measure of protection from harm. No one brought up any further mention of slicing his guts open, and the deer meat, tender and delicious, was doled out generously.

He was told that he'd be sharing a lean-to with Mosher and Johnson, his original captors, for the night, and after a large bottle of corn whiskey was passed around one more time, the men went off to their sleeping quarters with full bellies, mostly drunk, and for the most part happy. Murrell spent the meal sitting apart from his men, the woman still sitting near him, and always with one hand on his arm. In the firelight Murrell's face looked drawn and gaunt, and every once in a while he coughed and then spat off to the side.

After retiring to their lean-to, Mosher and Johnson lay down on smelly buckskin covers, and were asleep within minutes, to judge by their snores. Sleep eluded him, both because of the noise, and also because of his uncertainty regarding what he should do next. Fischer had landed him two days, or at most three, before the divergence. It had already been over a day since his arrival, and here he was, captive, with no obvious way to escape.

While it would be simple for him to get up quietly, and push aside the curtain covering the front of the lean-to, there was no clear course of action afterwards. He'd be lost, alone and weaponless in the dark woods, near men who knew the place and knew how to track him. He had no idea what direction the town was from the clearing. Plus, he had the notion that Murrell was not nearly foolish enough not to post guards who would sound the alert if Darren tried to make a run for it.

But why did Murrell want him? It was certain from the conversation that if he'd had family in the area, Murrell would have sent a message to them demanding ransom. But since he didn't, what was he planning on doing? Did the highwayman think he was lying? Was he going to try to contact Josiah McCaskill? That was the only name he'd mentioned other than Zebulon Bell, and he'd told Murrell he hadn't even met the Reverend yet.

He hoped no one would rough up Josiah. It was unfortunate that he'd mentioned the name, but somehow Murrell just pulled the information out. The man had a hypnotic presence. It was no wonder people came to hear him preach.

But all of that didn't give him any ideas of what to do next. He had to figure out what Zebulon Bell was up to, and why he and his daughter were connected to the divergence. Something important was going to happen in the next day or so, and he had to see if he could find out what it was. But how could he do that if he was stuck in the woods?

A quiet sound suddenly stilled his thoughts. There was a movement, visible because the canvas curtain at the front of the lean-to had been moved slightly, letting in a ruddy glow of firelight. Someone stirred inside the small space, coming toward him slowly and cautiously. Mosher and Johnson's snores didn't even stutter. Was it someone sent by Murrell to kill him while he slept?

No, there'd be no reason. If Murrell wanted him killed, he could have done it that afternoon. There were a dozen men right there who would have been happy to slit his throat.

A voice whispered, right next to his ear.

"Wake up."

His body tensed. If the next thing he heard was "Don't make any sudden moves or I'll cut you open," he was going to scream. Enough was enough.

"I'm awake," he said.

"Come with me. Quietly." The sibilant whisper, breathed with barely any sound behind it, was impossible to identify. It could have been any of the people he had met that day, or someone entirely new.

A hand pushed aside the curtain, and there was the same reddish glow. He caught the briefest glimpse of a profile—a straight nose, high forehead, well-shaped mouth, clean-shaven.

"Well?" the voice said, a little louder. "Are you coming?"

"I'm coming." He crawled out from under the scratchy wool blanket he'd been given, retrieved his glasses from the pocket of his jacket, and put them on. Then he followed the shadowy figure out into the chill night air.

The person motioned for him to follow around the back of the lean-to, and away from the fire.

"Only a little way," came the whispered voice. "And not for long. If you're discovered missing, there'll be an alarm raised."

They stopped in a little open spot, downhill and out of sight from the clearing where the fire was. His companion stood, listening and not speaking, for several moments. Finally he couldn't stand it any longer.

"Who are you?" he said.

The person answered with a laugh. "You don't know? I'm Murrell's lover. I thought you'd know immediately."

"You must be able to see like a cat in the dark. I can't see a thing."

She laughed again. "I needed to talk to you privately, away from the ears of your two friends. I couldn't leave you with them without warning you."

"Warning me? About what?"

"We don't have much time. Murrell is no fool. The men he surrounds himself with may be, but he is brilliant. He is also very likely insane. But there are three things you should know. The first is that he intends to kill you. He decided that as soon as you told him you had no money and no one knew where you were. He's keeping you alive because it amuses him to see what you'll do, but sooner or later he'll tire of that game, and have one of his men slit your throat. He's done it before. He kneels down to pray for the soul of the victim while it's being done. Second, you should know that he's very ill. Probably dying. He got consumption in prison, and was ill with it when he was released in April. He's been declining all summer, they say. When I took up with him last month, he was already probably beyond any help a doctor could provide. That could work in your favor. He sleeps a lot, and when he's not awake, his men get lazy and sloppy, and you might have a chance to escape."

"That sounds hopeful," Darren said. "What's the third thing?"

"When you go, I'm coming with you."

"But how can I help you? I'm a stranger here."

"I'm not coming with you to be helped by you, although part of it is I want to get away from Murrell and his men. I'm coming with you to help *you*. I know these woods like the palm of my hand, at least with the help of a little daylight. I can get you to safety."

"So you're from around here?"

"No, but I know my way around."

"Who *are* you?"

The laugh came again. "You haven't guessed? You *are* slow. I'm Brother Zebulon's daughter. I'm Jane Bell."

"*You're* Jane Bell?"

"Of course. Who did you think I was?"

"Well, I don't know. Some woman Murrell had lured in. Or maybe kidnapped. Why would I think you were Jane Bell?"

"I heard you talking about my father, and I figured you must know him from somewhere. I assumed you knew." She paused. "Why do you want to meet my father, anyway? He doesn't get many converts."

"I can't imagine he does."

Careful. There was no way to tell if she agreed with her father's beliefs, or if she considered him a wacko. Best to tread lightly.

"How did you come to be with Murrell?"

"I went to one of his prayer meetings. He draws quite a crowd. My father forbade me to go, which made me want to go even more. I'm not a child any longer, but my father thinks I am. So I went, and I listened to Murrell preaching, and then I noticed his men going behind the crowds and stealing from the people who were listening. And it made me laugh—here is this man talking about the Word of God, and how it is easier for a camel to pass through a needle's eye than for a rich man to enter the Kingdom of God, and at the same time he's taking people's belongings."

"So you went with him?"

She shrugged. "Murrell is everything my father isn't. Murrell is what my father would like to be if he had the guts for it. He's real, even when he lies and steals. He believes he's doing right, that when he prays for a man's eternal soul as his henchmen strangle him to death, he's doing what is righteous in God's eyes. My father tries to be tough, but it's in a thin, pathetic way, like watered-down liquor. He thinks by singing the Lord's praises while slapping each other around, he's some kind of Witness to the Suffering of Jesus. But all he is is a fraud." Her voice sounded sad. "You'll understand when you meet him."

"But why do you stay with Murrell if you know he's a liar, and probably crazy?"

"He's got something. There's something vital about him, something more than the dead souls and dried-up husks I've grown up with. If he wasn't dying, I might stay with him. But I know what will happen once he's dead. One woman, in amongst two dozen ruffians? Do you even have to wonder what my life would be like, once Murrell's protection is gone?"

"No. I understand."

And all the more reason to finish up with this conversation, and get on with figuring out how to get the hell away from Murrell and company. But Jane was still speaking, in a low, intense voice.

"So I want to go, the first opportunity I have. You seem like a kind man, and no threat to me. When I saw you, I thought, *I'll save him and myself at the same time.* I don't know if I'll rejoin my family. I'd have to eat crow for a time to patch it up, but my father would probably take me back if I begged him. I'm too useful as a nursemaid to my younger siblings to disown."

"Isn't there anywhere else you could go?"

"Not easily. I don't have a husband. A single woman on her own, with no man, is immediately thought to be a whore."

"That's not fair."

She shrugged again. "What is *fair?* A word someone made up. People make up words all the time, and a lot of them are words made up to give a name to a thing that's also made up. It might be that that's what people are best at—lying to themselves and others, and pretending the entire world doesn't know they're lying." She looked around her, and the hairs on the back of his neck prickled, although around him were just the ordinary night noises of the forest. "You should get back. If you think Murrell and his cronies aren't watching you, you're a fool. The two he put you with don't have a scrap of sense between them, but watch out for Crenshaw. He plays the clown for the benefit of the other men, but he's ruthless and smart. Murrell trusts him with any job that's too hard for the rank-and-file. And he enjoys his job. He *likes* cutting throats."

He swallowed. Even though Fischer had complete confidence in the computer getting him back to the Library in time to save his life, there was the story of the unfortunate Janowsky coming back in two separate chunks. It would be better not to risk it.

"I'll go whenever you're ready," he said.

"We'll have to watch for an opportunity. And you don't have all that long. My best guess, from watching when they've waylaid other travelers, is that Murrell intends to murder you tomorrow evening after supper. So some time tomorrow is going to be about our only chance. You'll have to be ready to jump as soon as I give the signal."

"I will be."

"Good. Now, let's get you back to your quarters, before someone thinks to check."

He followed her back up the hill, and soon the fire came into view. They slunk around the side of the lean-to, and he was relieved to hear the noises of Mosher and Johnson, still snoring loudly. No one else in the camp seemed to be moving.

"Until tomorrow," she said.

"Yes."

He pushed aside the curtain, and cautiously made his way to the spot, now cool, where his blanket was spread.

What if she was lying? What if she was the one who liked to play with a man before he was killed? He had no guarantee that she wasn't the one trying to lead him into a trap.

But then he pictured Murrell's lean, intense face and burning eyes. Whatever she was, he was better off with her than he would be with Reverend Devil. Murrell gave him the creeping horrors. And with that thought, he pulled up his blanket around him, and was asleep within minutes.

The next morning dawned clear and cold, and Darren woke to the dulcet tones of Mosher and Johnson stretching, yawning, and farting. The air was already not pleasant-smelling, but got worse quickly, so he pulled his glasses out of his pocket, put them on his nose, and exited the lean-to.

Murrell was already awake, and was in an intense discussion with Crenshaw by the fire. He looked worse than the previous day. His cheeks had a hectic flush, and he alternated taking drinks from a tin cup—probably whiskey, judging by his comments the previous evening—and coughing. When he saw Darren emerge, he gave a come-here motion of his hand.

He approached the fire, but didn't sit.

"Sit down, my friend, sit down," Murrell said. "God has

blessed us with a beautiful sunny morning. It will be shirt sleeves weather by noon, praise His Holy Name."

He sat down rather tentatively on a log. He kept his eyes on Crenshaw, who he half expected to pull out a knife and stab him on the spot.

Murrell seemed amused by Darren's timidity. "I trust you passed a good night. Slept soundly? I expect you're not used to our rough conditions. You have the look of someone who is used to feather beds."

Crenshaw snickered a little.

"It was fine," Darren said.

"And your companions? All congenial enough? Did you have any illuminating night time conversations?"

He didn't answer for a moment, but looked at Murrell with a slight frown. Did the preacher know about the talk he had had with Jane Bell? The question seemed innocent enough, but there was that knowing look in Murrell's expression that left one with the feeling he could see a man's thoughts.

"We mostly conversed in snores," he said.

Murrell laughed, and the laugh terminated in a cough, and he spat off to the side. "My apologies. Not the most genteel of behavior, but you must excuse it because I am ill."

"Not a problem."

"I am glad you are a forgiving man," Murrell said. "It is an excellent mark of character, and will come in handy to you."

Well, that sounded sinister.

"I was wondering again when you are planning to let me go," Darren said. "I mean, I'd love to join your band of Merry Men and all, but I really need to get down to Concord. I have business to conduct."

"Ah, yes. Business with the estimable Brother Zebulon. I am curious, why are you so eager to meet with him? What attracts you about his rather unusual brand of the Christian religion?"

"I've always been interested in the groups that practiced austerity. Self-denial. Mortification of the body. You know, like those monks who bashed themselves over the head with things."

Was that real? Or had he seen it in a Monty Python movie?

"I haven't heard of those," Murrell said. "But I understand that self-flagellation was widely practiced at one time. And as one who was once on the receiving end of thirty lashes across the bare back, I can tell you that it is an excellent way to sharpen your senses." He gave Darren a slight smile. "On the other hand, you don't have the look of someone who relishes pain. In fact, I'd have thought you were cut from the opposite cloth."

"Well, you know, looks can be deceiving."

Murrell smirked. "That they can. In fact, I have lived as long as I have by seldom taking anything on its face value."

He glanced over at Crenshaw, who watched him with a vicious-looking smile. He swallowed. "But you didn't answer my question. When can I leave?"

"Oh, perhaps, when you tell me the truth about what business you have in Concord. And when I am quite certain that you will not, when you get there, go to the first law authorities you meet and tell them where we are encamped."

"Why would I do that?"

"For one thing, because you hold a grudge against my fine compatriots, Mosher and Johnson, for knocking you off the path and bringing you here at knifepoint. It would be a forgiving man indeed who could overlook such a thing. And you, my friend, have not answered my questions, either. Why are you interested in meeting with Zebulon Bell? What does the miller have to do with it? And you needn't repeat your answer, that you intend to join the Church of Our Lord Jesus Christ Risen and Triumphant Through Suffering. You and I both know that this is a lie. So as between gentlemen, perhaps you can now tell me the real reason, or it will be my unfortunate duty to ask Mr. Crenshaw here to test out his new knife on your throat. Please understand that I would regret very much having to do so. Such things should not be necessary between equals."

He glanced at Crenshaw again, whose smile had turned positively predatory. He forced himself to turn back to Murrell, and then made a decision. He hoped fervently that this would the last time he had to explain all of this, because he was getting damned sick of doing it.

"Okay," he said. "The truth is that I'm from a hundred and fifty years in the future, give or take. I'm here because someone from my time went back and changed something, and I've been given the task of finding out what it was and setting it right. What he changed has something to do with Zebulon Bell and his family, so that's why I'm trying to talk to him. And if Mr. Crenshaw tries to kill me, he'll find that I'll disappear before the knife strikes home." He shrugged. "But he's welcome to try, because at the moment I think I'd be better off back where I started, as I seem to be accomplishing bugger-all here."

There. That'd give the creep something to chew on.

Murrell looked at him for a moment, an inscrutable expression on his face. "Well. I've had more than one poor lost soul beg me for his life. Many have told me heartbreaking stories about grief-stricken widows they'd be leaving behind, or destitute children, or poor, gray-haired, weeping mothers having to attend their sons' funerals. I've been promised wealth, promised silence, promised anything it would take. But your story—no, I've not heard anything quite like that." He coughed again, quietly, and wiped the sweat from his brow. "I don't quite know what to tell you, except that you amuse me, in a strange fashion.

"Crenshaw, I hate to tell you this, because I know you've been eager to try out your new blade, but I think we must give our guest a little more time. I'm not sure yet what I want to do with him." He looked at Darren again, and one dark, well-shaped brow rose a little. "Yes. You amuse me. And for now, that is sufficient."

He coughed again, and wiped his mouth on his sleeve, and there was a smear of blood on the stained tan cloth of the man's shirt. "I will take a rest now. I trust you to stay here in camp. While you are here, you are under my protection, and Crenshaw? That fact is to be made clear to our other companions. But should you leave the perimeter of the camp, I cannot be held responsible for your fate. Do we understand one another?"

He nodded.

"Excellent. And perhaps you would be so good as not to have further conversation with my friend, Jane. I would expect that even in your century,"—here he smiled a little again—"there is such a thing as observing the laws of decorum when it comes to speaking to another gentleman's woman."

He nodded again. He'd been right—Murrell knew he'd talked to Jane. But how? Did Jane tell him? Was she playing with him, too? No way to tell. Nothing to do now but wait and see what happened, and run when he got a chance... with or without her.

The morning dragged on. Boredom, coupled with the combined anxiety of not knowing if he was going to be executed, and wondering how he would complete the task he'd been given, made him twitchy. Darren saw no sign either of Murrell or of Jane Bell, but he did notice Crenshaw talking to several other men, who glanced over at him and snickered.

This did not improve his mood.

It was after lunch—roasted chunks of deer meat from the previous evening—that he saw an opportunity, and ironically, it came about because of his kidnappers, Mosher and Johnson. Mosher had been halfheartedly working at scraping some pieces of the deer hide when Johnson walked by and bumped him, causing Mosher to skewer the palm of his hand with his own knife.

Mosher let out a bawl, and turned around, clutching his bleeding hand. "Watch where you put your great ugly foot, you clumsy pig!"

Johnson rounded on him, and yelled back, "Who're you calling a clumsy pig, you snaggle-toothed goat?"

"Goat?" Mosher shouted. "If I was a goat, I'd be running scared from the likes of you. I know what *you* like to do with goats."

This prompted Johnson to tackle Mosher, and the next few minutes were filled with the sounds of fists hitting bodies, and inarticulate shouts punctuated by clear, and rather creative, insults.

"… god-forsaken son of a dog…"

"… lump-faced misbegotten fathead…"

"… ugly stinking mud-wallowing maggot…"

"… filthy flea-infested sheep-humper…"

Soon, the two had an audience cheering them on, and the fighting pair was lost to view from being encircled by an enthusiastic crowd. Crenshaw had moved toward them when the fight began, a scowl on his face, but at the moment Murrell's ill-favored second-in-command wasn't anywhere to be seen. Murrell himself was still apparently asleep in his lean-to. It looked like luck was on Darren's side, and his indecision lasted only a moment. There wouldn't be another chance like this. He couldn't afford to wait for Jane. He'd have to take his chances in the woods.

He dashed off into the trees.

There was a shout behind him. Someone had spotted his escape.

He didn't turn, but ran as fast as he was able to, dodging

between trees and fighting through clinging underbrush, and waiting any moment to feel a knife in his back.

His pursuer shouted again.

"Wait! Wait, it's me!"

He glanced over his shoulder, barely slowing.

"You're heading the wrong way!"

He slowed, and Jane Bell caught up with him, breathing hard.

"Did anyone else see me?"

"I don't know. I heard the commotion, and put my head out just in time to see you dash off. Murrell has been sleeping all this time. He's in a bad way today. But I think the noise roused him, too, and you can bet that when he sees you're gone he's going to send someone after you. Or probably more than one. You've got to get some miles behind you, and quickly."

She led him back a little way along the path he'd taken, but then they branched off to the left and downhill. The noise of the camp still drifted toward them. Whether it was the ruckus caused by the fight, or a more serious noise because they'd discovered he was missing, was impossible to tell.

"Come on," she said. "We need to get back to the road down to the town. It isn't that far. After that, it's less than an hour's walk to Concord."

"Do you think Murrell would come into the town to find us?"

She didn't answer for a moment. Finally she said, "He might. He's vindictive. He doesn't like losing. And he never forgets it if someone double-crosses him. If he figures out I had a part in your escape, I don't want to think about what he'd do to me."

"He knows. This morning, he told me not to talk to you again."

"Did he? Well. I guess I'd better never let myself get caught, then."

Her voice sounded light, but there was a tremor as she spoke the words.

"How good are they at tracking?"

"Good. Most of his men were born in the woods. They're like animals. Like wolves. Especially Crenshaw. He's the worst of the lot."

A voice spoke, from off to the side, in a conversational tone. "Oh, now, Miss Jane, that's downright hurtful. You sure do know how to stick a knife in a man's heart." And Crenshaw came out from between two trees, a long knife in his hand, and a nasty grin on his face.

She stopped, her breath catching in her throat, then backed up, and ran into Darren.

"Now, if you two will come back to the camp all peaceable, we can probably work this out."

Jane laughed. "Not likely. Unless you call cutting both of our throats 'working this out.'"

"Well, that's one way to work things out, don't you think?" Crenshaw lunged toward her. She jumped aside, and his knife missed by inches.

"Ain't you gonna defend the lady, schoolmaster?" Crenshaw gave a guffaw. "Ain't you got a schoolbook to beat me about the head and shoulders with?" This time he swung at Darren, and the knife nicked his cheek, drawing blood.

"Ow! Shit!" He clapped a hand to the side of his face.

"Listen at him swear," Crenshaw said, clearly impressed. "Maybe you ain't a schoolmaster after all."

"I told you that, you moron," he said, still holding his cut cheek.

"Moron, am I?" Crenshaw said. "You'll see how much smarter you feel when your guts are spilling out onto the ground." He lunged again, but this time Jane leaped under his swinging arm, and her knee connected solidly with his crotch. Crenshaw doubled up and collapsed to the ground.

"You… whore…" he gasped out, and tried to lift the knife,

but Darren stepped on his arm, and the knife tumbled from his grasp.

Jane picked it up, looking at it curiously, as if she had never seen such a thing before. Then she looked at Crenshaw, and changed her grip on the knife handle.

"No." Darren stared at her in horror. "You can't kill him!"

"Why not?" Her voice was calm, dispassionate. "He's killed many a man, and many a woman, too. He'll come after us if I don't."

"But you don't want to be like him!"

Crenshaw, still clutching his aching groin, was already struggling to get up. "You filth… I'll kill you both…"

And Darren did what was probably the only thing he could. He cocked his fist back and punched Crenshaw in the face as hard as he could.

He was no fighter—he had never hit another person in anger before—and he didn't anticipate how much the impact would hurt. It sent a shock wave of pain up his arm to the shoulder. He spent next few moments screaming obscenities and clutching his fist to his chest. But Crenshaw was knocked backwards, lost his balance, fell, and struck the back of his head on a tree.

After recovering his composure, but still massaging his injured hand, he went over to the fallen highwayman. Crenshaw's chest still rose and fell regularly, but his eyes were closed.

"Lights out," he said. "Let's get out of here."

Jane nodded, pocketing the knife. They jogged away between the dark trees, and soon the sight of Crenshaw's inert body, and the sounds of noise from the camp, were both lost.

"Thank you," she said, after a little time had passed.

"I was saving myself as much as I was saving you."

"No. I mean, thank you for stopping me from killing him. I would have done it, you know."

"I know."

"It would have changed me. I know that. I still would have done it, but it would have changed me. I've seen it happen since I've been with Murrell. When someone new joins his band, he makes the new man kill someone. It's like a proof of loyalty. Sometimes it's someone they've captured, like they captured you. Other times, he makes the new man kill one of the old members. Part of it is to keep the others in fear—*if you don't continue to be useful to me, and loyal to me, I might have you killed next.* And the new men change, once they've done it. You can tell. Even if they get away, or leave and start a new life, they'll never be the same men they were before. Killing someone like that, cutting his throat in cold blood, I think it destroys part of the killer's soul."

He shuddered. "I think you're exactly right."

All discussion ceased, as the afternoon moved toward evening, and they walked quickly, silently, through the never-ending trees toward the road to Concord and safety.

———

They struck the road at a little before sunset, and not far from the place Darren had been waylaid the previous day. Once on the road, they made better time. He was footsore and exhausted by this time, but they didn't dare slow for fear Murrell's men catching them.

It was nearly pitch dark before they came to the first house. It was a small log cabin, set back from the road, with a candle burning in the window and smoke curling from a chimney. This seemed like a good sign, and he went up to the door and knocked on it.

There was the sound of footsteps, and then a male voice spoke, without opening the door.

"Who are you and what do you want?"

"We're trying to get to Concord, and we need a place to spend the night."

"That don't tell me who you are."

"My name is Darren Ault. My… friend, here, is Jane Bell."

"You ain't one of them highwaymen, are you?"

"No. In fact, we're trying to get away from them."

"Then get the hell away from my house. I ain't sheltering you if them murdering savages is on your trail."

There came the sound of something being dragged in front of the door, then the footsteps receded.

"Look, you've got to help us!" he said, but further pounding on the door produced no result other than making his bruised hand ache worse.

Jane put a hand on his arm. "We need to keep moving. We'll get no further with him. There's an inn in the town that might give us shelter, although how we'll pay for room and board I don't know."

By this time, it was completely dark, and they stumbled more than once on unseen ruts in the road. At least its being dark meant that Murrell's gang was less likely to be able to track them.

Another ten minutes of walking brought them to the town, where there were candles in many windows, and ahead the sound of talking from a building that was obviously a tavern. The rushing of water sounded nearby, the stream that passed through Josiah McCaskill's mill, finally meeting a much larger river glinting under starlight in the distance. He went toward the tavern, with Jane following. He pushed his way through the doors, and stood blinking in the light of candles and oil lamps.

He had not counted on the effect of a stranger bursting into the room, his face cut and bloodied, wearing a dazed expression. Everyone turned toward them, and all conversation stopped.

"What…" said a fat, bald, copiously mustached man who

was holding three beer mugs in one huge hand. "What happened to you, stranger?"

"We were kidnapped by highwaymen."

That was all it took. He and Jane were immediately surrounded by people wearing concerned looks, voicing words of support, two of them murmuring prayers of protection under their breath.

"Not that Devil-Man who has holed up in the valley?" someone said. "The one who calls himself a man of God?"

"That's the one."

"And all you came away with was that scratch?" the innkeeper said, his voice lowered with awe.

"Well, I bruised my hand punching one of them in the face."

"You're one brave man," came a reverent voice.

"Or durn lucky," said another, somewhat more prosaically.

"Anyway, you both look like you need something sustaining," said the innkeeper. "A beer for the gentleman." He paused, and looked questioningly at Jane.

"And one for me as well," Jane said firmly.

A cheer went up from the assembled crowd.

So, as it turned out, he needn't have worried about having a place to stay. He and Jane both had a dozen offers before their beer was brought to them.

***

Darren was given a room in the inn above the tavern to sleep in, and his objections of "I haven't any money" were waved off by the innkeeper, whose name was Gillette.

"I'm happy enough to help anyone who has the backbone to stand up to those ruffians," Gillette said, as he showed Darren to his room. "A pity there aren't more like you."

Jane was taken in by an older man, whose name was Thurston.

"My wife'll put you up in our daughter's old bed," Thurston said. "Cora married last year and moved to Tennessee, so we've got the room. It'll be no bother at all."

By an unspoken agreement, neither of them mentioned that Jane was the daughter of the itinerant preacher who was, as far as they knew, still camped on the north end of town. It was uncertain how the citizens of Concord viewed the members of the Church of Our Lord Jesus Christ etc., and it was probably better to leave them thinking that she was just another poor, innocent victim of Murrell's wicked band.

Darren, for his part, was exhausted. He did no more than a cursory wash-up, and tried as best he could to clean the cut on his cheek, which was long but not particularly deep. Finally, he decided to leave well enough alone.

If the divergence was scheduled for that evening, it would just have to happen without him. After all, he'd done diddly-squal to stop the other two divergences, so there was no reason to think that he'd be able to stop this one, either. Let it be what Fischer said. A reconnaissance mission, in which all he had to do was watch what happened, and report back with anything important.

And, after all, he already had one vital piece of information—the name McCaskill. Josiah was a McCaskill. That had to be critical. But how could he be connected to Lee if he never married and had no children?

But maybe that was it. Maybe that was the divergence. Josiah was supposed to have married, and have children, like Per Olafsson was. But then, what did Jane Bell have to do with anything? The computer had said that Jane was the point of the divergence, not Josiah. And she was a good thirty years too young to be a candidate for Josiah's intended wife.

He slipped between the sheets, and pulled a deliciously comfortable goose down quilt up to his neck. At least he didn't have to worry about fleas and the Black Death here. He closed his eyes, and heaved a sigh of contentment. But a moment later, his eyes popped open.

Maybe that was it. Maybe Josiah McCaskill was supposed to have a son, and that son was supposed to marry Jane Bell. Jane wanted out of her dad's crazy bunch of religious wingnuts—that was why she took up with Murrell. But what if what was supposed to happen was that she was intended to fall in love with McCaskill's son, and marry him, and eventually have a son and a grandson who would be Lee's ancestors? That would explain why she popped up as the focal point of the divergence.

But that would mean that the line that got wiped out when Lee shot him was Lee's own ancestry, not his. How could that be? How could killing him change the history of Lee's family?

A headache clanged against the inside of his skull, and he closed his eyes again. It might be that Fischer could think about all of this stuff without his brain exploding, but he couldn't. And comfortably warm for the first time since his arrival in Kentucky, he drifted off into a dreamless sleep.

The next morning Darren woke to the slanting light of sunrise coming through the window, but there was a fine tracery of frost on the window pane. He yawned and stretched, got out of bed, and looked at the town below. Concord, or at least what he could see of it, was a cluster of buildings huddled around a dirt-road main street that skirted a wide river. The steeple of a church rose in the distance, and nearer at hand was a large, squarish building that could have been a courthouse. There were a few people milling about, but the whole scene exuded an air of rural small-town peace.

He pulled his clothes on. The shirt stank. Oh well. Not a

problem in a place and time where everyone smelled bad. He buttoned the jacket. The whole place was not what he'd expected. He'd pictured a frontier town with gunfights, and cowboys and Indians running around killing each other.

Another myth shot down.

The first order of business was to find a bathroom. A chamber pot stood in the corner, but he declined to use it, not being certain what—if anything—he was supposed do with it when he was done. He left his room and descended the stairs, and came back out into the main room of the tavern. Gillette the innkeeper was already up and bustling around.

"Passed the night well, my friend?"

"Yes, very well," Darren said. "But… could you point me in the direction of the outhouse?"

"Oh, certainly." Gillette gestured off down a hallway that passed the kitchen and a storage room. "Out the back door. You'll see it."

Ten minutes later, and a great deal more comfortable, he returned to the tavern, and before he could even ask found himself with a plate of bacon and eggs, and a mug of beer.

"Hell yeah," he said under his breath. He thanked the innkeeper warmly, and tucked in.

"I never did get your name." Gillette leaned on the bar and watched him eat.

"Ault," Darren said through a mouthful of eggs. "Darren Ault."

"German fellow, then?"

"My great-grandfather was born in Germany." Hopefully they didn't dislike Germans in 1844. There were all sorts of weird prejudices back then.

But the innkeeper just grinned. "My mother's Pennsylvania Dutch. I grew up hearing German as often as I did English. My grandma still hasn't forgiven her daughter for marrying a Scotsman."

"Yeah, I've got a bit of mixed ancestry myself."

"I expect we all do, if you go far enough back," Gillette said. "But tell me, Mr. Ault. How did you get mixed up with that band of villains? And that young woman, too?"

"I was kidnapped, right off the road, two days ago. She'd been with them a bit longer, I think." Better to be careful how much to tell him. Less said, less to repair afterwards. "I expect she was kidnapped, too, but we didn't have time to talk about it. We were too busy running away."

"You must have had a stroke of luck to have an opportunity to escape. I don't think many people meet up with Murrell and his men and live to tell about it."

"It *was* luck." He gave an abbreviated version of the fight between Mosher and Johnson, his flight with Jane from the encampment, and their run-in with Crenshaw.

"And that took a bit of bravery on both of your parts," Gillette said. "The young lady disabling him with a well-aimed knee, and then your knocking him out with one punch." He shook his head, and his grin returned. "Meaning no disrespect, but to look at you, I'd never have thought you had it in you."

"Surprising what anger and desperation will do." He finished the last of the beer, feeling much happier now that he had a full stomach. He didn't know that in the past they had beer with breakfast, but he could get used to it.

"That's the honest truth," Gillette said. "None of us knows what he'd do when it came to tight circumstances. And a good job that few of us ever have to find out, I'd say."

"Do you think Murrell will send his men after us?"

"I don't know, and that's a fact. He's not had the brass to come into the town, but he's been camped up there in the valley for nigh on two months now, and harasses anyone he thinks he can get away with. More than one has gone missing, mostly folks traveling alone as you were. I expect their dead bodies are hidden up in a hollow somewhere, and like as not will never be seen again and given a Christian burial, sorry though I am to say it. Groups are safer. They leave alone anyone who looks like they can defend themselves."

"How does McCaskill manage? He lives alone, and comes to town with his flour every week, he said."

"You know old Josiah?" Gillette's face lit up. "Sound man, Josiah McCaskill. No, they won't tackle old Josiah. He always travels in the daylight, and armed. He shot one of 'em that came near his wagon, I hear—blew the ruffian's ugly head right off his shoulders, so I'm told. After that, they left him be, and wise of 'em to do so, I say. Josiah won't hesitate to defend himself."

"Good. I'm glad to hear that."

"How do you know old Josiah?" Gillette asked.

"I, um, am a cousin on his mother's side. I'm here visiting from… North Carolina." He hoped that either the innkeeper didn't know anything about Josiah McCaskill's family, or else that he was remembering right about where Josiah'd said his parents had come from.

But the innkeeper nodded. "Oh, that's fine, then. Any relative of Josiah's is a friend of mine." He patted Darren on the shoulder.

"Say, I'd like to have a chance to talk to Jane. She's the woman I escaped with. She went off with a man who said he'd put her up for the night… where does he live?"

"Oh, that was Tom Thurston," Gillette said. "He's the town barber. He lives down the road a ways, close on the river side. His barber shop is right there attached to his house, so you'll see the sign. I expect he'll be up and about by now." He turned around and yelled into the back area of the tavern, "Toby! Come show Mr. Ault where Mr. Thurston lives!"

He frowned. Gillette's voice had changed, from the genial, hale-fellow-well-met tones he'd used every time he'd spoken previously, to a harsh command.

A tall, dark-skinned young man, dressed in a simple plaid

work shirt and heavy canvas pants, came out of the kitchen, and walked up to Gillette, his eyes downcast.

"Damn, boy, you are the slowest thing I ever did see," Gillette said. "Mr. Ault here needs someone to show him to Mr. Thurston's house. Bring him down there, and see that you hurry right back. There'll be people arriving for lunch right soon, and I'll warrant you've done almost nothing I've told you to do this morning."

"Yes, sir." Toby still didn't raise his eyes to meet either of theirs.

Shit. Slaves. He had forgotten all about slaves. Okay, this sucked. This completely sucked.

"I can find my own way, thanks," he said, his voice a little thin.

Gillette completely mistook his meaning. "Oh, no need for worry, Mr. Ault. Toby here wouldn't hurt a fly. He'll lead you right faithful. Right, Toby?" Again, there was an implicit threat in the last two words that hadn't been there when he spoke to Darren.

"Yes, sir," Toby said again.

"There, you see? Now, get right along, and Toby, see that you get back double quick."

Toby turned toward the door, and there was nothing to do but to follow.

What should he do? He followed Toby down the wood-plank sidewalk that skirted the main road. The river sparkled in its course, only a hundred yards away, and he passed several other people—all white—who smiled and nodded greeting at him, and ignored Toby as if he were a nonentity.

Which is what they thought. But what could he say to the man? "I'm sorry?" "I don't think like they do?" "In twenty years, there will be a war and in the end you'll be a free man?" "In a hundred and fifty years, an African-American man will be president of the United States?" If Toby even believed him, which was doubtful, none of that would make much difference to his life here and now. And would telling him all that change what was supposed to happen?

In the end, he said nothing, but felt conflicted and guilty about it even though he had no idea what else he could have done.

Toby stopped in front of a building that had a red-and-white sign saying "T. Thurston, Barber."

"Here, sir."

Darren said, "Thank you, Toby," in as kind and sincere fashion as he could, and Toby just turned away and made his way back toward the tavern.

"Well, that is the pits," he said under his breath, and walked into the barber shop.

Mr. Thurston looked up as he entered, and smiled recognition. "Well, if it's not the man who fought off the highwaymen. Welcome, stranger. I didn't catch your name last night."

"Darren Ault."

"Mr. Ault. Well, welcome. I'm Tom Thurston. Are you here for a haircut or shave? Or to talk to your lady friend?"

"The latter, Mr. Thurston."

"I thought you might be. She's in the house with Elizabeth. The two have been up since dawn, talking about heaven only knows what. You know how women are."

He didn't quite know how to respond to that, so he just nodded.

"Kind of you to check on her, but she's in good hands. I'll let her know you're here."

Thurston disappeared through a door at the back of the shop, and was gone for about five minutes. Darren looked at the collection of scissors and leather strops hanging from pegs on the wall, and a whole lineup of wicked-looking straight razors. He rubbed his stubbly chin. After all the talk by Murrell and his men of throats being slit, he didn't want any of those anywhere near his neck. He was perfectly fine looking scruffy for the next few days.

Thurston returned, followed by Jane, who as always wore an inscrutable expression. "Would you like to accompany me for the day?"

"Sure."

Thurston gave her a paternal smile, and she said, "I told Mrs. Thurston we'd be gone for much of the day. I will return by evening," and the two of them left the shop, and walked down the sidewalk. She rested one hand in the crook of his arm.

After they'd walked a little way in silence, she said, "I have to confront my father."

"You're not going back with him to stay, then?"

"No. I've thought about it. I can't do that. I love my father, but… I know what he is. And I know that sooner or later, probably sooner, the people of Concord are going to want him gone, and he'll up stakes and move on to the next town. I'm tired of living like that, and spending all my hours caring for my siblings, and pretending I believe the message he's peddling. I feel sorry for my mother, but she promised to love, honor, and obey him. I haven't."

"I understand."

"I wonder very much if you do," she said, her voice flat. "I wonder if a man *could* understand."

He didn't respond.

"Mrs. Thurston has offered me room and board in exchange for my help around the house and the shop. To be a servant."

"You'd do that?"

She shrugged. "They seem like kind people. There are worse lives. I would have been worse off with Murrell. I see that now."

"Isn't there something else you'd like to do with your life?"

"What? What options do I have? I've no schooling to

speak of, and no husband to support me. I've no choice, really."

"A friend of mine told me, not long ago, that we always have choices."

"He's wrong."

"She."

"Was it a woman, then?" She seemed surprised. "Well, *she's* wrong, then. We don't have choices. Or, at least not in the way you mean—that we are truly free to do what we'd please, without thought of consequence. Our lives run like a cart wheel in a rut. You simply roll along, your path chosen for you. If you try to jump out of the groove, you're likely to accomplish nothing but breaking your wagon's axle. Look where it got me, trying to do just that. Living with the worst man I've ever met."

"Did he treat you badly?"

She gave him a wan smile. "Me? No. He always was gentle with me. But that doesn't mean it was right. They call him Reverend Devil, did you know that?"

"That's what he told me."

"I think it may be true. Satan can be a gentleman, so they say. I believe it."

He frowned. "But wait a moment. Just because it went wrong once doesn't mean that you shouldn't ever try to make things better again."

"I haven't told you everything." She stopped, and turned toward him, and her hazel eyes met his for a moment in a gaze of singular intensity. They seemed to be looking directly into his mind. "I'm carrying Murrell's child."

He gaped at her. "Oh," he finally said. "Oh. Hell."

"Exactly. And I know my father would never let me live that down. Even though my child's father is an evil man, I would not want him to live in a household where he'd be thought of as a bastard. No child deserves that."

"You could tell your father Murrell raped you."

"But that would be a lie. I bedded him willingly. And more than once. And I enjoyed it, and felt no shame afterwards." She looked out toward the river. "And I still feel no shame about it. It was what I chose to do with my body, and that is all." She paused. "I told Mrs. Thurston I was with child by Murrell, and she said, 'Then we will see to it that the child grows up to take after his mother.' It is the best I could possibly hope for, and I have to take her offer. There will not be another like it, I think."

"I think you have a lot of sense." He felt foolish after he said it. It must have sounded hollow to her.

She just shrugged again. "I need to ask you a favor. I would ask you to accompany me to speak to my father. It may be that another voice beside mine, and a man's voice, to tell him about Murrell and his men, and how we escaped, will blunt the edge of what I have to say to him. I do not want to hurt him. But I do not wish to lie." She sighed harshly. "I want to speak to my father, tell him the truth... and then never see him again. Let his memory of me fade away and die."

"That may be the saddest thing I've ever heard in my life."

"Will you go with me, then?"

"Of course. I wanted to meet with your father in any case."

She gave him another intense look. "Thank you." She turned and they began to walk again. "That is kind of you." They went a little farther, and she said, "Why is it you want to meet my father? You said that to Murrell, and then said that you wished to join my father's church. But I didn't believe it then, and I do not believe it now."

"Neither did Murrell."

"So, why? How do you know about him? And why do you want to meet him?"

So much for not having to explain all this again.

"I'm actually not from this century," he said, a little tentatively.

She laughed. "What could that possibly mean?"

"I'm from the future."

She made a dismissive sound. "You needn't treat me like a child. I am not one. Such stories are for children."

"No. This is true."

Something in the way he spoke made her grip tighten on his arm, and she looked up at him.

"Prove it," she said.

"I don't know that I can."

"Then do not ask me to believe you. And in any case, what would some man from the future want with my father? He is neither very important nor very smart. He is not the man I would expect anyone from the future would take the trouble to visit."

"Nevertheless, there is a reason. And not only to visit him. To visit you."

"Why?"

He took a deep breath. "It's hard to explain, because I don't fully understand it myself. I was sent back here because another man—someone from my time—has gone back and changed things. Altered people's lives in such a way as to create chaos in *our* time. I was sent back to find out what he did, and to try to fix it. And somehow, one of the things he did has to do with you."

"Does it? I can assure you that I have never met anyone else from the future." Her mouth curled upwards a little, and he wasn't sure whether she was mocking him.

"It's possible you met him and didn't know it. You didn't know I was from the future, until I told you."

"That's true. What year have you come from?"

"The year two thousand sixteen."

Her eyebrows went up a little. "Indeed. That is far distant from this year. Things must be much different."

"They are."

"Tell me about your time."

"I don't know if I should. I don't want to tell you anything that will change what's supposed to happen. I mean, suppose I told you something about your future that was supposed to happen, and you decided that you didn't like it, so you made it not happen? It could create all kinds of problems. In fact, that's what we think Lee did."

"Lee?"

"The man from my time I am trying to find."

"Ah." She paused, and seemed to be pondering his words. "It is a strange story. I would, if I were you, not mention any of this to my father. He is a singularly unimaginative man."

He looked at her. "Do you believe me?"

She didn't answer for a moment. "No. You're probably telling the truth, but no, I don't believe you."

That seemed like such an odd assessment that he didn't have a ready answer, and for a while they walked in silence.

The noise of the crowds drifted to him before the tent came into view. He looked over at Jane. She seemed to be trying not to respond to the familiar sounds of a revival meeting, but her feelings showed in a tightness of her lips and a hard glint in her eyes. This was a homecoming that would not be a cause for rejoicing, for father or daughter.

It wasn't until they came up to the rear of the crowd that he realized that what was going on wasn't your typical evangelical revival. He knew a little about such things, which still existed in his twenty-first century world, even though rare. But he'd never seen, much less attended, one. He'd heard, however, about the speaking in tongues, the fainting, the crying out for God's blessing by one and all, that accompanied the frenzied shouts of the preacher to call on God's Holy Name and be healed.

This, by comparison, looked like outdoor theater. It was possible some of the audience took the whole thing seriously, but it was evident Brother Zebulon had by this time lost some of his luster, and the attendees were coming to his performances more for the humor value than to be touched by the Holy Spirit.

As he maneuvered his way up through the hundred or so people who were watching the spectacle, he heard, "Hit him again!" and "Harder!" as much as he heard "Amen!" and "Hallelujah!" And far more people were laughing out loud than was probably typical at a revival.

Several people were gathered under a large canvas tent, enclosed on three sides, with a plank floor like a low stage. All were in frantic motion. One of them was a tall, paunchy man, dressed all in white, and wearing a round straw hat. He was gesturing to the assembled crowd, and saying, "… the way to the Lord is through seeking out pain, *embracing* pain, so as to be one with Jesus Christ's suffering!"

A rail-thin man with a prominent nose and a shock of unruly black hair shouted, "Amen, Brother Zebulon! Amen! I want to be closer to the Lord!"

"Thank you for your devotion, Brother William!" the fat man said. "Prepare to receive the sacrament!"

Brother William held his hands up in the air and closed his eyes, and the fat man slapped him across the face.

The crowd gave a cheer.

"That wasn't much of a hit!" someone shouted. "My sick grandmother could hit harder than that!"

"Yeah, if he's still standing afterwards, you didn't hit him hard enough!" yelled another, and everyone laughed.

Brother Zebulon seemed well aware that his words were not having the desired effect. He pulled out a handkerchief and mopped his brow, despite the fact that the air was still chilly. "Now, brothers and sisters, the point is not to knock out Brother William here, but to bring him closer to the suffering Jesus felt! Are there any here who are feeling moved by the spirit of the Lord to come witness to the power of

Jesus? To feel what he felt? A step forward is a step closer to Jesus, brothers and sisters!"

A man near the front of the crowd suddenly lurched forward.

"Excellent, my friend!" Brother Zebulon broke into a broad, and rather surprised-looking, grin. "What is your name, brother?"

"What the hell?" The man scowled and then pointed into the crowd. "He pushed me!"

This elicited more laughter.

"Never mind how you got here," Brother Zebulon said. "The Lord works in mysterious ways, and through unexpected means. But here you are now. Are you going to witness the power of Our Lord Jesus Christ Risen and Triumphant Through Suffering?"

"Right now I think I'm gonna witness a little suffering on Johnny Dinkins's ugly face." The man rushed forward and tackled the man who pushed him. An appreciative roar went up from the crowd. Apparently this was even better than most of Brother Zebulon's revival meetings.

At this point, Brother Zebulon seemed to realize he was fighting a losing battle. "Well, brothers and sisters, I see that the time is not yet ripe for you to receive Jesus' message. Perhaps we should all retire to our homes and ponder the message we have heard today…"

But no one was listening. In fact, several other members of the crowd had leaped into the fray, and the whole thing was devolving into a small-scale riot.

Brother Zebulon, Brother William, and the five or six other people who appeared to be the revival leaders, backed away from the crowd until they were in a tight knot at the back corner of the tent.

Brother Zebulon said, "I think it's time to leave."

"For today? Or for good?" said Brother William.

"Both." Brother Zebulon pulled a flap at the side of the

tent, stepped out and strode away in the direction of several wagons and a cluster of smaller tents that stood about a hundred yards off.

Jane broke into motion toward the retreating figure.

"Father!" she called.

The man turned slowly, ponderously, and there was a moment where he simply frowned, as if he weren't quite sure what he was seeing. Then he said, "Jane?"

She slowed to a walk, and when she reached him gave him a perfunctory hug, which Brother Zebulon returned in a half-hearted, puzzled sort of fashion.

Darren came up behind them, embarrassed at having to witness this, and even more anxious about the greater confrontation that was sure to come.

"Jane..." Brother Zebulon said. "Where have you been? Your mother... your mother has been sick unto death worrying about you. We thought you might be dead."

"I'm not." Her voice was flat.

"But where were you?"

"I think you know the answer to that," she said. "Father, I went with Murrell. I've been there, up until yesterday, when this man helped me to escape. His name is Darren Ault, and he was being held captive by Murrell's men. He and I conspired to escape, and came into Concord last night."

Brother Zebulon looked at him, eyes narrowing suspiciously. "You were also taken up with that Devil Man?"

"No." He cleared his throat nervously. "They kidnapped me. All I wanted was to get away. If I hadn't, they surely would have murdered me by now. Your daughter helped me escape. In fact, if it hadn't been for her, I would never have succeeded."

Brother Zebulon turned back to Jane. "And you, my daughter... you were also kidnapped?"

"I think you know the answer to that, too, Father. I wasn't kidnapped. I went with him of my own free choice. But yesterday I knew it was time for me to leave, and I also knew that Murrell would not let me go willingly. When I saw this man, and realized what they were planning to do to him, I thought that I could escape, and help him to escape, too. Two have a greater chance than one alone. And so it proved. Here I am."

"Well," Brother Zebulon said, a little tentatively, "praise Jesus that the prodigal daughter has come back to us."

The corners of Jane's mouth twitched a little. "I'm glad you see it that way, Father. I wondered if you might order me to leave your sight."

Brother Zebulon shifted his weight uncomfortably. "Well, you know, forgiveness is commanded of us by the Lord."

She looked him straight in the eyes. "Does that forgiveness extend to a daughter who is carrying Murrell's child?"

Brother Zebulon's fleshy face paled. "You… you had carnal relations with… that man?"

She laughed. "What, Father, did you think I spent a month living in his camp, sharing his quarters, in chaste innocence? Yes, he and I were lovers. And I have his child here with me." She rested a hand on her belly, as yet flat. "Your grandchild."

Her use of that word made him wince, as if someone had stuck him with something sharp.

"Jane," he said, his voice stern, "you cannot be in your right mind. I must insist that you come back into the fold. I will not ask for your participation in our Holy Sacrament. You are far astray from the path, too far astray for it to do you good in any case. But you cannot simply stand there, brazen, and not be shamed into repentance."

"Do not talk to me of repentance. The kind of penance you would have me do is foolishness, and I cannot help but think the Lord God is far likelier to see it my way than yours. You will not lay a hand on me, not now, not ever, and if that means that I am never to see you again, then so be it. I have a warm place to stay, and a promise of employment. My child will not be born into abject poverty."

Several men stood behind Brother Zebulon, and from their aghast expressions, they had never heard any of Brother Zebulon's family confront him before.

"If you have discounted everything I have ever taught you," he said, "think at least of your mother."

"I do think of her. I pity her, far more than you know. I would at least say farewell to her, if you will allow it."

Brother Zebulon drew himself up, as much to save whatever face he had left before his followers as to make a point with his daughter.

"We shall see. I cannot visit this pain on her right now. I think we are soon to leave this town, and such a thing is hard on a woman. To tell her of your sins, and your horrid change of heart, and how you have embraced this wickedness—no, that I cannot do. Another time… we shall see." He turned to Darren, and for the rest of the conversation, acted as if Jane did not exist. "As for you, sir, I thank you for bringing my daughter back. I have no doubt that your part in it was valiant, and I hold you in no way accountable for my daughter's fall into evil. You seem like a good man…" A canny look came into his eye. "Perhaps you might be moved by the spirit to join our little band of holy warriors? You might know that we embrace pain, so as to become closer to the suffering of Our Lord Jesus Christ."

"Um…" he said. "Well, thanks a lot and all that, but I'm afraid I have to say no. I'm… um… otherwise affiliated."

"Oh? And by which doctrine do you live your life? There are many excellent sects in the wide world, although none—if I may say so—as pure as our own."

He frantically ran over all of the names of religions, Christian and otherwise, he'd ever heard of. His parents had been agnostic, and he'd been raised without much in the way of information about what sorts of things the rest of the world believed in.

"I belong to the… um… First Reformed Latter-Day Full Gospel Holy Knights of the Round Table," he said, all in one breath, and then added, "Of God."

Brother Zebulon looked impressed. "My word. I've never heard of them."

"We're a small sect," he said, which was truthful enough.

A roar went up from the crowd, which was apparently still cheering on the fight going on in front of the tent.

"Well," Brother Zebulon glanced around nervously, "I would love nothing more than to discuss doctrine with you, but I really must be going. You see… my family and I are being called by the Lord to move on, so I believe we should prepare for our departure."

"I understand. I'll head on back into town, then."

"Yes." Brother Zebulon pointedly avoided looking at his daughter. "I'm much obliged to you, sir, for the good deed you tried to do for me and mine, however it turned out. That it went awry is hardly your fault, as you acted out of nothing but good intentions." He raised his straw hat. "Good day."

"Good day." He and Jane turned back toward town, giving the tent and the rioting townspeople a wide berth.

After walking a little way, she said, "Well, that went as well as can be expected."

"Did it? I wouldn't call being cut off cold by your own father 'as well as can be expected.'"

"Father will come around eventually. He's a weak man, but not a bad one. He does not have the strength of will to hold a grudge for long. Right now, what is wounded is his pride. To have his eldest child caught out for fornication, and for her to be entirely unrepentant about it—he honestly doesn't care so much about me, or my eternal soul, as his own standing with his people. It would be worse if I had asked for absolution, begged him to take me back. He would have done so, but then he would have been caught in a cleft stick. He would have had to grant forgiveness to me, and after that, every time afterwards that he saw me and my child, he would have been reminded that his daughter had gone astray. And his followers would see that even those in his own family weren't as holy as he wanted them to think. It will be easier all around if I simply vanish, if his followers are allowed to think I was kidnapped and killed."

"Some of them were here. His followers. They saw you, you know."

"Doesn't make any difference. They tell themselves stories, you know? That's all they really do. Before three weeks have passed, and they're settled in somewhere new, they'll be talking about the terrible thing that happened to Brother Zebulon's daughter, how she was taken by a devil man, stolen away from the flock. I'll be worked into sermons as a cautionary note, but not too negative, being that I'm of Brother Zebulon's blood. I'll be the poor victim of Satan, that they tried to save, but the Evil One proved too strong. A martyr to the cause, you see? After a while, they'll all believe it, and it'll be as if it had really happened that way."

"That's sad." He looked down at the dirt road, unable to think of anything else to say.

"That's all any of us do. Tell ourselves stories, and repeat them often enough that we finally believe them, until we don't know ourselves what is real and what we invented." She smiled a little. "But perhaps after a while he will return here, and my father will be able to remember that he has a daughter. Perhaps he'll be able to find it in his heart to admit me as his child again. Or perhaps not. He is a petty, fearful man, and I think he knows that in his heart. He hates being reminded of it."

"You seem to know your father well."

"None better."

"Are you content with your choices?"

She shrugged. "Does it matter?" And then she looked up at him, a slight smile on her face. "I suppose it must matter to you, since you asked. You are a kind man. Do you have a woman, in your land and your far distant time?"

"No."

"Why not? Is there none you would have?"

Unbidden, the memory of Maíre Gillacomgain again came to mind—her beauty, her voice, her ready laugh, and especially the soft warmth of her mouth on his, when she kissed him in the rain after he freed her from the Vikings. Not that he'd ever get to kiss her again. She was dead and gone, over a thousand years ago.

"Just don't have any luck with women, I guess," he said.

"Your luck in other respects seems considerable. There are few who have survived being waylaid by Murrell and his men. And you came through your other adventures unscathed, did you not?"

"Yes, that's true."

"Then perhaps luck in love will find you some day."

"Perhaps." He studied her closely. "But you never answered my question. Are you content with your choices, now that they are made?"

"What if I said no?"

He didn't answer for a moment. "In the last place I visited, in Norway, I met a man who felt that everything in his life was wrong. That nothing was working out the way it should have. He seemed to me to be the most desperately sad person I'd ever met. And I'd like to think..." He paused. "I hope that you will be able to be happier than he was. Because all of his craving for a different life brought him only to a horrid end."

"And you would not want the same for me."

"No." He looked at her, and smiled, a little shyly. "Because I like you, Jane. You're a fine person. In my time, you'd be... oh, I don't know, you'd be a leader. Someone with your brains, and your courage and independence? You could do anything, be anything you wanted. You would be someone who could change things, who could take charge."

For the first time since they'd met, her face broke into a grin. "Such sugared words, they go right to a woman's heart. How can I not answer, after such flattery?" She stared off into the distance, where the river glittered under a fitful November sun. "So, then, yes. Yes, I am content. I have my child, however its father is a terrible man. I have my freedom. I have a place to live and employment to keep myself and my child fed. I am content."

By this time, they had reached the outskirts of the town, and Tom Thurston's barber shop was in the nearest row of buildings.

"And here we must go our separate ways," she said. "I to my fate, with which I am well content. And you?"

That was a good question. What would he do now? He hadn't seen anything much yet that qualified as a divergence, at least so far as he could tell. But how would he know? It could be anything. It could be causing Jane to walk on the opposite side of the road than she would have. It could be delaying her arrival at Mr. Thurston's by ten seconds, or speeding it up by ten seconds.

It could be anything.

"I don't know," he said. "I'm not sure what I'm supposed to do. I have to stay here until I've figured out what changed here, what piece of the past was altered by the man who caused all of this."

"I wish you luck," she said. "I have only to work as a maid, and give birth to and raise my child. And I think that even so, you have the more difficult task."

Darren returned to Gillette's Inn, where he was welcomed back with shouts of acclamation. Evidently the innkeeper had spent the morning being thronged by customers eager to hear the story of how Darren and Jane had escaped from Murrell's men, and it had lost nothing in the telling.

"*You're* the one who fought off a dozen of Murrell's ruffians?" one of the pub's patrons said, a little incredulously, looking him up and down.

"Well, actually," he began, but Gillette cut him off.

"Yes, Smyser, he's the fellow," Gillette said. "He's skinny but fights like a wildcat. I heard it from the girl, who said he laid 'em out flat when they tried to stop him."

It was probably better not to argue. He said, "I'm hoping it'll be all right if I stay here another day or two."

Gillette made a *pfft* noise, making his copious mustache flutter. "You're more than welcome. Wish all of my guests were fine upstanding young men like yourself."

He thanked him warmly, accepted an offer of stew and a pint of ale for lunch, and sat at the bar to eat.

At first, the inn's customers clustered around him, watching, as if they expected him to Do Something Valiant right before their eyes. He finally looked at them, shrugged, and returned to eating his lunch, and a little disappointed, they finally dispersed. Gillette refilled his mug with ale.

"Didn't mean to put you on the spot." The innkeeper thwacked him on the arm. "But business has been fine from them as wasn't here last night and wanted to hear the story, and no story's so good that a bit of embellishment can't make it better. So I figure, long as I can sell some pints to folks as wants to listen, I don't mind giving you free room and board. Bit of a trade, is how I see it."

"I'm really grateful."

"So, how long do you think you'll be in town? I'll warrant you'll be anxious to get back to—where was it you said you was from, North Carolina?—sooner or later."

"Yes," he said. "I'm sure I'll be leaving soon."

How he'd get out of there, though, remained to be seen. In

Scotland and Norway, he'd had to wait until someone tried to kill him to get back to the Library. What would he do if no one offered to chop his head off? Jump off the top of a building, or something? Or would Fischer bring him back if he was gone too long?

"Well, you're welcome to stay here until your business is concluded," Gillette said.

But that business showed no sign of appearing that day. He loitered around the inn, took an extended nap, and showed up back in the pub in time for dinner. Evening was coming on, and he decided that whatever was supposed to happen, it wouldn't be today.

Just as well. Even if it happened, he wasn't sure how to recognize it, or what to do about it even if he did. He had settled into a comfortable complacency, and was finishing a second bowl of stew—it seemed like the main dish served in the pub—when a young boy, perhaps only twelve or thirteen, burst in through the front door, a terrified expression on his face.

Gillette, who was in jovial mid-conversation with a customer, turned toward him, and one by one, the other people fell silent and looked at the boy, who came up to Gillette, a smudged and dirty piece of paper in his hand. The boy was panting, and visibly trembling.

"Mr. Gillette," the boy said. "I got a message, and he told me to deliver it to the stranger, he did. He said if'n I didn't get it right to the stranger, he'd come back and cut my throat right across. So you got to help me."

The boy pushed the paper into Gillette's hand.

"Now, Rich McCord, what are you talking about?" Gillette said. "Who told you that?"

"The man. He caught me, as I was comin' back from the forest. My dog had run off, and I chased him along, down by the creek a ways, and suddenly the man grabbed me by the shirt collar. He put his face right close to mine, and says, in this dark, terrible voice, he says, 'Boy, you from down in Concord town?' And I says, 'Yes, sir, I am.' And he says, 'You heared tell of a stranger down thereabouts, a strange man come down out of the forest with a woman?' And I said, 'Reckon I did hear tell of such a ones, mister, but I never laid eyes on 'em and I don't know nothin' about 'em.' And he says, 'That's all right, boy, I ain't expectin' you to do nothin' too serious about it. All I want you to do is find that stranger, and see as you give him this note. And make sure he reads it.'" Rich swallowed. "And then I remembered my daddy sayin' he'd heared from Mr. Thurston that the stranger was up here at the inn, so I thought I'd bring the note here on account of because I thought you'd know what to do with it. And the man, he says, 'You think you can do that for me, boy? Or will I have to track you down like a chicken-killing dog and cut your throat right across?' And I said that yeah, I'd do it, and told him not to cut my throat on account of because my mama would take on so if I was killed. And he laughed, and let me go, and I runned all the way back here."

Gillette unfolded the note, and read it, his face paling a little as he did so.

"What's it say, Mr. Gillette?" one of his customers said.

Gillette looked around, and his eyes found Darren's. "I… I'd best let the man it's intended for read it, before I say anything more."

He got up from his seat, and went and took the note from Gillette's hand. He looked down. In a precise, neat cursive script, he read,

My dear friend,

I was most indisposed to find out that you chose to leave our encampment, forsaking our hospitality without so much as a word of thanks. But standards of politeness are not, perhaps, so valued where you come from as they are here, so I am willing to put that much aside.

I cannot, however, abide by the fact that in leaving as you did, you took along with you my cherished companion, and injured one of my men. The first I take much amiss, and the second is, I am afraid, an unforgivable transgression in the mind of my compatriot Mr. Crenshaw, whose head and (I am sorry to say) privates are still much aching from the encounter. So it is my unfortunate duty to require you and Miss Bell to return to my encampment immediately to face justice for what you have done.

I realize your incentive for doing so is minimal, so I have taken the expedient of giving you some encouragement toward meeting my request. This afternoon, several of my faithful helpers secured the person of Reverend Zebulon Bell, my erstwhile companion's father, and have returned with him to my encampment. If by tomorrow evening at nightfall, you have not returned with Miss Bell, it will be my sad duty to find a nice sturdy tree from which to hang Brother Zebulon by the neck until he is quite dead.

I feel certain that you will see that there is really only one reasonable recourse that you have. My men will be waiting for you, with Brother Zebulon, at the creek crossing east of Josiah McCaskill's mill. I believe you know the spot. If you and Miss Bell arrive prior to sundown, you have my word that I will set Brother Zebulon free.

I hope to have the honor of your presence within the next day. In that hope I remain

Yours faithfully,

Reverend John Andrews Murrell

"What's it all about, mister?" one of the customers said.

"Well," he replied, and was amazed at how steady his voice was, "it's a note from Murrell. His men have kidnapped Brother Zebulon, and if Jane and I don't return to Murrell's encampment to 'face justice' for punching out some of Murrell's goons and escaping, they're going to hang him from a tree."

Someone gave a low whistle.

He turned to the boy, who was watching him, wide-eyed. "This man who gave you the note, did he have black hair? And a nasty expression? And a big scar up the side of his face?"

The boy nodded, his mouth hanging open a little.

"Crenshaw," he said, looking around him. "Murrell's right-hand man."

One of the customers gasped. "I heared tell of Crenshaw before Murrell and his rabble even got here. Murrell may be crazy, but Crenshaw is downright evil. He hurts people for the fun of it. You're lucky he wanted you to do something for him, Rich McCord, or like as not no one would ever find your body. Or maybe… just find *pieces* of it."

Rich gave a little whimper.

"You hush on up with that kinda talk, Perkins," Gillette said. "No need to be goin' on like that and scarin' folks half to death." He put a meaty hand on the boy's head, and ruffled his hair. "Don't you pay no attention to him, now, Rich. Just get on home to your mama and papa. You did what you was supposed to do, and you stay out of the forest for the next few days until all of this has settled down. Like as not Crenshaw has forgot all about you by now. Just run along home, and if your mama gives you a hard time about being late for dinner, as seems pretty likely, you tell her to come talk to me and I'll vouch for you."

"Thanks, Mr. Gillette." Rich hurried out of the inn door and disappeared into the early evening gloom.

Darren looked around at the frightened faces turned toward him.

"What're you gonna do, mister?" one of them asked.

And much to his own surprise, he heard himself say, "Well, I guess I have to go back."

The room erupted in shouts of dismay.

Gillette said, "Now, son, you can't do that. It'd be suicide. And they probably wouldn't kill you quick, neither. I've heard stories, I have. Them fellows is worse'n savages."

And to think he'd been worried about getting slapped in the face by the Whackers. That seemed like a hug between friends as compared to having his body parts removed one at a time by Crenshaw.

"I don't see that I have much choice," he said. "I can't let them hang Brother Zebulon."

"Why the hell not?" someone said. "He ain't much loss to the world, far as I can see."

"Came here to stir things up," another man said. "Preachin' his foolishness about seeking out pain. Well, I guess he found it, didn't he? He should be glad."

There were several murmurs of assent.

Darren looked around him at the questioning faces of the men in the pub. "Look, I see what you're saying. But listen, this is Jane's father we're talking about here. You think she'd be content to stand by and let this happen?"

Gillette frowned, and his forehead wrinkled up. With that expression, he looked uncommonly like a puzzled walrus. "Now, you can't mean to say you're gonna tell Miss Bell about this, and take her back with you to them ruffians?"

"No. I don't mean that at all. In fact, I want all of you to promise not to mention anything to Jane. The less she knows about this, the better. But if I don't do something, she'll find out sooner or later, because her father will be dead. I'm going to go up there and see if I can free Brother Zebulon. I'm the only one who can do it."

"You ain't immortal, boy," said the man who had suggested that Brother Zebulon would be no great loss. "And you seem worth a good deal more than that fat, hollerin', white-suited jackass. Tradin' your life for his ain't a fair trade, is all I'm sayin'."

"Don't assume I'll die," he said.

Gillette grasped him by the shoulder, and said, in a low voice, "Look, son, just 'cause I may have exaggerated a little about how y'all escaped from Murrell's men, don't let it go to your head."

"I'm not. I just don't think they can kill me."

This comment elicited nothing but a lot of silent stares.

"I know it doesn't make any sense to you," he said, "but I've already survived more murder attempts than a Mafia informant."

More stares.

"Dammit. I forgot, the Mafia doesn't even exist yet," He looked back up at them, and took a deep breath. His pulse accelerated, and a heady, heroic energy flowed through him. "Never mind." His voice rose, and he spoke commandingly to the assembled crowd. "In the last few days, I've had people try to skewer me with spears and behead me with swords, and I have come through it all without so much as a scratch. So I know I can save Brother Zebulon's life. I don't want anyone else to be in danger here. Heaven knows, I've probably done enough damage by telling you about all of this. But what I'm trying to say is, saving a human life is worth the risk. Which of you cannot empathize with Brother Zebulon's plight? Imagine yourself in that place—captive, afraid, alone, facing certain death if no one risks everything to save you. Think if you knew that someone said your life wasn't worth saving, left you to be hanged from a tree, having committed no crime. And the one thing I know is that I have to go alone. I know it may seem like suicide, but I've got to risk it. It'll be dangerous, but I know I can do it. If anyone rescues Brother Zebulon, it's got to be me!"

He stopped, breathing hard, and cast a flashing eye on the crowd. He expected his speech to elicit shouts of acclamation, rather in the fashion of the "They will never take our freedom!" speech from *Braveheart*. None came. The room was silent, except for the odd nervous cough and throat-clearing. Then one by one the crowd of onlookers melted away into the far recesses of the pub, and he heard, amongst the muttering, the words "damn ijit," "martyr," "well, we *tried* to talk him out of it," and "touched in the head, poor thing."

Apparently he wasn't cut out to be William Wallace.

Gillette clapped a hand to his shoulder, and gave him a smile.

He looked at the innkeeper's kindly face, and relaxed a little.

"So," Gillette said, "you got any next of kin you'd like me to notify?"

Darren scowled at him. "No. Nobody you could get a hold of, anyway," and retreated up the stairs to his room.

Later that evening, Darren lay on his back in bed, hands cupped behind his head, and stared at the ceiling.

Was this the divergence? Was this what he'd been sent here to change? To somehow save Brother Zebulon's life? If that was it, then why did the computer identify Jane as the focal point? It was back to the same old thing—not enough information. They knew the Reverend and his daughter were involved, but not how. Darren knew he was supposed to change something, but not what.

This was hopeless.

But still, even if his speech in the bar didn't quite have the results he wanted, hadn't it been the truth? He couldn't sit back and let Brother Zebulon be hanged by Murrell and Crenshaw and company. It wasn't right. And he was sure he'd been correct about one thing—he really did have the best shot at coming out of this unscathed, if anyone did. So far, the computer had done a pretty damn good job of saving his life.

Even if it hadn't quite worked out for Janowsky.

Still, there was no guarantee he'd succeed, nor that he'd come away without injury. Even Fischer had said the computer wouldn't retrieve him just because he was in pain.

"Shit," he said aloud. "This whole thing sucks. Oh, well, at least this is the last divergence. There's nowhere else for Fischer to send me after this."

And with that not very reassuring thought, he fell asleep.

Darren woke the next morning to the steady hiss of drizzle striking the window. Even under the goose down quilt, he shivered a little. The room had grown damp and cold, and between the time he dragged his chilled, naked self out from under the covers, and pulled on his chilled, smelly clothes, he felt like every trace of heat had been robbed from his body.

He stumped down the stairs—even with the big fireplace in the tavern, it was still uncomfortably cold—and sat down to his breakfast with considerably less cheer than he had the previous morning.

Gillette, however, greeted him with undiminished good nature.

"There's the brave soldier, ready to go into battle." He plopped down a mug of ale in front of him. "I'd offer you something better, seeing as how it's your last meal and all, but I'm afraid it's eggs and bacon again."

"It's fine. And I'm not planning on dying."

"No one does."

There didn't seem to be any arguing with that, so he set his attention to his breakfast.

And although he had really meant it when he told Gillette that he wasn't planning on dying—and he really believed that

Fischer's computer was reasonably reliable about getting him back to the Library before he was messily murdered—when it came right down to it, he was reluctant to set out. For one thing, it was still drizzling, and an icy wind was sneaking through the cracks in the walls. For another, Gillette's tavern was the most homelike place he'd been to yet. The 1840s weren't so far removed from 2016, despite the lack of electricity and indoor plumbing. It brought home to him all that he had lost about the familiar modern world. Leaving meant plunging headfirst back into the unknown.

But finally, there was no way to avoid it any longer. He pushed his plate and mug back, and stood up, wiping his hands on his pants. This seemed to be the convention. Nineteenth century Kentucky had apparently yet to invent the napkin dispenser.

"Heading out, are you?" Gillette said pleasantly. "Well, I'm mighty sorry to see you go, Mr. Ault. It's been a pleasure. We don't get much excitement around here, and I must say, it was nice seeing someone gettin' the best of them ruffians for once. Although here you go, throwin' your life away by givin' them a second chance. Sure I can't talk you out of it?"

"No, sorry. I've got to see if I can rescue Brother Zebulon."

"I figured. It's a pity. I'll let your cousin Josiah know you're dead next time I see him."

He gave a harsh sigh. "I'm not going to die. And incidentally, Josiah's not my cousin."

Gillette's broad brow creased with confusion. "I thought you said…"

"Never mind what I said. It's complicated, and I'm not going to explain it. In any case, I've got to go, so I'll just say thank you for the food and lodging. I really appreciate it. And look after Jane, okay? I mean, I'm sure she'll be fine with Mr. and Mrs. Thurston, but so far, she's had a hell of a life, and she's a nice woman. She deserves better. A lot better."

"I'll see that she's taken care of. But you don't need to

worry. Tom and Elizabeth Thurston are good folk. They'll treat her like a daughter."

He shook Gillette's hand, they said their farewells, and he exited into the damp, frigid drizzle, forcing himself to give only one rueful backward glance at the inn, with its warm food and goose down quilts, as he trudged up the road toward the forest.

The woods were silent, with no sound but the steady hiss of the rain. All of the normal noises—animals rustling, birds singing, the hundred little natural sounds that were ordinarily omnipresent—seemed stilled, as if all of the denizens of the forest were hiding until the sun came out. It amped up his nerves until they tingled. He found himself listening for sounds of pursuit, for the stealthy creep of feet in the underbrush as an unseen assailant paralleled his movement up the road, waiting for the right moment to attack. He strained his ears until he had a headache, and more than once had to force himself to relax when he realized he was clenching his fists and his jaw as if in preparation for an assault.

Three hours passed, and the assault never came. The creek trickled its way along the road, running the opposite way, downhill toward the river that passed beside the village of Concord. There was a point, he remembered, where the creek crossed the road, and he'd had to step across on wide, flat stones that had undoubtedly been laid in the water for that purpose. That was where Brother Zebulon was being held, where he would try to set him free, perhaps at the cost of his own freedom.

At this point, he'd was almost ready to welcome them killing him, if all it did was send him back to the Library. He wiped the rainwater out of his eyes to no apparent effect. But what if they decided to torture him first? Could he deal with being tortured? And yet, here he was, walking into a situation where there was at least one guy who probably would love to retaliate against him for Jane's having kicked him in the balls, most likely by removing his.

Maybe Gillette was right. There was no rational reason to do this. After all, by the twenty-first century, Brother Zebulon would be long dead, and he would still be long dead no matter what was accomplished here. Maybe he should see if there was a way to get back to the Library without going through all of this.

But some habit of perseverance, some unsuspected streak of courage he'd developed since he'd been launched on this bizarre adventure, wouldn't let him turn back. He was certain that somehow, he had to get back to Murrell's men, and do his best to rescue Brother Zebulon, whatever the cost to himself.

He slogged his way to the top of a hill, and looked down the slope ahead of him. The road, dim in the gray half-light, wound its way between the trees, and ahead he glimpsed a hint of movement—the creek, tumbling along in its gravelly bed. Somewhere near here, the letter had said, Murrell's men would be waiting for him.

He shuddered. The rain continued to fall. He was already soaked through and chilled to the bone, and the water dripped from his hair into his eyes. His leather shoes were caked with globs of ice-cold mud.

Also, he had to pee. Should have taken care of that sooner. He wasn't doing it now, that was for damn sure. Just his luck, Crenshaw would pop out from behind a tree while he had his pants down.

He started walking again, slowly, waiting for something to happen—being tackled by Mosher and Johnson, a knife point in the back, Crenshaw's nasty laugh. He reached the creek after five minutes' slow plod downhill, and stood there for a while, watching the water flow.

The rain continued to fall. And nothing continued to happen.

He swore under his breath, and stomped across the creek. One of the stepping stones turned under his foot, and his left leg plunged up to the knee in freezing cold water. He yelped, swore again, and ended up with his right leg in the creek while trying to extract the left one. Finally he was able to get back up onto the stepping stone, and sloshed his way up on to the other bank.

Now his teeth chattered uncontrollably. He stood there, looking around, hugging himself miserably, and trying to figure out what to do next.

Finally, all of the accumulated tension from the past days seemed to burst inside him. He looked around him, at the wet, dripping, bare trees, the muddy road, and the creek with its three big stepping stones, and he leaned back his head and yelled, "Hey! Whoever is waiting here! You'd better show yourself, or kill me, or something, because I'm sick and damned tired of standing here in the rain! Come on, you said you'd meet me here. Where the hell are you?"

No one answered.

And that was when a hand grabbed him by the upper arm.

He took a big breath to give a shout, but his captor's other hand went over his mouth, and all he said was, "Mmmmph!"

An annoyed voice whispered, "Jesus and all the saints, do you *want* to get yourself killed?"

It was Jane.

She took her hand from his mouth, and regarded him with one eyebrow raised quizzically. "What were you thinking, shouting like that?"

"I don't know," he said. "I felt like I had to do *something*. There's no one here."

"Well, shouting, 'Please come kill me' isn't very smart."

"It might be easier to get it over with."

She shook her head. "That's ridiculous. You haven't seen any sign of them?"

"No. And how did you find out? About…" He stopped, not knowing how else to explain her presence, but not wanting to mention Brother Zebulon's kidnapping explicitly in case she didn't have the whole story.

"How did I know Murrell had taken my father?" she said, her hazel eyes betraying no emotion. "Elizabeth Thurston told me. She had it from the wife of one of the men who was there last night when you received Murrell's letter. You can't keep a secret in a small town."

"Ah." He looked at her in what he fancied was a stern fashion. "You should have stayed home. It's not safe."

"Really?" She laughed lightly. "And let you have all of the fun? You sorely misjudge me. Also, if we succeed, this will even the score considerably between my father and me. I couldn't let such an opportunity pass."

"But where are they?" He glanced around them at the empty, dripping woods. "The letter said they'd be here, at the creek crossing east of McCaskill's mill. That's here, right?"

"That's here," Jane said. "But as far as where they are, that I do not know."

They proceeded slowly up the farther bank, and still saw nothing more than trees, rocks, and mud. His wet trouser legs stiffened as the water in them gradually froze.

This was idiotic. If they weren't here, they could be anywhere in the woods. And searching for them on foot would be impossible.

But then, off in the woods to the right, they heard a familiar voice shout, "Truly I say unto you, God knows what you have done!" before subsiding into quieter tones whose words were lost against the white noise of the creek and the drizzle.

Jane's head turned, like a hound scenting a hare. "Father."

"Brother Zebulon!" he breathed, and before she could stop him or he could stop himself, he sprinted off into the woods toward the voice.

He wasn't sure what he planned to do, whether he intended to fight the ruffians hand-to-hand until he won or they did, or to try to convince them to honor Murrell's terms and let Brother Zebulon go. In his chilled, exhausted, anxious brain, all he could think of was that he had to get to the ruffians first, before they saw Jane—that he had to keep them from finding out that she had come along.

He burst into a small clearing, where two dozen men stood. Brother Zebulon, still wearing his straw hat and white suit—now muddied and much bedraggled—stood on some kind of raised platform, with his back to the trunk of a tree.

Darren gaped for a minute, and then shoved his way through the crowd of men around him, shouting, "No! Don't hang him! I'm here! You have to let him go!"

Two dozen faces turned toward him in frank puzzlement. His former bed mates, Mosher and Johnson, were among them.

Mosher gave him a confused, gap-toothed grin. "What the hell you yellin' about? Hang the Reverend? Why the hell would I hang the Reverend?"

He looked around him, his thoughts bouncing from the inside of his skull as if trying to find a coherent explanation to catch on to, and failing. Finally, he looked up at Brother Zebulon, who gave him an angelic smile, and it was only then that he saw that Brother Zebulon didn't, in fact, have a rope around his neck.

"My son, you shouldn't'a troubled about me. The Lord has his hand over my head." Brother Zebulon gave a sweeping gesture around him. "You are looking at the latest converts to the Church of Our Lord Jesus Christ Risen and Triumphant Through Suffering."

As if to illustrate the fervor of their newfound beliefs, one of Brother Zebulon's converts reared back and socked the man next to him in the jaw. The recipient of the punch went down like a sack of corn.

"Whoo-eee!" shouted someone else. "Damn, Cooley, that was a good'un!"

"Hallelujah!" yelled someone else. "Praise Jesus!"

"I like this a hell of a lot better than them Methodists," the man who'd thrown the punch said, rubbing his hand and grinning, displaying far less than the standard-issue number of teeth. "Them Methodists don't talk about nothin' but singin' hymns and avoiding demon rum. Brother Zeb here is the genuine article."

Brother Zebulon smiled over his flock of new devotees.

Darren, on the other hand, felt like he'd been hit in the solar plexus. "I came all this way, in the rain, and I didn't even need to, because you'd all *converted*?"

Jane, who had come up silently behind him, whispered into his ear, "Not all. Where's Crenshaw? And Murrell?"

A chill that the rain and the wind were insufficient to explain shuddered its way down his backbone. "Maybe they ran off when the rest of the men found religion."

"I doubt it," she said. "Neither of them would ever give up. Not when there was a reason for revenge."

"Well, then, since your father is safe, maybe we should get ourselves out of here before they find us."

"That's not a bad thought." She turned to one of the men nearby—it was Darren's scraggly-bearded captor, Johnson—and said, "Do you know where Crenshaw is?"

Johnson looked at her through narrowed eyes. "Why you wanna know?"

"So we can avoid him."

Johnson stared at her, his mouth hanging open a little, and finally seemed to come to the conclusion that her answer was acceptable. "Oh, as for Crenshaw, he got mighty angry at the lot of us when we decided we wasn't gonna hurt Brother Zeb, here. We was supposed to torture him a little bit—you know, just so's when y'all showed up, y'all'd know we meant business. But then Brother Zeb started talkin' to us about the

Word of the Lord, and we all realized the error of our ways." Johnson put his hand over his heart. "So we beat the shit outta Crenshaw, and he took off toward Reverend Murrell back at the camp."

"Murrell's still there, then?" she asked.

"He was took real bad last night," Johnson said. "He wasn't in no shape to oversee the festivities, here, so he sent Crenshaw to do it. I 'spect that he and Crenshaw are plannin' together right now, tryin' to figure out how they'll get the better of us and string up poor Brother Zeb. But they ain't gonna do it, are they, boys?"

A cheer went up from the assembled group.

"So, you'll be all right, Father?" she said to Brother Zebulon.

Brother Zebulon was in a fine mood, no surprise given that if things had gone differently, he'd be very shortly due to be hanged from the tree he was standing next to. He looked down at his daughter with an indulgent smile.

"Don't you worry yourself none, child," he said. "I've more'n doubled my congregation in one go, and we're soon to head off to Tennessee with our newfound converts. When I get back to Concord, we'll pack up and leave." He looked up to the gray sky, which was still spitting rain, and said, "After your dear mother and brothers and sisters and I have finished giving thanks for my miraculous delivery from death."

"I think that's our cue to leave," Darren said.

She nodded.

They turned away from Brother Zebulon and his flock, and headed back toward the road. The rain was slowing down, but the wind had picked up, and the temperature was dropping. From the feel of it, there would be a hard freeze once the sun went down, and he was determined to be back in Concord by nightfall, now that his task of rescuing Brother Zebulon had been rendered irrelevant. The thought of the goose down quilt waiting for him in his room in Gillette's inn was enough to propel his feet forward.

After a few minutes' walk, he said, "I hope those ruffians don't turn on your father."

"I doubt they'd hurt him," she said. "Rob him and run away, once they realize that he's not going to find them sport the way Murrell did. But he has precious little to steal in any case. Once they get tired of hitting each other and shouting hallelujah, I suspect that they'll vanish one by one." She shook her head. "It's what happens to most of his converts. They seldom last long."

"I wouldn't imagine."

"What about you, Mr. I-Came-From-The-Future? Where will you go now? Has the disaster you were sent to fix been averted?"

"I don't know. I thought maybe that it was rescuing your father from Murrell, but it looks like he took care of that one on his own."

"How will you get back home, wherever home is?"

"I'm not sure. I guess I have to wait until the people in charge bring me back."

Except that he didn't have a home. Everyone was gone. The Library might be comfortable, but he couldn't stay there forever. And in any case, if he failed to bring back the human race, the Board of Directors was going to fire Fischer and Maggie, and then where would he be?

Suddenly, a terrifying image came to mind. What if everything and every place in the world still existed, but all the *people* were gone? He pictured the entire city of Seattle, all of the businesses and homes and apartment buildings and cafés and roads… all empty. Food still sitting on tables, never to be eaten, belongings dropped in place as the people who held them disappeared, papers being blown down streets filled with empty cars still sitting in the middle of roads…

He'd never given it any thought. Even after he'd accepted

that Fischer was telling the truth, that what Lee had done had somehow made the entirety of humanity disappear, he didn't consider what had happened to everything else. Did the whole Earth vanish, too, or was everything still there, just abandoned? The latter seemed like one of the most horrifying thoughts he had ever had.

And so it was that he was once more lost in thought when he was tackled from the side and knocked sprawling, landing flat on his back in the mud. A gobbet of mud spattered his glasses, and Jane screamed. A knee made solid contact with his gut, and his breath was expelled in a whoosh.

"Well, look here who we got. If it ain't the schoolmaster and Miss Bell, out for a nice stroll in the rain."

The blurred outline of Crenshaw's face grinned down at him. He had both of Darren's wrists pinned to the ground.

Crenshaw, however, looked like he hadn't been having an easy time of it. His right ear was torn and bleeding, and there was also blood around his mouth. One eye was swollen and already beginning to blacken. Most likely the results of the fight between Crenshaw and Murrell's men.

"I told you, you asshole," he gasped out, "I'm *not* a schoolmaster."

"Well, whatever you are, you'll be dead soon, so it don't make a difference."

He struggled to free himself, but Crenshaw leaned on him, and laughed in his face. "You a prayin' man? You might want to say one or two."

"Murrell still using you to send people to heaven while he prays for their souls?"

Crenshaw's smile vanished. "Murrell's dead. He died last night, coughin' up blood. So much for his God. As for me, I don't care one way or the other. I just like killin' people." Crenshaw looked over at Jane, who was standing, frozen, watching them. "And you better run, little girl, or I'll do the same to you. But not before I've had some other kind of fun with you first." He straddled Darren, placing his knees on his arms, and put his hands around his neck. Two dirty thumbs pressed against his Adam's apple. "Say goodbye, schoolmaster." He squeezed. Black starbursts exploded in front of Darren's eyes.

With a furious shriek, Jane leaped on Crenshaw. She grabbed him by his torn ear, and pulled. Crenshaw howled, and the pressure on Darren's throat suddenly lessened, and he was able to pull one hand free. He reached up and jammed the base of his hand into Crenshaw's nose.

The injured highwayman gave an inarticulate cry of pain, and fell to one side, and Darren was able to slither out from underneath him. He turned, and looked toward Jane—still fighting Crenshaw with a fury he would never have expected—and he said, "Jane, get yourself out of here!" And for the first time in his life, he leapt *into* a fight.

He expected the punches to hurt more. A couple of them made solid contact—one with his face, another with his upper chest—but he found himself grinning, even laughing, and fighting the harder as he realized with some amazement that he was actually winning the fight. Crenshaw was falling back, the look on his face changing from gleeful savagery to astonishment as he realized that he was being beaten by someone he had derided as a weakling. Finally, Crenshaw stopped throwing punches, and put his hands up to ward off Darren's.

He let his fists drop to his side. His chest was heaving, and he hurt in a hundred different places, but at the moment all he felt was exhilaration. "Now," he panted out, and was amazed at how tough, how completely *badass* his own voice sounded, "get the fuck out of here, and you'd better not even think of trying to bother Jane Bell or me again. Or anyone else."

But Crenshaw had been a dirty fighter since he was little. Without warning he kicked out a leg, hooked it around

Darren's, and swept him off his feet. Then he leaped on top of him, and the two rolled off into the underbrush.

But here fate took a hand. A branch slapped Crenshaw across the face, catching him squarely in the right eye, the one already bruised and blackening from his earlier fight with Murrell's men. He screamed an obscenity, and clapped a hand to his face, and Darren knocked him sprawling and in a moment had him pinned him to the ground.

Now what? He looked down at Crenshaw's bloodied face. The highwayman had intended to strangle Darren slowly, but there was no way Darren do the same to him.

He glanced around, but didn't see Jane. Perhaps she'd obeyed his command to run. Then he looked down at his adversary, who was still struggling, but feebly. Crenshaw's eye was bleeding from a tear in the eyelid, and he seemed to know he was done.

He couldn't just let Crenshaw go. He couldn't get caught out that way a second time. And with some horror, he realized that meant Darren would have to kill him.

He had no weapon, but he saw, within reach, a large rock. He picked it up, holding it tentatively. Could he take a rock, and smash someone's head with it? Was it in him? He looked down at Crenshaw, now completely inert, looking up at him with his one good eye. One lip curled back, exposing yellowed, crooked teeth. With all of his injuries, and scars, and his black thatch of hair soaking wet and matted with mud, he barely looked human.

"If you do it," Crenshaw croaked, "you better make a good job of it. Because if you don't, I'll hunt you down, you and the girl both. I'll find you. I'll cut your throat clean across. But before that, I'll tie you up and make you watch while I'll have my use of the girl until I tire of it, then I'll…"

And Darren struck Crenshaw in the head with the rock.

The voice cut off like someone had flipped a switch. But then, he felt a pull, as if he was attached to a giant rubber band, and the whole scene—Crenshaw's body lying in the muddy patch in the woods, the bare trees, the tangled underbrush—was yanked away from him. He had a momentary glimpse of the whole scene, viewed from above. He could see the road, with Jane's small form jogging down it—*She ran away, she's safe, thank heaven she's safe*—and in the distance the roofs of the town of Concord and the river, glittering in the vague gray light. Then his consciousness flew upwards and away, and everything went black.

part four

the city by night

. . .

"Jesus Christ," came Fischer's awestruck voice, "every time you come back, you look worse than the time before."

Darren looked up from his position—face down on the floor in Fischer's office—and decided that on the whole, he was happier face down.

"Are you badly injured, Mr. Ault?" Maggie asked.

"Can you die of bruises?" he asked, his voice muffled from having his mouth pressed into the carpet.

"I would imagine you could," she said.

"Then I think that's what I'm going to do. Just drag me away when I'm done."

"Come on," Fischer said. "You can't die without telling us what happened in Kentucky."

"Why not?"

"Because it's not fair to leave us hanging. Get up, you'll feel better. Maggie, is there any coffee left?"

"I believe there is."

"Can you get him a cup? Oh, and bring a towel. I don't want him sitting on any of the furniture in his current state."

Maggie's steps receded. He decided that however

appealing it was, he couldn't stay on the floor indefinitely. He slowly moved himself into an upright position, emitting a good many groans in the process.

"Jesus," Fischer breathed again, looking him up and down. "I believe… yes, I really do think. You've been in a fight, haven't you?"

"Yes."

"You poor guy. I feel almost guilty." Fischer frowned. "Wait… it wasn't the Whackers who did this to you, was it?"

He shook his head. "No. They turned out to be pretty harmless. The guy I got in the fight with was a highwayman named Crenshaw."

"Wow. He looks like he really worked you over. What did you do to piss him off?"

"It's a long story."

Fischer shook his head. "Okay, dude, that did it. I really *do* feel guilty. I didn't mean you to get the shit beat out of you by some nineteenth century gang member. I hate unfair fights."

"Oh, it wasn't an unfair fight. I won. In fact, I think…" He swallowed, and his eyebrows drew together. "I think I killed him."

Fischer's bright blue eyes opened wide. "You… you *killed* him?"

"I think so. I had him pinned to the ground, and he was saying all kinds of… you know, nasty talk. Threats. Like how he was going to hunt Jane and me down, and rape her and make me watch, and then kill us both. So I hit him in the head with a rock." He gave an apologetic shrug. "It seemed like the only thing to do at the time."

"What happened to this being a reconnaissance mission? You're not supposed to go into the past and *change* things. That's what caused all of this in the first place." He brushed his hair back, and it immediately fell across his eyes again. "And you're especially not supposed to *kill* anyone."

Maggie came back into the office with a steaming mug of

black coffee and a large towel. He accepted the former grate-fully, and she draped the latter across a chair, and indicated that he should sit, which he did.

"So," she said, in a conversational tone, "did I hear correctly that Mr. Ault may have killed someone?"

"That's what he said." Fischer's eyes still registered incredulity.

"Perhaps he should tell us the entire story. One isolated fact may not be of much consequence, however alarming it may seem."

He took a sip of the coffee, and then told them what had happened in Kentucky, from his meeting with Josiah McCaskill, his subsequent kidnapping by Murrell's cronies and meeting with Jane Bell, their escape, arrival in Concord, and confrontation with Brother Zebulon, and Brother Zebu-lon's miraculous conversion of almost the entire ruffian gang to Whackerism.

"Murrell apparently died," he said, "or he'd probably have stopped them from joining Brother Zebulon somehow. Murrell was one seriously scary guy. He had an absolutely convincing way about him. Listening to him, you found your-self believing what he said even while you knew it was false. If he were alive today, he'd be a major cult leader. He had something, that's for sure." He took another sip of coffee. "But once he was dead, and the rest of the gang abandoned ship, Crenshaw was left to his own devices. He wasn't going to fall for Brother Zebulon's religious message, and without accomplices, he couldn't very well have continued his career as a highwayman. But he could take revenge on Jane and me, and that's what he tried to do."

"But you stopped him?" Fischer still seemed unable to believe what he was hearing.

He nodded. "I know what you're thinking, and you're right. I'm not a fighter. I'd never been in a fight before, in fact, unless you count getting beat up by bullies in middle school.

But I couldn't let him win, you know? If I'd let him go, he'd have found Jane and hurt her. I had to stop him. I know you're going to say it was the wrong thing to do, that I shouldn't have interfered with what was supposed to happen, but I had to stop him. Jane Bell—she's a good person. She didn't deserve how her life went, and if I could prevent anything else bad from happening to her... well, I just *had* to." A flash of defiance flared inside him. "So, when I had a chance, I hit Crenshaw in the head with a rock. Yes, I'm pretty sure it killed him. And I don't care what you're going to say. If I had it to do over, I'd do it again."

Fischer held up both hands, palms outward. "Whoa, sport. I'm not going to argue with you, not while you're in this mood. I'm not a fighter, either."

"And remember," Maggie said, "just as with the unfortunate events that concluded your visit to Norway, it may not make any real difference in the long run. What happened to Per Olafsson was the result of his being in the wrong track. The same, we must suppose, is true of Miss Bell and Mr. Crenshaw. If I am correct, then once we reestablish proper tracking, Mr. Ault's actions may right themselves, along with everything else."

"We'll have to hope that you're correct." Fischer regarded him with one eyebrow raised. "Still. I have to admit that I'm impressed. There's more to you than I'd thought. Saving the damsel in distress, and all. Badass."

"I don't know if I'm a badass," Darren said, "but Jane Bell is about as far from a damsel in distress as you could get. A hundred years later, she'd be part of the women's rights movement. She landed a few good punches on Crenshaw herself."

"If I may make a suggestion," Maggie said, "I think we should focus on the information Mr. Ault gathered. In my opinion, there is one fact that stands out as being important —the rest is, as far as I can see, ancillary. And that is that the first person you met in Kentucky was named McCaskill."

Fischer nodded. "I agree. That can't be a coincidence. It's not like he was named Smith, or something else common. There can't be many McCaskills around. The name has to mean something."

"Is there a way to check to see if he was one of Lee's ancestors?" Darren asked. "Or, was supposed to be? I know everything's all screwed up, but you know what I mean."

"Of course." Fischer swiveled to face his computer. "We have the genealogy of every human on Earth in the database."

"Don't tell the people at Ancestry dot com," Maggie said. "Nor the Mormons. They'd be battering down the door."

"Fortunately, they don't know where we live." Fischer typed a few commands, moved the mouse around and clicked, typed again and hit "Enter," and then said, "What was Lee's middle name again?"

"Allen."

"Born in Spokane, Washington, as I recall?"

"Yes."

Fischer typed a bit more, and then moused over and clicked twice. Then he leaned back and cupped his hands behind his head.

A moment later, he brought his chair back to an upright position with a loud *thunk*. "What the hell?" He frowned at the screen.

"What?" Darren and Maggie said simultaneously.

"Well, it looks like we've isolated the problem." He turned the computer monitor around to face Darren and Maggie. On it was a branching family tree, starting on the left with "Lee Allen McCaskill" (a red notation under his name said, "CAUTION: No Valid Actual Track: Alternate Tracks Only! Use This Data For Speculative Track Analysis Only!"). The tree split, and split again, showing Lee's parents, and grandparents. But at generation five there was another message written in bright scarlet. The spaces for the parents of Lee's great-great grand-father, Stephen Patrick McCaskill, were filled in, "ERROR TYPE 2033-B. Data unavailable."

"My word," Maggie said softly.

"Another thing that isn't supposed to happen?" he asked.

"Yup." Fischer looked up. "Even if you never existed, you *have* to have ancestors."

"I don't even want to think about all the ways that doesn't make sense."

"Look, even for people who were never born, who are on alternate tracks, there are the parents they *would* have had if they'd been born. You see? There are different kinds of nonex-istent. People who only exist in alternate tracks are nonexist-ent, yes, but it's a circumstantial sort of nonexistence. It's contingent. This,"—he gestured at the screen—"*this* is *really* nonexistent. This is the real deal."

"Of course," Maggie said, "you do realize this forces us to a reevaluation of the problem."

"Oh, yeah," Fischer said. "Because we've been working from the wrong angle. We'd thought it was your ancestry that Lee wiped out. It looks like it was his own."

"How can that be?" Darren asked. "I mean, the same thing occurred to me when I met Josiah McCaskill, but I couldn't see how what Lee did would have any effect on his own family tree. It doesn't make any sense."

"Not on the surface," Maggie said. "But I think that's the only explanation. Now, we have to determine why."

"But wait," Darren said. "When you started out on this whole thing, you began with my grandmother's name, and tried to figure out where the divergences in *her* family tree were. You didn't start with Lee."

"No, you're right," Fischer said. "And if we had, we might have figured this out a lot quicker. But just because there are divergences in Lee's family doesn't mean there are none in yours. The fact is, you and Lee probably share a good many ancestors, so any divergences would show up in both lineages. And the farther back you go, the more likely that is to be true. In fact, most anthropologists believe that if you go back before about 1200 AD everyone currently alive in Europe descends, multiple times, from every single individual who left descendants."

"No one is currently alive in Europe," Maggie observed. "Nor anywhere else, for that matter."

"You know what I mean."

"Of course. I was being flippant, sir."

"So my point stands. If Lee was supposed to descend from Per Olafsson and Maíre Gillacomgain, chances are you do, too."

"So Lee and I are cousins?"

"Everyone's a cousin, Ault. It's impossible for it to work any other way. You can't keep on having everyone's family tree double at each generation farther back. Eventually a person's number of ancestors would exceed the population of the Earth at the time. At some point in the past, there were only two groups of people—the ones who are the ancestors of everyone on the planet, and the ones who were the ancestors of no one."

"Weird."

"So, you're a distant cousin of Maggie and me, too. We're all one big happy family."

"Well, that's just awesome, but it doesn't get us any closer to figuring out what caused all of this."

"He has a point, Fischer," Maggie said. "And it may not be the best time, but I should remind you that we're under a bit of time pressure."

"Time pressure?" Darren said.

Fischer shifted uncomfortably in his seat. "She's referring to the fact that the Board of Directors has issued us an ultimatum. While you were off cutting it up rough in nineteenth century Kentucky, Maggie and I and the other department heads were called into a meeting, where we were basically handed our asses by the Chair."

"In fact, we'd only just come back when you arrived here," Maggie said.

"The Chair isn't a happy woman," Fischer said. "She evidently considers the loss of the entire human race a bit of a... misstep."

"It wasn't your fault," Darren protested.

"No, but she's not seeing it that way. It was only some fast talking by Maggie that kept us all from being shown the door right then and there. She said, 'Perhaps it might alter your perception of the situation, Mrs. Holcombe, if you knew that we have an operative on assignment as we speak, working to rectify this situation.'" Fischer's imitation of Maggie's rolling Scottish accent was eerily accurate, and the corners of Maggie's mouth turned upward a little.

"And what did she say?"

"That we have twenty-four hours. No more, no less. In her words, 'at twenty-four hours, this situation will be resolved. If not, it will be under sixty seconds later that you and your entire administrative staff will be packing up their belongings and looking for employment elsewhere.'"

"Elsewhere?" Darren said. "*Is* there an 'elsewhere' at the moment?"

"I don't expect she cares," Maggie said.

"So I think we have only one choice. To send you on one last reconnaissance mission."

He winced. "*Another* one? Where to now? I thought that there were only three divergences?"

"Well, yes and no. There were only three spots the computer picked out. But remember that the computer wasn't exactly behaving normally. We don't know why it chose those three points as focal events in leading up to the evaporation of all of humanity. But there's one other place we need evidence about. And that's the events immediately preceding Lee's firing of the gun at your forehead."

"The present, you mean."

"More or less."

"What would that tell us?"

"Well, maybe we could find out what should have been the first thing we looked into—why Lee wanted to kill you." Fischer leaned back in his chair, and Ivan the tomcat appeared from underneath his desk and jumped into his lap, purring. Fischer scratched the cat's ears. "If we'd been thinking, we'd have sent you there first. Because, after all, that's really where the action is. Whatever happened—whatever caused all of this—it was consequent to Lee's shooting you. Everything before that happened afterwards."

"That sounds rather Zen, Fischer," Maggie said.

"No, but it's true. Whatever he did led to a temporal paradox. If we know why he had it in for Ault, it might give us a way to stop it. I wish we'd been smart enough to see that from the beginning. It would have saved a lot of time."

"Remember, we thought at first that Lee himself had escaped into the past and altered the flow of time. It seemed like a good idea"—the corner of Maggie's mouth twitched again—"at the time."

Fischer looked over at him. "There's a couple of things, though, that you should know. First, we don't have the leisure to give you a night's sleep. It's going to be a quick shower and change of clothes, and off you go, bruises and scrapes and all. And second... there's going to be a difference when you go to Seattle."

"A difference? What kind of difference?"

"The system has an internal safeguard, set up to prevent anything from interfering with people whose actual tracks haven't been locked yet. In other words, people who are still alive. As you've found out, through the Library you can go back in time, and witness events, and even interact with people, but only ones who have already chosen their own actual tracks. For people who are still alive, the present is… fluid. Things only freeze in place when a person dies."

"Rather settles the question of free will, doesn't it?" Maggie said. "Don't tell the philosophers. They do so enjoy debating the topic."

"So we have a way of preventing anyone from messing with recent events, and stopping people who are still alive from choosing freely. If you go back in time, but not far enough that the people in it are already dead… you can't actually talk to anyone. It's too risky. You could change your own timeline accidentally, or deliberately. You could try to talk to yourself, with alarming results. You could influence someone's choices, instead of the person choosing for his or her own reasons. So, to everyone there who was part of that temporal anomaly—in other words, to everyone who was alive, and who disappeared when Lee shot you—you'll be invisible and inaudible. You'll be able to witness what's going on, but not interact." Fischer paused, and then added quietly, "You'll be a ghost."

"It'd have been a hell of a lot less painful if I could have been a ghost in the other places you sent me."

"No doubt. Objects will still be solid, but you should refrain from messing about with anything. If you pick up a pencil, anyone looking in that direction will see a pencil magically float up into the air. Can't have that."

"I guess not."

"The good part is that no one will be able to harm you. After what you went through in Kentucky, that's bound to seem pretty appealing. But there's a downside. You've got only twenty-four hours. Less than that, because the clock started a little under an hour ago. So you'll excuse the rush, but we need to get you showered and changed, and then it's off you go, back to your home town. And if you don't figure out why Lee killed you and come up with a way to stop it, you'll be dealing with an entirely different bunch when you get back." He blinked solemnly. "And I don't think you'll find them as warm, charming, and lovable as I am."

Darren looked over at Maggie.

"I wish he were joking, Mr. Ault," she said, her face serious. "Mrs. Holcombe makes Fischer look like Winnie-the-Pooh by comparison."

"Oh," he said.

Darren was whisked up to his temporary quarters, where he found his original clothes—clean and dry—waiting for him in a neat stack by the bathroom door, along with a light windbreaker that looked brand new.

"Couldn't send you back to Seattle in March in nothing but a t-shirt," Fischer said.

"Thanks."

"I'll wait here while you get yourself cleaned up." Fischer dropped into an overstuffed chair in front of the television. "Don't take too long. Maggie wasn't joking that we're under some pressure."

He went into the bathroom, and stripped off his nineteenth century clothing. Bits of dried mud, twigs, and leaves pattered onto the floor. He considered cleaning it all up, then decided that it wasn't his problem, turned on the shower, and stepped in.

The hot water stung his scrapes and cuts, but overall, it was delicious.

Odd how every time he returned from the past, the best thing about returning was a hot shower. Airplanes and cars and computers and modern medicine notwithstanding, at that moment Darren decided that hot showers were the finest invention of the human race.

He stayed in as long as he dared—he didn't think Fischer

was above coming into the bathroom and dragging him out if he took too long— then got out, dried off, and looked at himself speculatively in the mirror.

His left eye was progressing toward black, and the opposite cheek had a bluish bruise and the healing cut he'd received from his first encounter with Crenshaw. There was a tender spot on the back of his scalp, probably from one of the several times he'd landed flat on his back. His upper chest had several more bruises. There was a long scrape on the side of his neck, and both hands ached—the result, he thought, of all of the punches he had landed. The human body was a harder target than he'd thought. As he got dressed, though, he couldn't help but give his reflection a roguish smile. Winning a fight, especially against such a deserving target as Crenshaw, had done something to him.

Crenshaw had to be stopped. And he was glad he had the balls to do it. For once in his life, he he hadn't wimped out.

He pulled on his boxers, t-shirt, and jeans, and went back out into the living room. Fischer had the television on, and was slouched in the chair, legs stretched out in front of him, watching some chick-flick-looking movie. Gwyneth Paltrow was running for a train, missed it, and turned away in frustration, as Darren said, "I'm ready when you are, Fischer."

The Librarian looked up, and punched the "Off" button on the remote.

"Okay." He gave Darren a quirky smile. "You know, Ault, you *do* look like a badass. I don't know if it's the bruises, or something different in your eyes, but something's changed. You look like you might actually be able to pull this off."

"I'll do my best."

"You've done pretty fucking amazing so far. You know, I gotta say… thanks. I know this hasn't been a pleasure cruise. I really appreciate everything you've done."

"I'm sorry about killing Crenshaw," he said. "I know that was against the rules."

Fischer shrugged. "He'd be dead by now anyway."

"I guess that's one way of looking at it."

"It's amazing how comforting taking the big-picture approach can be."

He sat down and pulled on his socks and shoes. "So, I really won't be able to talk to anyone?"

"No. No interactions allowed with living people, and as few as you can manage with everything else. That's the rule. The most important thing is to see if you can figure out what Lee McCaskill was up to, and what made him suddenly turn homicidal. He has to have found out something that triggered that, and whatever that something was is the key to this whole thing. So if we can fix that… maybe we can set everything else right at the same time."

"Understood."

"There's food in the backpack on the floor. Resist the temptation to try to eat anything you find when you get there. Or move anything. Or, really, *do* anything. You're an observer only. It takes some training to perfect this, but you have to try your hardest not to change things while you're there. You have no idea how often we've had to go back and fix stuff our own employees inadvertently screwed up."

He picked up the backpack and slung it across his shoulder. "I'll do my best."

"You'll be pulled back in a little under one day's time. We've timed it to give you until about ten minutes after Lee murdered you."

"I can't believe it, but that actually makes sense to me."

Fischer gave him a wry grin. "I told you, you get used to it. You should try to be there watching when the shooting happens, but then be ready to jump immediately afterwards. We'll get you back here an hour or so before the deadline. I know that doesn't give you a lot of time to figure this out. You'll have to work fast."

"I'll do what I can."

Fischer thwacked him on the shoulder. "That's what you've done all along. It'll be enough. It'll have to be." He paused. "Any final thoughts?"

"Just that this scares me more than any of the other jumps did."

"We're at the heart of it, now. This is the real deal, this time. Oh, and one last thing… don't freak out when you see yourself. Some people do."

"I'll try not to."

"Okay, then. Good luck. See you in twenty-four hours."

He closed his eyes, and everything went dark.

When Darren opened his eyes, he was standing on a street corner at night. Cars swished by him, but something about them was insubstantial, as if he were the only real object in a world made of phantoms. People walked past, lots of them, but they didn't look his way, and he had to jump out of the way of a young man propelling a skateboard down the sidewalk.

He looked up at the street sign. The intersection of 15th and Madison. Two blocks from his apartment, six blocks south of Lee's.

Where to first? It was more important to find out what Lee was doing, but there was something compelling about seeing himself, to know what it was like to look at his own body from the outside. The whole idea was simultaneously terrifying and fascinating. Without even consciously making a decision, he headed toward his own apartment building.

The city by night was familiar and unfamiliar, like the contents of a dream. A metro bus rushed by, and a gust of warm air washed, but the people whose faces looked out of the windows were translucent, gray specters, their edges blurred like an out-of-focus photograph. No one's eyes met his as he walked past, and once, a young man walking hand-in-hand with a laughing girl stepped suddenly to one side to avoid a cracked place in the sidewalk, and there was a clutch of nausea as the man's free hand swept right through his midsection.

Fischer was right. He was a ghost in a city full of ghosts. This was way worse than being in the past. It was like a nightmare he wouldn't wake up from for twenty-four hours.

He hiked another block, and found himself looking up at the tan stone façade of Kingswood East Apartments. The front of the building was a sickly yellow in the streetlight. He fished around in his pocket for his keys, and then put the key into the lock on the entrance… and it turned, no resistance, as if the interior of the lock mechanism wasn't there. He grabbed the handle, rattled the door. An elderly man in a tailored suit and a fedora with a small feather glanced around, gave the door an odd look, and kept walking.

Now what? He was locked out of his own apartment building. And even if he got inside the building, he still wouldn't be able to get into my apartment.

But luck was on his side. A middle-aged woman he'd seen before—she lived on the second floor, he recalled, and had two teenage kids—came bustling out of the door. He moved aside just in time. Not that it would have mattered, she would have walked right through him, but reflexes were hard to change. He ducked inside before the door closed.

The interior hallway led to an elevator, and farther along, a staircase. He opted for the stairs, wondering how the electronic controls on the elevator would respond to someone who, technically, wasn't there. With that not particularly comforting thought, he trotted up to the third floor.

His apartment was 304. He went up to the door, his footsteps making no sound on the worn indoor-outdoor carpet, and stood there, looking up at the three brass numbers he had seen so many times without even registering.

How could he get into his apartment? Would he—the Darren of one day previous, of two weeks previous, of what seemed a whole lifetime previous—even be inside? He didn't bother trying the key. There was no reason to suppose it would work. And after standing there for five minutes, he did what in retrospect was probably the only thing he could have done. He knocked on the door.

There was the sound of footsteps, and the door opened, and there was Darren, looking out into the hall, a perplexed expression on his face.

With a shock bordering on hysteria, he realized that he remembered this happening. He'd just gotten home from the bookstore—and there was a knock on the door—and when he opened it, no one was there. But there had been someone there.

It was him.

An almost painful shiver ran up his spine, and he nearly had the door shut in his face before he remembered why he'd knocked in the first place. As the door was closing, he slipped in, stepping right *through* his other self and into the familiar foyer of his apartment.

Darren watched Darren, as his shadowy doppelgänger went back into the apartment, and busied himself fixing an unimaginative dinner of canned ravioli, some reheated green beans from the previous night, and a bottle of beer.

What had happened next? He'd lived all this before, and yet couldn't remember a single thing from that evening. At that moment he realized how little he ever paid attention to what went on in his life. The big events, the major upsets, were all that stuck. Life, real life, was going on all around him, and for the most part, he ignored it into nonexistence.

No wonder Fischer had said most of the events in the past had no effect. No one paid them any attention, so they could have happened any number of ways, with the same overall outcome. It made the whole Butterfly Effect idea ridiculous.

He had just finished the last forkful of ravioli when the phone rang.

Right. Lee called. That was when he called and said he wanted to have dinner together. How could he have forgotten that?

The shadow Darren stood, went into the kitchen, and picked up the telephone.

"Hello...? Oh, hi Lee. What's up...? I know it has. But you've been busy with everything.... Sure. Tomorrow works fine for me. It's not like I have a social calendar or anything.... Cool. My place or yours...? Sounds good. And don't worry about cooking. I can pick up something on the way there. You got any prefs...? Okay, I'll figure out something. Maybe get some sushi from Sumo or something. Will Sherry be there?"

The Darren on the telephone frowned, a momentary crease of the brow, immediately smoothed. "Oh. Too bad. Okay, then, just us. Looking forward to it... Later, dude."

Shadow Darren put the telephone back in its cradle, and returned to the dinner table to finish the last of his beer while looking at a magazine.

But now the other Darren, the observer, remembered something about that conversation. There had been an odd tone in Lee's voice when he'd said that his girlfriend, Sherry, wouldn't be coming to dinner. Some strange little catch in the voice, a hesitation, there and gone again almost too quickly to notice. At the time, he *had* barely noticed it. It slid across his perception like a leaf on the wind, seen but not really registered. Subliminal. Forgotten as soon as observed.

Like most things in life.

Darren got up, carried the dishes to the sink, and then walked into the living room, dropped into a chair, and picked up the remote.

He did not want to watch himself sitting for an hour in front of reruns of *Buffy the Vampire Slayer*. There were more pressing things. He needed to find Lee, follow him around for a while. There was something here he wasn't understanding, and he wasn't going to figure out what it was stuck in his apartment staring at himself vegging out in front of the television.

Darren-the-Observer looked around his apartment. The whole place was strangely unfamiliar, as if it belonged to another life he'd led, decades ago. He padded silently over to a bookshelf, where the wooden box from his grandmother, Katherine Clevenger Ault, always sat. The box that Per Olafsson had thrown into his arms from a burning building, the one for which Per had made a beautiful silver key, a key that should have been hanging around his neck.

He half expected the box to be gone. Fischer had said that removing it from Norway had yanked it out of the timeline, and that in some abstruse sense, it didn't exist. But the box still sat there, its carvings polished smooth with time and the caress of many hands, in its accustomed place on the bookshelf, looking solid and heavy and real. More real, in fact, than the shadow Darren sitting in the recliner, settling in to watch television.

He gently ran his fingertips across the groove made by the incised figure of a dragon, let it take him back to his childhood, when he'd spent hours looking at the strange, mythological carvings, wondering what they were and who had made them. He wondered now, as he had then, how many hands had done the same thing, only now he realized how far back the box's history went. Almost seven hundred years.

He put both hands on the sides of the box, and tried to lift the lid. It was locked. Probably for the best. Fischer had cautioned him against so much as picking up a pencil. Even though one Darren couldn't see the other, all the objects in the room were clearly visible to both. Darren would certainly see it if he moved anything, to judge by the reaction of the old man who had heard the door rattle. He couldn't imagine what the reaction would be if the box lid suddenly, mysteriously swung open.

Besides, he should have known that he didn't open the box, or at least, that he hadn't noticed it. He'd have remembered that, because he was there, watching *Buffy*, and the box never moved. Perhaps Fischer and Maggie saw all the possibilities, saw everything in flux, but from his standpoint, it was much simpler. Everything is what it is, and there was no changing it. What was in the past happened a certain way— either with his help, or without it. There was no altering that.

That was when he remembered another thing that had happened that evening. While watching Buffy dispatch two creepy-looking floating dudes who had stolen her voice, the front door of his apartment had blown open.

He laughed to himself, but then felt a sudden chill. How many other little, random, inexplicable things had been due to people from the Library, people he couldn't see, watching him and manipulating their surroundings in small ways? That thought didn't bear too much consideration. It was simply too frightening.

He walked over to the door, silently turned the doorknob, and pulled it gently open. The Darren in the armchair looked up, frowned, and stood. Darren-the-Observer slipped unseen out of the door and jogged down the hall as behind him, he heard the apartment door close, latch, and lock.

It was a twenty-minute walk to where Lee lived, in a nice part of north Capitol Hill. But as Darren stood in front of the apartment building, he saw that the windows of Lee's place, a spacious and well-furnished corner apartment, were dark. Lee, apparently, was not at home.

Lee could be anywhere in the Greater Seattle area. Should he wait for him to get back home? Strike off and try to find him? He didn't have a lot of time. He was going to be pulled back to the Library in less than twenty-four hours whether he figured this out or not. He had to get information, and quickly.

He cast his mind back to the last time he'd seen Lee—that ill-fated dinner, sitting there at Lee's dinner table in front of trays of sushi and miso soup, and Lee looking uncomfortable and fidgety. And he remembered a piece of the conversation, the conversation that had ended with Lee pulling out a gun.

"You look tired tonight. Too many late nights with Sherry?"

Lee had jumped a little at the name. "No. No, it isn't that. I wish it was. Too many late nights in the lab."

"You need to take it easy, dude. You're gonna burn out."

"I'm on the verge. If I can get results, it'll make my career. I can't let it drop now, not when I'm this close. I've been there late every night this week."

"What are you working on?"

Lee's face had changed when he asked that, as if he'd come to some sort of a decision. "I don't think I can explain it, because I'm not entirely sure what it implies myself. But it's going to overturn everything we thought we knew about physics."

"That sounds momentous."

"Yeah." Lee looked down at his empty soup bowl, his handsome face still, unmoving, unreadable. "Momentous. Yeah, it is."

"You don't seem very excited about it."

"Excited?" Lee gave a grim laugh. "There's such a thing as knowing more than you should."

"Damn, Lee, what is wrong with you? I've never seen you like this."

And Lee had looked him right in the face, and said, "It's nothing. At least, nothing that this won't fix."

And he pulled out a pistol, and shot him squarely in the forehead.

***

That was all. No information. No statement of what Darren had done to merit murder. Just some talk about his research, and once again, that momentary catch in the voice when Sherry's name was mentioned. Either of which could have been relevant, or not. There was no way to tell.

However, the one thing that seemed likely was that Lee wasn't out partying, or with his girlfriend. He was in his lab on the second floor of the Physics/Astronomy Building at the University of Washington, working on whatever abstruse experiments about the arrow of time currently occupied his brilliant mind.

He glanced into a Starbucks, where a clock said 7:40 PM. It was a good hour's walk to the campus, perhaps more, and no guarantee he'd be able to get inside the building once he got there. But here fate took a hand—if fate wasn't what had, all along, been driving him to do what he did.

This time, fate took the shape of a portly gentleman with a briefcase, flagging down a taxi and shouting "U District" at the cabbie in unnecessarily stentorian tones.

Before Darren could question his decision, he'd slid behind/across/through the portly man and into the back seat of the cab, and then sat, watching the man set his briefcase on his lap and fumble with his wallet.

That was fortuitous. He wrestled his backpack from his shoulders and set it in his lap. It was like it was meant to happen. Of course, Maggie would disagree. To her, choice was the most important thing. There was no such thing as destiny, it was all up in the air until individuals made their decisions. And who was he to argue? Of course, that meant the Calvinists were wrong.

Oh, well, he'd never liked them much to begin with.

He looked at the man, who had opened his briefcase and was rummaging through some manila folders. He reached out one hand, and passed it right through the man's head. The man didn't react.

He yelled, "Hey, you!" right in the man's ear.

No response.

"Weird. At least if I was a real ghost, I could scare someone. This is more like being nonexistent."

As choice would have it—since he had ruled out fate as a determining factor—the portly man was headed to the Magnuson Health Sciences Center, a two-minute walk from the Physics/Astronomy Building. As his unwitting ride paid the fare and maneuvered his feet out onto the sidewalk, Darren slipped out and jogged lightly up the sidewalk and into the crosswalk on Pacific Street. Ahead of him was the glass and red brick façade of the building that housed Lee's lab.

And that's when he bumped into a little old lady in the crosswalk who was heading the other way.

"Oh, I'm sorry," he said instinctively, before it registered with him that he not only had struck another real, solid human being, but she was looking at him crossly and brushing her sleeve where he had hit her.

"Watch where you're going, young man," the little old lady said.

"I'm so sorry, how clumsy of me." He watched her trot away, giving off disapproval in waves. Then he turned and continued his way across Pacific Street, and it was only when he stepped onto the sidewalk that he realized what must be the truth, and stopped, his heart pounding in his chest.

Fischer said that he wouldn't be able to interact with anyone who had disappeared when the temporal paradox had occurred—anyone who did not have a locked end track. That is, anyone who was alive at the time.

So the little old lady must have died some time in the next twenty-four hours.

He turned and looked, but she had already vanished into the night.

Should he find her and warn her? But what good would that do? He didn't know how she died—a heart attack, a car accident, a fall down some stairs. Even if she believed him—which was unlikely—what, exactly, would he be warning her against?

He grimaced. This sucked. Maybe the Calvinists were right, after all. Or maybe both sides were wrong. Maybe *all* the philosophers were wrong. After all, even Fischer, who should know what was going to happen if anyone did, wished him luck with trying to figure out what was going on. Maybe everyone was just whistling in the dark, and pretending they knew what they were doing when no one actually had a clue.

The bulk of the Physics/Astronomy Building rose before him, a sprawling complex of classrooms, offices, and labs he had only been in once, a year ago, to meet Lee for lunch.

This time, his luck—or fate, or chance, or whatever—had its attention turned elsewhere. The front door was securely locked. He backed up and scanned the building. There were a couple of lights on, probably in labs or offices, but no way to see into them. His memory of his single visit to the lab was insufficient even to indicate which side of the building Lee's lab was on.

More than ever, what he had to do seemed impossible.

He walked around to the rear of the building, and saw that one of the only cars in the parking lot was Lee's trim little silver Audi. At least that meant his hunch was right. Lee was here. But the likelihood of his being able to pull another sneak entrance, as he did in his own apartment building, was slim. It wasn't as if there was going to be a lot of people going in and out of the Physics/Astronomy Building at eight o'clock at night.

He found a bench under a fir tree, and sat down. Waiting seemed the only option. How late did scientists work? He pictured all of the old science fiction movies, with scientists in basement laboratories hovering at midnight over bubbling beakers of green, viscous liquids. Lee's lab wasn't like that—it was gleaming and spotlessly clean, and filled with equipment made of shining metal and glass—but still, he couldn't shake the image of the mad scientist, working alone at night, and periodically giving the obligatory maniacal cackle and rubbing of the hands together.

What had Lee found out? It had to be something connecting Lee and him. Why would killing him "fix" what was wrong?

He leaned back, his brow furrowing. Lee had spent years working on experiments involving time. What if the physicist had somehow got a glimpse of the future, and saw something he didn't like... something involving him? Something involving Sherry?

He sat up, an astonished expression on his face. Did Lee see him with Sherry? Like... *with* her? But how on earth could that happen? It's not like he would ever...

But the more he thought about it, the more sense it made. If Lee had somehow, through one of his experiments, caught a glimpse of the future, and it was a future where Sherry left Lee for him, that would explain why he did what he did.

He had known Lee since they were children, and knew Lee's personality to the last detail. Honest to a fault, as straight an arrow as there ever was, but don't ever deceive him, don't ever lie. He remembered the one time he'd seen Lee get into an actual fight, in high school—when a supposed friend had started a rumor about Lee, to the effect that Lee had lied on his application to get into National Honor Society. As if he'd needed to. As if that was even credible.

But it hadn't mattered. Lying about Lee, and worse, insinuating Lee himself had been dishonest, had resulted in a bloody nose each, a split lip for the guy who had started the rumor, and three days' suspension for both. It had been the only time he had ever seen Lee in trouble at school, and afterwards, he was completely unrepentant.

Could that be it? Could he have seen Sherry, somehow, improbably, cheating on him with Darren, and decided that his deception—whether now or in the future—could only be fixed by getting him out of the way, permanently?

The temperature fell rapidly, the cool dampness of a Pacific Northwest March day being replaced by a gnawing, bone-deep chill. He huddled beneath his windbreaker, trying to will his teeth to stop chattering.

An hour passed by, then two. The noises of the city by night gradually faded down to a dull roar as the majority of Seattle's residents found their way home for the evening. He didn't have a watch, but he looked up at the moon, faint and fitful behind a haze of clouds, and guessed it was close to 11 PM. And that was when the side door of the Physics/Astronomy Building opened and Lee came out.

He was dressed impeccably, as always, in a long, elegant jacket, a gray scarf, and a dark British-looking driving cap. He carried a briefcase, and tugged his jacket around him as he trotted down the stairs.

Darren jumped up and ran toward him, resisting the impulse to call out. Lee wouldn't hear him. No one would, unless the doomed little old lady was still around, and she certainly wouldn't want to hear what he had to say.

Lee clicked the automatic key on his key chain, and the silver Audi's lights flashed twice. There was a *thunk* as the locks turned. Lee got inside, started the car, and turned on the heater, but didn't close the door immediately. He remained with one of his long legs outside, and pulled out his cell phone.

Darren slipped through him and clambered over the stick shift into the passenger seat, wishing as it jabbed into his thigh that the objects in this queer ghost world were as insubstantial as the people were.

"Hi," Lee said. "I hope I didn't wake you… I wanted to see how you were doing… No, I'm not worried." He smiled, and laughed a little, but the laugh seemed forced. "I don't know, I was thinking about you… Oh, I'm just finishing up at the lab… No, don't worry about me, I'll be done with this round of experiments soon, and then I'll have more time…" His voice got softer. "Yeah, I miss you, too… I know, it's been way too long. Soon, I promise… Take care… I love you, too… Bye."

Lee shut off his cell phone with a harsh sigh, and shoved it into his jacket pocket. He put his car into gear with what seemed unnecessary force, and his face set in an angry scowl, he backed up and then drove out of the parking lot.

That was it. Lee was checking up on his girlfriend because he thought she was cheating. His forehead wrinkled in incomprehension. How could Lee think that? Why on earth would Sherry want him over Lee?

Then, with some amazement, he realized his recent adventures had shown that he was not quite as hopeless in the romance department as he'd thought. With a renewed pang he remembered Maíre Gillacomgain kissing him—*Unfair, just completely unfair*—and even Jane Bell, who had clearly not been interested in him as a lover, had thought it odd that he had none.

Maybe Sherry, in their two or three casual encounters, had somehow gotten a crush on him? He tried to recall what had happened during those meetings, but couldn't think of anything of significance. Nothing she'd said had indicated anything more than mild interest in someone who was her boyfriend's childhood pal. And certainly, nothing he could remember saying was anything that could be construed as flirtatious.

But what other explanation could there be?

It was after eleven, so the Seattle gridlock had tapered off, and the drive to Lee's apartment only took twenty minutes. Lee pulled his car into a parking space, shut it off, and got out so quickly that Darren almost got his hand caught in the door.

He followed Lee into the building. That would just be awesome. Stuck in the past with a broken hand, invisible to everyone except a poor little old lady who might already be dead. But he got into Lee's apartment without mishap, followed Lee around while he took off his jacket, opened the fridge and got a bottle of beer, and did other completely mundane things. Lee sat down in a recliner, opened a science journal of some sort, and proceeded to read for twenty minutes while drinking his beer.

He watched Lee, waiting for something to happen.

Nothing did.

All of this had been of dubious benefit so far. He looked around for a place to sit—maybe Lee couldn't see him, but he'd be mighty alarmed if a rocking chair suddenly moved or the sofa cushions dimpled under the pressure of an invisible butt. He finally took his backpack off, sat down cross-legged on the floor, and went into a semi-doze.

Lee set down the empty bottle by the recliner, tossed his magazine onto an end table, and got up. Darren became alert once more, but it turned out Lee had just decided to go to bed. He turned the light off and walked out of the room, a light in a farther room came on, there was the sound of tooth-brushing, peeing, a toilet flushing, and then footsteps. Then the quiet swishing of Lee getting undressed, followed by the noise of bedsprings creaking.

The lights went out.

This was pointless. He could have gotten a good night's sleep in a real bed, and showed up tomorrow morning, and it wouldn't have been a problem. He unzipped the backpack Fischer had given him, pulled out a plastic bag with a peanut-butter-and-jelly sandwich, and took a bite.

Instead, here he was. Stuck, accomplishing nothing but eating a sandwich, while in less than a day all of humanity was going to vanish, and he hadn't the first idea of what to do about it.. Fischer may have been a little hasty in his vote of confidence. He finished the sandwich, then took off his windbreaker, bundled it, and set it down on the floor. Then he curled up on his side, his head on his makeshift pillow, and fell into an uneasy sleep.

Darren woke up in the middle of the night, groggy and confused, unable at first to remember where he was.

He'd been in so many places and so many different time periods in the last week that it was getting to the point that he never knew where he was going to wake up. He reoriented his brain. Seattle. Lee's apartment. The present, or close enough.

He sat up, and looked around. Light came from Lee's bedroom. The gleaming red digits on the digital clock on a bookcase stood at 2:14. There was the sound of footsteps, and Lee came out of his bedroom, wearing jeans and pulling on a shirt. His blond hair was tousled with sleep, but he didn't bother to comb it. He sat down on the sofa, donned socks and shoes, then grabbed his jacket, wallet, and keys, and headed for the door.

Darren jumped up and followed him, remembering at the last moment to take his backpack and windbreaker, which was still wadded up on the floor where it had served as a pillow.

They walked silently out of the building and then across the parking lot. Fog shrouded the city, and even the ubiquitous traffic noise was muffled and distant. Lee got into his car —Darren once again narrowly missing getting caught in the door—and pulled out onto the street.

They'd only gone a couple of blocks when he realized that they could only be going one place—back to the lab.

Lee's face was knotted in a frown as he drove. He was speeding—in fact, he ran a stop sign once he saw no one was coming from the cross street, muttering, "Fuck it," under his breath as he did so. He spoke out loud a couple of times, once mumbling something Darren couldn't hear well enough to understand, and another time saying something like, "… way to check if it's certain or only possible."

Back to the empty parking lot next to the Physics/Astronomy Building. Darren clambered over the stick shift, and dove out through the car door as it closed, scraping both palms on the asphalt. He got up, swearing under his breath, and jogged after Lee, who stroke toward the entrance with an I'm-On-A-Mission pace.

"I'm going to need a month to recover from all of my scrapes, cuts, and bruises," he mumbled, as Lee used a card key to let himself in.

Lee, of course, didn't respond, but pulled the door open, letting himself and Darren into the fluorescent-lit hallway.

Up a set of stairs, down a further hallway, and up to a door festooned with *Far Side* cartoons, an engraved plate that said "High Energy Physics Laboratory," and a handwritten sign underneath that said, "Unauthorized Individuals Will Be Vaporized." A sign next to the door read, "DANGER! When the red light is on, lasers are in use in the lab. DO NOT ENTER WITHOUT APPROPRIATE PROTECTIVE EYEWEAR."

The red light was off, to his relief. Lee went in, flipped on the fluorescent lights, and hung his coat on a hook. He went past several heavy tables laden with gleaming equipment that sprouted wires and cables like Medusa's reptilian coiffure.

The brushed nickel front of each was festooned with dials, knobs, switches, and digital displays, dark at the moment. Heavy glass windows showed dimly-visible arrays of lenses and magnets. There were legends Darren only vaguely understood—*Sync. Frequency scaler. Rate scaler. Event timer. Mode select. Attitude. Beam collimation. Scatter. Magnetic field strength. Freeze/resume. Flux density. Reset.*

Lee sat down in front of a row of machines, and flipped a switch. There was a whir and a hum as power began to flow through it. Displays lit up, and something in the middle that looked like a flat-screen television glowed with a gray, neutral light. Lee pulled a notebook from a nearby shelf, opened it, flipped a few pages, and stared down at the page with a scowl of an intensity that looked as if it should cause the pages to ignite.

Darren came up and looked over his shoulder. There was neat, even script at the top of the page. After an indecipherable list of dial settings and equations, it said,

Split quantum state established at 14.5 keV/m^3 multiple at 23.8 keV/m^3 Projection begins at higher energies—stable threshold achieved. Images appear to be stable and from forward time sequence. Confirmed 9 March 2016.

The brightness on the screen gradually increased, and the whole thing became a pale, flat gray, the color of high clouds on an overcast day. Lee leaned over and adjusted more dials and switches. Digital readouts glowed red, their numbers communicating nothing to Darren other than awe at Lee's brilliance, something he'd felt during their entire friendship.

Lee used the dials labeled "Rate scaler" and "Flux density," gradually turning one clockwise, waiting, then turning the other, then waiting, back and forth. The brightness on the screen reached a pure white. Lee stared at blankness, his forehead creased, waiting for something, his eyes registering a combination of anger, frustration, and longing.

There was a sudden crackling noise, and the numbers on one digital display jumped. The solid white image on the screen streaked, fragmented, and rippling ghost images played across its surface. He continued to turn the two dials clockwise. A second crackling noise, then a third and a fourth in rapid succession. The images on the screen darkened, resolving and fading like faces behind a curtain blowing in the breeze.

Another gradual twist on the dials. The images clarified further. They were definitely human forms, but still vague, shifting and merging with the gray background. Then there was a rush of white noise, like a burst of radio static during an electrical storm, and the picture cleared, resolving into sharp-edged faces like pen-and-ink sketches. Three people were there, images surreal and incomplete but nonetheless recognizable. Darren's heart pounded against his ribcage.

He'd known who he'd see. He'd known, from the moment he heard Lee talking to his girlfriend.

He just hadn't wanted to believe it.

The three people on the screen were Lee, Darren, and Sherry.

The figures moved around each other in a jerky, angry way, the lines bending and merging on the screen. One, then another of them spoke, to judge by the movement of their mouths, but there was no sound. Lee's figure gestured with one hand. He was clearly in the grip of some high emotion.

With a swirl and a blur, the images of Darren and Lee collided. They were fighting, wrestling, their faces twisted with anger. Sherry stood a little way away, her mouth open, eyes wide and horrified.

Then her image was rocked backwards. A dark, jagged mark appeared in the middle of her torso. She looked downwards, the horror in her expression changing to astonishment, and then her knees buckled and she collapsed to the floor. The two men separated, their chests heaving with exertion, and turned toward Sherry's inert form.

Darren held a small, but deadly-looking, handgun.

Lee—the real Lee—pressed the button marked *Freeze/Resume*, and sat for a while as motionless as the image on the screen. Darren looked in wonder at the lines depicting his own, familiar face, lines twisted almost out of recognition by rage. Or was it fear? Or a sudden, dawning comprehension? It was impossible to tell. Drawings were only that—a bunch of lines, about which you had to create the underlying meaning. But there was no denying what else the image depicted. Sherry, bleeding her life away from a gunshot wound to the chest. Darren, standing over her holding a gun. Lee, his back to the viewer, only a part of his profile visible, but every pixel in the image radiating grief.

So, that was it. He was not going to have an affair with Sherry. He was going to kill her. And Lee decided to kill him first, to stop it from happening.

A voice in his head, sounding breathless and terrified, said, *It can't be. It can't be true. I would never kill anyone.*

But he had. He had killed Crenshaw. He had him pinned down, helpless and injured, and hit him over the head with a stone. He'd killed once, he could do it again.

But that wasn't the same thing. Crenshaw was a rogue murderer. He'd done it to protect Jane.

Could there have been a reason that he killed Sherry? It was in the future. There was no way to tell how far into the future it was. Maybe between now and then, he'd have come up with a perfectly good rationalization for killing her.

Just like he'd done with Crenshaw.

A wash of vertigo swept over him. He felt disassociated, like he was floating. He could feel his heart pounding against his ribs, and the shuddery sensation of adrenaline pouring into his veins, but a part of his brain just let go. Separation, floating upwards and away.

No. Get a grip. The voice in his mind sounded a little like Maggie Carmichael. *You have a job to do. Don't you dare go weak sister on us now. You know that the future isn't written, isn't locked into place, until the people who make the decisions get there and decide what it's going to look like.*

That was Lee's mistake—he got a glimpse of the future through his fancy machine, and decided that it was inevitable, that he had to do everything he could to stop it. And look what happened. His actions created a paradox that wiped out everyone.

Don't like the idea of this being the future? Then use your brains, Darren Ault. Lee propelled himself from one horrible possibility into another, worse one, one where not only his girlfriend but the entire human race was destroyed. You've got more perspective, Darren. You've learned how this works. Maybe that's why you ended up in the Library. So you could understand enough to make the right decisions when the time comes. So you could see enough of how our decisions now create the future that you will do what it takes to make sure that everything is put right again.

But that would mean that there is one right path, and that everything is meant to happen a particular way. Right?

Don't think about it too hard, came Maggie's voice. *It's a mystery. There's a way in which we are free to choose, and a way in which what will happen a billion years from now was foreordained one microsecond after the Big Bang. That's what the proponents of free will and the proponents of predestination don't understand— they're both right, and they're both wrong, and neither one really understands the reality. As for you, you have to trust that when you act from your heart, guided by your brain, that things will unfold as they should.*

Really?

Yes. Maggie's voice became a little wry. *Of course, you must also remember that this is all just a bunch of voices in your head. Probably best not to put too much stock in what they tell you.*

He gave himself a little shake, and looked back down at Lee, who still stared at the screen. His face was wet with tears, but he wasn't sobbing. He sat there motionless, eyes streaming, looking at the image of his best friend holding a gun that was still pointed at the crumpled body of his dying girlfriend.

How could he stop this from happening? And why had it happened in the first place? Darren didn't even own a gun.

But Lee did. Darren knew that. Because in eighteen hours, it would be pointed at the middle of Darren's forehead, propelling him into the Library of Timelines and the rest of humanity into oblivion. But even if it was Lee's gun, it was Darren's hand that it rested in, Darren's finger that pulled the trigger.

Lee reached out and pushed *Freeze/Resume*. The images started moving again. The figure of Darren dropped the gun, turned toward Lee. Lee ran to Sherry, partly lifted her from the floor, his form curled over her as if he could shield her from death. Then his face turned toward Darren, his handsome features pinched with hatred and rage, and his mouth opened to snarl words that neither of the men standing there could hear.

Lee grabbed both of the dials, gave them a sharp twist to the left, and the screen went dark. Then he sat there, staring, his eyes still flooded with tears he did not even bother to brush away as they spattered his shirt.

It was a glimpse of the future. Of one possible future. Somehow, Lee's machine had allowed him to see one thing that could happen, and finding that out changed everything. But how could he fix it?

The first thing to do was to stop himself from going over to Lee's apartment. Maybe that wouldn't fix things permanently. It wouldn't stop Lee from hunting him down somewhere else. But at least it might give him a little more time. That's what he needed... time. It was after midnight, already the Big Day. Doomsday for Humanity. *Homo sapiens* had survived the Rapture and the Mayan Apocalypse, but this one was going to be the real deal, tonight at a little after 7:30.

And then an idea—a tiny flicker, like a firefly in the woods on a moonless night—shimmered before him. At first, he pushed it away as ridiculous, facile, a *deus ex machina* that couldn't possibly work. Could it be that simple? To stop the world from ending, that was all he had to do?

But that's what it boiled down to. There were millions of events that had virtually no effect on anything, and a small handful that had profound ones. The problem was, you never knew ahead of time which were which. But he knew one thing that could prevent a catastrophe, at least for a little while. After that... well, there still remained to be determined why Lee shooting Darren had caused a paradox that had destroyed the entire human race. But right now, stopping it seemed more important than figuring out why it had happened.

Lee suddenly backed his chair up, narrowly missing running the wheel over Darren's foot. He stood up, then with the side of his hand pressed three switches simultaneously. With an electronic sigh, the hum of the machine died into silence. He strode over to the coat hook, retrieved his jacket, and was through the door of the lab almost too fast for Darren to follow him.

He tailed after Lee at a near-run, down the stairs, down a long half-darkened hallway lined with the closed and locked doors of classrooms, labs, and offices, toward a sign marked *Exit*. Lee thrust the door open, and Darren slipped out behind him into the raw March night.

It was still completely dark. He guessed the time was about 3:30, and there wasn't even a hint of pearl gray on the eastern skyline. Lee's long stride propelled him across the parking lot, there was a flash of light as he used his remote to unlock his car doors, and he opened the door of the silver Audi.

Darren leaped toward the door, and missed. The door slammed shut, narrowly missing his arm, but it closed on the strap of his backpack. He struggled to free it, unsuccessfully. He thought, briefly, about casting aside Fischer's command not to mess with things, and opening the car door.

But before he could talk himself into it, Lee threw the Audi into reverse, and he was yanked backwards. His butt made solid contact with the blacktop, but the impact dislodged first one arm and then the other from the backpack's straps. Lee's car glided away, the backpack, and the food it contained, still hanging from the door, invisible to everyone but Darren.

He struggled to his feet, brushing off the seat of his pants, as the Audi disappeared around a bend in the road.

"Well, fuck!" he shouted. "*Now* what do I do?"

There was, of course, only one thing he *could* do. He started walking back toward the bridge across Portage Bay and his only way to get back to his apartment.

As he trudged down Pacific Avenue toward Roosevelt Way and the bridge to Capitol Hill, his face set in a scowl, it started to drizzle.

"This is ridiculous," he said, pulling his windbreaker closer around him. "Fischer should have chosen someone tougher than me to save the human race."

But of course, Fischer *hadn't* chosen him. He had been chosen because, improbable as it seemed, he was somehow the linchpin. What he did, whether he lived or died, mattered.

Cars swished by, their drivers invisible shadows in the dark. The blocks slid past in the chill, damp night, most buildings only illuminated by streetlights, their owners away or asleep.

Like he desperately wanted to be. Like he would be first chance I got. Because what he needed to do couldn't be done till this evening in any case, so damned if he wasn't going to find a dry place to have a nap first.

He crossed the Roosevelt Way Bridge, staying as close as possible to the guardrail to avoid being sideswiped. The cars could easily kill him, even if their drivers couldn't see him. He made it across Portage Bay safely, then followed it down toward Capitol Hill and his apartment building.

It was 4:30 and the eastern sky showed a faint streak of light by the time he once again stood in front of the Kingswood East Apartments. His doppelgänger would still be inside, sound asleep under a down comforter, and wouldn't wake for several hours. The bookstore didn't open until ten, and except for days when he had to do inventory or work on his tax papers, he could sleep in until nine and still get there with plenty of time to spare.

But someone must have to get to work early, and would come through the door to let him in. He sat down on the bumper of a car facing the entrance, and composed himself to wait.

Forty-five minutes later a very grumpy-looking middle-aged man with a briefcase and a paunch came through the door, and Darren by this time was so cold and miserable he almost didn't react in time. But he made it through the door before it closed and locked, into the comparative warmth of the foyer, then bounded up the stairs toward the third floor. He stood in front of the door for a moment. Phase one of his plan was complete. He could relax for a little while. With a sigh, he lay down on his back on the floor with his hands cupped behind his head. He was soaking wet and still chilled to the bone, but even so was asleep within a minute.

Darren woke up after several hours of uncomfortable and fitful sleep to the sound of someone thumping around on the other side of the wall. He opened his eyes slowly, feeling once again that confusion that came from a combination of insufficient sleep, stress, anxiety, and time travel. It took him a moment to realize that the sound was his alter ego opening the coat closet, as always banging the external door with the closet doorknob. There was the sound of a door closing, and then the outside door being unlatched.

He sprang to his feet, and as soon as the door opened, he jumped forward, and he and his other self switched places. The door closed and locked behind him.

Maybe he was getting the hang of being a ghost. He glanced around the inside of his apartment and tried to catch his breath.

He walked over to the window, and watched himself exit the building, and disappear around the corner toward the parking lot. After a moment, his blue Toyota Corolla pulled into traffic and disappeared toward the bookstore.

Okay, dry clothes. Food. Nap. In that order. He went into his bedroom, and retrieved boxers, t-shirt, and cargo pants, and pulled off his clammy, damp clothing. He trotted off to his bathroom, toweled dry, and then returned to the bedroom to dress.

He paused with one leg in the boxers. Wouldn't he notice the wet clothes in the hamper? Then he shrugged. If he noticed, he noticed. They were his clothes, and it wasn't like he usually thought much about what he was wearing in any case.

Then he stopped, his eyes widening a little.

The clothes in his dresser belonged to this timeline. So if he put them on, when the other Darren came home, he'd see empty clothes walking around. Like the Invisible Man, or something. But he couldn't spend the rest of his time here bare-ass naked, even though it was his apartment, and no one could see him.

And he didn't even want to think about Fischer's reaction

if he showed up back in the Library with no clothes on.

He pulled off the boxers, and stuffed them and the clean, dry clothes back into his dresser with a disgruntled snort. Then he picked up his wet clothes, still lying in a heap where he'd dropped them on the floor, and brought them over to his little clothes dryer, which stood in an alcove near his bathroom, on top of an equally tiny washing machine, pushed them in, set it, and pressed start.

The clothes would take a while to dry. He could walk around naked until they were done. Next order of business, though, was food. Fischer had cautioned him about eating anything. Why? He was ravenously hungry. The last thing he'd eaten had been the peanut butter and jelly sandwich the previous evening, and before that, he couldn't even remember.

What possible harm could eating something do, other than there being food missing? Like with his clothes, he was only minimally aware of what was in his fridge. The idea of his recognizing if an egg or a couple of slices of bread were gone was ridiculous. A real hot breakfast, that was what he wanted.

He once again paused, this time with his hand on the package of bacon.

Wait. He was invisible to everyone, but nothing else was. Fischer had said that if he picked up a pencil, people would see the pencil floating up into the air. So, if he ate something, would everyone see the food as it sat in his stomach... and then intestines... just kind of floating there, moving around... and then...?

He set the bacon down, his feelings of hunger replaced by mild nausea.

Maybe he'd skip breakfast after all.

"Well, hell," he said. "This whole thing sucks. No one can hear me or see me, I can't put on clothes, and I can't eat. Just *peachy*. Well, at least I can take a nap."

He went back into the bedroom. He never made the bed. The down comforter was still pulled back in a rumpled snarl, just as he'd left it that morning.

If he was asleep, he wouldn't be aware that he was hungry. That was his last thought as he finally, deliciously, slid between the sheets of his own bed. He pulled the comforter up, and drifted off into a dreamless sleep.

When Darren woke up from this second, and much more satisfying, nap of the day, he could tell that a great deal more time had elapsed. The gray light slanting through the window was different. His stomach had reached new and alarming levels of hunger pangs. He rolled over. The clock read 4:37. He had slept for over six hours, and still felt as if he could easily have closed his eyes and slept for another six. But his alter ego would be home at a little after five, to take a quick shower and then head off to Lee's, and his rendezvous with a pistol.

He got up, straightened the blankets into as close to their original positions as he could recall, and padded barefoot out into the living room. He retrieved his clothes from the dryer —still slightly warm—and put them on. He tossed Fischer's windbreaker over the back of a chair, and returned to the living room to wait.

He sat on his sofa, watching the minutes tick away. He would have to move quickly once his chance came. The only opportunity would come when his alter ego was in the shower. A tremor passed through his body. If this didn't work —well, there wouldn't be a second shot at it. He would be propelled thereafter on an inexorable path that would lead to Lee's apartment and the gunshot that would end everything.

At 5:15, right on schedule, there was the sound of a key in a lock, and his past self walked into the apartment, humming tunelessly under his breath. He carried a folder stuffed with papers. Business tax forms, which were to be delivered the following day to his accountant, a day that he hadn't known would never come. He tossed them on the kitchen counter, opened the fridge and got out a beer, then consulted his watch and gave a snort of annoyance.

With a sudden surreal feeling, he realized that he remembered this happening. He was going to have a beer, then realized he needed to take a shower because he was all dusty from hauling boxes of books down from the bookstore attic, and he wouldn't have time for both. He'd put the beer back and opted for the shower.

His alter ego put the beer back in the fridge, and headed for the shower.

Darren-the-Observer followed him into the bedroom, and watched—feeling weirdly uncomfortable—as his other self undressed and headed for the bathroom. There was the sound of the shower being turned on, and the squeak of the curtain being pulled back.

Now. This would be his only chance.

He went over to the bed, where his doppelgänger had thrown his clothes, picked up the jeans, and rooted around in the pocket. He pulled out the car keys, wondering for a moment what his other self would have done if he'd walked out that moment, and seen the key ring hovering motionless in mid-air. Then he carried them out of the room, went into the kitchen, opened a cabinet door, and deposited them inside an open box of Froot Loops.

Then he returned to the sofa to wait.

Ten minutes later, a freshly-washed Darren came out, wearing a clean pair of boxers and pulling on a Dave Matthews Band t-shirt—the same set of clothes he had been wearing on his arrival at the Library, he noticed with a shudder. The ones still wore. He picked up the jeans from the bed, gave them a superficial look and evidently decided they were clean enough, and donned them as well. He walked to the phone, selected a menu from a tattered stack between the phone and the wall, and after a moment's perusal, dialed.

"Hello?... yes, I'd like to place an order for pickup... Darren... 387-9806... Yes, I'd like the Golden Dragon Platter... let's see... a side of yellowtail sashimi... and two cups of miso soup... Yes, that's it... Well, as soon as you can... Okay, I'll be there in a half-hour. Thanks."

He hung up and reached for his jacket. Then a frown crossed his face. He reached into his pants pocket, and the frown deepened. He checked his jacket pockets, then went into the bedroom and looked on, then under, the bed.

Here's where the two timelines diverged. He had no memory of this happening. And of course, he wouldn't. He belonged to the other time line, the one where he went to Lee's apartment and got shot in the head.

There followed a rather random wandering around the apartment. He pulled back sofa cushions, the down comforter and pillows, looked under the recliner and kitchen table and end table. He gradually became more agitated, and began talking to himself.

"I know I had them when I came in... otherwise I wouldn't have been able to unlock the door... I don't think I set them down anywhere, I just put them back in my pocket because I knew I'd be leaving..."

He did not, fortunately, think to look in the box of Froot Loops.

A half-hour later, frustrated and irritated, he called Sumo to tell them he wouldn't be in to pick up the sushi. They were clearly annoyed.

"Look," he said, "I'm sorry. But I've lost my car keys and I don't have any way to get there. You'll have to sell it to someone else. Someone's bound to order that tonight, right? I can't do anything about this."

They apparently accepted this with some reluctance, and

he hung up with a loud snort.

Afterwards, he called Lee.

"Hey, dude," he said, "I'm gonna have to take a rain check on our dinner tonight. I've lost my car keys… yeah, seriously. I had them when I came home, and now they've evaporated… No, look, I've already cancelled the sushi and they were pissed off about it. I should have thought to tell them that, but I didn't, and honestly, I'm feeling irritated and not much like visiting. I *hate* losing things, and I have to find them, or I'll have to take the bus to work tomorrow, and I'd really rather not do that. So can we do it another night…? Okay, thanks… Sorry."

He hung up, frowning a little.

He gave a perfunctory effort to further searching—which, of course, turned up nothing—and finally gave up and plunked down onto the sofa.

And the minutes ticked toward 7:30.

Darren-the-Observer went over and stood in the middle of the living room in front of his other self, who had picked up a *Time* magazine and was idly leafing through it. And at 7:34 and 5 seconds, Saturday, March 12, 2016, for one fleeting moment the two Darrens saw each other, and two pairs of identical eyes flew open wide in astonishment.

Then there was a snapping noise, like an overstretched rubber band breaking, and the two of them were thrown toward each other. There was a confused, jumbled second during which two brains with different experiences intersected, fused, questioned, and finally integrated.

Then he opened his eyes. He was sitting on the couch. The magazine was face down on the floor. The seconds ticked past and then away from 7:34 and 5 seconds Pacific Standard Time, and nothing happened.

And he stood, went into the kitchen and opened the cabinet, and from a half-empty box of Froot Loops retrieved his missing keys.

part five

accidents and
corrections

· · ·

Darren stood in the kitchen for a moment, feeling like a deer facing a hunter. It couldn't be over. Just like that? He stood, completely still, for about five minutes, waiting for something to happen, but around him his apartment was as calm and quiet and ordinary as ever. He had a peculiar sensation of remembering two separate versions of the previous five minutes—he could distinctly recall looking for his keys, but he could equally distinctly recall *watching* himself look for his keys. He gave a little shake of his head, as if to clear the fog, and then willed himself to think about something else, and the sensation faded. He was back to being himself, one person, plain Darren Ault the bookstore owner.

But before he could think of what he should do next, there were two things he had to check. Neither of them were really that critical, given that he had bigger things to think about, such as how to keep Lee from killing him the next time they met, and wiping out the human race again. But still, curiosity makes powerful demands, and before he could settle his mind into how to prevent another catastrophe, he had to have the answers to two questions.

He went over to the dinner table, and looked at the chair where he'd thrown Fischer's windbreaker.

It was gone.

He smiled. Things were being righted. The windbreaker certainly didn't belong here. Perhaps it had gone back to the Library, or maybe it had just vanished. Whatever obscure Law of Conservation of Stuff governed objects from the Library had probably pulled the jacket out of this time line and sent it back where it belonged.

He returned to the living room, and walked up to the bookshelf. His grandmother's wooden box was still in its accustomed place on the shelf. He reached inside his t-shirt, and there, hanging from a slender chain, was the key Per Olafsson had made 650 years ago. He pulled the chain over his head, and with a strange feeling of trepidation fitted the key into the lock. It turned smoothly, the bolt shooting back with a soft *snick.*

He lifted the lid, and removed the knick-knacks, smiling as he recalled Per's amusement at the term, setting them on the shelf next to the box. Then he reached in, and pushed on the bottom of the box to slide it over and open the secret compartment he had never dreamed existed.

The mechanism was stuck. Who knew how long it had been since it had been opened? Had anyone since Per Olafsson's time known that there was a way to open the bottom of the box? It was impossible to tell.

Finally, with a little crunching noise, the false bottom came free, and the base plate slid to the side. He tipped the box over. The thin wooden sheet swung on its hinges, creaking slightly, and two slips of paper fluttered out and landed on the floor. Both were yellowed with age, and looked fragile, as if rough handling might crumble them to dust.

He picked them up, and opened the first. It had a brief message, in dark, blocky letters, written with a rough charcoal pencil:

DAREN KARLSSON Takk Per O.

Darren smiled. His maternal grandfather was from Denmark. He knew enough of Scandinavian languages to understand. Per Olafsson, using his peculiar second sight, had sent him a message down through the centuries—even though in this timeline he and Per had never met.

The silversmith was an odd, odd man. He gently set the first piece of paper down on the bookshelf. But he hoped that whatever happened to Per in the end, it wasn't burning to death in his own workshop. He hoped Per found his lover, and they had their children, and all was as it should have been. Since Per had thanked him, it must be something like that, but he probably would never know for sure.

He opened the second piece of paper. This one was in a modern, rather scrawly handwriting. It read,

Yo, Ault! Awesome job. I never doubted you for a moment. But I have good news and I have bad news. The good news is that what you did fixed the divergence, the human race is back safe and sound, and Maggie and I aren't going to be fired. The bad news is we're going to need you back in the Library in about an hour or so, which will give you just enough time to… well, to finish up. You'll see. And we've got a surprise for you here, once you're done, which (if you don't fuck things up tonight) will make the bad news into good news.

Sorry for being ambiguous, but Maggie tells me I can't give you any hints, because that would influence what you do, and you know that's against the rules.

Anyhow. Good luck with stuff.

See you soon.

Fischer

He was rereading the note for the third time when the telephone rang.

He set the note down on his bookshelf, next to the box, and went to pick up the telephone.

"Hello?"

"Darren?" came Lee's voice.

His heart gave an unsteady little jump. "Yes?"

"I… I need to talk to you. I was hoping that we would talk at dinner, but I can't…" He stumbled, stopped. His voice was ragged.

"What is it?"

"I don't want to discuss it on the phone. It's important that I see you in person."

Okay, this was unexpected. Should Darren tell him what he'd seen, and then assure him that Sherry was in no danger? Or would that freak him out worse?

Stall for time. Think, think…

"I don't know, Lee. I lost my car keys."

"I know. You told me. But I could pick you up."

"And go where?"

A pause. "To my lab. I need to show you something."

Of course. Something he'd already seen.

"How does your lab have anything to do with me?" he asked, trying to keep his voice light.

"You have to see for yourself."

Okay. Fischer said he had to finish things up tonight. So this was it. He had to trust in Fischer's confidence that things could still turn out all right.

He took a deep breath. "Okay. Come pick me up, then."

There was a brief pause, as if Lee was trying to decide if there was more to what Darren had said than what appeared on the surface. Then he said, "Good. I'll be there in twenty minutes."

Darren spent the next twenty minutes trying to keep from panicking. What would happen if Lee shot him again? Would he once again be thrown back to the Library? Or this time, would he simply die? How could he convince Lee he wasn't a threat to anyone, least of all Sherry Christensen?

He went down to the foyer, and watched for Lee's little silver Audi to pull up. Which it did, right on schedule. He went outside, and heard the door click shut and lock behind him with a stark finality. Would this be the last time he'd ever see his apartment? No one ever thinks of that. Any time someone sets foot away from home could be the last time, and no one even considers it.

Lee watched him walk up, his face inscrutable.

Darren let himself into the passenger side. "How's it going, Lee?"

"I'm all right."

"You seem like you're on edge. You need a vacation, dude. I'm worried about you."

Lee laughed mirthlessly. "Sherry said the same thing about me on the phone, not ten minutes ago."

He looked at Lee sidelong. "What did you tell her?"

"That I'm at a point right now that I can't simply let it drop."

The rest of the ride proceeded without either man speaking. The only noises were the swish of the windshield wipers, the hiss of the tires on the wet pavement, the sound of cars passing.

Lee pulled into the empty parking lot of the Physics/Astronomy Building, and then turned, frowning, as a second car followed. It was a trim little red Mazda. Lee stared, gave a strangled cry of anguish, and his grip tightened until his knuckles were white.

The Mazda pulled up next to Lee's car. The door opened, and Sherry Christensen stepped out.

Lee's head drooped until his forehead almost touched the

steering wheel. Then he looked back up, glancing momentarily toward Darren—who had never seen anyone look so completely despairing—and then let go of the steering wheel, opened the door, and climbed out to meet Sherry.

"Hi, sweetie," she said with a smile.

Lee looked up at her, and said, in a weary voice, "Sherry… what are you doing here?"

"When I talked to you, you sounded so exhausted… I was worried about you. So I thought I would meet you here, and maybe I could keep you company while you worked, and then… afterwards, we could go out for drinks or something."

Darren stepped out of the car. They were on a collision course. His heart beat a staccato rhythm against his ribcage. It was fated to happen. How could he prevent what was inevitable?

"Hi, Sherry," he said, trying to keep his voice steady.

"Oh, hi, Darren!" Her voice was light and friendly. "I didn't know you'd be here. I guess it's a party?"

Lee looked from one of them to the other, and seemed to come to a conclusion that made his broad shoulders sag, but a grim set came into his jaw. "I guess… I guess you both need to see this."

He turned and walked off toward the building, not bothering to lock his car.

Darren glanced at Sherry to find her looking back, her eyes questioning. *Do you know what this is about?* she seemed to be asking, and he gave a helpless little shrug.

Lee unlocked the door with his card key, held the door for Sherry and Darren, and then led them up the stairs to his lab. An eerie sense of déjà vu came over Darren. He'd done this, not twenty-four hours earlier, but at that time unseen and unheard.

Into the spotless lab, past tables with towers of equipment, toward one specific device near the back of the room. Lee sat down at the controls. The machine was activated, the dials turned, and with a static crackle the screen came to life. And again, just as the previous night, the figures moved together, swirling and merging, vague at first and then clarifying, becoming recognizable.

A gasp sounded behind him, as Sherry recognized the three faces.

"What… What are they doing? What is this showing?"

"Just watch." Lee's voice was tight.

And as before, the figures on the screen wrestled, Sherry's image backing away until she recoiled and collapsed, a darkening stain on her shirt, and Darren turned toward her, still holding the gun.

Freeze/Resume.

The real Darren looked at Sherry, who stared at the screen as if transfixed, her eyes wide.

"What does this mean?" she finally said, her voice high and thin.

"You know the answer to that," Lee said, still facing the motionless figures. "I've told you enough about my research that you should be able to figure it out. This device… it uses what is known about the present to predict the future. I'm still trying to understand completely how it does that. I started with using it to predict particle positions, which it did flawlessly. I scaled it up, and it still worked. It showed me what was going to happen. And it was always right." He gave a humorless chuckle. "If I'm right, it throws the Heisenberg Uncertainty Principle and Schrödinger's Cat right out of the window simultaneously."

"But you know that can't be true," Darren said. "The future is fluid. It depends on choices."

"Apparently not." Lee stood, and in his hand was the pistol, as Darren knew it would be.

Sherry gave a little cry of alarm, but did not move.

"Lee, this doesn't have to be the future." He worked to keep the horror he felt from showing in his voice.

Lee smiled, but his eyes held nothing but despair. "It has to happen this way. We fight. In the fight, the gun goes off. I've watched it happen a hundred times. It has to happen."

"Nothing *has* to happen."

Lee made an angry, dismissive noise. "How do you know that? You're not a scientist. You're a bookstore owner."

"How do I know that? I know it because I was here, standing behind you, at 2:30 this morning, when you watched this little screenplay on your magic machine, and made the decision to kill me in order to stop it. I know it because you were going to kill me at dinner tonight—right? I know it because it all happened before, and when it did, it caused a catastrophe." He shook his head. "I still don't understand why. But the result of all of this is that I *know* the future isn't somehow fated. I'm sorry if this destroys your theory, and puts you out of the running for a Nobel for the time being, but you're wrong. I was able to stop you tonight, and I'll stop you again. Put away the gun. Sherry doesn't have to die."

"It's going to happen!" Lee shouted. "You can't stop it! Don't you think I'd stop it if I could? My device has never been wrong…"

"It is this time."

Lee gestured at him angrily. "Go ahead. Try and take the gun away from me. If this is going to happen, let's get it over with!"

"It's *not going to happen*. I will not fight with you."

"You will!" Lee said, through clenched teeth. "You don't have a choice. It will happen! What this device shows always happens!"

This was it. This was the point where the decision was made. Either he talked Lee down, or everything spiraled out of control.

"Maybe because you always did what it took to make its predictions come true. Maybe because you didn't know that you could decide any other way." He shook his head. "I will not fight with you. You know what will happen if I do. We can stop it, you and I. We can change the future."

Lee looked from him to Sherry. The moment hung suspended.

"How do you know all of this?" Lee said. "How did you know what I was intending to do?"

"It would take *way* too long to explain that," Darren said, "and I suspect I don't have the time to tell you. Let's say that I have it on good authority."

Lee didn't answer for a moment. And for the first time, doubt entered his eyes. Finally he said, "Then why did I see these images? If they're not true, then why?"

He shrugged. "I don't know. I know someone who could probably answer that question, but he'd probably say that in the long run, it doesn't matter. Everything that's happened up to now is done, and has led us to this place, and led all three of us to know what we know. But what we do with that knowledge now is up to us." He smiled, and he felt the tension drain from his body. "It always is."

And in the room, something changed, like a record skipping a groove, only now the timeline spun smoothly away, spiraling into the future. The moment passed, an irrevocable instant in time that would lead to... something different. Something other than what Lee had seen, something other than Darren bouncing through history trying to fix what had gone wrong. All of that now lay in an alternate track. The cause, the divergence, had all along been due to what was going to transpire in this room. What decisions Darren and Lee made.

What may have been fated from the beginning. Maggie would have had an opinion about that. Darren, at the moment, didn't care.

Lee let the arm holding the gun drop to his side. "I'm... sorry," His voice cracked, and he collapsed back into his chair.

He set the pistol down with a thump, and put both hands over his face.

"It's okay," Darren said. "It's all okay, now."

Sherry went to Lee, put her arm around him, and he leaned into her, his strong frame shaking with sobs.

"Okay, guys?" Darren said, after watching them in increasing discomfort for nearly a minute. "I think I'm going to leave, now. Two's company, and all that sort of thing. You two have a lot to talk about."

Lee looked up at him. "I…" His voice was hoarse, and he wiped his eyes with the back of his hand. "I'll give you a ride back to your apartment."

"I don't think you need to. I'm not going to my apartment. I'm sort of… going away, apparently."

"Where?"

"Back to the Library."

"What Library?"

He grinned. "The Library where I learned how to make sure that tonight would end the right way."

Lee frowned. "That makes no sense at all."

He ignored the comment. He had the feeling that the hour Fischer had given him to right everything was about to run out, and there were a few things he couldn't leave unsaid.

"Anyhow, I might be back. I might not. I'm not sure." He shrugged. "It's amazing how okay I am with that. And if I don't come back, there's this antique wooden box in my apartment I want you to have." He pulled the key out from inside his shirt, and slipped the chain over his head. "This is the key that goes with it."

Lee took the key from his hand. "I have no idea what you're talking about."

"Neither do I, really. We're all floundering in the dark, and trying to make things work out for the best, based on incomplete information. It's amazing we don't screw things up more often."

Lee looked at him, and for the first time since all of this started—it seemed like ages ago—his frown was replaced by a faint smile. His features smoothed out, and Darren got a glimpse of the kind, loyal face that he had known since they were children together.

"You know, buddy, you never *have* made much sense. It's a good thing I'm the one who went into science."

"Yeah." Darren grinned. "Good thing. Anyhow, I guess this is goodbye for now. I hope you two have a good… future."

And that was when he felt a pull, as if he'd been yanked by some painless hook attached to his belly button, and then there was the now-familiar sensation of being launched through space.

Or time.

Or both.

And he opened his eyes, and found himself, clean and dry for a change, in Fischer's office. Fischer and Maggie stood there, Fischer wearing a broad grin that made his narrow face look even more elf-like, and Maggie with only a slight upwards turn of the corners of her mouth, but an approving look in her steely eyes. As soon as he appeared, both of them applauded.

"Bravo, Mr. Ault," Maggie said. "Well done. Really, quite masterful."

"Yeah, Ault, you knocked our fucking socks off," Fischer said. "Honest to god, I didn't think you had it in you. That'll teach me to judge by appearances."

"I didn't think I had it in me, either."

"Well, in any case, you fixed the divergence, and that's what counts."

"I guess I did."

"So, are you ready to go?" Fischer rubbed his long hands together.

"Go? Go where?"

Fischer looked at him, and one pale eyebrow rose. "You haven't figured out what our surprise is, then?"

"No."

"Wow. I thought that by now you would have put the pieces together."

"Just tell him, Fischer," Maggie said.

"Oh, come on. Let me have my little fun. You know why Lee tried to kill you, right?"

"Sure." Darren frowned. "Because he got a glimpse into the future. Or a *particular* future, where I was responsible for his girlfriend's death."

"Right. Can you believe it? Sonofabitch accidentally hacked into the Library's main computer, and got into the timeline projections. I'm upgrading our security program as we speak so it won't happen again. See what happens when you people find out what could happen in the future? Fucks things up royally."

"That's an understatement."

"But have you figured out why killing you obliterated the whole human race?"

"No. That part I still don't see."

Fischer gave a second-long glance at Maggie, who returned a nearly imperceptible little nod back to him.

"Okay." Fischer drew a deep breath. "So remember how we thought something had interfered with your ancestral line? But then we found out that one of the people you met in Kentucky was named McCaskill, and so that led us to the surmise that what had actually happened had interfered with Lee's line, not yours?"

"Yes."

"So, somehow there was a divergence that occurred that took out one of Lee's ancestral lines, starting back in the tenth century. But we know Lee didn't go back there and do it. Just killing you did it. Right?"

"Right," Darren said, slowly, his eyebrows drawing together.

"And we know that the computer picked out Maíre Gillacomgain, Per Olafsson, and Jane Bell as being the focal points. We don't really know why the last two were selected. If I were forced to guess, I'd say that it was because in each of those two places, there was an intersection with something having to do with how you'd respond when Lee confronted you in the lab tonight. You needed to know about where your grandmother's wooden box had come from, and see Per Olafsson's connection to you. You had to meet Josiah McCaskill, and see his connection to Lee."

"So?"

"You know, you sound *really* hostile when you say that word," Fischer said. "Anyhow, the important one was Maíre Gillacomgain. The reason she's important is that she is Lee's maternal ancestor. We knew that, right?"

"Yes."

"Well, his paternal ancestor, Ault, is… you."

"Me?" he said, his voice rising a full octave.

"Yup. That's why it created a temporal paradox when Lee killed you. He was killing his own great-great-etc. grandfather."

"That's impossible."

"Sorry, dude. Now that the computer has reset, tracking has been reestablished, and all it took was a simple check. You're supposed to go back to Scotland, and do the horizontal tango with your red-haired girlfriend. Because you will father a child who will be Lee McCaskill's direct ancestor. One of your descendants, one Ingrid Nilsdottir, will be born in Oslo, Norway in 1325. She's Per Olafsson's long-lost wife. One of *their* descendants, five-hundred-odd years later, will end up in North Carolina, and marry poor lonely Josiah McCaskill. They'll have a son, David McCaskill, who then marries Jane Bell. The whole interlude with Murrell never happened. She and David McCaskill have three children before his death at Gettysburg. Their eldest son, Stephen Patrick McCaskill, was Lee's great-great grandfather."

"But… me?" he said. "I'm supposed to go back to Scotland and marry Maíre?"

"Well, not necessarily," Fischer said. "All you technically have to do is have sex with her. But by all means, marry her if you want to."

"Fischer, don't be crude." Maggie made a *tsk*-ing noise under her breath.

"Well, it's *true*," Fischer said.

"But what if she doesn't want me? She has a say in this, after all."

"I dunno, Ault. Given that Lee exists, I'd say you've pretty much got a sure bet, here. That should be a confidence-booster."

Darren swallowed, and just stared at him.

"Bow-chicka-bow-wow," Fischer said. "If she's as cute as you say, you should be pawing the ground right now."

"Well, sure. I'm just finding this a little hard to believe."

Which was an odds-on contender for Understatement of the Year.

"No harder to believe than anything else you've been through, Mr. Ault," Maggie said. "When you take the long view, it really all makes sense."

"On the other hand, you can refuse." Fischer gave a little shrug of his narrow shoulders. "Then the divergence happens again, and the entire human race vanishes, and you'll spend the rest of your life in the Library with yours truly. So you can go back to Scotland, and look forward to making sweet love to your Hieland Lassie, or you can stay here and reshelve books for a living. Your call."

"I'll go to Scotland."

"I kind of figured. So, this is goodbye, then. Probably permanently, this time."

"Probably?"

"We might check in on you. You know, see how you're doing in the fathering-offspring-to-save-humanity department. I've got some vacation time coming, and I've never been to the Hebrides before."

"That'd be awesome," he said, rather unconvincingly.

"Geez, Ault, you could at least fake some enthusiasm. You could hurt a guy's feelings." Without warning, Fischer pulled him into a surprisingly powerful hug, and then let him go. "You done good. Seriously. Thanks for everything."

Maggie, for her part, reached out her hand, and gave him a stiff little handshake. "Most impressive, Mr. Ault. My most sincere gratitude."

"Um… you're welcome," he said, and for the second time in ten minutes, he was launched into darkness.

The wind and rain hit him in the face like a cold, wet hand. There was the glow of a campfire, and the sounds of movement and angry voices nearby. Then, without warning, the hulking shape of a man bore down on another figure standing there, small and defenseless. A well-muscled bare arm reared back, and thrust forward, and a barbed spear flew toward the smaller figure.

It was only then that he realized that the smaller figure was… himself.

With an audible pop—he could almost hear the air molecules recoiling to fill the gap he'd left behind—his double vanished. The spear sliced through the space his body had occupied less than a second earlier. It hit the ground with a loud *chunk*, and stuck, its wooden shaft quivering.

The Viking leader gave a shout of alarm and dismay. He ran forward, retrieved his spear, and stared uncomprehendingly at the spot where, by all reason, his prey should be lying dead, skewered through the breastbone.

Darren felt in his pocket, and found there—thank heaven at least this part of the timeline had stayed the same—his key ring with the electronic airhorn his mother had given him. He crept up behind the Viking leader, who was still frowning at the bare spot on the sand as if he couldn't quite believe his eyes, and blasted the air horn right in the man's left ear.

The Viking leader gave a remarkably girly scream, dropped his spear, and ran.

Darren picked up the spear and swung it around, and shouted, "Yeah! Take that! And don't come back!" He gave another blast on the air horn, and heard, in the distance, another terrified yell.

"Eeeeeevil spirits!" the Viking shouted, his voice fading into the distance. "The island is filled with eeeeevil spirits!"

Even in tenth-century Scotland, discretion was the better part of valor. Time to get out of there.

Still holding the spear, he ran off into the darkness, back toward the spot where Dugal's hut had once stood.

He could help them rebuild. And if Fischer was right, he'd spend the rest of his life here. And the bookstore, and his apartment, and Seattle… he'd never see them again.

It was amazing how little that thought bothered him.

Somewhere in the darkness ahead was Maíre and her family. His future lay here, in the past. He didn't know what would happen—if his life would be long or short, if it would be happy or tragic—but at least he knew he would live long enough to tell Maíre what he'd recognized the moment he saw her.

That he loved her, and that whatever time he had left, he wanted to spend it with her.

He reached the top of a hill, and then turned and looked back toward the ocean. The faint light of dawn was spreading on the horizon, and the undersides of the clouds were stained with red.

He smiled. It wasn't like he needed anything more than that. It was more than most men ever get to know. And it was enough.

And he turned, and ran down the hill toward the rest of his life.

epilogue

. . .

epilogue

. . .

Maggie set a cup of coffee down in front of Fischer. "All of the tracking is reestablished, then?" she said, standing next to his desk, her hands clasped behind her, looking a bit like a headmistress from a traditional girl's school addressing one of her charges.

Fischer didn't look up from his computer screen. "Yup. We've run full-scale diagnostics. No other divergences found. I think we're home and clear."

"Quite a near thing, that was."

"Oh, yeah. I thought we were done, there, a couple of times. But Ault was a trooper. A lot smarter than I thought he was, at first."

"Should we have told him about his own ancestry, sir?"

Fischer shook his head. "Toward what end?"

"There were two reasons his premature death triggered a temporal paradox. You only told him one."

Fischer looked up at her, and cocked an eyebrow. "He only needed to know one."

Maggie pursed her lips. "I suppose you're right."

Fischer leaned back in his chair, then picked up his coffee and took a sip. "I mean, I told him, remember? Anyone with

European ancestry is very likely to be descended from everyone who lived in Europe in the thirteenth century who left descendants. If he can't put two and two together, I'm not going be the one to burst his bubble."

Maggie's eyes glittered behind her round eyeglasses. "Perhaps, given Mr. Ault's personality, it's best if he doesn't know."

Fischer gave her a wry smile. "It puts a new twist on that song from back in the nineteen forties, do you know it? 'I'm My Own Grandpa.'"

"I am not an aficionado of twentieth century novelty songs, Fischer."

"No," Fischer said. "Somehow, I don't expect you are."

also by gordon bonnet

The Communion of Shadows

Sephirot

Descent into Ulthoa

The Shambles

Kári the Lucky

Kill Switch

The Fifth Day

Gears

Snowe Mysteries *(beginning re-releases 2023)*

Book 1: Poison the Well

Book 2: Dead Letter Office

Book 3: Face Value

Snowe Mysteries *(available now)*

Book 4: Past Imperfect

Book 5: Room for Wrath

Book 6: The Obituary Collector

Book 7: Slings and Arrows

The Boundary Solution Series (stay tuned for re-releases)

And More…

Stay tuned for releases *(and re-releases for ones you may have missed)*

Sign up for Gordon's Little Bustard Books Newsletter and Obscure Weird Tidbits at his website: http://www.gordonbonnet.com

about the author

Gordon Bonnet has been writing fiction for decades. Encouraged when his story "Crazy Bird Bends His Beak" won critical acclaim in Mrs. Moore's 1st grade class at Central Elementary School in St. Albans, West Virginia, he embarked on a long love affair with the written word.

His interest in the paranormal goes back almost that far. Introduced to speculative, fantasy, and science fiction by such giants in the tradition as Madeleine L'Engle, Lloyd Alexander, Isaac Asimov, C. S. Lewis, and J. R. R. Tolkien, he was captivated by those writers' abilities to take the reader to a fictional world and make it seem tangible, to breathe life and passion and personality into characters who were (sometimes) not even human. He made journeys into darker realms upon meeting the works of Edgar Allen Poe and H. P. Lovecraft during his teenage years, and those authors still influence his imagination and his writing to this day.

This fascination with the paranormal, however, has always been tempered by Gordon's scientific training. This has led to a strange duality: his work as a teacher, skeptic and debunker on the popular blog *Skeptophilia,* while simultaneously writing paranormal and speculative novels, novellas, and short stories. Gordon explains this, with a smile: "Well, I do know it's fiction, after all."

He blogs daily, and is never without a piece of fiction in progress—driven to continue (as he puts it) "because I want to find out how the story ends." From historical fiction (*Kári the Lucky*), to murder mysteries (the Parsifal Snowe Mysteries, beginning with *Poison the Well*), to paranormal fiction with a humorous twist (*Periphery* and *Lock & Key*) to the truly terrifying (*Gears* and *Descent into Ulthoa*), Gordon's fiction has something for all tastes!

Find him conversing with his dogs (and perhaps his wife) in Trumansburg, NY, or the following platforms:

- YouTube *https://youtube.com/@skeptophilia1509*
- Skeptophilia blog *http://www.skeptophilia.com/*
- Books and stuff *http://www.gordonbonnet.com*
- Twitter *@TalesOfWhoa*
- TikTok *@LittleBustardBooks*
- Instagram *@skygazer227*

Or, ya know, the Google.

www.ingramcontent.com/pod-product-compliance
Lightning Source LLC
Chambersburg PA
CBHW032152190726
48290CB00005BB/1525